DIVISIBLE MAN™
TEN MAN CREW

by

Howard Seaborne

ALSO BY HOWARD SEABORNE

DIVISIBLE MAN
A Novel – September 2017
DIVISIBLE MAN: THE SIXTH PAWN
A Novel – June 2018
DIVISIBLE MAN: THE SECOND GHOST
A Novel – September 2018
ANGEL FLIGHT
A Story – September 2018
DIVISIBLE MAN: THE SEVENTH STAR
A Novel – June 2019
ENGINE OUT
A Story – September 2019
WHEN IT MATTERS
A Story – October 2019
A SNOWBALL'S CHANCE
A Story – November 2019
DIVISIBLE MAN: TEN MAN CREW
A Novel – November 2019
DIVISIBLE MAN: THE THIRD LIE
A Novel – May 2020
DIVISIBLE MAN: THREE NINES FINE
A Novel – November 2020
DIVISIBLE MAN: EIGHT BALL
A Novel – September 2021
SHORT FLIGHTS
A Story Collection – Coming 2022
DIVISIBLE MAN: NINE LIVES LOST
A Novel – Coming 2022

PRAISE FOR HOWARD SEABORNE

"This book is a strong start to a series...Well-written and engaging, with memorable characters and an intriguing hero."
  —*Kirkus Reviews*
  DIVISIBLE MAN [DM1]

"Seaborne's crisp prose, playful dialogue, and mastery of technical details of flight distinguish the story...this is a striking and original start to a series, buoyed by fresh and vivid depictions of extra-human powers and a clutch of memorably drawn characters..."
  —*BookLife*
  DIVISIBLE MAN [DM1]

"Even more than flight, (Will's relationship with Andy)—and that crack prose—powers this thriller to a satisfying climax that sets up more to come."
  —*BookLife*
  DIVISIBLE MAN [DM1]

"Seaborne, a former flight instructor and charter pilot, once again gives readers a crisply written thriller. Self-powered flight is a potent fantasy, and Seaborne explores its joys and difficulties engagingly. Will's narrative voice is amusing, intelligent and humane; he draws readers in with his wit, appreciation for his wife, and his flight-drunk joy...Even more entertaining than its predecessor—a great read."
  —*Kirkus Reviews*
  DIVISIBLE MAN: THE SIXTH PAWN [DM2]

"Seaborne, a former flight instructor and pilot, delivers a solid, well-written tale that taps into the near-universal dream of personal flight. Will's narrative voice is engaging and crisp, clearly explaining technical matters while never losing sight of humane, emotional concerns. The

environments he describes…feel absolutely real. Another intelligent and exciting superpowered thriller."
—*Kirkus Reviews*
DIVISIBLE MAN: THE SECOND GHOST [DM3]

"As in this series' three previous books, Seaborne…proves he's a natural born storyteller, serving up an exciting, well-written thriller. He makes even minor moments in the story memorable with his sharp, evocative prose…Will's smart, humane and humorous narrative voice is appealing, as is his sincere appreciation for Andy—not just for her considerable beauty, but also for her dedication and intelligence… Seaborne does a fine job making side characters and locales believable. It's deeply gratifying to see Will deliver righteous justice to some very bad people. An intensely satisfying thriller—another winner from Seaborne."
—*Kirkus Reviews*
DIVISIBLE MAN: THE SECOND GHOST [DM4]

"Seaborne…continues his winning streak in this series, offering another page-turner. By having Will's knowledge of and control over his powers continue to expand while the questions over how he should best deploy his abilities grow, Seaborne keeps the concept fresh and readers guessing…Will's enemies are becoming aware of him and perhaps developing techniques to detect him, which makes the question of how he can protect himself while doing the most good a thorny one. The conspiracy is highly dramatic yet not implausible given today's political events, and the action sequences are excitingly cinematic…Another compelling and hugely fun adventure that delivers a thrill ride."
—*Kirkus Reviews*
DIVISIBLE MAN: TEN MAN CREW [DM5]

"Seaborne shows himself to be a reliably splendid storyteller in this latest outing. The plot is intricate and could have been confusing in lesser hands, but the author manages it well, keeping readers oriented amid unexpected developments…His crisp writing about complex scenes and concepts is another strong suit…The fantasy of self-powered flight remains absolutely compelling…As a former charter pilot,

Seaborne conveys Will's delight not only in 'the other thing,' but also in airplanes and the world of flight—an engaging subculture that he ably brings to life for the reader. Will is heroic and daring, as one would expect, but he's also funny, compassionate, and affectionate... A gripping, timely, and twisty thriller."
—*Kirkus Reviews*
DIVISIBLE MAN: THE THIRD LIE [DM6]

"Seaborne is never less than a spellbinding storyteller, keeping his complicated but clearly explicated plot moving smoothly from one nail-biting scenario to another. As the tale goes along, seemingly disparate plot lines begin to satisfyingly connect in ways that will keep readers guessing until the explosive (in more ways than one) action-movie denouement. The author's grasp of global politics gives depth to the book's thriller elements, which are nicely balanced by thoughtful characterizations. Even minor characters come across in three dimensions, and Will himself is an endearing narrator. He's lovestruck by his gorgeous, intelligent, and strong-willed wife; has his heart and social conscience in the right place; and is boyishly thrilled by the other thing. A solid series entry that is, as usual, exciting, intricately plotted, and thoroughly entertaining."
—*Kirkus Reviews*
DIVISIBLE MAN: THREE NINES FINE [DM7]

Any reader of this series knows that they're in good hands with Seaborne, who's a natural storyteller. His descriptions and dialogue are crisp, and his characters deftly sketched...The book keeps readers tied into its complex and exciting thriller plot with lucid and graceful exposition, laying out clues with cleverness and subtlety...Also, although Will's abilities are powerful, they have reasonable limitations, and the protagonist is always a relatable character with plenty of humanity and humor...Another riveting, taut, and timely adventure with engaging characters and a great premise."
— *Kirkus Reviews*
DIVISIBLE MAN: EIGHT BALL [DM8]

THE SERIES

While each DIVISIBLE MAN ^{TM} novel tells its own tale, many elements carry forward and the novels are best enjoyed in sequence. The short story "Angel Flight" is a bridge between the third and fourth novels and is included with the third novel, DIVISIBLE MAN - THE SECOND GHOST.

DIVISIBLE MAN ^{TM} is available in print, digital and audio.

For a Cast of Characters, visit **HowardSeaborne.com**

For advance notice of new releases and exclusive material available only to Email Members, join the DIVISIBLE MAN ^{TM} Email List at

HowardSeaborne.com.

Sign up today and get a FREE DOWNLOAD.

ACKNOWLEDGMENTS

This is the Divisible Man's fifth mission. The flight crew deserves a medal at this point. Stephen Parolini is always first up the boarding ladder and leads the mission with impeccable editing. Waist gunners, Rich "Maddog" Sorensen and Judethe "English Ace" Johnson defy the odds by volunteering for each test flight, bless them. The ground crew at Trans World Data—David, Carol, Claire, April and Rebecca—work miracles to keep the ship flying while the G-2 Section, Kristie and Steve, stare for hours at reconnaissance photos so I can concentrate on flying. No preflight inspection is complete without a great crew chief, Roberta "Eagle Eye" Schlei, whose amazing copyediting spots the gremlins lurking in every paragraph.

And thank you, Robin—call sign "Polly Pureheart"—for being the perfect copilot.

*For all the boys with one more
takeoff than landing.*

PART I

PART I

1

_____

Dammit!

I floated in the high heat of the barn, near the roof. Pinprick shafts of sunset's last light angled through the air around me and through me.

I tried again.

DOWN!

Nothing.

FLOOR!

Nothing.

"Shit!" I barked.

"That doesn't sound good." Andy's voice rose from the open barn door below and behind me. I rotated in the air, using the strange core muscle that runs down my center when I vanish. For months the sensation of a controllable pivot point had been reliable and consistent.

At least that works.

"God, it's hot in here, Will. Why not do this outside? It's a beautiful evening."

She stepped out of the framed light and into the shadows of the barn loft. In short shorts, sandals and a tank top, my wife reminded me once again why I love summer. Tonight, she tied her flowing auburn hair in a high ponytail, lifting it off the back of her slender neck for the sake of cooling. In each hand, she held a glistening bottle of Corona with a green lime wedge jammed in the neck.

I pushed the thumb slide on the power unit in my hand. Unseen, a six-inch carbon fiber model airplane propeller turned, blowing prop-wash air across my forearm, pulling me forward. I performed a spiral around one of the central barn beams and eased to a landing on the uneven wooden floor.

Fwooomp!

I reappeared in stride, startling Andy. It's been a year, and this still catches her by surprise. She extended the cold beer to me. Free of the cool sensation that *the other thing* wraps around me, the barn heat hit me.

"Seriously," she said, "it's fifteen degrees warmer in here."

"Yup. Old barns. You should stack hay bales in one of these some-time when it's 110 in the loft."

Andy adopted a distant gaze, fixing her gold-flecked green eyes on me and not on me at the same time.

"What?"

"Oh, just picturing you, shirtless, all shiny and sweaty, heaving around fifty-pound bales. My beefcake farmhand."

I took her musing as an invitation and stepped closer. "Want some slippery sweat on your skin? Some hay in your hair?"

"Yuk. It is way too hot in here."

"What kind of seductive farmer's daughter are you?"

"My father is a lawyer and a corporate CEO. He wouldn't know a plow from a cow unless you itemized them in an annual report. Let's get out of here."

Leaving the barn, the cool evening air washed over my skin and made her point. We walked toward our rented farmhouse. The rim of the sun slipped beneath the horizon, abandoning a pale blue, cloudless sky and offering the false promise of an endless twilight. I sent a splash of delicious chilled refreshment down my throat.

"You didn't answer."

"What?"

"Why do that in the barn? It's a beautiful evening."

I shrugged. "I dunno. That's my original training space. Area Fifty-One. It feels...comfortable. It's safer, too. I'm being cautious—trying something I don't understand. You don't want me to go shooting off into space."

"I appreciate the caution." She slipped her hand in mine. "Any luck?"

"No."

She didn't press and thankfully didn't offer suggestions. *Maybe you need to focus. Maybe you have too much on your mind. Maybe you shouldn't try at all.* The last thing I needed was Andy coaching from the sidelines. That happened in my head without her.

And how are you doing?

Getting nowhere faster than usual.

On several occasions while in the vanished state I propelled myself by simply *thinking* a direction or objective. The first time it shot Lane Franklin and me through the window of a burning building. The second time it lifted Andy and me to the ceiling of a motel room seconds before a now-dead Nazi shot up the bed we slept in. The third time—the longest sustained event to date—it launched me halfway across Essex County carrying Andy's nearly-drowned sister Lydia to a hospital.

For months I've tried to recreate the effect without success.

"Maybe it's a by-product of adrenalin," she offered. "We don't know what happens to your physiology when you do what you do. Mix in a shot of a chemical compound that jolts the human body the way adrenalin does—I don't know—maybe it supercharges you."

"I don't think so. I've pumped plenty of adrenalin inside *the other thing* and nothing happened. I think it's something else."

"Like what?"

"Mental. Brain waves. Neurons firing in the right combination with those wires in my head. The difference between generated thought and a flash of pure instinct."

"Speaking of those wires—"

"Yeah, yeah. Stephenson wants me to see him for an updated scan. We just did that, for chrissakes!" I sometimes wonder if the neurologist we trust with my condition is more interested in me as a specimen than as a patient.

"That was in February, dear."

"Nothing changed in February. Nothing is changed now."

5

Andy answered with a skeptical expression that dismissed my base-less assumption.

Change the subject.

"Hey, it's a gorgeous night. Let's take a joyride."

She stiffened slightly. My wife does not like vanishing and flying with me. Our first experience together introduced the possibility of first dying from hypoxia, then from hypothermia. That was followed by a near-death incident involving a tall building. I hoped a gentle scenic tour of Wisconsin farmland on a summer evening might scrub the bad memories.

"Slow and easy. Just for fun," I said. "I'll even let you drive." I held the propulsion unit out for her.

"Oh, no. Not me. And you've been drinking." She pointed at my half-finished beer.

"All the more reason for you to drive." I flipped the bottle onto the lawn. Foamy gold spray spun from the neck.

"That's a shameful waste."

I took her bottle and repeated the gesture with excellent aim. The bottles clinked together in the grass.

"Works best if we snuggle," I said. I put my left arm around her and pulled her close. Catching a sparkle in her eye, I leaned into a kiss and held it. She kissed back energetically.

Fwooomp!

We vanished.

She pulled her lips from mine. "God! I told you! That's just weird!"

We began to float. She tightened her hold. I tapped my toes on the gravel and started a vertical ascent.

"Wait! How many propeller-thingies do you have?"

"It's called a ZAP."

"No, it isn't. How many?"

"Just the one."

"No! Will, go get your vest! We need backups!" She transmitted urgency through fingers digging into my waist. Andy's fear of floating out of control like an untethered astronaut was well-founded.

Choosing not to sabotage this exercise with an argument, I aimed the power unit straight up and pulled the slide into reverse. The prop hummed. We ceased ascending and slowly dropped to the driveway.

Fwooomp! We reappeared. She stepped away abruptly.

I turned to make a quick trip to the house when we both heard a vehicle approaching from the west on our narrow country road. A car rolled into view a quarter of a mile away. Twilight remained strong and the car ran without headlights. I stopped and watched it approach. Instead of rolling past on the whisper of its tires, the car decelerated and eased into our driveway.

"Do you think he saw us?" Andy asked quietly, as if the driver, inside a closed vehicle seventy feet away, might hear her.

"Not a chance." I strolled to the grass and picked up the two Corona bottles. Most of one had drained out, but the other still carried a healthy third of the golden liquid. I handed Andy the empty along with a mischievous grin.

The car, a mid-sized silver Nissan sedan, crunched to a stop on our gravel driveway. Reflections in the windshield obscured the driver. With an eye trained by my police detective wife, I noted the Iowa plates.

The driver stepped out.

"Oh, shit!" I muttered out of the side of my mouth. "I know that guy!"

"HI! BEAUTIFUL EVENING!" The driver eased around his door and closed it. He walked casually, pitching a disarming smile our way. The smile conflicted with the shoulder holster he wore over a black polo shirt. A semi-automatic handgun hung under his left armpit.

I eased the power unit into my back pocket and slipped my right arm around Andy's waist. In my head, I closed an imaginary grip on a set of imaginary levers. Pushing those levers forward would make us vanish in less time than it would take for the man to reach for and touch his weapon. Andy tensed beside me. There wasn't time to explain.

Instead of reaching for his weapon, he slipped his right hand into his trouser hip pocket and pulled out a flat black wallet.

"Detective Stewart?" he asked Andy.

"And you are?"

He flipped the wallet open. "Special Agent Lee Donaldson." He didn't need to add "FBI" because the imprint on his ID left no doubt.

7

"May I?" Andy reached for the wallet. He gave it to her. She examined it closely.

It's fake, I thought. *It has to be!*

"What can I do for the FBI, Special Agent Donaldson?" Andy handed the wallet back to him.

"First off, I apologize for dropping in like this. I had hoped to see you at your office, but when I called, your dispatcher said you were off duty. I just got here and thought I'd at least drive by. I saw you from the road and decided to take a chance. I hope you don't mind."

"That will depend on the nature of your visit. Got here from where?"

"Pardon?"

"You said you just got here. From where?"

"Oh!" He chuckled. "Sioux City. I'm with the Sioux City field office."

Bullshit!

"And what does the Sioux City field office of the FBI want that a phone call wouldn't handle—not meaning to sound rude."

"No, no. You're quite right. It was my bad to just drop in like this without calling. If you'd rather, I can make an appointment. However, I would ask if you can make time for me tomorrow. I have to be back in my office first thing Monday morning."

"That is a shitload of driving," I commented. "All the way here from Sioux City today, then all the way back again? Must be important."

Donaldson glanced at me. I put him in his mid-forties. He had the same military bearing, the same buzz-cut hair and the same drill instructor jawline I remembered. His eyes were a muddy green brown, but they powered a sharp gaze. He briefly studied me. I searched his expression for recognition, but he showed no sign.

There's no way this is a coincidence.

"This is my husband, Will."

I traded a handshake. As expected, he closed a tight grip, which I returned in kind.

"Pleased to meet you."

"Beer?" I lifted mine.

"Thank you, no. But I wouldn't turn down a glass of water." He turned to Andy. "That is, unless you prefer to meet with me tomorrow?"

8

Andy shook her head. "Nonsense. You're here. Come inside, please."

Rather than head for the back door, Andy led us past Donaldson's parked car to the front of the house and the screened porch.

"I'll get you that water," she said. "Please, make yourself comfortable." She gestured at our motley collection of wicker furniture and the old chaise lounge I like to occupy on summer evenings. Then she hurried away through the house.

Donaldson remained standing but turned to face the front yard. "This is a nice property. Quiet. Family farm?"

"Rental." I considered stopping there. Freezing him out. Then I thought about Andy's motivation for taking us around the house to the porch, rather than through the house via the kitchen. "It's quiet, alright. Except when they're picking the corn. We're practically an island in cornfields here. You must be used to that sort of thing in Iowa. Oh, and then there's the manure spreading. Once in a while, they buy some liquid manure from a couple dairy farms that have big vats on the west side of town, and they fling some pretty ripe stuff. It reeks for a few days. Mostly at the tail end of winter." I went on for a few minutes about farming, about our landlord, and about Essex County. I was about to launch into a monologue about Essex County Air Service when Andy reappeared. She handed Donaldson a tall glass filled with ice and water.

"Thanks," he said. "Did I check out?"

She smiled and held up her phone. "You did."

He returned the smile. "What got your guard up?"

"I did," I said quickly. "I recognized you when you drove in. I told her the last time I saw you was at the wedding at Cinnamon Hills. You were private security for some rich guy." It was a two-part lie in that there hadn't been time to tell Andy how I knew Donaldson—and Cinnamon Hills wasn't the last time I saw this man.

The last time I saw this man, I was about to put a gun to the head of his billionaire boss, Bargo Litton.

Andy took the news in stride.

"Affirmative," Donaldson acknowledged. "I supervised security for Litton Industries until about eight months ago. Before I worked for Mr. Litton, I was with the FBI for sixteen years. After my service for Mr. Litton terminated, I went back to the FBI."

Andy maintained a straight face. "That's unusual. That the FBI would rehire someone who left."

"You mean someone who jilted government service for the private sector? Yes, it is. May I?" He gestured at one of the wicker chairs. We all sat. I chose a chair beside Andy, rather than my lowrider lounge. "I had to pull in a mountain of favors and do some serious begging. I spent most of my career in L.A. Now I'm in Sioux City. You can do your own math on that one."

"You didn't like private security?" I asked.

He shrugged. "Things changed. Mr. Litton's needs...evolved."

Evolved, hell. I scared the piss out of the old bastard one night and made it clear I could do it again, whenever and wherever I wanted, regardless of the money he threw at his security apparatus. I left Litton helpless and furious. A breach of security at that level must have cost Donaldson his job.

Which doubled my unease.

"I guess I have law enforcement in my blood. You understand, Detective."

"I do. It's not the easiest path."

"Amen, that."

"So, Special Agent, what caused you to drive halfway across the Midwest on your day off? Your office said you're off duty until Monday. Or are you working off book?"

"Sharp. I'm starting to see your fingerprints on the Parks case."

"Is that why you're here? Parks? That wrapped up months ago."

"No. Not Parks. Or Seavers."

Andy tipped her head. "Brogan?"

"Three for three. That's an impressive track record."

"For a small-town cop?" Andy bled a little of the warmth out of her tone. "I also took down a sinister gang of nativity scene vandals last winter."

"I'm not one of those feds who thinks local LEOs are all hicks, Detective. Skill and intellect deserve recognition wherever they're found. Your department is lucky to have you. A federal agency would also be lucky to have you."

"Recruiting? Is that what this is?"

"No." He shook his head. "Well, not yet anyway."

"Then it's Brogan," Andy deduced. "You would be better served by contacting the prosecuting office. The Brogan case is still playing out."

"A little more each day, it seems. Six congressmen resigned. More on the chopping block. Senate hearings. The media's been in a frenzy for months."

"I'm not involved in the politics and I do my best to stay out of the media," Andy said. "My concern was Olivia Brogan's role in a murder and an attempted murder. What's your concern?"

"The same. Obliquely."

Andy waited and watched. Donaldson sipped his water. Beyond the porch screens fireflies initiated luminous courtship flights above the lawn.

"Josiah James." Donaldson cut the still evening air with the name.

Andy stiffened.

"Proof that a turd can walk and talk," I said without hesitation.

"That and more," Donaldson nodded, backing me up while working to ignore the increased tension between him and my wife.

"Then 'obliquely' is a good choice of terms," Andy said coldly, "because James was peripheral to Brogan. She funded him. As far as I know, that's all."

"James was part of the noise that set off your bomber, Braddock."

"So was Fox News. So was the man in the White House. Neither have been indicted. Josiah James is an overblown conspiracy theorist selling his brand of racist talk radio to half a dozen remote station groups in the hinterlands."

"He claims to be syndicated on more than two hundred stations nationwide."

"He lies. It's nowhere near that."

Donaldson lifted his eyebrows. "You've researched Mr. James." Andy didn't comment. "You're right. James lies. He's a living example of the cliché about moving lips. Until a few years ago he was just another nut job using the internet to vent the worms in his head. Then he polished his image with some tech and some outsourced marketing savvy. Even got the attention of the President."

"I've seen the tweets."

"Olivia Brogan and others like her—Litton included—poured gasoline on that fire with cash. Next thing we know, James is inspiring people to homebrew plastique. Your guy Braddock, to name one. James calls him a 'freedom fighter' now. He regurgitates and enhances the story every few weeks."

"One man's terrorist…" I muttered.

"Your name comes up now and then, Detective. Did you know? Along with Off—"

Andy interrupted him. "Special Agent Donaldson, you drove eight hours—"

"Seven."

"—seven hours on a Saturday, on your own time, to come here and discuss a tangent to a case I worked. That tells me I'm right about you working off book. And not to make assumptions, but it strongly suggests that your supervisors would not approve."

"Very few supervisors appreciate genuine initiative."

"I didn't give you away—just so you know—by calling."

"Thanks."

"Given your posting after returning from the private sector, I will also guess that you spend your days running background checks on political appointees, and that your hopes of promotion are nil. Am I hitting the ten ring?"

"Like a pro, Detective. Care to go the distance?"

Andy sat back and thought for a moment while Donaldson watched her. He appeared amused by Andy's deductive effort.

"Fine," she said. "You're here to enlist an ally. You want me to use my access on the Brogan case to dig into James. No. You *need* me to dig into James because your office has already shut you down. Correct?"

Donaldson glanced at me. "Your wife is everything I've heard."

"And then some."

"Yes," he said to Andy. "I need help and I need it discretely. Outside of my office."

"Why?"

"Because the Bureau is hypersensitive about the appearance of political motivation behind an investigation."

"PR answer. Not good enough."

"Because James has ties to the President."

"Fifteen minutes of fame shared by two ruthless opportunists."

"Because James is a cancer."

Andy shook her head. "I don't like him either. For reasons I'm sure you can imagine. But that doesn't mean I'm willing to launch an investigation off book or use my badge for personal vengeance. Are you?"

"What?"

"Out for personal vengeance? Or is this a play to restore your employment with Litton Industries?"

"No."

"Revenge then. Against Litton for terminating you."

Donaldson chuckled. "No, this has nothing to do with Litton. And Litton has nothing to do with me, except for using his influence to guarantee I finish my twenty at a desk in Sioux City." He leaned forward, resting his elbows on his knees and clasping his hands together. For a long moment he stared down at those hands.

Twilight slipped into dusk and cool air drifted through the screens, falling around us.

"Josiah James may lie about his syndication, but he is a cancer and he is spreading. He got a pat on the head from the President and it might as well have been a shot of rocket fuel. He's been pushing his radio syndication hard in the Midwest and middle west. His hate and crazy conspiracy shit plays like a pop tune to the fringes in rural markets.

"A few months before I moved to Sioux City, he pitched one of the radio stations there. The flagship property in a multi-station group. The Nedritch Group. They own stations in Iowa, Nebraska and Kansas. Get a foot in the door with the flagship station and it's one flick of a switch to syndicate to the whole group. The deal would have expanded his market by forty percent. A big leap."

Donaldson drew from his ice water, then continued.

"Nedritch turned him down flat. The group isn't what I'd call progressive, but they're moderate enough that the James brand of venom would never play on their air. That's what everybody thought, anyway."

"He got the deal?" Andy asked.

Donaldson nodded. "Two months ago. Flagship and five affiliates. And not some three AM slot, either. Daytime talk. A first for James."

"Okay. He's upped his game. Maybe he's stretching his fifteen minutes of fame with the White House. Maybe he promised to tone down the crazier shit," I said.

"No. That's not it."

"What then?" Andy asked.

"In early April we had a missing child case. Amber alert. A seven-year-old boy was abducted from his yard. Unquestionably foul play. Three days into the nightmare, the family received an anonymous tip that the kid was in a storage container. He was. Cold, but unharmed. Somebody locked him in there with a box of candy bars and a sleeping bag. Never touched him. My stock isn't worth much around the office, but since the SAC called for all-hands-on-deck, they let me in on the scramble. I was assigned interviews with extended family. They saddled me with the grandparents, which is usually an exercise in making note of suspicious foreigners they can't seem to name."

"But not this time," Andy said. "Nedritch."

Donaldson pointed a finger at Andy.

"Himself. And a few weeks later, James cut his deal with the radio group," Andy continued.

"Nobody was interested in my assessment. Nedritch denied any connection and refused to see me after the first interview. His people told my SAC that there was nothing further to discuss once the boy was home again. They made a point of telling me to stay away."

"Wait." I held up a hand. "You're saying that James kidnapped the kid and the ransom was a deal for syndication? Extortion? That's one hell of a stretch. Nedritch must have money, resources, political pull. Why wouldn't he lay on extra security? Twist some arm with the Iowa state police? If what you're saying is true, he had to have been furious."

"He may have been furious, but he was also pragmatic. All the extra security in the world won't stop harm from finding you if the perpetrator is crazy, determined and patient."

He had us there. I played a similar card with Litton. Despite his story, I wondered again if Donaldson knew it was me that breached Litton's security.

Impossible.

"Nedritch has nine children, seventeen grandchildren and four great-grandchildren. They're spread out all over the country. What you might call a target-rich environment. How do you protect them all? Denouncing James wasn't an option. People who do that become talk topics on his show. It's not a position I'd like to be in. The man is a master at dancing just this side of the defamation line. There have been eighteen suits brought against him for libel and defamation, and none of them stuck. James hounded a county sheriff for a year after he got stopped on an OWI. The sheriff lost in the next election."

"You're not exactly gilding your case for joining the cause," Andy said. "Asking me to use my ties to the Brogan prosecution so I can poke around Josiah James—and risk him setting his sights on me—isn't what I'd call appealing."

"No. And you're right. I am not trying to gild the case. Or minimize the risk. I'm stuck in a career backwater. It won't matter if he targets me. I don't have a family he can threaten. I've got nothing to lose."

"She does!" I said.

"Why come to me?" Andy asked.

"Because you have a personal stake in seeing James taken down."

And there it was.

I looked at Andy and she looked at me. Pain traveled across that glance like lightning.

"You're talking about Mike," she said.

"Mike Mackiejewski," I added. My throat locked up. I thought of Mike and of Corey Braddock, the boy who *wasn't* a bomber. I thought of Lane Franklin.

Lane had been collateral damage in a tragedy sparked by Ben Braddock and the venom and hate broadcast by Josiah James. But Lane had survived and gained strength in her inimitable way.

Corey Braddock and Mike Mackiejewski—Andy's subordinate and friend—had not.

"I'm so sorry," Donaldson said, "about Officer Mackiejewski. That was a double tragedy."

"Don't think you're going to come here and use Mike's suicide to sign me up on some revenge crusade, Special Agent," Andy said harshly. "Not when you used to collect your paycheck from Bargo Litton. The only difference between Litton and James is that Litton outsources his hate mongering and murder."

Donaldson hung his head again. He spoke without looking up. "You're right. I did work for Litton. I did a job as a professional. A job I was damned good at. I also saw things and heard things and I should have questioned but didn't. Now I can."

Andy rose and stood with her arms folded. I read the set of her jaw and knew the conversation was over.

"I need help, Detective."

"If the Brogan investigation opens a door to a probe of Josiah James, I will go through that door like Tactical. But I will not use my connection to the Brogan case to get you out of a dead-end desk job, Special Agent."

Donaldson gave it a moment. He took a sip of ice water. He slowly took to his feet.

"Understood." He nodded to punctuate the point. I waved a hand at the screen door. He followed my gesture down the steps and onto the front lawn. Darkness had nearly consumed the dusk and he slipped into silhouette as he moved out of the porch light toward his car. Andy and I followed him halfway there. At the driver's door he paused and looked up at the sky where stars glittered against blue-black.

"The thing about Sioux City I can't get used to is the weather. My time with Litton was in the desert." He looked across the roof of the sedan. "Ever been to the desert? It can be beautiful."

He ducked into the sedan.

We watched him back onto the road. After a few minutes his tail-lights winked out in the west.

"Fuck!" I said. "He may not know it was me that got to Litton, but he knows we were there."

Andy turned and walked back to the house without a word.

2

"Nothing?"

"That's what I'm saying."

"You're fucking kidding me."

Pidge hopped up on the propane-powered airport tug. She wiggled on the seat, adjusting it to the full forward position so that her child-sized feet would reach the pedals.

I lifted the tow bar attached to the Piper Navajo's nose wheel. She turned the key and brought the tug to life, then eased forward on my hand signal. I snapped the bar into the tug hitch and climbed onto the fender. She dropped it in reverse and backed the win-engine airplane away from the gas pumps.

"Why?"

"Whaddya mean, 'Why?' Will! You've got this freak show thing in your head! You should be out there using it!"

We've had this conversation. Five people know what I can do—not counting a drug trafficker who thought I was a ghost. Pidge is one of them.

"To do what?"

"Kick some ass like we did in Chicago!" Pidge twisted in the seat and grabbed the back of the fender, steering in reverse across the ramp toward the open hangar. The ramp lay Sunday-quiet. I had taken a short charter run during the afternoon, picking up a construction work crew in Muskegon and delivering them to Essex. After landing Earl's Beechcraft Baron, I pulled the Education Foundation's new Navajo out of the hangar to gas it up for a morning trip. While I wrangled the gas hose, Pidge brought the Essex County Air Service Piper Mojave in for a landing on Runway 13, completing a two-day trip. By the time I finished fueling, she had the Mojave shut down and ready for a push into the hangar. I disconnected the tug from my ship and gave her a hand. She returned the favor, mostly, I am convinced, to take up her favorite topic with me.

She poked a finger at me. "Go out and take down some bad guys!"

"Okay. Fight crime. Sounds good. So…what? I'm supposed to hang out at the bank, waiting for it to be robbed? Then what?"

"Fly down on their asses!"

"Oh. Sure. Some guy with a gun. I'm supposed to fly down and kick his ass. You saw how that worked out in Montana. Pidge, I have no inertia. I'm weightless. If I punch the sonofabitch it just sends me in the opposite direction. High school physics."

"Go join the fucking CIA, Will! You'd be the perfect spy."

"Oh. You mean infiltrate the Kremlin?"

"That's what I'm talking about!"

"I don't speak Russian. Or Arabic. Or any other language. I can't read the Russian signs that say, 'This Way To Secret World Takeover Laboratory.' People don't sit around chatting about their evil plans."

We approached the hangar. Pidge wheeled the big airplane past the open door and started an arc away from the building. She stopped, shifted to a forward gear, and deftly maneuvered the fuselage to align with the center of the hangar. She eased the Navajo backward until the tip of the nose cleared the threshold. After she stopped, I jumped down and released the tow bar. I lifted the bar into a steel tray on the side of the tug. I expected Pidge to back away and roar off, but she killed the motor and sat looking at me.

"You have no fucking imagination, Stewart. If I had the ability to do what you can do, shit, I'd be hitting all the casinos—"

"Grand larceny."

"—I'd be sitting on a beach somewhere with a pile of cash—"

"Traceable."

"—screwing a different hardbody cabana boy nightly."

"That, I could see. But the beach? You'd flip out without flying."

"I'd buy a Gulfstream. How do you think I'd get to the fucking beach?"

"You'd get bored."

She didn't deny it. "What about you? And this?" She waved at the Navajo behind me. "I mean it's a beautiful bird, but are you really going to do this? Just fly Sandy Stone around on her Foundation business?"

"I'm in the rotation for charters. So's the airplane, on lease-back."

Pidge snorted. "Your wife is holding you back, man. That's the reason you keep hanging around here. That's the reason you don't take your show on the road and really do something with it." She read my look. "What? You know I'm right! Hey, I love Andy, but she needs to get her shit together, too. She should be working for the FBI and the two of you should walk right into the director's office and tell him what you can do. She can be your handler."

Pidge's mention of the FBI on the heels of Donaldson's visit sent my thoughts wandering. The pause I gave it only encouraged Pidge.

"You know I'm right!"

"I need to fly," I said.

"Fuck that. You can fly like all of us dream about flying. I've seen you change, Will. I mean it. In the last year. When they took away your ticket, you were like some fucking junkie. Itchy. You were dying to get it back. And then you did. And I shit you not, you're not the same. You don't have the fire for it. I mean, yeah, this is a good gig, talking the Foundation into buying a Navajo so you can cart Sandy around the country. But the charter thing for Earl? Half the time I think you're just doing it because you can't come up with a way to tell him you're done."

"You're full of shit."

Pidge squared herself at me. "You know he thinks you're going to take over this flying circus someday."

"You're completely full of shit."

Pidge simply grinned and shook her head. She twisted the key and fired up the tug. Flourishing middle finger salutes with both hands, she backed away from the hangar and roared away.

I strolled to the side of the hangar and hit the button to bring down the big folding door. After it thumped into place, I walked across the polished concrete to the exit, stroking my hand across the left wingtip as I went.

So full of shit.

I stopped at the exit door and looked back at the airplane, white and gleaming despite the darkness in the hangar. She sat poised and proud on her landing gear over a spot that once contained the shredded pieces of another Navajo, the one that spit me out over an Essex County marsh. The wreck of my accident had occupied this same hangar until someone unknown—at least to me—hauled it away. Now a nearly-identical new bird filled the void, as if born from the ashes.

My mind ran forward to the morning and the trip scheduled for just after dawn. I probed myself, looking for the thrill, the expectation that the next flight always awakened.

I gave it a minute. Then two.

I locked the door and went home.

3

Sandy Stone initially ran the Christine and Paulette Paulesky Education Foundation out of the home she inherited from her father, the late State Senator Bob Stone. Perhaps naively, she tried to conduct the business of the one hundred million-dollar fund from her dad's old office while staying true to her first love, teaching kindergarten. She thought that by enlisting the help of a board of directors consisting of my boss, Earl Jackson, my wife and me, she could field requests for funding, evaluate grant proposals, and dole out the Foundation's funds to deserving schools, teachers and education programs.

That was her first mistake. Earl was the only member worth his salt as a businessman, but his Attila The Hun personality clashed with the nuances of philanthropy. Andy was earnest in her efforts but found herself too busy in her job as a newly promoted detective with the City of Essex Police Department. Except for having created the fund by putting a gun to the forehead of Bargo Litton, one of the richest men in the world, I was utterly useless.

Sandy made her second mistake by throwing a huge Open For Business sign out through press releases and social media. Pleas for funding poured in, some of them legitimate, many of them scams. Sandy tried judging the cases on her own. That proved overwhelming. She then tried assembling her board to wade through the requests. That failed. None of us had the time.

One problem was the money. Aside from the fact that it attracted flies, it was too damned much. It needed to be invested, accounted for, reported, taxed, not taxed, and God-knows-what-else before distributing a dime. Earl jumped to Sandy's rescue and tapped an acquaintance, a human computer and accountant named Dewey Larmond. I asked my landlord, James Rankin, a farmer with the largest landholdings in Essex County, for the use of his attorney to assist Sandy in navigating the Foundation's legal limitations. Still, the more help Sandy got, the farther she drifted from the primary task of giving money to schools in need.

Two pieces fell into place to make it work.

The key piece came in the form of the Foundation's first full-time employee, Arun Dewar, a fresh graduate of the Northwestern University School of Business. To hear Sandy tell the story, Arun didn't interview for the job as much as roll in and announce he would be taking over. Just over five feet tall, looking more like a middle-schooler than a business school graduate, Arun spoke a mile-a-minute with an accent more British than Delhi. He sank his formidable intellectual teeth into the task of running the Foundation. He set up shop in one of the empty offices at the hangar at Essex County Airport and soon had the place wired for phone, internet and his boundless energy.

"If the business of this Foundation is the advancement of education, then one obvious mandate is to see education benefit from the unwavering and uninterrupted expertise of one of its stellar practitioners," Arun told Sandy on day one. "You." At which point he gathered up the stacks of applications littering Sandy's home office and loaded them into his Toyota for a trip to his new office in the hangar.

That was in late May. I wasn't sure I'd seen a day since when that red Corolla wasn't parked outside the hangar.

I contributed the second rescue element. I proposed that the Foundation use money left over from another case Andy and I worked to purchase a Piper Navajo. The seven-seat airplane offered Sandy a way to travel quickly and efficiently to small town schools applying for funds. When it wasn't being used for Foundation business, Earl leased it to fill the gaps in the busy Essex County Air Service charter schedule. Arun quickly connected with Rosemary II, Essex County Air's unflappable office manager, and the two of them conspired to handle all planning and scheduling for the aircraft, including maintenance.

Monday morning, after Donaldson's weekend visit, I showed up for a predawn preflight to find Arun had the hangar lit up and his espresso machine pumping.

"Good morning, Will!" Arun flashed his bright smile at me as I maneuvered my flight and overnight bags into the office. "Coffee is ready. And there are scones. Miss Stone will be here in thirty!" No amount of effort on Sandy's part convinced Arun to call her by her first name.

"Wheels up in forty-five, then," I found myself trying to match the young man's energy, which was absurd absent my first coffee of the day.

Arun and his spotless white shirt disappeared into his office. July had been warm so far, and the air conditioning in the hangar offices struggled to keep pace, but Arun never failed to show up in a white shirt and tie with a suit coat on a hanger behind his office door.

He called out to me from behind said door.

"Do you have the updated itinerary? I emailed it to you last night."

"Sure," I said, pouring myself a cup of salvation. "Probably. Maybe. Can you print one for me?"

A sheet of paper appeared at my elbow.

"When are you going to add email to your phone, Will?"

I took the neatly printed trip itinerary. "When…" I tried to think of something pithy involving Hell and frost, but the caffeine had yet to jump-start my brain. "Ah, screw it."

Arun dashed back into his office. I looked over the schedule. As a practitioner of precise time management, I admired Arun's to-the-minute plan for the three-day trip. The first leg took us to Bloomington, Indiana for a morning meeting with allowance for an early lunch to follow. The second leg took us to Nashville for another round of meetings and an overnight, with additional meetings on Tuesday morning. An early afternoon departure then took us west to Springfield, Missouri. Another overnight. Meetings on Wednesday, then home. Arun listed arrivals, departures, allocations for ground transportation, hotels, blocks for lunch—I double-checked to see if he wrote in bathroom breaks. He had.

Sandy initially invited me to accompany her to the meetings. I told her I would love nothing more than schmoozing with school superintendents and school board members, touring science wings and preschool programs, but I had already scheduled the time slot to poke sharp sticks in my eyes. Plus, she had Arun at her elbow.

Besides, I had other plans.

SANDY ARRIVED at the hangar within half a minute of Arun's predicted ETA. I had just finished filing flight plans and updating my weather briefings. I use an old desk in the hangar. The fresh air feels good in summer, and it removes me from Arun's incessant ministering of minutiae. Through a glass wall between the hangar and a small lounge, I watched Arun hustle to handle Sandy's overnight bag while bombarding her with details about the day. She, however, spotted me and waved a hand that worked on Arun like a Pause Button. She dropped her purse and launched in my direction.

The dark expression on her face suggested trouble. I leaped to the inevitable conclusion.

Dave.

Sandy Stone is an attractive young woman. Exponentially beyond attractive. Dave Peterson, my pal and fellow Essex Air Pilot, is smitten with her, and he worked on me for a couple months to broker an introduction. She shot him down before his wheels left the turf. Andy and I felt bad for Dave but understood her position, and in fact had warned Dave. Sandy was only a few months past the worst ordeal of her life—a storybook marriage blown to hell by the murder of her father, and then her own near-death experience at the hands of her new husband. She simply wasn't ready for a relationship and she told Dave so. He took it with dignity in her presence but went down hard in her absence.

Now she marched toward me across the polished concrete floor of the hangar wearing the same look my wife wears when I've done something I've been told not to do. I immediately wondered what crime Dave had committed, and just as quickly groped my mind for an alibi.

"Will," she said (not "Good morning, Will" and not smiling).

"It's not my fault."

"What?"

"Standard greeting for any woman wearing that look."

"What? No." She glanced back to confirm that Arun was occupied. He shuffled folders in a leather briefcase. Turning back to me, she gestured for me to walk with her. We moved toward the open hangar door and the first hints of morning light. "The FBI came to see me yesterday."

"A certain Special Agent Donaldson?"

She nodded, again checking to be sure Arun wasn't suddenly behind us. He has that ability. "You know him?"

"Only because he came to the house to talk to Andy. What did he want from you?"

"He asked me a lot of questions about the Foundation. About you and Andy."

Shit.

"Like what? What kind of questions?"

She lifted her crystalline blue eyes high to her right. "What was my connection to Litton Industries? How long had I known Mr. Litton? Was the Foundation set up through Todd before the wedding?" She put her hand on my arm. "He wanted to know what your involvement was. Before becoming a board member. And the same about Andy. He asked how you both know Bargo Litton. I didn't know that you did."

"I don't." It came out too fast. She looked at me, questioning. "At least not as any kind of acquaintance. I mean, everybody knows who he is. Doesn't mean you know the guy. What did you tell him?"

"I told him that before I or any member of the Foundation board would be divulging proprietary Foundation business, he'd better explain the nature of his inquiry."

"I can tell you the nature of his inquiry. He used to work for Litton. He got fired. I think he's having trouble getting past that. What did he tell you?"

"Nothing. I mean, the usual. 'The FBI doesn't divulge the nature of its investigations.' Do you think he's pursuing something about the Foundation?" She looked worried.

"No. Before he came to see you, he stopped at our place. On Saturday."

"Why?"

"He says he's investigating Josiah James." Sandy made a face, like she caught a whiff of something bad. "Yeah, that guy."

"Well, what on earth does that have to do with the Foundation?"

"I doubt it has anything to do with the Foundation. Look, I wouldn't worry about it. He came looking for help from Andy. The guy is probably just being thorough. Checking us out."

"I suppose, but…when this all happened, with Dad, with Todd…you know I wasn't at my best. I wasn't very clear when Litton's attorneys contacted me about the Foundation. It happened in a blur."

That's because it wasn't Litton's attorney. James Rankin's attorney set up the Foundation. That Sandy didn't remember his role at the time came as no surprise.

"A lot happened."

"I know, but should I be worried? Do you think there's something wrong? Should I contact Mr. Litton?"

"No, no, no." I shook my head. "There's nothing wrong, not with the Foundation. Until someone tells you otherwise, everything was done by the book and according to Litton's wishes. Plus, I hear that these days, the guy has gone all Howard Hughes. Nobody knows where he's hiding. Leave it alone. The Foundation is fine. Like I said, that FBI guy wanted Andy's help with James. I think he was just doing a little background check on her."

"What if Litton wants his money back?"

I laughed. "Then you'd already be up to your eyeballs in attorneys."

She let the laugh infect her and produced a wry smile. "I suppose that's true."

"Just let me know if you hear from Donaldson again, okay? I'll want to tell Andy."

It seemed to calm her.

Like magic, Arun appeared at her shoulder. "Miss Stone, I believe we're within our departure window."

"Well, then, let's kick the tires and light the fires!" I clapped him on the back.

4

Early morning summer flight lets you bore holes in a glass-smooth sky before the sun has a chance to cook up thermals that lace the flight path with turbulence. Our ride to Indiana had the quality of floating. The sun climbed into the sky along with us, casting platinum reflections across the metallic surface of Lake Michigan off our left wing. Chicago Center gave me the usual extra vectors around O'Hare, but I didn't mind. The engines sang. My fingers whispered to the controls. And the thrill I had been looking for after Pidge challenged me showed itself. Neither Sandy nor Arun accepted my offer of the right front seat. The cockpit and the sky were all mine.

Two hours and seven minutes after lifting off, our wheels kissed the pavement of Runway 17 at Monroe County airport, the sole airport serving Bloomington. I found a place to park, waved off the lineman offering fuel services, and set about offloading Sandy and Arun. A cluster of suits stood outside the FBO; Sandy's welcoming committee awaited, hats in hand. They all looked like English teachers. I made excuses about seeing to the airplane and sent Sandy and Arun across the ramp into their care.

As the engines cooled and ticked, I climbed back into the cabin and took a seat facing aft with my feet up. I pulled out my phone.

"Hey," Andy said cheerfully.

"What're you up to?"

"Shooting pictures of VINs out on Al Raymond's back lot. Probably getting poison ivy."

I pictured it. Andy on duty favors jeans and a pullover top unless an interview calls for something more businesslike. In the rising summer heat and because she's on duty, she would have her hair tied up or braided.

"Why?"

"Oh, don't ask." She made it sound like her efforts wouldn't crack the case of the century. "Usual Disclaimer?"

"Usual Disclaimer."

"That woman who works in his shop—his chief mechanic?"

"Yeah?" I wanted to say Godzilla because anyone who ever had to deal with the woman walked away knowing how Tokyo felt after a rampage.

"She got drunk last night."

"Destroyed the Ginza Line?"

"What? No. She was with Al at Sully's and she got in a fight with him. They broke one of those video poker machines by the bar. Al ducked out, but she was still there when Sims pulled up. He hauled her in for disorderly."

"Sims? Wow. Points for bravery." Officer Terry Sims might be the smallest cop on the Essex PD roster. Andy is taller by a hand.

"She went on a rant about Al. Taught Sims a few new words. But also claimed Al's been trolling in Milwaukee with his flatbed. Pulling older models onto the truck like he's towing a parking violator, then stashing them in his yard."

"Ah, so you get to chase the wild goose in the back lot."

"I think she's full of it, although that rumor about Al has surfaced before."

"Speaking of full of it, guess who stopped to see Sandy yesterday."

"Special Agent Donaldson," Andy said, continuing her unbroken run of marching one step ahead of me.

"Oh. You talked to her?"

"She left me a voicemail this morning. I didn't get to follow up with her yet."

"She's off touring now, but I talked to her." I relayed what Sandy told me about her meeting with the FBI. Andy pondered it across cell phone silence for a moment.

"You do know that proving the two of us were in that desert motel is child's play for an experienced FBI agent," she said.

"Don't you need a warrant to search someone's credit card history?"

"Depends." An answer I often get from my law enforcement wife. "But it hardly matters. The question here is whether he's poking around us for what happened with Litton, or is he really pursuing James?"

This was new. "James? Going after James?"

"I've just been thinking."

I had already decided, the night Lane watched Mike Mackiejewski kill Corey Braddock with a shotgun blast, that Josiah James would pay for his role in the tragedy. I vented my feelings with Andy, who has a habit of talking me out of murder. Nothing she said changed my mind about making James pay. It just meant I would have to make it happen my way.

"Are you saying you want to help Donaldson?"

"That's not for discussion at this moment, Will."

"I can't tell if that's encouragement or a warning."

"A request, love. To talk about it when you get home."

"Fine."

"But I can answer your question. I have no intention of working with Donaldson."

"Good."

"Listen, gotta go. I think there might be a family of raccoons under this car."

"Love you!"

5

There are four major hospitals in the Nashville area specializing in the care of children. Of the four, according to my limited research on the web, the Marjorie Ellenwell Children's Hospital and Center for Cancer Care fit my target specifications. Not that the Monroe Carell Hospital at Vanderbilt or the Children's Hospital at TriStar Centennial fell short. I picked Ellenwell because it boasted of advanced research in the treatment of leukemia.

Fucking leukemia.

In the seven months since committing an act of absolute insanity on an Angel Flight into Marshfield, Wisconsin—and then finding out *the other thing* may have saved a dying child—I've been in and out of half a dozen children's hospitals. Always at night. Always unseen. Except for the first one I visited, no one sanctioned the visits. At Children's of Milwaukee, Christie Watkins, an oncology nurse who rode through the night with me over Marshfield, got me in the door, took me to the rooms of the sleeping children, and later reported the mix of miracles and disappointment that followed my visit.

Christie is one of the five people who know what I can do. She's one of only three people who knows that when I wrapped *the other thing* around Emma Parrish, it killed the leukemia that was killing her.

Christie called me four days after she gave me a middle-of-the-night tour of Children's Hospital in early January. I didn't expect the jolt of anticipation, seeing her name on my phone screen. She caught me driving home after work. I pulled over to take the call.

"Three of them! Will! It worked on three of them!"

"Slow down, Christie."

"Screw that! I've been dying to tell you! I waited. I wanted to be sure. But as of the start of my shift tonight, we have three kids here whose current condition cannot be explained. All three had leukemia. Two were advanced. And now—Will! *You did this!*"

She choked up, fought it, then plowed on. And on. About doctors baffled by the unexplained remission. About pharmaceutical reps elbowing each other aside to claim that their particular regimen deserved credit. About three emaciated kids who were suddenly ravenous, full of energy, full of life. About tests and test results.

The more excited she got, the greater the fear I felt welling inside.

I asked her about the other four. We had seen seven kids the night she took me on the tour. Seven rooms where, behind closed doors and under Christie's watchful eye, I lifted light little bodies off the sheets and closed *the other thing* around them. Most slept. A few moaned. All were tiny and tearing my heart apart.

"Inconclusive," Christie replied. "But I'm watching them. Maybe it takes time for—"

"What's the common denominator? Among the three?"

"Well, the diagnosis for each one is different. Complicated. There are factors of—"

"Christie! High school graduate, here. What's the common denominator?"

"Leukemia."

"And the others?"

She launched into a list of Latin medical names—a mixed bag of horrors inflicted on children. She said, "We'll know more after another round. Maybe the others need a higher dose. When are you coming back?"

I didn't answer.

"Will! You *have to* come back! We have to do more testing!"

"No. We're done."

"Will—!"

"Christie! You promised me. You made me a promise about this." It was her turn not to answer. "Listen. I will pursue this. On my own. But you won't know. That's how this works. You won't know I've been there or who I touch."

She gave it a beat. "Can we discuss—"

"I need time to figure this out."

"Please—"

I ended the call.

That was in January. Since then, I visited three more hospitals devoted to treating childhood cancer. I've broken and entered, sneaked in with shift-change employees, or most often, arrived during visiting hours and merely floated in a corner until well past midnight. Once silence and low light took command, I eased my way through empty halls, squeezing past partially open doors to find children in restless sleep. Some wore bandages over clear plastic IV tubes. Some were bald and thin. Some recoiled at the touch of a stranger in their sleep. Twice, the children woke as I held them above their beds. One cried out, "I'm flying!" I had to warn her that she must remain quiet or the magic would end. She solemnly promised to be quiet but begged for more, so I flew her around the room, pushing off the walls, careful not to topple any of the equipment at her bedside. She giggled in delight.

When I left that room, I prayed she would be one of the miracles. But then I prayed for all of them.

Getting in and out is anything but easy. I don't know if they've always been so rigid about security, but a children's hospital is a fortress at night. They're locked up tight, with single-point entry and exit, armed guards and myriad cameras. While none of that stops me, it does make the mission difficult.

I don't know how it works—what I'm doing—any more than I know the origin of *the other thing.*

I don't learn the names of the children. I try to find kids fighting leukemia in its various forms, but it's nearly impossible for me to know the specific diagnosis. There's no "chart" hanging at the end of the bed. In-room computer terminals blink at me, but I have no access and would hardly know how to read the chart if I managed a log-in. There are signs. Specific sections of the floor. Physical indicators. My aim may not be perfect, but I'm pretty sure I can tell the difference between a child on chemotherapy and a retired banker recovering from a triple bypass.

I tell myself that I'm experimenting, the same way I've been experimenting with self-propulsion in the barn. The effect of *the other thing* on sick children may be science, but what I'm doing is far from scientific method. It is literally shooting in the dark.

I haven't asked myself why I'm doing it, because that's a stupid question. I can do it. Therefore, I should do it. In a dark hospital room, looking at a sleeping child, the equation is simple.

The hard questions come outside the room when I consider how this aspect of *the other thing* fits in the world of medicine, moral obligation and money. I've already glimpsed the answer to that in the face of the Angel Flight nurse, Christie Watkins. I see what she wants, and it scares me.

I SLIPPED AWAY from Sandy and Arun after we checked into the Holiday Inn Express near the airport in Smyrna—which I chose for landing near Nashville because the services are less expensive and more convenient than those at the international airport, and because it was closer to the rural school district on Sandy's itinerary.

I waited thirty minutes in the room, just to allow for the possibility that Arun might rap on my door with last-minute itinerary changes. When he didn't appear, I left the hotel, caught a cab, and took a short ride to Ellenwell. The cab dropped me at a main entrance to the modern, five-story hospital. Revolving doors ushered me into an atrium decorated with green palms, a small pond and a fountain. A grand piano occupied one corner, playing something light and jazzy on its own. Opposite the piano, a long, curved information desk faced the doors. Behind the desk, a young woman welcomed me with a warm smile.

I glanced at my watch as I walked up. "How am I doing on time? Do I have enough to hit the gift shop before visiting hours end?"

"Which floor will you be visiting?"

I had no idea. "Children's. Cancer treatment. I forget..."

"Three. You've got about fifteen minutes. Visiting hours end at eight for the children. But I need to register you. Who are you here to see?"

I glanced at the small gift shop tucked in the corner of a hallway behind the expansive desk. "Tell you what," I said, pulling out my phone, "while I go get my niece a teddy bear, I'll call my sister. She's upstairs now. She can come down and either validate me or take the bear up to her daughter."

"Okay, but you'll need a badge to get onto the floor, so have your sister meet you here."

"Got it!" I hurried toward the gift shop. Noting cameras everywhere, I diverted to the men's room just beyond the small shop. No cameras in the men's room. No men, either.

Fwooomp! Holding a grip on the door handle, I vanished. Pressing one hand on the wall, I pulled the door open and slipped through.

The hall remained blessedly empty. I pulled a propulsion unit from my flight jacket pocket, snapped a propeller in place, and thumbed it to life. It pulled me back toward the atrium. I kept the power level low, barely a growl. Jazz piano covered the sound.

The young woman at Reception devoted most of her attention to a book spread on the desk in front of her, but she glanced back at the gift shop as I passed her. She hadn't forgotten about me.

A bank of elevators rose the full height of the atrium behind the front desk. In the fashion of modern architecture featuring atriums, each floor offered a view of the greenery and fountain below. I ascended, counted off three floors and passed over a waist-high railing onto a carpeted hallway.

"Damn. I like this place," I said aloud when I spotted a sign that read *Children's Oncology.* The sign pointed down the hall, underscoring my point with Pidge. Without good signage, sneaking around unseen is futile.

I held a glide a few inches above the carpet and floated down the hall, vigilant for visitors or staff. Luck stayed with me. Neither appeared. The hallway split at a Y junction, and more good signage directed me forward. Patient rooms lined either side of a hall sporting brightly colored doors and cartoon characters from the Disney library. A clear plastic frame at each door displayed hand-drawn artwork and featured the first name of the room's occupant. Marcy. Tobie. Jean. Cody. Most of the artwork looked tender-aged, as Andy would call it. One sheet, however, showed significant talent and skill, suggesting the occupant might be older. Older kids pose challenges.

I came up on a nurse's station serving as a hub to four hallways branched in cardinal directions. Three women and one man in pastel scrubs worked at various computer terminals around the station.

A man and a woman in civilian clothing, each tugging the hand of a toddler between them, emerged from one of the rooms and moved down the hall toward me. I pushed the power slide and rose toward the ceiling, extending my legs to let them pass beneath me. They called out "Good-night" to the staff at the nurse's station and continued toward the elevators.

Beyond the nurse's station I found a small lounge. In one corner, a television broadcast silent images over closed captions. The opposite wall offered kitchen features: a sink, refrigerator, microwave and one of those glorious little single-serving coffee makers. I settled in a hover facing the counter and spent some time figuring out how to brew a cup without anyone seeing poltergeist objects move above the countertop. With coffee made, I settled in to kill time in the muted company of ESPN.

Christie Watkins taught me the basic routines common to many hospitals. Ellenwell seemed to uphold those routines. The seven-to-seven rotation staff spent the first part of their on-shift hour getting their patient assignments and reviewing charts. At eight they fanned out for the first of a night's hourly assessments and to administer medications. Parents leaving filed out. Parents staying the night prepared for restless sleep on cots and couches. At nine, the nurses repeated the hourly assessment routine. Most of the patients remained awake but followed the lights-out instructions of the staff. From then on, hourly, the nurses slipped into their assigned patient rooms for assessment, checking IV and infusion connections, and caring for those whose pain denied sleep.

I waited until almost eleven-thirty before striking out.

Some of the doors near the nurse's station were closed to protect the patients from noise, but most kids seem to want their door partly open at night. Slipping into those rooms without moving the door was easy. Once inside, I let my eyes adjust to the dark. The rooms maintain a design consistency. Bathrooms to the left or right of the door. Beds perpendicular to the entry. The beds were designed for children, small and low.

In my first room, the bed was a crib and the child within not quite a toddler. A woman lay under a thin blanket on a couch beside the crib. Even in the dark, even in slumber, I saw wear and worry in the woman's cheeks.

I maneuvered over the side of the crib and reached in. I removed a blanket, careful to avoid tangling with the plastic IV line taped in place on the child's arm. I placed my hands on either side of the child's ribcage over its fuzzy one-piece sleeper. Initially, I had feared pushing *the other thing* around someone unless I held them in a full embrace. I feared not enveloping them completely, with dreadful consequences. I've since grown confident that all I need is a firm touch.

The child wiggled and made a soft sound, a nearly-inaudible signal that magically transmitted to the mother, causing her to stir restlessly. I waited. Both settled back into sound sleep.

I pushed.

Fwooomp! Gone, the child had no weight. I lifted it to my chest— boy or girl, I had no way of knowing in the dark. I smelled its baby-scented scalp. It floated helpless against me, serene in its dreams. The IV line hung in the air, vanishing where it met the edge of *the other thing*.

I don't know if duration matters, but I floated over that crib for a long time, holding the child against my chest with one hand and the top rail of the crib with the other. I listened to its shallow breathing long enough to be made drowsy by the gentle rhythm. Eventually, wary of the on-the-hour nursing assessment due soon, I shook off the sleepiness dragging my eyelids down and eased the child back to the mattress.

Fwooomp! It settled and fussed, alerted by the shift in gravity when it reappeared. Fussing caused the mother to stir. This time she lifted her head and looked. Seeing the blanket out of place, she sat up and reached into the crib to cover her child. She stroked its head.

I slipped out the door, fingers crossed.

Working between the clockwork care visits of the nurses, I entered eight rooms over the next four hours.

Nearing the end of my rounds, I came to the room with the crisply drawn name display. Swirls and delicate lines surrounded the name Anastasia. The door hung open far enough to let me glide in.

She sat on her bed with a sketch pad on her knees. A girl of twelve or thirteen wearing an elaborate twist of colorful kerchiefs over her bald head. Her skin glowed, pale under a single desk lamp positioned on a small table beside the bed. Her eyes were Asian, but I lack the knowledge to guess her national origin. She focused dark eyes intently on the strokes of her pencil across the paper's surface. I eased closer to examine her drawing.

The picture portrayed a girl. Thin. Hairless, like the artist who drew her. She was rendered upright above a pond. She floated several inches above the surface of still water. Her hands were open, and her arms were spread at her waist; her face was upturned. The scene, to my eye, was expertly rendered. Delicately shaded. Perfectly proportioned. This girl had talent. And I had a dilemma.

Show myself. She freaks out.

Make her vanish. She freaks out.

Move on.

And what if she's one of the miracles?

The pink tip of her tongue peeked from the corner of her mouth, a signal of deep concentration. She deftly wiggled the pencil lead, shading the eyes of her image. Making them smoky. Making the girl in the picture darker, sadder.

Making up my mind for me.

Fwooomp! I edged into the room, fully visible.

"Hey."

She startled, looked up and blinked at me. The pencil hung frozen over her picture. "Who are you?"

"Doctor?" It came off as a lame guess.

I got the look, the one that belongs exclusively to preadolescent girls. "You don't look like a doctor."

"Visiting art critic?"

She reflexively turned the picture away from me. I saw the call button beside her on the bed. She didn't reach for it.

"Lemme see." I pointed. "Come on. Please."

"Are you another therapist? Did my parents send you?"

"At this hour? I saw your light. Come on. Show me. I won't tell anyone." I realized saying those words to a preteen girl in the middle of the night while lurking around a children's hospital carried a huge creepy factor.

She studied me long enough to convince herself that she had studied me, then eased the sketch pad toward me. Although I'd already seen it, I took a long moment to study it. Whatever I said next might save her life.

"I see this as the moment of transition. Am I correct?"

She nodded.

"Is she already across? Because she casts no reflection on the water."

She nodded again, this time bringing her eyes up to read me, looking for trust she didn't expect to find.

"Are you going to tell me I'm really good?"

"Nope. Everyone tells you that. And you can't be sure they mean it —or if they're just being nice because you're sick. I want to ask you something." I pointed at the picture. "Do you think you're ready for that?"

She didn't hesitate. "My mom and dad aren't. But I am."

"You sure? That floating thing looks scary." I gestured at the foot of her bed, at the open space in the room. "Want to try it out first? Take it for a test drive?"

The *look* came back, complete with tucked lip and knit brows. I decided I wouldn't want to be her parents; this one would be a challenge. I reached out and closed a gentle grip on her sketch pad. She let me take it. I placed it on the tray beside the bed. I stepped to the foot of the bed and held out my hands.

"I'm not getting out of bed with you! I'm going to call someone." Her hand fell to the call button.

"Wait! Let me show you something. Okay? Here." *Fwooomp!* I vanished. Her eyes opened wide. Astonished pupils floated on bright white—hunting for me in the empty space at the foot of her bed. "Relax. I'm still here." *Fwooomp!* I settled on my feet and held out my hands. "Come on. Try it with me."

She stared at me, deeply uncertain, fear growing on her face. "Are you—? Is it time? Are you here for me?"

"Oh hell, no! I'm just here to give you a ride. So you don't have to be afraid."

"I'm not afraid!"

"Honey, everybody's afraid. If they tell you otherwise, they're lying. C'mon."

I held out my hands.

She wiggled to her knees, then to her feet on the bed. The heavy plastic infusion line running into the top of her gown tugged at her. She reached up, closed a valve and pulled it free.

"Should you be doing that?"

"I do it all the time."

She took two hesitant steps closer and her hands came forward to meet mine. I gently closed my larger hands around hers.

"No giggling," I warned her. She suppressed a smile.

FWOOOMP! I pushed a little extra hard and *the other thing* snapped around us.

"Heeee!" she squeaked.

"*Shhhhhhh!*" I worried about the open door and the cluster of night nurses down the hall. The girl's breathing grew urgent, louder. "Relax. We're going to float now. Like in your picture." My feet left the floor. I flexed my ankles for a light push-off. Her hands clamped on mine like vices. She rose with me. "I'm going to let go with one hand. Just relax." I had to pull my right hand out of her tight grip. She wobbled and began flailing. "Easy! Easy! Just hang loose. Just float." She calmed down.

We floated free of the bed. In short order I had to touch the ceiling to stop our ascent. I used the core muscle to rotate her around me like a dancer. She didn't giggle or laugh like Lane, but her rapid breathing telegraphed her excitement. We toured the small dimensions of the room. I kept her aloft for what felt like a long while, though it may only have been minutes.

Eventually I guided her to a position over the bed.

Fwooomp!

She reappeared and bobbed on the mattress. I dropped to the floor beside her. She stood frozen, astonished, searching her body and mine.

"Is that—is that what it will be like?"

"I don't have a clue. Here. Sit before you fall down." She dropped onto the mattress. The preteen skepticism was gone. She stared at me with wonder. She maintained a rigid grip on my left hand.

"Anastasia, this wasn't a preview of death. You shouldn't be thinking in those terms. But, no matter what happens, you don't have to be afraid," I said. I had to hustle the words out. My throat threatened to close. I peeled my hand free, picked up the sketch pad and looked at the image again. "May I have this?"

She nodded. I handed the pad to her. "You have to sign it."

She released a shy smile, found her pencil and added her name to the lower right corner in flourishing cursive. She dotted the i with a heart, then tore the sheet off the pad and handed it to me. I folded it carefully and slipped it into the breast pocket of my flight jacket.

"Thanks."

"What's your name?"

I considered lying to her. Giving my name might be one too many clues left behind. A kid telling a story about a strange man who made him or her disappear and fly won't gain a lot of traction, but when you start adding a name and possibly an image from a security camera, things begin to take shape. It brought Donaldson to mind. A dangerous man collecting puzzle pieces.

"Will," I told her, despite caution and logic. "And listen to me." I leaned in close to her, picked up her hand again and squeezed. "Do you feel this?" I squeezed harder. Pinched.

"Uh-huh." She winced at the pressure.

I let her hand go. She rubbed it. "That was real. This wasn't a dream. Whatever you think for the rest of your life, I promise you, this wasn't a dream. I can't explain it, but don't ever doubt yourself. Got it?"

"Got it."

"Okay. I gotta go. And yes."

"What?"

"You are good." I patted the drawing in my pocket.

Fighting an overwhelming urge to kiss her on the forehead, I backed away, vanished, and pulled myself out of the room as she stared at the empty space I had occupied.

6

I made my first solo flight after just six and a half hours of training. Every instructor I've ever flown with has told me I have a touch. I was sixteen and full of myself. My confidence grew disproportionally. A few weeks after that first solo, around the time I had fourteen or fifteen hours, I was practicing takeoffs and landings. I had this thing *down.* I was hot shit. On the fifth or sixth landing I guided the Cessna 152 down the final approach toward the runway numbers I'd been hitting the way Robin Hood hits bullseyes. Just as I eased the nose up to flare for the landing, a rogue gust of wind swept across the runway. The aircraft ballooned skyward, what with the big barn-door flaps hanging out. My airspeed dropped and the aircraft heaved off to the left. Grass replaced asphalt below me. I slammed the throttle forward for full power but felt the shudder of a stall. At that point I hung thirty feet in the air in the worst possible position. Without forward speed, the wing ceases to produce lift. Instead of flying, I sat in an aluminum can about to fall to earth. To this day, I'm not sure how that little trainer clawed its way out of a crash. I remember wallowing along above the edge of the taxiway, feeling the flaps resist forward speed. I don't remember raising the flaps. I don't remember climbing out and flying the traffic pattern back to another landing. I remember touching down and braking to get off the runway as fast as possible. And I remember sitting there, shaken, thinking I needed to taxi back to the hangar to get the hell out of this machine. I don't remember consciously deciding instead to taxi to the end of the runway for another takeoff, and then another landing. Possibly the most important takeoff and landing of my career. I don't remember either.

Floating outside Anastasia's room with her sketch tucked in my jacket, I wanted to get out of that hospital and never return. I wanted to be done with it. I wished that the Angel Flight had never happened, and I had never learned that *the other thing* does more than let me vanish and float. I looked for good signage that would allow me to escape. And I would have.

Except for Benny.

Benny's door sign had an airplane on it. He either had my artistic talent, or he was somewhere in the preschool age range. The airplane had two wings and a tail and a scribble for a propeller. A stick figure sat in the pilot's seat with a round head and a big fat grin. The name Benny was spelled across the bottom of the page in uneven, block letters, but this kid wanted to make sure everyone got it. He wrote "me" above the airplane and used an arrow to point at the pilot.

Benny.

I took one look at Benny's sign and knew I had to make one more takeoff, and one more landing.

If the sign wasn't enough, I heard a child's voice call out from within his room. "Yeeeeooooowwwwwwnnnnn!" It translated easily for me.

"Benny! Go to sleep!" One of the nurses called out from across the hall. I prepared to hustle out of the way, but she didn't move from her station. Apparently, dealing with Benny in the middle of the night was routine.

"Okay!" Benny called out cheerfully.

I used my propulsion unit to glide through his door and into his room.

Benny sat on his bed in the dark, nowhere near asleep. He waved his hand above his head, pushing a small die-cast airplane through the blue skies of his imagination. His arm wore tape for an IV plug, but the plastic tube was disconnected and hung dripping at the side of his bed.

I waited a minute to make sure he didn't let loose with more airplane noises. He had been warned. Keep it quiet, and no one would come in and force him to duck under the covers. He operated his airplane in silence.

When I felt reasonably certain he wouldn't draw trouble, I reappeared.

Fwooomp!

Benny scarcely gave me a glance.

"What are you flying?" I asked, whispering.

"Airplane." There was a hint of *dummy* in the reply.

"I can see that," I shot back. "What kind of airplane?"

He looked at me. I would have guessed four or five, but I've found that kids waging war with cancer run small. His face read slightly older. Seven? He had the signature bald head, but didn't wear a cap, although I saw one on his nightstand. It advertised Southwest Airlines.

"Lemme see it," I said. I put my hand out. He surrendered the toy to me, but with an expectant look.

"F4U Corsair," I said. "You can always tell. They have the gull wing." I pointed out the wing shape on the blue toy. "Navy fighter. One of the best."

Benny looked at his toy with new appreciation. I bent down, resting my elbows on the protective bars of his bed.

"I'm a pilot," I said.

"For real?"

"Gimme five." I held up my hand which he slapped vigorously. "As real as that. I fly airplanes all the time."

"My uncle is a pilot. He gave me this. And he gave me a hat."

"Does he ever take you flying?"

Benny shook his head. *Well, what kind of crap is that?* A kid like this, you gotta take him flying.

"Ever been in an airplane?"

"We rode in an airplane to come here!"

"One like that?" I pointed at his Corsair.

Benny shook his head. "It was really big! It was orange!"

"I like this blue one better. How would you like to go flying right now?"

Benny's eyes lit up. His whole body shivered suddenly, like he'd taken a mild electric charge.

"Okay. But we pilots obey the rules. First rule, be really, really quiet. The nurses will make us stop if they hear you. Can you do that?"

His head bobbed a solemn vow of silence.

"Alright, then. You're my copilot. This is going to feel funny. Put your airplane down and stand up."

He stood. I reached out and picked him up off the bed. He was thin and light. He threw an arm around my neck.

"Can I wear my hat?" He pointed. I plucked the hat from the nightstand and dropped it on his head. He grinned.

"Okay, copilot. Here we go!"

Fwooomp!

We began a slow rise. I expected a giggle or an outcry, but Benny fell silent.

"You okay pal?"

He didn't speak.

"What's wrong?"

"When are we going to fly?" he whispered.

"Um…" My feet were already six inches off the floor, but I realized that from Benny's perspective this wasn't all that impressive. I wondered if he even noticed that his body had disappeared. I checked the clock to see how much time we had before the next hourly assessment. "Okay, hang tight. And keep quiet!"

"Shhhhh!" he signaled.

I pulled the power unit from my pocket and rotated. A shot of power took me to the door. After scanning for trouble, I cleared the hall and eased out. I pushed the power to a low, subaudible growl. We eased forward and I aimed upward. The grip on my neck tightened and Benny wiggled, telling me he was sure as shit flying now.

We took to the hallway, rising. Benny's breathing quickened.

"What do you think?" I whispered when we were well out of earshot of the nurse's station.

"Cool!"

We passed the Y junction and eased down the hall toward the elevators. Beside the elevators, the waist-height railing overlooked the atrium. I pushed slightly higher and we floated across the top of the railing, out over the huge atrium, three stories up.

"WOW!" Benny cried out, full voice. I had expected his arm around my neck to strangle me, but he remained relaxed.

"Shhhh!" I checked. The reception desk was empty, as was the atrium. Still, a kid calling out at three a.m. might set off alarms.

We flew. We flew figure eights. We flew down to the fountain and back up to the skylights at the top of the atrium, higher than the fifth floor. We circled and dove and climbed and Benny broke the rules and giggled and laughed. I had to shush him when a man in blue scrubs hurried across the atrium floor below us. The man fingered his phone as he walked. If he heard a tiny boy giggling in the rafters, he didn't pay it any mind.

I watched the time. When the session began to feel long, I gave Benny a last circuit, down to the floor, around the piano, which someone had unplugged, then back up to the skylight. It was time to go home.

Back on Benny's floor, we passed the lounge with the coffee station. A clock showed that the minute hand had edged past three-thirty. The coffee called out to me. I decided this was going to be an all-nighter and resolved to grab a cup on my way out of the hospital.

The television hanging on the wall opposite the coffee station stopped me cold.

Josiah James's puffy head filled the screen, his mouth working furiously, baring canines. Big bold graphics splashed across the screen behind him.

JOSIAH JAMES AMERICAN REVOLUTION TOUR

Quick cuts of the American flag waving, of jets screaming overhead in formation, of battleships and marching American soldiers joined the onscreen barrage of images. The big metallic title graphic returned with another image of James, this one striking a noble and patriotic pose with his face turned skyward. A series of city names and dates appeared.

A tour.

The asshole was taking his show on the road.

I hung there staring when a long, low muttering sound broke the silence.

"I farted!" Benny announced loudly, giggling.

"BENNY, GO TO SLEEP!" someone called out from the nurse's station.

45

I turned my head to where I thought his ear was and whispered, "You sure did! Something stinks!" He laughed.

"BENNY!"

The Josiah James commercial faded to black, but I found myself smiling at Benny's contribution to the sound track.

I took Benny back to his bed and warned him that pilots need their sleep and airplanes need to rest. I put his die-cast Corsair on the night-stand along with his hat and tucked him in.

He checked his airplane and hat, gave me an inscrutable look, then closed his eyes.

I slipped out.

One more takeoff and landing.

7

"Hey." Andy's voice.

"Hi!" I said it a little too brightly.

"Were you sleeping? Oh, god! I'm so sorry!"

The room was dark, but decent hotels have decent curtains. I rolled up on one elbow to check the night stand clock. Eight oh five. Hell, yes, I was sleeping. For all of about an hour.

"No, no," I said automatically and for no intelligent reason.

"You're a bad liar, especially when you're half asleep. I'll call you later."

"Wait!" I sat up and worked some saliva around in my mouth. I keep a water bottle by the bed in hotels. "No, it's fine. I had the alarm set for whatever time this is anyway."

"Liar."

"How did your raccoon hunt go?" I reached for the water bottle.

"Al's no dummy. If he's poaching parked cars in Milwaukee, he's not stupid enough to hide them in his back lot. We didn't find anything, but yes, there was a family of raccoons under that car. I told Al to call that wildlife rescue place down in Fredonia."

The water cleared my throat. I rubbed lingering sleep from my eyes.

"Did you grill Godzilla?"

"Who?"

"Al's mechanic."

"Will, that's terrible! But, yes. Except once she sobered up, she shut up about the whole thing. How's the trip going?"

"Good, I guess. I can't speak for the meetings, but the flights have been superb. The throttle jockey up front has a masterful touch."

"I can attest to that."

"Oh, don't do that to me at this hour of the day. Hold that thought."

"How long?" she asked, all but purring.

"As far as I know, we're on schedule to be home for dinner tomorrow." We slipped into small talk about dinner, menus, shopping and household minutiae. Asleep or not, I liked that she called. The sound of her voice soothed emotions rubbed raw when I make hospital visits.

She brought up Friday night.

"What about Friday night?"

"Do we have plans?"

"You're the keeper of the calendar," I said. "You tell me."

"Are you scheduled?"

"Not with Sandy. Why?"

She hesitated for a second, then said, "I can get off a little early. What about a weekend in Milwaukee?"

"Are you asking me out on a date?" My mind already raced ahead to thoughts of a nice dinner, a nice hotel and Andy... "I'd have to check with my people."

"Well, have your people contact my people. Now go back to sleep."

Fat chance of that.

8

"What's he doing here?"

I stopped. Andy took another step, then turned to me with an entirely insincere look of innocence.

We stood at the entrance to the back lounge of Elsa's, an upscale restaurant on Cathedral Square in Milwaukee. The Friday night crowd gave the place an electricity that made me glad I'd come.

A visit to Elsa's is a treat, a must whenever we run away to the big city, garnished with superb martinis and the best cheeseburger I've ever tasted. The bar draws a crowd, especially on weekends. Being an old married couple more interested in what awaits back at the hotel, we don't close the joint, but we linger over a great meal and romantic conversation blessed with brimming martinis. The crowd building around the time we make our exit strikes me as a 'see and be seen' demographic. I suspect that later in the evening, Elsa's is a busy hookup bar.

The front of the long, narrow restaurant features the bar and traditional tables. The back lounge is darker and offers low leather chairs and small round tables. Andy and I usually choose the subdued atmosphere of the lounge.

Greg LeMore, a wiry MPD detective with raging facial stubble, sat at a corner table for three. His presence did not contribute to the ambiance I had in mind.

"Uh, I invited him," Andy said. She stepped intimately closer.

"Don't bat those beautiful lashes at me, woman. Was this your plan all along?"

"No!" Her hands found my waist. "I mean, yes. But seducing you remains a priority. I want you to keep that in mind while we talk cop shop over dinner with Greg." She pecked me on the cheek and bounced away.

LeMore issued a broad smile as he traded a hug with my wife.

"Will!" He shook hands with me. "Good to see you!"

"Good to see you, too, Greg," I said. He pulled a chair for Andy. I slipped into another beside her. LeMore took the third seat in the triangle.

I like LeMore. Under a low-key countenance, he's a sharp, nerdy detective with the Milwaukee Police Department. He's been an invaluable resource for Andy on several occasions. My appreciation for LeMore outweighed my disappointment that Andy and I wouldn't be dining alone.

A waitress checked in with us, laying small square napkins on the table in anticipation of drink orders. Andy favors the Cosmopolitan. I ordered a Kamikaze. LeMore waved off a drink and asked for water.

"I'm on the clock," he said. He nodded at Andy. "Chief Schultz said to tell you your desk is gathering dusk."

Andy may have blushed slightly. Deputy Chief Don Schultz's standing offer of a job with the Milwaukee Police Department was a high compliment to Andy.

"Please give my best to the Chief," Andy said politely.

LeMore sat back and looked us over.

"You two look good. It's been a while! And may I say, Andrea, holy shit! Brogan!" Andy offered a humble shrug. LeMore grinned. "Don't give me that, Detective. That was impressive! I take it you were in on that, too, Will?"

"Not me," I lied. "I'm just a float in the parade."

"Yeah, right." LeMore looked us over a second time, noting Andy's dress and my black jacket over a black shirt and tie. "Wait a minute.

You two look like you're doing date night. Jesus, Andrea, what the hell am I doing here? We can meet up tomorrow."

"No! Greg, no. It's okay," Andy pleaded. "Will and I are spending the weekend. This is fine."

LeMore adopted a skeptical look. "Okay. But I'm not third-wheeling your dinner." He reached back and pulled a file folder from a shoulder bag slung on the back of his chair. He offered a wry smile. "You can go through this at your hotel tonight if you have nothing better to do."

"Thank goodness," I said.

LeMore said, "That guy is a piece of shit. Undiluted. We dug into him after Braddock tried to blow himself up a block from the Pfister Hotel. It's like James and his conspiracy bullshit was hard wired into Braddock's head—which carries no weight in court, of course."

Andy flipped the file open.

"Anyway, there's some background on James. Interesting connections and associates. I wrote up a ton of notes on his web presence, his business model, and some of his recent political moves. I emailed you a long list of links, too. Articles about the guy, his tactics, some of his nefarious practices. People have been watching. The Nebraska state attorney's office had an interest for a while, but no matter what gets reported, nothing seems to stick to the guy. Our DA poked around him, too."

Andy turned pages, absorbed. Too absorbed to notice the questioning look on my face.

"James?" I asked. She didn't hear me. Or chose not to.

Greg leaned forward and pointed at one of the pages. "I wrote up some notes on his web structure, the servers he's using."

"Josiah James?" I asked.

"Yes, dear," Andy said absently, or tried to make it seem so.

"He scored a big infusion of cash in the last couple years. He's got some big-bucks equipment and serious firewalls."

If Andy and I were to discuss this, it clearly wasn't happening across the table from Greg LeMore.

"Did you hack into him?" I asked LeMore.

"Firewalls, Will. That's what they're for. To keep people out. It's not like in the movies where some joker taps on a keyboard and plows right through."

Andy looked up. LeMore looked her in the eye. "We all heard about Officer Mackiejewski. If giving you this balances the scale for Mike, you have my full support. But if you're going to do something stupid, tell me now and I'll take it with me and burn it."

"Doing something stupid is my role," I interrupted.

Andy gave LeMore a solemn nod. "By the book."

"Fuck the book. I just don't want you putting yourself in the shit over this piece of crap." She closed the folder and tucked it between her purse and the wall beside her.

"Second that," I said. Our drinks arrived. Martinis poured to the rim. The server landed them on the napkins without spilling a drop. Unable to lift them, Andy and I unabashedly leaned over the table to slurp the first sips.

"Did you know James is touring?" LeMore asked.

"We just found out," Andy said.

"He's following Great Leader's 'rally' model. He's also recording the rallies and using them as broadcasts. That's partly how he draws audiences. He bills it as the live recording of his show, so people think they're going to be on TV. It's not live, of course. He edits the shit out of it. There have been hecklers, protesters, people trying to call him out and disrupt. None of that makes it into the final cut. Also, he's not drawing big crowds, so he edits to make them look bigger than they are. I called one of the venues in Nebraska. Talked to a manager there who told me that James's people herded everyone into the front floor section to make it look like standing room only. Then they moved the whole bunch onto bleachers behind him and handed out signs to wave while he strutted around the stage."

"The Big Lie," Andy said. "Why is that so hard for people to grasp? He lies, of course, in the stories he reports—the statistics, the sequence of events. It's all easy to fact check, but then he lies about the fact check. And anything or anyone that comes out against him is 'fake news'—"

"All hail Dr. Goebbels," I muttered.

LeMore grew intense. "That's the craziest part! James pretends to be part of the press. He uses that news set to make himself look like a legitimate news organization. Which is *another* lie, because it's just a glossy set in a low-rent warehouse in Lincoln, Nebraska. He ambushes known political figures just to get his picture taken with them, then he inserts the images into his video graphics to make it look like he's Ted Koppel. Most of the people in those images have never heard of him! His content is all bullshit, but his image manipulation is masterful!"

Andy and I stared at LeMore for a moment. He shrugged.

"Yeah, I get a little worked up. How much of his stuff have you seen?"

"Too much," Andy replied. "I dug into it around the time—when Mike—when it was bad. I had to. The bastard said some things about Mike, about the Braddock shooting—it was hard to take."

"He's a snake. Out of one side of his mouth he cries about truth—"

"He wouldn't know truth if it bit him on the ass," I said.

"—and out of the other side he's telling the Ben Braddocks of the world to mix up plastique in the kitchen sink," LeMore said. "It's easy to get caught up in the emotion. Trust me, I know. My grandparents were Armenian. I can't take James's shit about immigrants. That shithead is second-generation Greek, for God's sake! Another 'let me in and slam the door behind me' immigrant bigot."

"I shouldn't say this at a table with two cops," I said, "but I'd like to see him fall in a wood chipper. Accidentally, of course." The idea wasn't new. Andy squashed my suggestion months ago.

LeMore, the senior detective present, grew emphatic. "You've got to stay between the lines, Andrea. I mean it. From behind the badge, you can only look at what he's doing that's criminal. If you get near him, you better have cause. If you get caught poking around him without cause, he'll scream all kinds of lies about you until someone who matters takes notice and that shit will fly right back in your face."

"Ever hear of an FBI special agent by the name of Donaldson?" Andy asked.

LeMore shook his head.

Andy explained, including Donaldson's story about the radio syndication.

"Kidnapping." LeMore's eyes grew wider. His wheels turned. "That's something we can sink our teeth into."

"We?" she asked. "What happened to Detective By The Book?"

"Yeah," I piled on. "What happened to stay the hell away from this snake?"

LeMore grinned. "As if you'd listen. And as if I'm going to miss another wild ride with you two!"

The server appeared. I held up my hand for her to stand by for a moment.

"Have you had the cheeseburger here?" I asked LeMore.

"To die for."

"Then stay. Please," Andy insisted. "Will and I have all night to drink and get silly. I want to talk more about this."

I studied my wife long enough for her to notice and look back at me with a flash of guilt.

This wasn't what I expected. And I wasn't referring to our inter-rupted date.

WE GROUND through the subject of Josiah James for several hours with LeMore. The meal came and went. LeMore declared himself off the clock and joined us in a cocktail, a scotch that smelled like burnt rubber. He and Andy bashed James back and forth across the table like tennis pros hammering the ball. The two of them knew enough to write a biog-raphy—from James's earliest days in college as a campus evangelist to his current arch-conservative attempt to construe his venom as the voice of Real America. They pulled out the file and LeMore pointed out pages that suggested possible criminal angles. Andy surprised me. Not the degree to which she had researched James, because Andy doesn't do anything half-assed. She surprised me because she had clearly nurtured an interest in putting an end to the man. Until now she had suppressed my proposals for squashing James like a bug—although that may have had something to do with the fact that most of my suggestions ended in a gaudy murder, usually involving a fall from something high.

We broke up the conference around nine-thirty. I felt bad about tying up the table so long and left an extravagant tip. Outside Elsa's glass front door, on a sidewalk infused with something that glittered, Andy and LeMore made plans to talk again at the end of the week. She promised to review all the material he had assembled. He promised to scare up more. He hugged my wife, shook my hand, then hurried off.

The still night hung warm and humid around us, with the electric charge of approaching thunderstorms in the air. The forecast projected a line passing through southeastern Wisconsin after midnight. Our hotel, carefully selected because Rosemary II gave Andy a Groupon that promised the second night free on select weekends, stood only a few blocks away. I hooked Andy's arm in mine and led her across the street for a stroll through the Cathedral Square park. The lighted face of the Cathedral of St. John the Evangelist cast a warm artificial twilight over us.

Greg LeMore's departure terminated the topic of Josiah James. I wanted to talk to Andy about him—not so much about him, but about her awakened interest. I sensed that she didn't, and since I can only take Josiah James and his ilk in small doses, the moment moved on.

We let the conversation wander. First commenting on Elsa's, then on the park, then on the city lights around us. I nurtured a lively buzz, having downed three of the oversized Kamikazes. Andy, a lightweight, went two rounds with Cosmos, but left the last third of her second drink for me to finish. Between the food, the drink and the touch of a beautiful woman beside me, I cruised happily on autopilot through the winding paths of the park.

"This is nice."

"Uh-huh."

She pulled me closer. We traded glances.

"Romantic," she said.

"Sure is."

We strolled past the bandstand on the eastern third of the park. A banner proclaimed Jazz In The Park every Thursday night during the summer. Andy and I have seen a few of the outdoor shows, sitting on a blanket with a bottle of wine between us.

"So, can I ask a question?" she asked.

"Anything."

"This strolling through the park thing…is this some kind of movie you see playing in your head, or would you rather take me back to the hotel and tear my clothes off?"

If not for her high heels, I would have run.

SOMETIME AFTER TWO A.M., I slipped my arm from beneath my sleeping wife's head and eased a pillow in its place. I slid off the bed and stood for a moment appreciating her shape on the sheets. Faint light defined the slope from her shoulders to her waist, the rise and curve of her hips. The room was warm, but I leaned down and lifted the sheet over her.

I slipped silently away to use the bathroom. The plumbing made excessive noise when I finished, but I sustained the effort to avoid waking her by turning the light off before opening the door.

She sat at the room's desk with a light on.

The sheet I had pulled over her hung around her, wrapped loosely across her bosom, leaving her shoulders bare. She leaned over the open file LeMore had given her. Her long hair, after-sex wild, hid her face until she turned and looked at me.

"Well, don't you know how to make an entrance."

"I wasn't expecting lights. Maybe I better put something on."

She appraised the situation. "I'd rather you didn't." She closed the folder.

"Find something interesting?"

She stood and moved toward the bed, then stopped, letting the sheet fall. "I believe I have."

Convinced she wasn't referring to the file, I went to the desk and killed the light. I found her in the dark and we tumbled back onto the bed.

I was wrong. Just before speech became impossible, she said, "He's doing one of his rallies in Des Moines next week. I want to go."

I hoped she wasn't expecting a discussion. Josiah James was the farthest thing from my mind.

9

"Who was it?"

"Stephenson again." I closed the screen on my phone and undid my seat belt. I helped Andy secure her headphones.

"Did he leave a voicemail?"

"He never does. I think he's paranoid about leaving recorded messages."

She didn't move from the copilot's seat. Outside the cockpit window, I saw the fuel truck approach across the Des Moines airport ramp. I wanted to catch the guy and top off.

"What do you mean 'never'? How often has he been calling?"

"I don't know," I said. "Couple times."

"Couple?"

"Six." I suppressed a grin. *Six out of eight!*

"Will!"

"I need to catch this fuel truck." I lifted myself out of the seat, twisted and scooted down the short aisle. I released the cabin stair door.

"You have to call him back!" Andy called after me.

I ducked out and dropped to the ground. The ramp was hot in the midday sun. Motivated, Andy wasn't far behind.

"Will, why aren't you picking up his calls?"

"Just now? Because I was expertly piloting a high-performance aircraft through three hundred miles of pop-up thunderstorms."

She followed me around the wing. I waved to the fuel truck driver who angled his tank truck toward the nose of the Navajo.

"When we get to the hotel, you're calling him." She moved in front of me and planted her hands on her hips. I'm taller and haul around fifty-five pounds more than she has, but I know formidable when I see it.

"Yes, ma'am."

While Andy found the restroom in the FBO, I finished securing the aircraft, handling the fuel ticket, and hustling our overnight bags from the plane into the air-conditioned office. I gave the airplane a glance as we prepared to transition to a rental car. She sat on the ramp in bright sunlight, white against a darkening western sky. Seventy or eighty miles away lightning flickered in rising cumulus tops.

"Hang on," I told Andy. I went back to the desk and flagged down the young man working reception. "Hey, we just came in with that Navajo out there. Twenty-One Hotel Whiskey. We'll be here overnight. Can you pull it into a hangar for us? I'm worried about hail."

"Uh..." he looked around for someone with more knowledge or more authority. "I can ask. I think so but let me get your number to confirm."

I recited my mobile number. "Thanks. It's chocked, but the brakes are off."

I caught up with Andy outside the FBO entrance.

10

"This place is a dump," Andy observed. She leaned forward to look through the windshield.

We sat in the parked rental looking at a cream brick building with a lumpy, stained dome roof. The overall effect suggested one of those pale fungus bulbs that materialize in a damp, dark woods. A sign above a span of entrance doors said *Coliseum*. I think the Romans would have taken offense. Behind us, the cracked asphalt parking lot stretched to a chain-link fence that sagged between leaning posts. On the other side of the building, a scrubby field stretched to where state highway 65 cut a north-south line across the Des Moines River. The field gave the impression it was once used for additional parking.

"What was it supposed to be?" Sitting here in the middle of nowhere, someone surely planted this monstrosity for a reason.

"It was supposed to be a country music festival venue. Ten or fifteen years ago. I think. It's mentioned on the website. Seems like the grand plan failed. Now it sees marginal use. James is on the calendar for tonight. There's a gun show in two weeks. And there's some seventies hair band playing in September. That's it."

"You sure you want to go in? Have you had your shots?"

"We're early." Andy sat back.

Early or not, the parking lot already contained a couple dozen cars.

Our rental was by far the newest and nicest. Half were pickup trucks, and of those, half had tailgates plastered with stickers proclaiming the political leanings of the vehicle's owner. Calling them 'conservative' seemed euphemistic.

A line had formed at the doors. Beer bellies hung over jeans accessorized with wallet chains. John Deere caps slouched over puffy, overweight faces. A few women wore the tights currently in fashion which let no panty line or cellulite bulge go unseen. T-shirts displayed personal statements ranging from Confederate flags to calls for imprisonment of various political figures. If James planned on pulling together a rally crowd for his cameras, he had slim pickings.

I became more conscious than usual of my wife sitting next to me. Outside of a calendar, I didn't think many in this crowd often encountered a woman who looked like Andy.

Coming here had been her idea, although I had already determined I would attend one of the shows on the Josiah James tour. My plan had been to do it as a tangent to one of Sandy's trips. Andy's surprise invitation to LeMore, her awakened interest in James, and her declaration she would attend his Des Moines rally caught me off guard. Until our evening with LeMore, her attitude had been to let this rabid dog lie. When I asked her about the sudden interest, she told me Donaldson's visit triggered the change. If so, it suited me.

Her presence altered but did not derail what I had in mind for James. It simply introduced a need to improvise.

"I'm not sure going in the front door is the best idea," I said.

"I'm not going to badge my way in. I'm not here to draw attention I don't need."

"How tight can security be for a dump like this? A couple of rent-a-cops, maybe?"

She didn't answer. More cars and trucks arrived. A steady stream traversed the dirt road leading to the parking lot. I checked the line. The one vehicle I had hoped for had not appeared.

"Do you think Donaldson will be here?" she asked. It startled me. She had seen me looking, but I had not considered the possibility.

"Why would he be here?"

"Iowa, dear. This is his home stomping ground. And this is the only date James has on his schedule for Iowa."

"Christ, Dee! If he sees you here, he's going to think—or figure out —that you're doing exactly what he asked you to do! Then what?"

"Doesn't mean I'm going to help him."

I wasn't sure she had that right. Donaldson had all but threatened us with his desert comment.

Just as I formulated an argument for Andy to abort, the vehicle I'd been looking for pulled into the line of cars. Andy pointed.

"What are they doing here?"

There was no mistaking the television news remote truck with its retractable transmission tower and the bold graphics emblazoned on the sides.

I didn't respond. I can get away with omission, but generally fail any attempt to lie to Andy.

I had called all four television stations in Des Moines. Getting one out of four to show up was all I needed. The van followed the flow into the lot but veered away from the cars seeking parking spaces. It rolled past us and positioned itself at the side of the building, blatantly ignoring Fire Lane warnings. A young woman jumped out of the right front seat. A moment later, the boom on the top of the van unfolded and rose.

Less than a minute later, the venue doors opened. Four men walked out. Three of them looked like football linebackers. They wore black tactical clothing and belts with conspicuous holstered weapons. No badges. Andy blew out a soft breath.

"So much for rent-a-cops."

The fourth man in the group wore a business suit. He approached the young woman and began a conversation. Andy pulled out her phone and lifted it into position to snap several photos through the windshield.

From the driver's side of the van, a man in a t-shirt and cargo shorts emerged, swinging a camera onto his shoulder. Immediately, one of the linebackers put a flat hand in front of the lens. A rapid discussion followed between the woman and the man in the suit. I expected the encounter to become confrontational, but it took on the appearance of a negotiation. The man, about Andy's size, silver-haired and carrying himself with authority, waved a hand between himself and the reporter. She spoke energetically, holding her microphone and her ground. He listened. After a moment he nodded, gave a short speech enumerating his points with his fingers, and then waved for them to enter the building. The security men took point and brought up the rear. All disappeared inside.

"I wasn't expecting that," Andy said. "It looks like the James people weren't either. I wonder why local news would cover this? More to the point, I wonder why they would let them in?"

"Are you kidding? That's mainstream coverage. James would eat that up."

The anonymous tip I called in had been crafted to serve the local news stations' underlying lust for a scoop. *James plans to jump into the race for President. He's planting people in his audiences who are supposed to start up chants demanding he run. The code words are "Declaration of Independence." When that happens, turn your cameras on the audience and you'll see the shills start up the chant. He's wants to announce in Iowa, but he wants it to look spontaneous. You can catch him in the act.* It was a thin fabrication layered over an even thinner fabrication. I hoped it was laced with just enough conspiracy spice to draw out a hungry reporter.

I was mildly surprised it worked.

"Why don't you let me get us in there?" I suggested to Andy. "We can try a back entrance. There has to be a loading dock."

"We're not breaking in. We go in the front door." She twisted around until she faced the back seat. She unzipped her overnight bag and rummaged through the bag until she pulled out the Metallica t-shirt she likes to sleep in. She unbuttoned the white blouse she wore over jeans. "Hey. Can I get a little privacy here?"

"Would you do the same for me?"

She cracked a smile and continued stripping off her blouse. "Not a chance."

I sat back and watched. Smiling the whole time, she laid her blouse across the back seat, then maneuvered into the t-shirt. Twisting back to face forward, she reached down and grabbed two handfuls of t-shirt and tied a knot just below the line of her bra, exposing her midriff above her jeans. She then broke her hair free from a ponytail and shook it over her shoulders.

"Your sunglasses," she said, holding out her hand. I plucked them from a pocket. She put them on. "How's this?"

"Every guy in that line is going to hit on you."

"Good. The distraction might come in handy." She reached for the car door.

"Hold on." I laid my hand on her shoulder bag. "Gun and badge are in here?"

"Yes."

I shook my head. "Those goons in the black bad-guy costumes are serious, which means I'll bet you dollars to donuts they're checking bags going in. Might even have metal detectors. Do you want them to know you're a cop?"

She bit her lower lip, thinking. "Do you think I should leave it here?"

"No. I'll feel better if you have it. Why not let me take it in? You go in the front door. I'll try the back. If I can't get in, I'll bring it back here, stash it and join the line. If I can get in, I'll find you and drop it in your lap."

"No breaking and entering!"

"Deal."

"Okay."

Good. Because that's what I had in mind all along.

It was my turn to twist in the seat. I pulled my old fishing vest from my overnight bag. I had already loaded it with three fully charged power units. I felt the pocket to confirm their presence. Then I touched another pocket. The weapon I had acquired for this trip was also present and accounted for.

After returning from Nashville, putting the Foundation's Navajo to bed and waving Sandy and Arun on their way, I stayed behind in the hangar. I fired up the office computer and found what I wanted on Amazon. I used the Foundation's credit card, the one meant for gas, hotels and travel. I didn't want the purchase showing up on any card that Andy monitors. The idea was too crazy to explain, and I gave strong odds that she would shoot it down before it ever left the ground. I had the package delivered to Essex County Air Service and paid extra for express shipping.

The weapon occupied the right front pocket of the vest.

I slipped into the vest. Andy handed me the shoulder bag. I felt the weight of her Glock and the extra magazine she carries. I shoved the compact bag into my vest and looped her shoulder strap around my neck.

We searched our surroundings. The line snaking away from the building stretched into the parking lot but angled away from the corner space we had selected. The lot filled quickly now. I had hoped it wouldn't, in part wishing there weren't that many American citizens lured by Josiah James's ludicrous conspiracy fabrications and dangerous hate mongering. The Heartland disappointed me. People streamed from their cars to join the lines. Couples. Parents with kids. Seniors. More disturbing than the numbers was the look of awe and excitement on most of the faces. Some of these people came to see a show. Many came to see their messiah.

"Dee, promise me you won't do anything to call attention to yourself in there."

"You either. Leave him alone. This is not a friendly crowd. This is purely research."

For her. Not for me.

"Are we clear?" I looked around. No one strolled near our car. People crossing the lot eyed the line, hurrying to get a place that guaranteed good seats.

"Wait! Put in your earpiece!"

I had nearly forgotten. I located the Bluetooth earpiece and slipped it in my right ear with the microphone extending along my cheek. She pulled the rental keys from the ignition and stuffed them in her jeans pocket.

"Be careful," Andy warned.

Fwooomp! I vanished.

She climbed out of the car, stepped to my side and opened the door. I used a grip on the roofline to heave myself free and upward.

"Clear."

She closed the door and locked it, then hurried to join the crowd.

ANDY'S SATCHEL posed no problem. It lost its weight when it vanished along with me but remained snug in the vest. I snapped a propeller onto a propulsion unit and eased the power slide forward. It hummed and pulled me. Thirty feet above the parking lot, I tracked a path over

Andy's head as she walked to join the line. Men and women alike watched my wife. She used their attention to her advantage and initiated an animated conversation with a small group when she joined the line. I understood her tactic. She didn't want to pass through the security line as a lone wolf. Chatting with others helped her fit in.

I left her smiling and laughing with new friends and angled toward the domed building. The bulging roof was made of a white composite material. Large green mildew blotches and rust lines from the hardware that secured the panels added to the structure's derelict look. I crested the top and angled downward. The back side of the building joined a cracked asphalt lot. An eighteen-wheeler and half a dozen cars and SUVs sat on the weed-infested pavement. The truck positioned its trailer against the loading dock. As I cleared the roof, I saw that the dock door was open. Perfect.

Music throbbed from within the building. I descended, reversed course, and eased through the space between the trailer roof and the top of the open door. My eyes required a moment to adjust to the dark interior. Wary of hitting a hanging cable or light or fixture, I used the power unit to stop.

The cluttered floor below might have belonged to any warehouse, but racks of lights, scaffolding and ropes above me established this as a backstage space. Crates, boxes, tool kits and tarps had been cast about after disgorging their on-stage contents. The set James used had been unpacked and assembled hours ago.

Several large cloth backdrops, extending from the black plank floor to the ranks of steel trusses above, shielded the stage from the backstage area. Feeling confident in my adjusted vision, I tracked forward to the edge of the nearest panel. Rounding it, I passed from the gritty backstage world to the false polish of the stage and set. At center stage, on a riser, the gleaming glass surface of a broad news anchor desk reflected bright overhead spotlights. Upstage of the desk rows of illuminated LCD screens formed a backdrop. Racks of black speakers poured out a driving rock anthem. The bass beat slammed against my diaphragm. The LCD screens blinked through fast cuts in time with the music. Flags. Military hardware. Farm equipment. Shots of national monuments and pretty girls. And slogans.

Tear Down Fear With Truth.

Take Back America.

Fight to Preserve Freedom.

Stop The Invasion.

With this last slogan, live-action scenes of dark-skinned people hurling rocks at police played across the screens. The images came and went quickly. Cuts of riots. Cuts of people running amid chaos. Cuts of police holding the line.

I stopped. One scene showed a group of black youths harassing, then assaulting, a young blonde woman. The cut was shaky and grainy, suggesting it had been taken by a bystander, but it also flashed the familiar wavy lines that intrude when video shoots video. I stared. It looked familiar.

"Son of a bitch," I muttered to myself. The scene had been lifted from a movie. Another scene followed, showing masses of people surging toward a bridge. I recognized it from a Will Smith film about zombies.

The mash-up panorama of plagiarized fear rolled on. I turned away. Twenty feet above the stage, I pointed the power unit at the auditorium's seating, which formed a half-circle around the stage.

People filed in, hurrying forward to find seats nearest the stage. Sections to the left and right had been roped off so that the crowd would fill the center section. Men acting as ushers stopped people from moving into seats farther from the stage. They waved the audience forward, funneling them, admonishing them to leave no empties.

Two main doors fed the audience into two main aisles. More and more people filed in, moving quickly, energized by the thundering music.

Andy stepped into the darkened auditorium and as I expected, separated herself from the patrons surging forward. She edged sideways beside the last row and stood examining the space around her, the unused second tier of seating above and behind her, the stage, and the linebackers in black stationed at the foot of the stage.

I hit the power and accelerated toward her, then reversed strongly to stop above her. The buzz from the propulsion unit was easily drowned out by the grinding rock music. I lowered myself over the last seat in the row and tapped her on the shoulder. She nodded while resisting the impulse to flinch or look for me. She lifted her left forearm, extending it perpendicular to her body. I extracted her satchel strap from around my neck and maneuvered the bag into position so that the strap would snag her arm. I let it go. A cold electric snap slapped my hand. The bag reappeared and succumbed to gravity. Her arm hooked the strap. She lifted it over her shoulder. Then she untied the t-shirt knot and let her shirt fall around her hips. She pulled her badge from the purse pocket and snapped it in place on her belt under her shirt.

She slid into the seat in the last row.

We waited.

Forty minutes later, playing to a crowd that filled only half of the center section of the auditorium, the Josiah James show began.

11

―――――

The auditorium went dark. LCD screens faded to black. Two cameras mounted on floor dollies moved into position stage-left and -right. A third on a crane swung in over the heads of the first row.

A voice, deep and polished, thundered in the darkness.

"While you breathe the last whiff of free American air, neocons and progressive puppets are preparing arrest warrants for heroes of the new revolution!" The voice stirred electric anticipation in the crowd. "While liberals ship your dwindling food supply overseas, the deep state is preparing starvation camps for those who oppose leftist tyranny!"

The crowd rumbled its outrage.

"While fighters like Josiah James uphold American values with their dying breath, gay and lesbian anarchists plot to burn The Constitution!"

The crowd roared. A few of the patrons seated below me shouted obscenities at such a heinous idea.

"While your mothers and sisters bar their doors against the rapists and murderers streaming across our borders, demon leftist Democrats are moving to pass laws that will take away your God-given right to defend yourself!"

This was too much to bear. Men took to their feet, fists raised.

"One man stands between you and the deep state liberal hordes!"

Feet stomped. Music swelled.

"One man carries the light of Truth in the black darkness brought by diseased homosexuals!"

Pounding drumbeats joined the roar of the crowd. The LCD screens flashed to life, spreading giant metallic letters across the stage, flashing in time with the drums.

JOSIAH JAMES

The crowd shouted the name.

"JOSIAH JAMES!"

"One man holds the Bible in his hand and Jesus in his heart and rages against the ruin of Western Civilization!"

"JOSIAH JAMES!"

"One man defends the supremacy that made this nation GREAT!"

"JOSIAH JAMES!"

The pace accelerated. Music thundered.

Suddenly the entire stage erupted in light and pyrotechnics. James appeared. He marched through swirls of smoke into a pool of bright light, holding his right fist high. A cameraman onstage shadowed him. James's head, rendered giant-sized, appeared on the LCD screens.

The crowd howled.

Hovering above the chanting audience felt like hanging over a pit full of vipers. My chest constricted. I suppressed fear that *the other thing* might fail me and drop me into this mob to be torn apart.

I twisted to check on Andy. She watched the spectacle from her seat at the back.

This is a really bad idea. I felt a stark irrational fear that a spotlight would land on my wife while James denounced her as a spy from the stage.

James held his pose. The screens shifted from his portrait image to a giant multi-panel image of the American flag. Martial music played.

In any other setting, Josiah James might have gone unnoticed. The only thin thing about him was his short black hair. A bald spot caught and kicked back spotlight reflections. His hands were pudgy. His belly pressed on his belt. He might not be considered fat, but in a poster for fitness, James would be the Before image.

In an orchestrated whirlwind of light, smoke and noise with his fist thrown high, James looked like a man fantasizing himself as Hero.

The music tempo accelerated. He marched, first left, then right. He pointed at his adoring fans. With each stab of his finger, isolated patches of frenzy erupted in the crowd. He performed this back-and-forth maneuver with his cameraman trailing until the screens changed again. Blazing computer-generated chrome and sparkling graphics appeared, displaying his name. The announcer's voice boomed.

"From over three hundred broadcast stations, from the largest internet news platform on the web, backed by dozens of reporters gathering news from our bureaus worldwide—ladies and gentlemen, the award-winning, ass-kicking, take no prisoners defender of truth and justice! The salvation of freedom! The pillar of the righteous! Here now to bring you the voice of Real America—JOSIAH JAMES!"

I didn't think the crowd had the capacity to get louder, especially over the blasting music, but the space filled with the sound of people screaming themselves hoarse.

James stopped his left-right march. He bowed, waved, pointed. He placed his hand solemnly over his heart. He turned to the waving flag on his LCD screen and saluted.

The music took up a new beat. James bolted into a short-stride run, leaping the small riser and jogging to the chair behind the broad glistening desk. The boom camera and both floor cameras moved in. The crowd continued cheering. I looked down. Most of them dropped into their seats. Looking closer, I saw that many had stopped cheering and were settling in for the show. Yet the crowd noise hit a crescendo. It dawned on me that the frenzied cheering came from speakers lined up below the lip of the stage.

James took up the seated anchorman position familiar to his internet fans. He reached under the desk and pulled out a sheaf of papers, tamping them together. He gazed out at the audience and pounded the desk with his fist. He reached under the desk again and pulled up a big desktop microphone, the kind last seen in radio broadcasts of the fifties. Utterly unnecessary, except as a giant symbol. He leaned into the silver monster microphone.

"Thank you! Please, be seated!" The crowd was already seated. The recorded cheering continued. He waved his arms. "Please! You're too kind! Thank you!" For several minutes he worked the humble celebrity host routine against the prerecorded cheers of an adoring audience.

The television news cameraman and the on-air reporter took up a position near the stage. The cameraman shouldered his camera and fixed it on James, but occasionally swung it to capture the center section audience. Standing nearby, two of the black-clad security men watched over the news team.

The news crew reminded me of my mission. I patted the device in my pocket. Operating the propulsion unit with my left hand, I eased toward the stage, mindful of the swinging boom camera. The rapt crowd settled in. Many raised their phones to record video of their hero. Good. I needed to act before they tired of holding their arms high.

James attacked the big microphone with his snarling gravelly voice. He promised his audience that what they were about to hear would shock them. He lamented that it was his sad duty to report to the great Americans here tonight a news story so depraved, so heart-stopping, that words failed him. He shouted out familiar names from mainstream headlines. The President. The Speaker of the House of Representatives. Senators. He gushed over some and sneered at others. He railed against fake news networks that refused to acknowledge the REAL TRUTH (on cue, the words appeared behind him in four-foot letters) he was about to share. He informed all present that not only would they hear Real Truth, but more Real Truth was available on CD and DVD at the kiosks in the lobby, along with t-shirts, hats and other authentic Josiah James paraphernalia—cash and all major credit cards plus Pay Pal accepted.

I floated across the edge of the stage. Rows of lights blazed down on James from above me. I pulsed the power unit to reduce my forward flight to a crawl. Using the core muscle running down my center, I rotated my body to a horizontal position, belly down, facing James below me. I approached the riser and desk. Eight feet away. Seven. I flicked the power unit to take me lower. Six feet. Five.

"Ladies and gentlemen! Good Americans! Before I get to my lead story for the night, before I can muster the strength to share with you horrifying details I have acquired from multiple reliable sources—and at great risk—before we confront the treachery and villainy that has seeped into our government, into the very fabric of America—I need you to know that I am here tonight in defiance of countless threats against my life!"

He paused. The screen behind him flashed DEATH THREATS.

"That's right! You would not believe it if I told you how many actionable threats have been posted against me. You would not believe me if I told you the names of the gay, and liberal, and lesbian, and neocon, and progressive traitors we have traced these threats to! The government agencies plotting against me on behalf of Hillary Clinton!"

The crowd booed.

"The Hollywood elite!"

More booing.

"The homo *New York Times*!"

Shouts and epithets joined the booing. James bobbed his head emphatically.

"Names you see praised in fake news headlines! Names you see every day! Names of politicians taking your money to spend it on abortion!" Boos. "On serums that make our children gay!" More boos. "On secret programs to bring murderers and rapists and drugs across our borders!" More boos mixed with curses.

I reached in my pocket and closed my hand around the device.

Three feet away. James's bald spot glistened with sweat. His polished desktop acquired spots of spittle. I pulled the device from my pocket and held it as close to him as I dared, allowing for the possibility that he might flail his arms or jump to his feet abruptly.

I waited for the right moment. Glancing back, I noted that the news crew had fixed their camera on James.

"Bombs! Poison! Snipers! My team has uncovered plot after plot against me! But do I waver?"

"NO!"

"Do I falter?"

"NO!"

"I will never waver! I will never falter!" He dramatically held up a hand. I'd seen this gesture in his online broadcasts—the pregnant pause holding his breathless audience hostage for the next shocking revelation. He leaned closer to the microphone and lowered his voice to a secretive semi-whisper that thundered around the room. "I need to share something with you. Something that will tear open your soul."

I extended my hand and squeezed.

Brrr-rrrr-rrrr-ppppt!

Benny's proud and joyful declaration filled my mind. *I farted!* The sound from the rubber device in my hand dominated James's dramatic silence.

James blinked. A giggle rippled through the crowd. James glanced sharply at the side of the stage where his black-clad stage manager stood holding a clipboard. The stage manager stared at him, wide-eyed, mouth hanging open.

"I—I am here tonight to sound a warning call to all of you!" James struggled back into his monologue. The ripple of giggling died under his thundering voice. "This may be the most important message ever to reach your ears!"

I squeezed again.

Bpppt! Bpppt! Bpppt!

The tiny rubber device in my hand sang out, a farting virtuoso. Three ninety-nine on the internet, plus shipping and handling. Tonight, worth more than the New York Philharmonic.

James shifted in his seat, a move which underscored his guilt. Giggles grew into open laughter. Under a sheen of glistening sweat, James's complexion turned scarlet. I glanced at the audience. More hands came up with phone cameras aimed at the stage.

James fired a look of rage at his stage manager. The stage manager shrugged.

James grabbed the microphone and stood up abruptly. The move came close to me, but I had allowed for it and remained clear.

"People! There are forces lined up against me, against all you good Americans in this room today. There are forces that will do anything to take me down!"

Pfffft! Braaaaaaaapppppt! I had practiced. The small handheld device generated a surprising variety of highly authentic fart noises. The long. The short. The staccato.

The crowd broke into open laughter.

"This is not right! This is not right! That wasn't me!" James cried out.

I pulsed the power unit and moved into position behind him, then swung my legs down.

James shouted against the laughter flooding the stage. "We're having—we're having technical diffficul*ties! Listen to me! Listen to me!"*

I swung my foot forward and tapped him on the ass.

Pffffft! Pffffft! Braaaap!

He jumped, whirled around searching.

The crowd roared laughter. Cameras rose high over heads. I saw the news cameraman edging closer to center stage, fixed on James.

The red in James's face went white. He froze, quivering. Off-stage, the manager hurled his hand across his neck over and over, signaling James to cut, to end it.

I pulsed the power unit and rose slightly, then backed into position above James again. He glared at the audience. The microphone shook in his hand. His jaw, hanging open, quivered.

One last shot. I reached down.

Brrrrrraaaaaaaaaaaaaapppppppp!

The crowd grew hysterical.

James dropped the microphone as if it had burned him. He stood shaking his head, shouting.

"That's not me! We're being attacked!"

A voice from the front row called out, "You got that right! Whooooeee!"

"They got a pill for that!"

He looked at his stage crew for help. None came. He hesitated, then bolted from his place behind the desk. His feet tangled in his rolling chair. He stumbled, caught himself on the desk, regained his feet and darted off the stage.

Laughter followed him, then morphed into a loud rumble. People turned to one another to repeat and imitate what they had just seen. A few young men shoved their hands up into their armpits and offered their own flatulent refrain. Those with cameras stopped recording and began to play it back, breaking into laughter again as the playbacks repeated. People tapped their phones rapidly.

Sending the video into the night.

Worldwide.

I felt the knot of tension in my arms and legs begin to ease. I calmed my breathing. I hadn't realized how tightly wound I had become. The rubber device in my hand felt slippery with my sweat. I carefully pushed it back into my pocket, then used the power unit to rise over the audience.

I looked for Andy in the back row but failed to find her. The seat she occupied earlier was empty.

"Ladies and gentlemen, ladies and gentlemen, please be seated. We are experiencing technical difficulties and will continue shortly." The voice making the announcement sounded high and strained. It was not the polished professional announcer from the intro recording.

"Technical ass difficulties!" someone cried out.

"Him that smelt it, dealt it!" another shouted, harvesting more laughs.

People rose from their seats. A few, phones in hand, perhaps unable to get a signal, hurried up the aisle.

"Josiah James will return shortly!" The announcer voice sounded uncertain.

My phone buzzed in my ear. I touched the button.

"Hi there!"

"Outside," Andy said tersely.

The call ended.

Uh-oh.

I thumbed the power slide and began a circuit of the auditorium that would take me across the stage, through the darkened backstage and out the open loading dock. Before transiting the black backdrop, I looked down to see the news cameraman set up on his talent. A light mounted on his camera illuminated the young live-on-the-scene reporter as she spoke into a handheld microphone, trying to be professional while suppressing a grin that wouldn't quit.

The silver-haired man I had seen earlier dashed across the stage, waving his arms and shouting at the linebackers standing a few feet away frozen in confusion.

I didn't wait to see what happened. It hardly mattered. The security men had no options. Video from the news camera had already transmitted to the truck in real time—and from the truck to the control room at the station. I passed over the stage and hooked around the backstage panels.

"Credit where credit is due," I said aloud, gliding over increasing backstage chaos toward the exit. "James was a contender, but you're the reigning fart champion, Benny!"

12

Boiling black clouds towered overhead when I emerged from the loading dock. Stormfront wind knocked me off my flight path as soon as I cleared the protection of the building. The anticipated line of storms announced its arrival with a volley of thunderclaps and strobe lightning flashes. I needed full power to hold a course over the roof. Below me, people streaming from the building darted for their cars and trucks.

I glanced to my left and saw a dust cloud boiling up as a microburst front roared across the landscape. With no weight and no inertia, I was about to become a dandelion fluff in a maelstrom.

I had no choice. I dove hard for the surface near where Andy stood with her arms folded beside the rental. Fat raindrops splattered the pavement and sheet metal on the parked cars. Dust driven by the wind hit my back just as my feet touched down.

Fwooomp! I reappeared and staggered, pumping my legs to catch up with my forward speed. Another second and the gusting wind would have scooped me up and sent me to Illinois.

"Get in the car!" I shouted at Andy. She stood still long enough to affirm that I had arrived, then jerked open the driver's door and dropped into the car.

Sheets of rain hissed across the parking lot and hit me the moment my hand closed on the door handle. I dropped into the passenger seat with a cold sheen of rain on the back of my shirt.

"Holy crap! I hope they got the airplane inside," I ran my hands down my face to wipe away the rain.

Andy said nothing.

I pinched my shirt and pulled it away from my skin. I shook it to knock a few drops of water free. Trouble sat beside me. I shook my fingers through my hair and wiped the drops on my pants. Rain fell in buckets. It roared on the roof of the car.

Having nothing left to stall the inevitable, I turned to my wife.

She sat rigid in the driver's seat, staring at me, eyes blazing.

"Dammit, Will!" She locked her jaw.

"What?"

She hesitated for a moment, digging deep for the words she needed to make her idiot husband understand.

"Do you have ANY idea why I came here?"

Trick question. I wasn't about to answer.

She shook her head, a gesture that suggested I wasn't worth an explanation.

"What?"

"I came here—I came here—" She hitched a breath and I saw something I didn't expect. Water glistened in her eyes.

And then I knew.

It had been months. She held this in for months.

When Mike Mackiejewski took his own life, alone in a car parked at the edge of the city's utility lot behind the police department building, Andy had been shocked but not shocked. She had been closer to Mike than anyone. She had seen him struggle. Despite counseling and the support of his entire department, despite Andy's personal pleading, Mike never reconciled shooting Corey Braddock. Andy told him over and over that the circumstances gave him no choice. Had Braddock reached for a real detonator, the shot Mike took would have saved countless lives, including his own.

But it wasn't a detonator. It was just a phone plugged into a portable speaker playing out Corey Braddock's shy adolescent adoration for Lane Franklin, feelings that were forbidden under his father's doctrine of white supremacy.

Although she worked to save him, Andy couldn't prevent Mike from ending the pain in the only way he knew how. Andy grieved, but mustered stoic strength for the public eye. She shed private tears but banded together with her fellow officers and they buried their pain behind stone faces as they buried their brother officer.

"God, Will! You don't understand anything!"

"What, then? Tell me."

"I—I came here—*dammit*!" She turned away.

"Talk to me, Dee!"

Her head shook, then lowered. I saw her hand form a fist and wondered if it was headed my way.

"I came here to kill him!"

The moment the words left her lips, I knew they were wrong. She knew they were wrong.

"No, you didn't."

"HE'S RESPONSIBLE!"

"Yes. He is. But you didn't come here to kill him."

She spun on me. "How do you know? What do you know? I've done it before!"

"That has nothing to do with this."

"I did! I did, Will! I—" A sob broke through her anger. "I—oh, dammit! Damn you! You're supposed to know me—!" She struggled to sustain anger, but a tear fell from her eye and ran down her cheek. Her lower lip quivered.

"I do know you. I know that—that this has been eating at you. I know that you've been bottling it up. But I also know that you didn't come here to kill him. You came here to *want* to kill him."

She lifted her eyes to look at me. The connection broke through her anger and she shook suddenly. She sobbed. "*I—I wanted so badly to want it!*"

I leaned across the console and pulled her to me. She cried against my shoulder.

"*Oh, G—G—God! Mike! That p—poor boy!*"

"You had no way of knowing, Dee! No way!"

"*I suh-suh-sent him in there! I told him! I told him to stop Corey, wuh-wuh-whatever it took!*"

I pulled her tighter.

"Jesus, Andy, you would have done the same thing. You and Tom and Jeff and every cop on the force would have taken the same shot. You all had the same intel."

"I'm so sorry! I'm so sorry!"

We sat for a long time with the rain falling hard, inside and outside the car. There's no counting the minutes at a time like that.

Eventually, Andy pushed herself upright. She rubbed her eyes with the back of her hand. Her face glistened, her eyes glowed red, and her nose ran. I stabbed a hand into my overnight case and pulled out a t-shirt and handed it to her. She refused it.

"There are no tissues in the car." I pushed it into her hands.

She wiped her face and blew her nose. She hitched in several deep breaths and blew them out, then sank back in her seat.

"God, I'm so sorry." She pushed her fingers into her hair for a moment. "It was James. All along. I tried to tell myself he was just one of the voices pushing Braddock. But after—when he started saying those things about Mike, about Essex PD—calling Braddock a hero—"

She raised her eyes to me.

"I wanted him to pay. I've had this pain for so long," she began to cry again, sucked in a huge breath and blew it out to force the tears away. "I hate myself for wanting that."

"Stop. I mean it. Stop. Dee, listen to me. Wanting it is only human."

She hitched a sob and suppressed it with another breath drawn and released.

"Hold on a sec," I said. I pulled my phone from my jeans pocket and began tapping the screen. The 4G connection seemed strong, but it still took a moment to find what I was looking for. "Here." I held out the phone for her.

Josiah James Gas Attack, the search engine read. A lineup of videos ran down the page.

"We killed him." I slipped my hand in my pocket and closed it around the weapon I had used to kill Josiah James.

Andy threw her hand over her mouth. She spasmed again, a burst of laughter, another sob.

"We—" I squeezed. *Braaapppt!* "Oh, excuse me. That was bad."

Andy giggled helplessly between hitching sobs.

"I'm so sorr—" *Pfffft! Brop! Brop!* "Oh, jeez, it must have been something I ate. I'm really sorry."

She laughed. She shook and laughed and sniffled and wiped the water from her eyes. I held up the phone and the little rubber device. "We killed him, Andy."

She stroked her finger up the screen, revealing a long line of posted videos. She let go of a long cleansing breath.

"We did. We killed him in the best possible way."

She reached up and touched my cheek.

"You're a genius."

"I am! I'm a fucking genius!"

She abruptly twisted across the console, threw her hand behind my head and pulled me into a kiss. She shared the tears on her cheeks with my cheeks. I kissed back, pulling her closer, awkwardly, delivering love she asked for like medicine. I expected this to last a moment, but she kept coming, pulling me into her with both hands. She heaved herself across the console onto me.

"Does this seat go back?" she whispered desperately in my ear. I fumbled with the side of the seat, clawing at the upholstery until I found a lever. I pulled it. We fell flat into the back seat.

13

"Wake up," Andy jabbed my shoulder. "C'mon! James is giving a press conference. We have to go."

I rolled over and checked the hotel alarm clock. Six-oh-four. *Jesus.*

It had been a good night. No. A great night. After the rain and the release of grief and the gymnastics in the car, we left the rundown Coliseum and checked in at the Holiday Inn across from the airport for more gymnastics. Then we dressed and found a bar that served Corona and pizza. We caught the James video on the local news affiliate whose reporter and cameraman had scooped the story. We drank to James's newfound celebrity as a running fart joke. We persuaded the bartender to flip through the cable news channels until he found the story being played as a humor piece (with unabashed glee from the mainstream anchors) on MSNBC and CNN. Back in the room again, I pulled up the iPad and we scrolled to check YouTube. The viewer count qualified the best of the videos as having gone viral.

Andy laughed. It was the kind of laugh that's never far from tears, but it made her light again. Maybe not whole yet, but able to begin living with the void Mike left behind.

Utter exhaustion caught up with us. We collapsed into sleep in each other's arms. Our plan had been to return to Essex at a leisurely pace in the morning.

Andy's wakeup call felt anything but leisurely.

Gaining my bearings, I found Andy fully dressed and growing impatient.

"Bring your vest," she instructed me.

I may be able to vanish and float, but my real superpower is being able to dress and clear a hotel room in five minutes.

"Why?" I asked. "I mean, so what? So, he's giving a press conference. He's not going to change anything. It's going to look pathetic."

Andy drove. I tightened my seat belt.

"Pull up his web page," she said. I worked my phone. It took a few minutes. When the page appeared, I read aloud.

"*Terrorist Attack at Rally. Middle eastern suspect with ties to ISIS apprehended.* Jesus, Andy. This is bullshit. Nobody's going to believe this crap." I scrolled down. "He's claiming that foreign agents hacked into his equipment at the rally to play obscenities and jihadist slogans over his audio. Uh...here. It says one of the agents, crying 'God is great!' in Arabic and carrying explosives, was apprehended by 'heroic security personnel.' Andy, this is all crap, like all the other crap he pumps out. It will be easy to disprove."

"His followers don't fact check. And when fact checks are published that show what a liar he is, they cover their ears."

"Monumental bullshit."

"Of course, it's all bullshit!" Andy cut across two lanes and scooted through an intersection on a yellow turning red. I uttered a prayer of thanks for the Sunday morning absence of traffic.

"I gotta give it to the asshole, he's creative. It says here the suspect has been turned over to Homeland Security and was taken by armed guards to a military jet and flown to an undisclosed black site. And check this out—'Homeland Security officials have been instructed to deny any knowledge of the incident.' The perfect lie." I closed the iPad, partly to escape the feeling of getting dirty that came from James's website, and partly to keep my eyes on the road. "Why are we bothering with this? Nobody's going to believe it. The video went viral."

"His followers will believe it."

"Who cares?"

"Will, he's news right now, which means he's going to have coverage. Not just one station. He's going to draw a crowd. He's not stupid.

Running and hiding would have been the worst idea. He's fighting back."

"So?"

Andy looked over at me. I wished she wouldn't.

"So, we fight back, too. We put the nail in this bastard's coffin. Right there in front of the cameras."

"I'm not following."

"In front of all those *microphones*!"

I got it. "Ahhh! You vixen! You have *so* gone over to the dark side!"

She didn't agree out loud, but a dimple peeking at the corner of her mouth betrayed her.

ANDY TOOK THE SURFACE STREETS, zigzagging left and right on Des Moines' neat perpendicular streets. Finding the Hilton Downtown was easy. Finding parking was not. Located adjacent to the Iowa Events Center, the hotel sat at the epicenter of whatever convention happened to be in town. A row of news vans parked in front of the hotel only made matters worse.

"What time is this happening?" I asked.

"His website said seven. I think he hopes he'll make the morning news shows."

My watch said we had ten minutes. "There!" I pointed. Andy shook her head.

"Fire hydrant."

"Uh-huh. And you're a cop."

Andy gave it enough thought to conclude it wouldn't fly but decided the citation would be worth it. She pulled the car into a tight U-turn and veered across two lanes to the curb. We made a suicidal dash across the street to the Hilton entrance.

The lobby hummed with voices. Open and airy with a few low gray cloth sofas positioned around the room, the space was large enough to accommodate a milling, growing crowd. Reporters with cameras clustered at one end of the lobby where a podium had been set up in front of a blank white wall. Two of James's black-clad linebackers stood six steps away on either side of the podium. They looked even more dangerous in the light of day. As we entered, James's harried stage manager rushed into the room with two American flag stands in his arms. He stood the flags against the wall directly behind the podium. He took a moment to consider camera angles and geometry, then adjusted the flags accordingly. The last-minute preparation energized the waiting cameramen and reporters, who edged closer. A semicircle formed around the podium.

I checked the ceiling. A sparking fixture hung dozens of star-like bulbs from thin wires. The whole thing looked like a net waiting to snag me. I would have to get at James from the side.

"You need to—*you know*. Quick!" Andy urged me.

"Yeah, but where?" We both looked around. She grabbed my hand. "C'mon!"

She pulled me through clusters of people. Some were clearly waiting for the celebrity to appear. Others had the look of hotel guests who had no idea what was happening but weren't about to miss it. Smartphone cameras came out, held at the ready.

Andy led me to the area near the check-in desk, then skirted the desk until we came to a short empty hallway. She looked around. Two clerks divided their time between customers at the desk and watching the media circus. Everyone else fixed their eyes on the podium.

Andy glanced left and right, then pushed me ahead of her.

"You're good!" She released my hand.

Fwooomp!

Acting as if nothing had happened, she slid away, weaving through the loose crowd toward the podium. Both security men positioned near the podium watched her as she took up a position to one side. Their interest in her gave me a chill.

I tapped the floor to rise, bumped against the ceiling, then stabilized. I scrambled for a propulsion unit and propeller. Once assembled, I tested the unit. I probed my right-side pocket and felt the rubber device. I decided not to pull it out until reaching a position near the microphone.

James would come to the podium and launch into his story, claiming that the flatulence attributed to him was a terrorist attack, propaganda promoted by his enemies to prevent him from revealing Real Truth. It would play with his devoted followers. It might even play with some of the mainstream.

Until his sphincter muscle betrayed him again in front of a phalanx of news cameras.

A commotion to my left provided a jolt of urgency. James, flanked by four more members of his security team, marched down a hall and into the lobby. One of his cameramen backed away ahead of him, focusing on James. The white-haired man I saw negotiating with the on-air reporter at The Coliseum now cleared the way for his cameraman.

Without pausing, James stepped to the podium. Lights from the news cameras ignited, illuminating James and casting his shadow on the wall behind him. He aimed an angry, steel-eyed glare at each news camera in turn.

I pulsed the power unit and floated across the top of the lobby, wishing it had a higher ceiling. A few of the taller heads below me were within reach.

Andy glanced upward from her position at the periphery of the half circle closing around James.

He placed both hands on the podium and struck a pose. Anger. Defiance. I'd seen this pose on his streaming video. Fully in character, he waited for all eyes to find him.

The room hushed.

I reached in my pocket and closed my hand around the rubber device.

Alright, Benny, let's do this.

I pulled the device from the vest pocket and extended my arm toward the podium microphones.

From a space between two of the front-row cameras, an elderly man wearing an ill-fitting suit caught my eye. He squeezed past two of the on-air reporters. He stepped forward, centered himself in front of James, and in one smooth motion raised his right arm.

No pause. No hesitation.

Six shots from a revolver cracked the silence, slammed eardrums, and drilled Josiah James through the chest in a tight cluster. The sixth bullet was through him and out his back before he began to slump.

James dropped to the floor.

Andy's voice cut the split second of silence that followed the gunfire.

"DROP IT! DO IT NOW!" Below me, in my peripheral vision, I saw her arms come up in a firing stance, weapon in hand.

Someone in the crowd shrieked. Everyone moved backward abruptly, isolating the old man who had fired. His hand opened. A snub-nosed revolver tumbled free and fell to the carpet.

James's hulking security team pointed at Andy and shouted, "GUN!" Two of them abruptly broke to their right for Andy. The first to reach her grabbed her right arm and heaved the gun in her hand upward. The second threw his arms around her.

I reflexively pointed the power unit to attack but stopped when a new voice took command of the chaos.

"FBI! EVERYBODY DOWN! NOW! NOW! NOW!"

Every head in the room ducked. Some dropped bodily to the floor. The old man who had fired stood motionless, staring at the dead heap that had been Josiah James.

Special Agent Lee Donaldson—appearing out of nowhere—calmly pressed the barrel of his weapon into the cheek of the goon wrestling with my wife.

"FBI! Back the fuck off, you no-neck asshole! She's with me."

PART II

14

"Will!"

The sound of my name carried over street noise. I turned around.

"Will Stewart!"

"What?" I called out to what appeared to be an empty sidewalk spanning a line between the Hilton and the convention center.

"Over here, dumbass." The voice belonged to a woman. It came from the curb where a Toyota Prius sat with the passenger-side window cracked. I took a step closer and leaned down to peer through a narrow opening.

The Prius driver looked at me from behind big round sunglasses. She wore a scarf over her head. The getup suggested a *femme fatale* from an old spy film.

"Call me dumbass again and this conversation is over before it starts."

"Yeah? Walking up to a stranger who calls you from a strange vehicle qualifies you as a dumbass."

"Hey! You called out to me. If that's how you feel, adios!" I drew myself erect and turned.

"You need to get your ass out of town. Off the grid. Gone."

"Says who?"

"One of the only two *real* friends you have!"

The window hummed up and sealed. The Prius performed its trick of whispering away down the street, leaving me standing and staring. Whoever she was, if her plan was to make me feel like a dumbass, she had succeeded.

15

Andy hurried toward me. The police officer on the other side of a panel of thick glass waited, timed her arrival, then buzzed the door open. She thanked him and slipped through. The ballistic glass barrier was a retrofit to the Municipal Court and Public Safety Building, which had been built by Franklin Roosevelt's New Deal. Modern glass or not, the building retained the cold marble acoustics common to government buildings of its era. Andy tipped her head and suggested we talk outside.

After the encounter with Ms. Prius I wasn't sure I wanted to stand out in the open.

Andy led me out the narrow entrance and down the first set of steps to a row of planters that doubled as anti-vehicle barriers. Foot traffic in and out of the station building was light. I had expected a media circus since Andy, Donaldson, the shooter and the corps of Des Moines police that joined the scene of the shooting had moved across town to the police station. Then I realized that the television crews would be running their live remotes from the scene of the shooting at the Hilton.

Andy stepped close and kept her voice low.

"James was pronounced dead on arrival at the hospital."

"I could have pronounced him dead on arrival at the carpet. Who was the old guy?"

"His name is William Andrew Henry. Age eighty-six. No criminal record. Last known address is a nursing home in...uh, shoot! Someplace in Missouri. I have it written down." She reached for her satchel and the police notebook she carried. I stopped her.

"That's okay. Did he have a reason for shooting the bastard? Aside from public service?"

"He wouldn't say. He just kept repeating, 'I confess to the murder of Josiah James and waive my right to an attorney.' That's it."

"Seems cut and dried. What's the deal with Donaldson?"

"You called it. He was here—off book, he told me—to investigate James. He wasn't at the rally. He said he's already had encounters with James's security team and knew they would pick him out of the crowd. He claims he wasn't interested in the performance, although he told me he wishes he had been there to see the guy implode—or rather explode." Andy cracked a thin smile at Donaldson's joke.

"Well, I guess his work is done. James is gone. The shooter is in custody and has confessed. All wrapped up." I looked at her. "Oh, please do NOT tell me you think it's all too neat! You're not letting Donaldson drag you into whatever he's doing, Andy! We need to get out of here and go home. The sooner the better. Those storms that went through last night are going to brew up again and this time they're hitting Wisconsin."

"Will, I can't. I need to be here at least another day. I was a witness and an arresting officer on the scene. You know how this goes."

"You were an off-duty out-of-jurisdiction officer."

"With arrest powers," she corrected me. "I've got to give statements, file a report. The DA won't even be in his office until tomorrow."

I didn't like where this was headed. She read my expression and posture. "And no, I have no intention of getting involved with Donaldson."

"I'm telling you, Dee. He's got an agenda and I'd bet anything it involves his old boss, Litton. Donaldson is not our friend."

"I'll be careful."

"I appreciated him pulling that baboon off you at the Hilton, but you are definitely not 'with' him!"

"I didn't need his help. I was one second away from putting that baboon in the hospital. Listen," she came closer and slid her hands around my waist, "I'll handle this quickly. Trust me."

I gave her a reluctant sigh. "I do trust you. I don't trust Donaldson. So what does this do with our plans? You're supposed to be at work in the morning—"

"I already called Tom. He spoke to a deputy chief here. I'm on TDA to the Des Moines Police Department for tomorrow."

"Right, but I'm supposed to fly Sandy and Arun to someplace called Ekalaka, Montana."

"Montana again?"

"I know. Anyway, we're supposed to fly out tomorrow morning. I need to get back today. That was the plan when we borrowed the airplane." I let that last sound a little sulky, since the plan had already been blown to hell by a nursing-home escapee on a one-victim shooting spree.

"Day trip or overnight?"

"Supposed to be a day trip."

"Then go. Leave now before the weather becomes a factor. Do the trip with Sandy tomorrow. We'll talk during the day and if everything works out, you can pick me up on your way home tomorrow evening. I really don't see them needing that much from me here. The man confessed. It's not like he's a threat to society. He's almost ninety"

She let a distant, distracted look fall over her face. I recognized the expression and gave her a moment.

Coming back to me, she shook her head.

"What?" I asked.

"Uh…nothing."

With Andy, nothing is always something. I also knew when not to press.

"I had a weird encounter on the way here." I told her about Ms. Prius.

"Did you get a plate?"

"Uh, no." She scolded me for the rookie mistake. I asked, "Who on earth would know I was here?"

"I told Tom. Did you tell Sandy or Arun?"

"Not directly. I let Rosemary II know we were taking Twenty-One Hotel Whiskey, but that was just so she didn't book it out for anything."

"I don't like this."

"I know. Donaldson comes out of the woodwork. And now this. I bet they're connected."

"That's a bit of a stretch. Still, this isn't good."

"Which makes me feel great about leaving you here!"

She stepped back and patted her satchel. "I'm a cop, dear. I'm surrounded by cops. I'll be at a desk in the Des Moines Police Department. You're the one who is vulnerable. You should go. Straight to the airport, and just go."

"I need my flight bag. It's in our room at the Holiday Inn."

She made a face. "You can't find your way to Wisconsin from Des Moines? Really? It's across the big river, turn left at the big lake."

She was right. All I had to do was program the Essex County Airport identifier into the on-board Garmin navigation system. Put the airplane on autopilot and it's like having the horses drive the carriage home.

"I want you to go straight to the airport. In fact, I'm going to get you an escort!" She wheeled and started back up the steps.

"Dee, no! I don't need a damned police escort out of town!"

THE YOUNG OFFICER reminded me of Mike. Mid-twenties. Athletic. A perpetual grin on a friendly face. He asked me about Andy, about her meteoric career path. Word of her identity made its way around the Des Moines station as soon as they did a background check on the off-duty officer making the James shooting arrest. Andy emerged as a minor celebrity, given recent high-visibility cases. The officer assigned to deliver me to the airport in one piece made meeting her sound like a rare treat.

I don't trust other men around my wife, but the young officer's questions were peppered with a professional awe that put me at ease. I also trust my wife implicitly, although sometimes she is annoyingly blind to the intentions of men around her.

He delivered me to the FBO and parked at the curb. I protested when he climbed out of the squad car.

"This is fine. You don't have to go in. I'm sure you need to get back to the station."

He grinned. "No, man. I really want to see your airplane. If that's okay? I love airplanes. Always wanted to learn to fly."

Maybe he did. Maybe he didn't. Maybe my wife instructed him to get me on the airplane and not leave until the wheels left the ground. Because that's what happened.

16

The weather system that marched through central Iowa and soaked my shirt in the Coliseum's decrepit parking lot reanimated on Sunday afternoon. I had hoped to make the three-hundred-mile dash from Des Moines to Essex County before a squall line formed. Wheels up at noon, it was a race. A direct flight path was quickly blocked by a line forming between Mason City and Dubuque. The line hadn't reached the Mississippi yet. I deviated north, rode through some rocky turbulence between Minneapolis and Eau Claire, then hooked for an end run into Essex county. High, white cumulus chased me all the way, putting a pretty face on murderous intent.

The skies darkened as I rolled the Navajo into the safety of the Foundation hangar. Hefty raindrops knocked on the hangar's metal roof. I lowered the door quickly.

Arun intercepted me in the office. Nothing surprised me about finding him working on a Sunday afternoon, although his attire caught my eye. No shirt and tie. A polo shirt over khakis. He tried to drag me into a review of the planned itinerary for the Montana trip.

"Can you send it to my email? I want to try and get to my car before the skies open up." I pointed at the window, where the landscape had taken on a greenish darkness. Thunder rolled in the distance.

"You don't read your email, Will. I'll print a copy." He glanced at the darkened window. "Fine. Go."

I made the dash to the car with my keys in hand.

My keys.

Andy's car.

"Shit!" I completely forgot that she drove to the hangar. I stood there for a moment, stupidly hearing the echo of a stranger's voice in my head.

Dumbass.

White lightning flashed against a green-black sky. An instant thunderclap warned me that the strike landed nearby. Time to get the hell back inside. I made it, but not before my shirt and hair were soaked for the second time in twenty-four hours.

"I forgot," I confessed to Arun. "Andy drove and I don't have keys to her car." I thought it over. If not for the weather, I would simply vanish and fly my way home using a propulsion unit. That is, if I had one. My vest and three charged units remained in Andy's rental car at the Des Moines Police Station. I also had two spare units—*in my flight bag in the hotel room in Des Moines.* "Piss poor planning," I muttered to myself.

"No worries!" Arun said. "I'm nearly finished here. Let me drive you home. I will pick you up in the morning!"

"You don't mind?"

"No bother at all!"

Arun produced a pair of umbrellas for the dash to his car. Why he had two, I didn't ask. We dropped onto the cloth seats of his Corolla and slammed the doors behind us. Rain turned the windshield opaque until Arun fired up the four-cylinder and threw the wiper blades in motion.

"It's like a damned monsoon!"

"I have no idea," Arun said. "I've never been to India." He backed away from the hangar and started toward the highway.

"I didn't mean to presume."

"Oh, my family is from India. My father and mother moved to London while I was in utero. I was born in London and grew up there. My parents divorced when I was ten. Father stayed in London and I finished school there. Mother moved to Chicago. That's why I applied to Northwestern."

"Nothing like family to complicate life."

Arun agreed and went on to explain the challenges of having parents separated by the Atlantic. I interrupted to tell him which way to turn on to the highway. He pointed out that he knew the way, having studied it in case he was ever required to provide transportation.

I sat back and watched the sheets of rain. We turned off Highway 34. Traffic lightened and spray from other vehicles diminished.

Just before we reached the turn onto County Road N and the empty country mile on which my rented farmhouse sits, we slowed to pass a stopped van. The van's right wheels rested on the six-inch gravel shoulder of the road. Its lights were off and its hazard flashers were not illuminated.

"Abcress Plumbing." I read the bold lettering on the side panel as we passed.

"Clever."

I glanced at the van's side window, expecting to see the plumber working his phone, more than likely checking the next appointment. The seat was empty.

"How so?"

"Abcress. The first three letters of the alphabet. That's probably not a real name, but rather a ploy to gain prominence in alphabetical listings in a directory."

"Nobody uses a directory anymore. Someone keeps dropping a skinny Yellow Pages on my driveway, but it goes straight into the recycling bin."

"A victim of the digital age. The proprietors of Abcress Plumbing appear to be trapped in the receding recent past."

"Turn right up here," I said, forgetting for a moment that Arun had already mapped our course. "How so?"

"Abcress. A-B-C gave them prominence in printed alphabetical listings, but micro-marketing techniques in the digital age require a different approach. They would be better served painting their phone number or web URL on the side of the van."

"Didn't they?"

"No."

I twisted in the seat, but the rain blurred my view of the parked plumbing van. Arun made the turn onto County Road N. Waist-high cornfields sprawled on either side of the road.

Abcress. I didn't know the name. I knew Mark Bergandorf's name. Mark owns half a dozen plumbing and heating vans with his name, number and URL plastered all over the blue panels. Mark often joined the Saturday morning crowd at the Silver Spoon Diner. Several of his plumbers have visited the farmhouse to deal with our antique plumbing.

Thinking it through, I realized I didn't know the name of *any* other plumbers in Essex.

"That's ridiculous," I muttered, pulling out my phone.

"Indeed, when you consider the fact that those vehicles are on the road constantly. Visual marketing serves in transit as well as when parked in service of a customer. A *de facto* endorsement."

I wasn't listening. I opened my phone screen to Google and tapped out the name and Essex. Service is merely okay out on our remote road. The little wheel turned, searching.

The screen popped up. No listing for Abcress Plumbing appeared. The hairs on the back of my neck rose. I don't like using the voice application on the phone, but we approached my driveway.

"Okay, Google. Plumbers. Essex County." The wheel turned.

Arun eased off the gas. The farmhouse materialized out of the rain. A lightning strike froze the raindrops in midair for a split second. Thunder shook the car and vibrated through us.

A list of plumbers appeared.

Abcress wasn't on it.

Arun turned in the driveway. The sound coming from the car wheels shifted from hissing on the wet pavement to grinding on the gravel driveway. I looked at the house. At the yard. At the barn behind the house. I twisted in the seat and checked the road behind us. The visibility was poor. A quarter of a mile away I barely saw the dark shape of the van by the side of the road.

Poor visibility—that might help.

"Pull up there, Arun," I pointed. "Right up on the grass. Yes. Right up by the back steps."

I checked the line of sight. Trees in the front yard stood between the back door and the van.

Arun hesitantly stopped halfway off the driveway with his right-side wheels on the lawn. The car sat just a few feet from the backdoor steps.

I checked the yard. Except for the boughs of trees bending low under the weight of the rain, nothing moved.

"Wait here."

"Is there a problem?"

"Might be. Just wait here."

I grabbed the umbrella and positioned it near the top of my door. I opened the door, stabbed the umbrella out and pressed the release button. It popped open. I pushed the door open and pulled myself out, tipping the umbrella slightly to shield me as much from the rain as from the sight line to the parked van.

This is silly.

I took three steps, leaving Arun's car door open behind me. I held the umbrella high and angled right to appear large on the sight line to the parked van. Rain pelted my exposed left side. On the first step up to the back stoop, I pulled the umbrella shut and dropped into a crouch, then duck-walked back to the car and crawled in beside Arun. I closed the door and slid down in the seat until my knees were jammed in the space under the dash.

"I'm sorry, Will, is something—?"

"Back out. Easy." He stared at me. "Don't look down at me. Someone in that van is watching. Just back out and go east. Don't go back the way you came."

Arun obeyed, holding his head up and concentrating on the task of backing out of the driveway. He fumbled with the shifter at first, betraying tension.

"Should we call the police? Is someone breaking in?"

"No. I don't think so. Just back out—that's it. Good. Now go east. Nice and easy." I reached under the seat and found the manual release for the seat track. I pulled the lever and the seat jolted backward, giving my knees relief. I stayed below the line of the window. "Nice and easy. Casual." We rolled forward. Rain drenched the windshield. The tires hissed on the pavement. "Speed limit is forty-five here. Keep it at that, Arun."

"Did you see someone?"

"Not exactly."

"Did you see signs of a break-in? Because we should call the police, Will!"

"I didn't see signs of a break-in." He glanced down at me. "Eyes front, Arun. Just drive. Tell me what you see."

"The road."

Our stretch of County Road N runs for one mile between stop signs. The farmhouse sits near the western quarter of that span. The eastern three quarters runs arrow-straight and flat between James Rankin's cornfields until it encounters the next stop sign.

"Bloody hell!" Arun exclaimed. I wasn't sure I'd ever heard him say something crude.

"What?"

He swallowed, tightened his posture and fixed a death grip on the wheel. "Just stay down, Will! Stay down!"

"Talk to me, pal. What are you seeing?"

"There's another of your servicemen here."

"A what?"

"Your plumber. Abcress. There's another van here. By the side of the road. This one has a driver sitting behind the wheel. We're passing it...now!"

I squeezed myself down.

"He's looking at us," Arun said through clenched teeth, frozen, facing forward. I buried my face. A dark lump in the passenger seat might be anything—but not if it had a face.

"Did he move? Is he moving?" I asked.

Arun watched the mirror.

"Not yet. Not yet...still not moving. I believe you're right, Will. He appears to be watching your house."

"He's too far away to see anything."

"Will! What's going on?"

"Your guess is as good as mine. Drive to the stop sign and turn left."

"Is your wife still in Des Moines?"

"She is."

"You should call the police!" He reached for his phone.

"No. Turn left at the stop sign."

I felt the car decelerate. Arun eased off the gas and began braking. He held a full stop for a second, then turned and accelerated.

"There's a small hill ahead. Go over it. Then you go down into a slight depression. I want you to stop at the bottom. I'm going to get out. As soon as I do, take off immediately, got it? In case they're watching, you've got to make it look like you didn't stop when you come up the other side. Don't show your brake lights until we're over the crest. Use the parking brake to slow down. Don't let them see brake lights!"

Arun eased off the gas slightly to bleed away what little speed he had acquired. I felt the car rise, then drop. We continued for a few seconds until Arun braked abruptly. He brought the Corolla to a full stop using the hand brake between the front seats. I slid up against the dash.

I threw open the door and heaved myself out. There was nothing pretty about it. I crawled out onto the pavement on all fours.

"What do I do?!" Arun called after me.

I hesitated, projecting paths and outcomes.

"Go back to the hangar. If you don't hear from me within the hour, go home! And don't call anyone! No one!" I threw the door shut behind me and pulled myself to my feet. Arun's worried face remained fixed on me through the wet window. "Go! Go! Go!" I shouted. I slapped my hand on the thin metal roof.

He stomped the accelerator. The wheels spun briefly before the anti-slip system chattered. His car hissed forward in the rain. I pulled my phone from my shirt pocket and pressed it into the hip pocket of my jeans.

I jogged across the pavement and hopped over a small ditch. Water clinging to the tall grass soaked my jeans. Rain soaked my shirt and ran down my face. I hurried through the tall grass into the corn, which was better than waist high in this field. A few stalks had wide leaves that arched toward my chin. It had been a good summer with sun and rain alternating in a combination that makes the corn and the farmers happy. The field would provide ample cover if I needed it.

I crouched and waited to see if the van or anyone else followed Arun's diminishing taillights. Nothing passed.

This wasn't ideal. I had no power units. I also had no idea how vanishing would work in the rain. It's not exactly vanishing if you leave an empty human outline in falling raindrops. During the winter I had used *the other thing* in a heavy snowfall, expecting to see the snow pile up on my shoulders. It didn't. I had never tested this in rain.

"As good a time as any," I said aloud.

Fwooomp! I disappeared.

I held my arms out, trying to see their shape. Expecting to see a glistening outline of a person. After a moment, concentrating intently, I saw something, but not what I expected. If I looked closely—if I tried to follow a falling raindrop—I saw it vanish when it hit me.

I held my hand up in front of my face. Still unable to see any sign of an outline, I eventually spotted drops falling at a different pace than the rain around me. These were drops falling, disappearing, then reappearing as they fell away from my hand.

Not bad. Worse, however, was the constant cool electric snap I felt as each drop broke away. Anything I release from within *the other thing* causes a momentary sensation of an electric charge. The larger the object, the greater the sensation. It doesn't hurt, but it can be annoying. Now, as dozens of raindrops fell off my arms, I felt each of them as a tiny jolt. Like the pinpricks caused by paresthesia when a pinched sleeping nerve awakens.

The next thing I noticed was that I wasn't rising. My feet were light on the mud between the corn rows, but I wasn't floating free of gravity. The steady rain hitting my body from above drove me down, much the same way a wind pushes me. This gave me an idea.

I faced the road and hopped. I soared up from between the corn rows. I had wildly overdone the hop. I floated completely across the highway. For a moment I worried that the goof would result in an uncontrollable ascent, but my assessment of the effect of the rain proved true. Under the pressure of the falling rain, I sank again. I came down in the tall grass lining the ditch on the opposite side of the road.

"Okay. That works."

Fwooomp! I reappeared and hiked out of the tall grass, back onto the pavement. I crossed to the right side of the road. No sense in trying this and splatting myself on the grille of some gravel truck.

I jogged forward, took half a dozen steps, then—

Fwooomp!

I pumped the last step against the pavement and soared. The road fell away below me. I ascended above the small hill that had hidden

Arun's car from the parked van. The van appeared well ahead and to my right. I glanced to the west, searching for the first van a mile away, but the visibility was only half that. My house was barely outlined in the rain.

For a second time, I worried about continuing to rise, but once again, the falling rain provided pressure that turned my upward shot into a parabolic arc. After covering most of a hundred yards, the pavement came up to meet my feet. I hit the ground running, pumped two steps, and at once the act of taking a step and pushing the pavement launched me again.

The heavy wind from the gust front was gone. Rain fell almost vertically. A slight wind drift pushed me left. I came down the second time in the lane for oncoming traffic. Not good.

I adjusted my path and concentrated on taking lighter steps. The launch corrected my trajectory and didn't go as high. I covered only thirty or forty feet before returning to the pavement. The van sat not far ahead. Two or three more jumps.

A new worry blossomed. I realized that I might run out of the rain shower. Thunderstorm cells generated the rain, which meant they might only be a few miles across and moving quickly. Without the rain coming down, I might launch without any pressure pushing me back down.

It took only two more jumps to reach the van. At the end of the last jump, I bent my knees to absorb the momentum of my body. The move prevented me from bouncing away from the road surface. I carefully continued forward doing a flat-footed walk, letting the rain hold me down, restraining the spring action my ankles apply in ordinary walking.

The van sat like its companion, with two wheels off the road. The driver wore glasses and a ball cap, occasionally looking down at something. His lips moved. I couldn't tell if he was talking to someone in the back of the van or via phone or radio. He kept watch on the road leading to my house.

I contemplated pulling my phone out to take a picture. I'd done it before from within *the other thing*. It's not easy. And in the rain, despite its protective case, my phone would be slippery. I decided to wait.

I carefully stepped to the front of the van and looked inside. The driver continued talking. I was close enough to hear the muted conversation, but not the words, not over the metallic drumming of rain on the roof of the van. I tried to see into the back of the van, but darkness and rain on the windshield impeded my view. I was, however, close enough to see that the driver didn't wear a work shirt with his name embroidered over the pocket. He wore a tactical vest over a black polo shirt.

Like Donaldson.

Who the hell are these guys?

I stopped just ahead of the bumper and resolved to try my phone after all. I reached for my phone when I heard the ignition turn.

The driver pulled the gearshift lever down.

Shit! I stood directly in front of a vehicle about to plow right into me!

The side mirrors flashed through my mind—something to grip. *Too far away.* The wipers might give me a hand hold. *Moving.*

The van lurched forward.

I dropped. I used the core muscle to lift my feet off the pavement and swing them parallel to the front bumper. I grabbed the bumper and pulled myself up against the grille. The van shot forward, heading west on County Road N. The driver paid no attention to the rain. He accelerated to well over sixty or seventy in the short three quarters of a mile. Something had become urgent.

Wind pressure pushed me against the front of the van. The road streaked by just inches from my right elbow. I formed a plan to heave myself off the front left corner of the vehicle. Angular momentum would throw me out across the corn, but the falling rain would drive me down.

Or not.

The driver decelerated abruptly. He turned into my driveway and bounced across the gravel toward a duplicate van already sitting beside my house with its rear door panels swung open as a similarly black-clad man hopped out.

The van stopped. The driver jumped out joined by a fourth man who had been in the rear of the van. They hustled toward my back door, where the first two men climbed the steps. It took them only a second to open the door. They did it so quickly I wondered if Andy and I forgot to lock the house. The squad of intruders disappeared inside.

It pissed me off.

I rotated myself, then pulled my body on a vector that took me to the top step outside the back door. Clearing the space first, I pulled myself through the frame into my mudroom.

Inside my home, men shouted out.

"Clear!"

"Clear!"

Doors slammed open. Feet stomped upstairs.

I shoved myself across the mudroom to a closet. I pulled the door open and found what I needed. Two of my early generation power units lay on a shelf. These were units with the propellers already fixed. I picked up one and instantly knew the case had no batteries. I picked up the second and got the same result. I shoved them under my wet shirt. They vanished.

The first-generation power units used C cell batteries. I had purchased a pile of them at Costco. After switching to rechargeable batteries, I moved the unused C cell batteries to the Battery Drawer in the kitchen. Andy used them for household flashlights.

I shoved back, floated across the mudroom toward the open door, caught the door jamb and pulled myself through. I caught the kitchen table.

Someone shouted from upstairs, "Get the scanner!"

Scanner? Shit!

Cold fear shot a shiver down my spine. Feet pounded through my dining room. A man in full tactical gear hurried through the kitchen, into the mudroom and outside. I pulled myself over the high-top table to avoid him.

I gripped the table. Gray indecision closed in on my vision. This is how it happens in a panic situation. Thought ceases. Motivation turns to water. This is why pilots train and rely on training—so that thought isn't required.

I had no training for this. I hit the fight or flight decision point, and paralysis preempted both.

Batteries! I heaved myself over the table and grabbed the kitchen countertop. Hand over hand, I edged across the floor, past the kitchen sink, to the point where the Battery Drawer hung under the countertop. I glanced back to clear the room, then pulled the drawer open.

The C cells nested in their plastic packing. I jerked the plastic layer up. Batteries tumbled all over the drawer. Loudly. Feet pounded on the stairs. Two or three sets.

I grabbed a set of batteries and dropped them down my shirt collar. Then another. They were cold against my skin, but with my shirt tucked in, they stayed. I grabbed a third set and held them in my hand. They remained visible and weighed me down.

Using the weight of the batteries, I turned and ran—or carefully bounded. Each step used leg muscles trained to carry my hundred-eighty-something-pound body, not a few ounces of batteries. Too much pressure, and I would bound right into the ceiling. I concentrated on using the friction of my boot soles against the floor.

Boot traction sent me in the direction of the mudroom door. Now it was a question of timing. Someone had gone outside to get some sort of scanner. Was he close? Was he coming back in? Because he was about to encounter two C cell batteries floating out the door.

I made it to the door and saw a clear path to the back door. Beyond, the man who had gone outside now climbed the steps with a black plastic case in hand. I wouldn't beat him. I stuffed the batteries down my shirt where they vanished.

Whatever he carried was not yet deployed. He would need to get in, open the case and remove the device. Whatever it was, I decided it was meant for me.

How is that possible?!

I had a minute, maybe two.

I gripped the door jamb to the mudroom and swung myself through, then stretched out my legs and extended myself parallel to the floor, away from the door, still holding the jamb.

He passed in front of me and hurried to the kitchen where he was met by two more men, one of them the glasses-wearing driver of the van.

"Fuck, it's raining cats, dogs and cows out there!" the man carrying the case exclaimed.

I didn't stay to watch. I wanted to, but if they were pulling out a device capable of seeing me, I needed to be gone. Completely gone.

I twisted and heaved myself toward the back door. Midway across the mudroom I curled into a cannonball shape and rotated my body. The shot wasn't my best and I banged into the side of the door jamb. I quietly cracked the door open and slipped through.

Rain pressure immediately pushed me down. I floated far enough to clear the back steps, then my feet touched the wet grass. One step and I kicked off, this time with no attempt to be gentle or apply finesse. The shot arched over the parked vans, higher and higher, over the yard between the house and the barn, which gave me an idea.

I hit the top of the arc. Rain pressure pushed me back down. The trajectory took me back to Earth short of the barn. My feet landed on the gravel in the farmyard. I gave it my best guess and kicked off again. The barn sank in front of me. I cleared the roof, then continued sailing upward.

Stop! Stop! Stop! The four-panel barn roof sank below me. The cupola set midway down the center of the roofline, passed below me. Rain pressure finally halted my climb. I descended on an arc that would either put me at the edge of the barn roof farthest from the house, or not. If not, I expected a bad crash in a tangle of old fencing and farm junk overgrown by weeds and buckthorn behind the barn, in between two old silos.

The roofline came toward me and it didn't look good. Just as it became clear to me that I would miss and sail over the edge—

FWOOOMP! I pushed hard and reappeared in a snap. Gravity took me. I fell the last ten feet to the peak of the barn roof, stumbled and felt my feet go out from under me. My butt hit the roof peak. I skidded toward the edge. My feet went over the edge. I twisted and clawed to gain a handhold but felt nothing except asphalt shingles. My legs slid off the roof into empty air. Under my shirt, one of the propellers gouged my ribcage.

Fwooomp! I vanished. Gravity lost interest in me. For a moment I continued the trajectory over the edge of the roof.

Despite *the other thing* my heart nearly stopped as I slid off the edge of the roof.

I grabbed the woodwork beneath the overhang and held on. My body extended like a flag before the rain pressure pushed me down.

My heart pounded.

SILO!

The thought came to me uncalled. Something grabbed me at the core, by the muscle at my center. My body jerked away from the roof, pulling my hands free. I shot across the open space between the roof and the old cement silo. I flew around the dome to the back side and found the rusting iron handholds.

I stopped.

I grabbed one of the handholds and pulled myself down against the concrete silo dome. I hooked my feet on an iron bar below me and reappeared.

Fwooomp!

I held on in the rain, panting.

"Six months of trying and now you get it to work?" I gasped for breath.

The rain chilled my skin; the protection of *the other thing* was gone. I let it soak me and ignored the shiver it brought on. I hooked one arm through the iron handhold, rolled over and leaned back against the wet, cold concrete, closing my eyes against the rain.

Sixty feet up, lying on the wet silo dome, I waited. The rain eased by degrees. Occasional flashes of distant lighting and slow thunder made me feel exposed. But not as exposed as the idea that men were in my house, looking for me.

How is that possible?!

17

My clothing soaked through while I waited on the top of the silo. I peeked over the dome top twice. The first time, nothing had changed. The second time, I saw the intruders fan out in the yard—two headed for the garage and two headed for the barn. Neither carried any kind of device, nor did my glimpse show me that they had deployed infrared headgear.

I didn't push my luck. I slid back down and remained out of sight. After a while, my hand cramped from the grip on the iron bar. The thunderstorms had been generated by a cold front, and the air behind it lived up to the name. I shivered. When I couldn't wait any longer, I rolled onto my belly and crawled to the apex of the silo dome for another look.

Gone. The yard was empty. No men. No vehicles.

It took a few minutes to fish a power unit and batteries out of my saturated shirt. I immediately dropped one battery. It tumbled down the concrete dome and bounced off the lip. My dexterity suffered from the cold, the wet and the tension. I forced myself to slow down. The idea of climbing down the side of the silo fully visible and under gravity's influence did not hold any appeal.

I carefully installed a set of batteries and tested the power unit. The prop buzzed.

Fwooomp!

I vanished, fired up the power unit and flew myself off the silo dome. The rain had stopped. I did a precautionary circuit around the yard, then farther afield, checking the surveillance positions occupied by the two vans. I detected no sign of anyone watching.

I returned to the house, landed on my back step and reappeared. I found myself locked out. It took me a minute to get my keys out of my soaked pants pocket and let myself in.

I checked the entire house to be certain I was alone. I considered the possibility that they had left something behind to watch or listen. Spy camera technology is shockingly small and accessible. If they did, there was nothing to do about it until Andy returned. I left the power units and batteries in the mudroom, kicked off my boots and stripped down to my cold, wet skin. If they were watching, they got a show. I dropped the wet clothes in the laundry room.

Upstairs, I dried off and dressed. I went back to the mudroom where I packed two power units (this time with batteries) into a light flight jacket. I put on the jacket and hurried out of the house. The light rain had turned to drizzle. Sunshine cut through gaps in the western clouds lending a summer after-rain sparkle to the land.

I jogged to the barn, ducked into the loft and dialed my phone.

"Pick up! Pick up! Pick up!"

You've reached Detective Andrea Stewart. Leave a message.

I stabbed a finger at the red button to end the call.

"Shit!"

Think!

I did a quick web search and dialed again.

You've reached the Des Moines Police Department. If this call is an emergency, hang up and dial 9-1-1. If you are calling about...

I tapped 0. A not terribly enthusiastic voice greeted me.

"I'm calling for Detective Andrea Stewart. This is her husband calling."

"There is no Detective Andrea Stewart in the department, sir."

"Right! You're right! She's not from your department. But she's there today—"

"Sir, would you like the directory?"

"No! Listen, Detective Stewart is a visiting off-duty officer who was present at the Josiah James shooting. She's there today. Working with the FBI—with Special Agent Donaldson. I need to speak with Detective Stewart. It's urgent!"

"Hold, please."

I stood in the empty barn, tensed every muscle I had, and looked for something to punch.

Several minutes passed.

"This is Sergeant Leonard, media relations. I understand you have a question about an incident today?"

I slapped my forehead and took a deep breath.

"Sergeant Leonard," I said calmly, "I do not have a question. I—"

"This is the media relations office. I can tell you that we're not issuing a statement or any information at this time about—"

"Sergeant! Shut the fuck up and listen!"

"Sir, there's no need—"

"You have an officer in jeopardy! Listen to what I have to say!"

The line fell silent.

"My name is Will Stewart. My wife is Detective Andrea Stewart. She's TDA with your department and the FBI on the investigation related to the Josiah James shooting. Do you follow me so far?"

"Like I said, there's no need—"

"Good! Find her. Put her on the line. It is a stone-cold fucking emergency!"

"What is the nature of your emergency?"

"I need to speak to Detective Stewart!"

"Are you in danger?"

"At the moment…no. But Detective Stewart may be."

Silence.

"Sir, can you be reached at the number I see on my screen?"

"Yes!"

"And your name again?"

I gave it.

"I will take this message to the appropriate persons. If it checks out, you can expect a call back, but I advise you to watch your language."

The call ended.

I stood staring at the phone for a moment, hating the device, the sergeant in the Des Moines Police Media Relations office, and the world on general principles. I closed my eyes and collected a long breath.

Then I walked across the barn floor to the wall that faced the house. Through a knothole in the wood plank wall, I looked over the yard to see if my visitors had returned. Nothing.

The hair on the back of my neck told me this was not a safe place to be.

And Des Moines wasn't a safe place for Andy.

I didn't trust my phone but for the moment had no choice. I touched the screen again, brought up my contacts and tapped one.

"What's up?"

"Pidge, remember when we were having a beer at the Hyatt in Chicago, and I got that call? From the Irishman? And I left you a message on the table?" I crossed my fingers that Pidge would catch on.

"What the fuck are you talking about?"

"Drinks. Hyatt. I got a call. I left a message on the table. I—"

"Okay! Okay! I got it! Copy!"

"Good. I need your help. Where are you?"

"Where do you think I am? Up to my ass in laundry."

"Well drop everything. I want you to meet me."

"Is that squawk code for real?"

"It is. I want you to meet me where you dropped me off the first time you ever dropped me off. The first time I ever got out of an airplane you were flying. Got it?"

"Uh...I think so. What the fuck?"

"Not on the phone. Half an hour."

I ended the call. Paranoia told me to dismantle the phone and leave it in the barn, but I still hadn't heard from Andy. I increased the ringer volume to the max and pocketed the phone. It would have been better to have my Bluetooth earpiece—but that was sitting in my flight bag in a hotel room in Des Moines.

"This is what I get for listening to my wife," I muttered.

I pulled a power unit and broke into a run through the open barn door. On the third step—

Fwooomp!

SHAFTS OF SUNLIGHT scanned the glistening, rain-washed countryside between rows of ragged clouds. The clouds marched like camp followers behind the line of thunderstorms which, by now, were bearing down on the western shores of Michigan. Fresh puddles in low-lying areas reflected the sky as I flew over them. Steam rose in ghostly wisps from the wet landscape.

The runways at Essex County Airport looked good for the wash they had received, dark and clean. I flew a course that took me over the cluster of hangars on the north side of the field. Arun's Corolla sat in his favored parking slot beside the Foundation hangar. Earl's truck and Rosemary II's sedan were absent, it being Sunday. A cluster of cars sat in the FBO lot. One belonged to a weekend girl named Kelly who worked the counter and phones until five. The rest belonged to one of the part-time instructors and a couple of renter pilots.

No sign of plumbing vans.

"Really? Plumbing vans? Like something out of a stupid action movie," I said over the whine of the power unit and hiss of the relative wind against my ears. The sound of my own voice made me feel marginally better. Whether out of anger, or fear, my muscles and nerves were tightly wound.

Andy's voice intruded my thoughts.

Were they armed?

I realized I had no idea.

What did they look like?

I didn't look at their faces.

License plates on the vehicles?

"Nice job, idiot," I told myself.

I looked for, but didn't see, Pidge's Honda, but I was early. Rather than burn up my limited battery power, I turned and followed a line parallel to runway 31/13. The southeastern end of the runway terminated near a small river that wandered the southern perimeter of the field. I aimed for the Century fence that divided the airport property from the banks of the river. I pulsed the power unit to bring myself into a hover beside the fence for a moment of indecision. Do I stay out of sight? Do I reappear? I needed to see my phone and settled on the latter. A stand of trees shielded me from Highway 34 and a half mile separated me from the airport parking lots. I would see them coming if they came.

Fwooomp!

I dropped into the short, wet grass.

My phone showed no sign of a call from Andy or DMPD.

Jesus Christ! What part of "emergency" is so hard to understand?

I took a moment and thumbed a text to her. "Emergency. Call me. ASAP!"

Send.

Pidge's Honda Civic appeared in the distance, rounding the cluster of hangars and wheeling onto the runway 31/13 parallel taxiway. She drove with her headlights on. Light spray flew from her wheels.

What if she's not alone? What if someone has a gun to her head?

I walked up a slight slope to the taxiway where I had once watched her make her first solo flights. Three takeoffs and landings, each one perfect.

She rolled to a stop and dropped the window. I checked the back seat. Empty. She sat close to the steering wheel in denim shorts and a t-shirt. Her short blonde hair hid beneath a faded Essex County Air Service ball cap. She looked me over from behind her Ray Bans.

"You know, I will always take you seriously if you give me the emergency squawk code. Don't ever fucking abuse that."

I looked to see if any other vehicles moved half a mile away at the hangars. "Did you see anyone out of place? Anybody follow you?"

"No. What the hell?"

I told her what I knew.

"Any idea who the motherfuckers are? What they want?"

"Not a clue who, but my guess is they got wind of what I can do and want to get their hands on me. Or it." I walked around the car's front bumper and slid onto the passenger seat.

"How? Have you been showing off? Who else knows?" I shrugged but had already started compiling the short list in my head.

"It's better if I don't go into that. I need your help. I'm worried about Andy. She's in Des Moines." I explained. Starting with Donaldson and ending with the James shooting and the weird warning on the street.

Pidge grinned at me. "That was you? You whoopie-cushioned that fucker? Damn, Stewart! It's blowing up the internet!" She threw a congratulatory punch into my shoulder. "You motherfucker!"

"Forget that, Pidge! I can't reach Andy."

"She's probably just busy. Will, she's with a bunch of cops." The look on my face told her I wasn't buying that. "What? You think the same people will go after Andy?"

"I don't know. I don't know a lot right now, but I need your help. I need to get back to Andy, but they may be watching the hangar. I want to make it look like you're taking out the Foundation Navajo."

"Where?"

"You're not taking it anywhere. I'm taking it to Des Moines, but I don't want them to see me. I need it to look like you're flying."

She sat thinking.

"Just pull it out, taxi out here, hop out and I'll take it from there," I said.

"Okay. And how's it going to look when I wander back across the airport without the airplane? Or I drive off? That's a dumbass plan."

I wasn't pleased to be called a dumbass for the second time in a day, but she had a point.

"Why not take me with you? If you want to sell this to whoever you think is watching, sell it." I didn't answer. "C'mon, man! I don't have anything scheduled tomorrow. You're gonna come right back anyway, right?"

"I'm not sure about that. If Andy and I can't get back I was going to ask you to take a Foundation trip tomorrow. Montana."

"In what? You're taking the airplane."

Shit. This was getting more complicated than I hoped.

"Where in Montana?" Pidge asked.

"Ekalaka."

"Eka-what-the-fuck?"

"It's on the eastern end of the state." I had an idea. "Get your phone out. Call Sandy Stone." I gave her the number. Pidge made the call and handed me the phone.

"Hi, Pidge, what's up?" Sandy sounded cheerful. It felt out of place for the moment.

"It's Will."

"Oh. What's going on?"

"Which would be worse for you? Dropping everything and meeting me at the airport as soon as you can for the Montana trip? Or cancelling the trip?"

"Is there a problem?"

116

"Uh…for the moment let's call it a weather judgment."

"More storms?"

"Something like that."

"Okay. I guess…I guess I can be there in about an hour."

"See you at the hangar."

The call ended. Pidge reached for her phone, but I waved her off. I dialed Andy's number.

You've reached Detective Andrea Stewart. Leave a message.

I poked the red button to end the call. Again.

"This is not good," I said. "Let's go."

Pidge stared at me. "Are you gonna…you know…?"

"Yeah, yeah."

Fwooomp!

"That is just the shits!" She threw the Honda in gear.

18

The Foundation hangar has the big door, the office door, and a side entrance the size of a one-car garage door. I've tried to tell Arun to use the side entrance and park his car inside the hangar, but he insists such a privilege belongs to his boss. Sandy doesn't use it, either. I gave Pidge the code and had her pull her car inside, then close the door. I quickly reappeared before Arun poked his head into the hangar to see what was going on. He hurried toward us as we hopped out of the car.

"Hey, Arun," I said. "Have you met Pi—"

"Cassidy!" Pidge blurted out. I turned around to see her toss her ball cap into the back seat and shake her blonde hair out. "Cassidy Page." She approached Arun with her hand extended and a look on her face that reminded me of something she once said when she caught me staring at Andy across a room. *You look like an eleven-year-old girl watching a unicorn slide down a fucking rainbow.*

"Arun Dewar," he said taking her hand. She smiled at him and threw a quick swipe at her hair.

"Nice to meet you! I'm sorry, I'm a bit of a mess!"

"Not at all! You look quite nice."

I couldn't be sure because the lights were not on in the hangar, but it's possible Pidge blushed. Arun turned to me.

"Will! I've been waiting for your call. What happened? Is every-thing alright?"

"I'm not sure. Part of it, I honestly can't discuss. And we don't have time. Sandy is on her way here. We're launching within the hour." I braced myself for Arun to panic.

"You'll have to excuse me," Pidge said. "I need to run over to the office and get my overnight bag. It was lovely to meet you!" She backed away, then swung into a rapid walk to the exit.

"She seems nice..." Arun watched her go. I've seen Pidge snag men's eyes with her walk before.

I waved a hand in front of Arun's face. "Did I mention that Sandy is on her way and we're leaving?"

"I'm sorry...what?"

PIDGE TOOK FAR LONGER than necessary to fetch her flight bag. My nerves jittered. I worried about Andy. I wanted to get moving.

I checked weather and filed a flight plan with Pidge listed as pilot-in-command. I called Kelly in the Essex County Air Service office to request that she send over the fuel truck. That meant opening the big door. That meant I had to duck out of sight. I told Arun to go outside to instruct the kid on the fuel truck to top all tanks. Arun grew mildly flustered at the prospect of handling aircraft operations, but the kid operating the fuel truck knew the drill.

The fuel truck came and went before Pidge showed up clicking her roller bag wheels across the seams of the concrete hangar floor. Lurking out of sight in the office, I didn't see her until she stepped through the glass door.

I had to blink.

"Is that—are you—? What are you wearing?"

She looked around for Arun. I heard him rifling through file drawers in his office. "It's a fucking dress, moron," she snapped at me.

"I know. But it's—um, how do I put this? It's not—"

"Slutty? Bite me."

I shut up. The dress was like something Andy might wear to a church picnic. It had—*flowers*! On top of that, Pidge had brushed her hair and if I wasn't mistaken, applied makeup.

Arun popped out of his office. "Miss Page. You look lovely!"

"Thank you, Arun. Please—call me Cassidy."

I made a face at Pidge who smiled sweetly at Arun, who pried his eyes off Pidge just long enough to tell me, "I'll just be a minute, Will." He backed into his office.

I looked at Pidge. "Cassidy?" She made sure Arun was out of sight, then flipped me off with both hands.

Sandy showed up ten minutes later with a single overnight bag. Arun joined us with his own bag and a briefcase.

"Flight plan is filed. Weather looks bumpy but VFR all the way to Des Moines," I told Pidge.

"Des Moines?" Sandy asked.

"I'll explain on the way. Pi—er, Cassidy, would you help them load? I want to wait here until we're ready to roll out. I'm afraid you're going to have to pull it out. I don't want to be seen." Anticipating Sandy, I turned to her and said, "Again, I'll explain on the way." Sandy doesn't know about *the other thing* and I had yet to come up with a good lie for all this. Ideas ran through my mind, most of them casting Donaldson in a dark role.

Arun wore a giant question mark expression. "Is Miss Page joining us?"

"Miss Page is flying, Arun."

I thought Pidge might curtsey. I fully expected Arun to stop breathing.

"I need to make a phone call," I said.

Pidge led Arun and Sandy to the hangar. I pulled out my phone, checked for missed calls or a text from Andy and found nothing. I tapped up my contact list and picked out Earl Jackson's name.

"It's your nickel."

"Hi, Boss. I need to ask you something. Last winter, when that crew came and took away Six Nine Tango, did you ever find out who that was?"

"Insurance company. Why?"

"Do you know where it went?"

"Shit. Who knows? Those number jockeys at the insurance company would have farmed it out as a salvage."

"How does that work?"

"While you were still eating Jell-O and peeing into a diaper in the hospital," he said (*thanks for reminding me*), "their guy came out and took a look at the wreck to make sure we weren't pulling a swap. And to see if there was anything worth selling off. The moment I filed the claim it became their airplane."

"Which they farmed out to a salvage company."

"The suits weren't going to do it."

"Can we find out who did the salvage? Where it went?"

"Why? Didja leave your favorite pen in the cockpit?"

I didn't want to explain. Or lie. "Can you take this one on faith, Boss? It's coming from Andy."

A small lie. But I knew Earl never said no to my wife. Still, with or without dropping Andy's name, Earl doesn't like mystery. I crossed my fingers against the silence on the line. I pictured his expression. A face on Mount Rushmore before the sculptors smoothed out the granite.

"Might take me a couple days."

"Thanks, Boss."

The call ended. Pidge tapped on the glass wall between the office and hangar. "Let's go!"

I followed her into the hangar, keeping the airplane between me and the open door. I hopped up the airstair into the cabin and settled on the floor behind the last seat, below the sight lines of the windows.

Pidge hooked up the powered tow bar we use when we're not using Essex Air's tug. She eased the big twin out of the hangar, secured the tow bar, then ushered Sandy and Arun onboard. Last up the airstair, she pulled it shut behind her, threw me a smug glance, and moved up the aisle. Settled into the cockpit, she turned. "Arun, would you care to ride up front?"

"I'd be delighted!" He closed the open briefcase on his lap and shuffled into the copilot's seat, leaving me wondering how many times I'd made the same offer and he declined, citing his duty to go over trip details with his boss.

Sandy turned her curiosity in my direction.

"I'll explain when we get in the air."

19

I didn't lie to Sandy as much as reroute some facts. The weather forecast continued to call for isolated severe thunderstorms, but most of the action was predicted for north of us, around Minneapolis. It was enough, however, to suggest that traveling today was better than tomorrow. About hiding my face from prying eyes around the airport, I told her I didn't want Dave Peterson to spot me because he's always looking to grab a beer after work—which was true. Mention of Dave ended Sandy's pursuit of the subject. As for why Pidge was flying, I confessed that I asked her to take over the trip because I expected to join Andy in Des Moines—or so I dearly hoped. Sandy drew her own amused conclusions about Arun's sudden interest in riding up front.

"YOU STILL HAVEN'T HEARD from Andy?" Pidge took me aside after setting Arun and Sandy up on the curb to wait for a taxi to a hotel. It had been determined that they would spend the night in Des Moines since the tiny town of Ekalaka, Montana, population 358, had no overnight accommodations.

"No. I called the station and they said they do not give out the whereabouts of their officers."

Pidge read the look on my face. "Fuck."

"I'm going over there now. Somebody has to know where she went."

"Want me to come along?"

"No. Get them settled. Anywhere but the Hilton." I wasn't sure the media circus would be over—or if they would have the blood out of the carpet. "If you don't hear anything from me, take them up to Montana in the morning."

"And then?"

I shrugged. "If you still don't hear from me, take them home."

She gazed through the glass front doors at Sandy and Arun. Arun waved us to hurry when the first of two cabs pulled up.

"Hey!" I said, reeling in her attention. "Don't you chew him up and spit him out!"

"He *is* pretty."

"I mean it. Arun is the best thing to happen to the Foundation. Think of him as flight crew." Pidge has a rule. She doesn't sleep with pilots. A few on the Essex Air roster tried and got shot down.

She put on an innocent expression, looked at me in her guise as a petite child-woman, and said softly and sweetly, "Fuck you, Will Stewart. Go take care of Andy."

20

The short-lived glow of dusk faded to black by the time I reached the Des Moines Police Station. I asked the cab driver to wait. Inside, the night desk officer listened to me through the ballistic glass barrier, then disappeared to speak to someone higher up the command chain. I thought the effort would bring a detective or senior officer to the front desk, but ten minutes later the same officer returned and told me that, yes, Detective Stewart had been there, and no, she was not present at the moment, but yes, he would be happy to take a message and give it to the lead detective on the James case, and no, neither he nor anyone he talked to knew Detective Stewart's whereabouts or the whereabouts of Special Agent Lee Donaldson. He suggested I call the FBI field office in Sioux City.

Outside the station feeling the damp warmth of a summer night and no relief from the cold tension inside, I tapped my jeans pocket and the flat plastic room key card from last night's stay at the airport Holiday Inn.

The cab driver took me back the way we had come and dropped me under the hotel entrance overhang. I paid him and declined his offer to wait.

I waved at the night desk clerk and crossed the tan marble lobby floor, skirting a family clustered for a trip to the hotel pool. I took the stairs to the second floor. Halfway down the hall, I realized I'd been so intent on getting to the room that I never checked the parking lot for plumbing vans or the lobby for men sitting around in tactical clothing. Andy would have enforced greater caution. I was off my game, propelled by stark worry.

I slipped the card into the door slot for room 224, expecting it to fail.

Click! Green light.

It startled me. It meant Andy hadn't checked out. I wasn't sure if that was good or bad.

And what if someone is in here?

I pushed the door open. The room waited in darkness.

"Dee?" I called out. "Are you in here?" No sense creeping into my wife's hotel room at night and having her shoot me.

I flipped on the light. "Hello?"

No answer.

I eased the door shut behind me.

Flight bag. Overnight bags. Nothing had changed since our hasty morning departure. We didn't think to put the Do Not Disturb sign on the door, so the room had been made up. The bed was neat, untouched. Fresh folded towels replaced the ones we had used. My flight bag lay unopened. Both small overnight cases remained zipped, one on the desk and one on the dresser in front of the television. Andy refuses to put a suitcase on the floor or on the bed of any rented room as a precaution against collecting bedbugs.

Nothing out of place—except my missing wife.

I dropped into the room's singular chair, tense and weary.

"Now what?"

For perhaps the hundredth time in the last six hours, I pulled out my phone and searched for a message, a missed call, anything. Like some magic lamp, I wanted to rub the damned thing and make Andy's number appear on the incoming call screen. I tried again.

You've reached Detective Andrea Stewart. Leave a message.

"Christ!" I ended the futile call.

Options ran through my head. Sit and wait. Call Tom Ceeves and raise an alarm. Call Des Moines PD again and raise holy hell. Call the Sioux City field office of the FBI and try to locate Donaldson. Pull a power unit and start flying concentric circles around Des Moines, Iowa until I spotted my wife's auburn hair from sixty feet up.

My mind played ping pong, bouncing from one option to another, accomplishing nothing except to make my head ache and my eyelids heavy.

"I suppose that's another option," I told myself, standing up. "Accept that she knows what she's doing and can handle herself. Get a good night's sleep and see if she shows up." I thought about it for a moment. "And if she doesn't...?"

There would be no sleep. I settled on the idea of calling her boss in Essex. I would roll him out of bed and start the chain of command rattling.

Click!

The room door lock snapped my attention to full alert. Andy! But what if it's not? Men in tactical gear quickly came to mind.

I stared at the lock. At the door. It opened half an inch, then stopped.

If that's Andy, she would have walked right in.

This isn't right!

FWOOOMP! I snapped out of sight. Too quickly. I had nothing to grip. I had a dark geometric patterned carpet below and a flat white ceiling overhead. No handles, no light fixtures.

I reached down and pinched the bedspread as a temporary anchor.

I stared at the door. It remained frozen. Someone stood outside, waiting, listening.

Trying not to disturb the smooth surface of the bed, I moved to the corner of the mattress farthest from the door. From there, I pinched the edge of the curtain shielding the room from the parking lot. The flimsy hand hold wouldn't allow radical movement without moving the curtains and betraying me, but by degrees I eased around the corner of the mattress into a narrow space between the bed and the wall where I hoped no one would be walking.

My eyes never left the door. Whoever had released the lock was either in no hurry or was preparing a forceful entrance.

I held my breath.

The door swung open rapidly. It banged the wall. A black Glock semi-automatic handgun, held high, swept across the dimensions of the room, across me. For an instant, I fixed my eyes on the soulless black muzzle hole at the tip of the weapon. Then I changed focus and looked up the line of the barrel into intense, squinting eyes.

Donaldson.

He moved into the room by the numbers. Weapon raised, swinging to every new corner and space as he stepped forward. He diverted briefly into the bathroom, flipped on the light and satisfied himself that it was empty. He stepped far enough into the room to clear all the corners.

I considered assault. I calculated the angles. I felt a boiling rage, convinced that if anything happened to Andy—*he knew!*

I flexed my knees, coiled and prepared.

"Clear!" he called out, relaxing his stance, swinging his weapon back into his holster.

"I'm telling you, I did not leave that light on."

Andy stepped into the room with her own weapon in hand. She marched past Donaldson and made the same moves I'd made ten minutes ago. Checking the luggage. Checking to see if anyone had been snooping.

"My bag hasn't been opened," she said. Andy positions the zipper slightly open, leaving seven teeth exposed between the slide and the end. If anyone tampers with it, even if they close it again, she can detect the violation.

"Probably the maid service." Donaldson pointed at the bed.

"Hotel staff is trained not to leave lights on. Saves electricity." Andy checked my flight bag and my overnight bag. Looking less than fully satisfied, she turned to Donaldson. She spoke curtly, professionally.

"I have to meet with the DMPD chief of detectives at nine."

"Looks like I will see you there."

"Good night, then."

If Donaldson expected anything more to happen, the woman standing before him with a gun in her hand gave no sign of it.

He nodded at her and slipped out, snapping the door closed behind him.

My heart hammered.

Surprising Andy with a weapon in her hand did not seem like a good idea. She stared at the door for a moment, then she lifted the flap on her shoulder bag and slid the gun into the holster affixed inside. I tried to decide if I should just appear or if I should say something first. While arguing with myself, Andy pulled out her phone and eliminated the question.

She dialed. My phone rang. She swung around, startled.

"Dee, I'm here," I said. It didn't help. She jumped back a step and uttered a clipped shriek.

Fwooomp! She jumped again as my feet hit the floor.

"Dammit, Will!" She raised her hands briefly, as if to ward me off, then pressed them to her chest. "You're going to give me a heart attack! Don't do that!"

"I didn't exactly have a choice!"

"What are you doing here?!" A lock of her hair fell across one eye, a warning accompanying the anger rising in her voice.

"What's *he* doing here?"

"His job. Answering the question *any* officer would ask after seeing a light on in a hotel room!" She gestured at the curtain, slightly parted. "More to the point, what are *you* doing here?!"

"What the hell is up with your phone?"

"What are you talking about?" She looked at the device.

"I've been in a panic all afternoon, trying to reach you!"

"My phone's been on the whole time—" She stopped. "What on earth?" I stepped closer. We both looked at her screen. "Six missed calls? A text? Will, I never got any of this until just now!"

We stood facing each other, wound up, angry, worried. I pointed at the door. "What are you doing with *him*? I thought we agreed."

She held up a hand. "This case has changed."

"Case? You're on a case now?"

"We need to talk." She stepped back. "I'm sorry. I didn't mean that the way it sounded. It's just—*what are you doing here*?!"

"Going home wasn't exactly safe haven, Dee." I said it like an accusation, tinged with anger of my own—as if the raid on our home had been her fault. I instantly regretted it. I raised both hands in surrender. "I'm sorry."

I reached for her. She hesitated, glared at me, then took a step. We pulled each other close. I drew in the scent of her hair. She pressed her hands against the muscles in my back.

I moved my lips to her ear and whispered, "We need to get out of here. Now."

I TOYED with the idea of trying to make Andy, both overnight bags and my flight bag vanish, but I had not yet tried to carry a load that size. The roller bags also had metal in the handles, which *the other thing* sometimes breaks. We settled on old school sneaking.

Andy left the room first and moved the rental car to the nearest exit. I stacked the bags and rolled them out. If anyone watched us, I didn't see them. Five minutes later we hit the road with the bags in the trunk of the rental. Andy alternated between fifteen under the speed limit, with a few cars tailgating us or honking their horns, and fifty over the limit. She blew through two red lights. She drove around the same block twice, reversing the square with a U-turn, checking her mirrors.

"If someone's following us," she concluded, "they're using a drone."

"I wouldn't rule it out." I glanced up to see if the rental had a sunroof. It didn't. "God! I hate paranoia!"

"Where to?"

"If not for having Sandy and the crew here, I would have said go to the airport, load up and fly out."

"Sandy's here? Will! *What is going on?*"

She drove. I explained. Everything up to the minute. When I finished, she stared at the lane ahead, eyes squeezed into a hard-boiled squint. I gave her time to think—to move the pieces on the board in her head. Andy had a keen mind's eye for detail, and in a cloud of seemingly unrelated clues can often find the obscure element crying out for attention.

"One question," she said at length. "Pidge put on a dress—a *nice* dress?"

"Swear to God."

21

"Here?" I asked. "This is where you want to spend the night?" Andy angle parked facing the Des Moines river and killed the engine.

"There's no safer place."

"Have you checked their Yelp ratings?"

"Leave the bags in the trunk."

We got out, locked the car, ignored the meter and jaywalked across the street to the Des Moines Police Station. Andy and I both looked over our shoulders, but nothing moved in either direction on 1st Street. The imposing pillared façade, incongruous on a waterfront street populated by low warehouses, offered a sense of security as we climbed the steps. We hurried inside.

A perfunctory chat with the front desk officer led to a display of Andy's credentials. She dropped names—Special Agent Donaldson and a detective named Sontag, informing the officer that she'd spent the better part of the afternoon in their company. She mentioned that she was on Temporary Duty Assignment and gave the name of the authorizing assistant chief. We were told to wait while the night watch commander was fetched. A sergeant named Hodges with a football lineman's body and a smile as big rolled up to the window. He recognized Andy.

"Can't get enough of us?" He grinned, granted access and led the way down a hall.

"I came to drop off my notes and file a report. How's it been here?"

"The circus moved here from the hotel to set up their reporters on the front steps for their live remotes. Then they all took off. The phones finally died down about an hour ago."

"Phones?" I asked.

"Tips from psychics, conspiracy crap from the James Nation, you name it. People telling us Deep State forces looking to overthrow the President ordered the hit. People telling us the victim wasn't really Josiah James. One guy said the NFL killed him because James was about to expose them for replacing players with robots. One lady called —like three times—claiming she was married to the shooter—only it was a man with a different name who was shot down sixty years ago in the war."

"Which war?" I asked, attempting the math and coming up with 1959. Too late for Korea. Too early for Vietnam.

"Does it matter?" He waved us into a break room. I smelled coffee and drew a bead on what looked like a fresh pot. I pointed and looked to the sergeant for permission. "Help yourself! How was your field trip with the FBI?"

"Not productive," Andy said. "Detective Sontag stayed in Princeton. Special Agent Donaldson will report in with your captain in the morning if he hasn't already filed something by…" Andy stopped for a moment, thinking, then went on as if a switch had been thrown and reset, "…phone…I'm sure. But if you can set me up with a terminal, I'll file my report."

"Gimme ten," he said. "There's some pizza in the 'fridge. Please eat it. If you don't, I will, and that's a bad idea." He patted his substantial belly and strolled out.

I found a pair of clean mugs and poured coffee. Andy stepped to the hallway and surveyed both directions. Assured of privacy, she took the coffee and pulled me to a table as far from the break room entrance as geometry and space would allow.

"Who in God's name was at our house?!"

"I don't know what to tell you. Somebody who knows."

"Oh, this is not good." Andy clamped a hand on my forearm. "I don't understand why you came back here, Will! Why not go to Tom?"

"Right. And what do I tell the chief of police? People are looking for me because I can disappear. 'Well, then why didn't you just disappear, Will?'" I tried to mimic Tom Ceeves' deep voice and did so poorly. "And not to cast blame here, but I might have stayed in Essex if I had been able to reach you!"

"You came all the way back here because I didn't answer my phone? Will, that's crazy!"

"You never ignore your phone."

"*I didn't ignore my phone!*"

Her voice rose and mine followed suit. "Dee, those guys failed to find me. Plan B might have been to go after you for leverage. Especially with Donaldson conveniently planting himself close to you!"

"Donaldson may not be showing his cards regarding you and me, but he is a dedicated FBI agent working a case."

"Until we find out otherwise."

We both gave it a beat. I tried the coffee. Too hot. "This has to do with that woman in the Prius. And if you recall, we both thought her warning referred to your pal in the FBI."

Andy made an equivocating gesture with her hand. "I'm not so sure…"

"This is what I mean about Donaldson. You're getting sucked in by the guy!"

"Will, think for a moment. That woman warned you. And a few hours later someone showed up *at our home*. Why would she be here, warning you in Iowa when the threat is in Wisconsin?"

"She said 'get off the grid.' I think that applies to *everywhere*."

"Are you sure those men were looking for you?"

"They waited for me. They watched Arun drop me off."

"That suggests to me that they're *not* connected to the woman. If she was with them, and those guys were specifically waiting for you to come home, she would have told them you were *here*!"

She had me on that one.

"It means her warning was legitimate," Andy added. "And if she's got knowledge enough to warn you, she has knowledge of who they were and what they want. I would really like to talk to her."

Andy launched into the questions I had anticipated. Questions I was unable to answer about faces, license plates, descriptions. She kindly hid her disappointment but picked up her phone.

"Who are you calling?"

"Essex. I want to put patrol on the alert for those plumbing vans. I also want to see if Jeff can look at some traffic cam footage and spot them. What time did all this happen?"

"Around three-forty. Right when the storms rolled through."

Andy made the call and chatted briefly with the Essex PD's night duty sergeant. She asked him to pass the information to Jeff Parridy, the department's other detective. She seemed satisfied with the result. I wasn't as sure. Jeff isn't exactly a ball of fire. Trolling traffic cam footage for Andy wouldn't make him happy.

"Dee, I know you're getting involved in the investigation here—"

She cut me off. "Your safety comes first, Will. I'll file a report tonight. Then we go home. Donaldson can chase down the rest of it without me."

"What's to chase down? The man who shot James is sitting in a cell, somewhere in this building, I presume."

"He is..." She glanced at her watch. "Look, this is still the safest place to be tonight. I'll string out the report writing. You can use that couch and grab a nap. In the morning we'll go with Sandy to—where was it?"

"Ekalaka."

"Sounds like it qualifies for 'off the grid.'"

I reached across the small table and took her hand. We squeezed a few silent messages to each other, massaging both our hands and the rough edges of raised voices.

"Okay. My turn. Where were you today?" I asked.

"Doing my job. Here," she pulled out her phone and slid it across the table, "you tell me if there's something wrong with my phone, because I don't see it."

Not wishing to reawaken her anger, I let the phone lie and took a deep breath. "Let me rephrase the question. How was your day at the office, dear?"

She sipped her coffee and used a moment to organize her thoughts. Her tension eased. "Well, you were there for the thrilling start."

"Yeah, and I'm not going to lie—it wasn't what I wanted."

"I'm glad to hear you say that. It wasn't what I wanted either." She glanced over her shoulder at the hallway. Satisfied once again that we were alone, she leaned close and lowered her voice. "Last night. When we were at that rally. When I said I wanted…you know…"

"I know."

She shook her head. "Part of what stopped me was that it would have martyred him. And now that's exactly what happened."

"Don't be too sure. That flatulent footage will live for a long time on the internet."

"So will the shooting. I can practically hear the conspiracy theories clawing their way out of the sewer. Nobody will care that James's security biffed their job completely and fixed on me when the shooter was standing right in front of them."

I remembered the way James's hired security had watched Andy. The old man with the gun had stepped through the camera line entirely unnoticed. "What's his deal?"

"Usual Disclaimer?"

"Usual Disclaimer."

"That's what I spent my day on. The arrest, processing, booking, war room, the whole enchilada—that part of it was worthwhile, thanks to Donaldson stepping in and vouching for me."

I made a face at her.

"I'm just saying…"

"Did he do that thing the FBI does and jump the investigation jurisdiction?"

"The FBI doesn't do that. Only on TV."

"Yeah, but I thought our boy was working James off book. That's gotta make him a little possessive."

"Donaldson is officially assigned to a task force with DMPD on the James shooting. Out of the darkness, into the light."

"And he's pulling you into it right along with him." I leaned back on my stool and folded my arms across my chest. "Now…just why would he do that?"

"Simple. Donaldson still wants me along because of my access to Brogan. We talked about it today, after the shooting. He's made no pretense about it."

"But now he has legitimate access." I waved a hand between us. "Hold the phone! Why is he still interested at all? James is dead. Not to speak ill of the dead, but that turd has been flushed."

I think she wanted to scold me, *pro forma*, but a dimple at the corner of her lips betrayed a stifled laugh. She suppressed it and picked up her phone. She opened the screen, opened her camera gallery and tapped one of the first images. She stopped and held up the phone.

"Remember him?"

The photo showed the façade of the Coliseum. The television news van was sliced off the frame on the left. A cluster of people occupied the center of the picture. The young female news reporter had her back to Andy's lens. Facing her, the white-haired man I had seen at James's rally.

"Of course. Who's the suit?"

Andy put away her phone and pulled out Greg LeMore's file which she had folded and stuffed in a side panel of her bag. She flipped to the back of the sheaf of papers. She pulled one sheet free and turned it to face me. A small image showed the same man in a boardroom portrait pose.

"I should have recognized him last night. He was here, in Greg's notes. That…is retired United States Marine Corps general Winslow Pemmick." The man in the photo had the look of an ex-Marine. Neat. Trim. Squared away. His hair had been cut short, but not buzz-cut short. He had lines etched in the corners of his eyes and no excess jowl fat over sharp chin and cheek bones. Like other former Marines I'd met, this man, perhaps thirty years my senior, looked capable of kicking ass without breaking a sweat. I flashed back to seeing him move across the stage at the James rally. Quick and in command.

Andy went on. "According to Greg's notes, he joined the James organization two years ago as an advisor. That turned into a vague position with the media company—some sources have it listed as vice president, some as media director. Donaldson thinks he invested— significantly—right around the time James changed his game from a guy broadcasting late night conspiracy crap out of his garage to a web presence with all the glitzy news show trappings. He thinks Pemmick is the catalyst for James' radio syndication growth."

"He's the guy that made James?"

"You remember that exchange between James and the President?" The online interview gained a lot of mainstream media coverage, and the James name along with it. I nodded. "Donaldson thinks Pemmick was the conduit for that. That Pemmick still has connections with the national security apparatus."

"Which explains how a nutball like James gets fifteen minutes of fame with the man in the White House."

"Possibly. So, guess who is now the majority owner of the James Media Group."

"What? How did that come to light?"

"Jeez, Will, you've really been out of the loop today. Pemmick held a news conference this afternoon. He promised to carry the James torch forward and bring the holy wrath of God 'down on the traitors trying to stifle the voice of Real Truth by murdering a great American hero'—his words. He promised to do so as the new head of—and majority owner of—the Josiah James Media group."

"Is that why Donaldson won't let go? He thinks this guy is involved? That makes no sense. Murdering James would be killing his golden goose. James put the rant in rave. What would be the point?"

"True. However, one more note on the new owner and CEO of James Media— Donaldson also found out a few days ago that James Media is the new owner of Nedritch Communications."

"Owner?"

Andy nodded. "That's right. James didn't close a syndication deal with Nedritch. He bought him out. Donaldson said the FCC fast-tracked approval of the station license transfers—which smacks of White House influence. And my guess, as well as that of Special Agent Donaldson, is that a certain child abduction swung the deal."

I whistled softly. "That's cold."

Andy picked up her phone and thumbed the screen.

"Who are you texting?"

"Greg. I want to see if he can flesh out the information on Pemmick."

I tapped the photo. "Okay, I get why FBI Guy is interested in James's business partner. But I feel like we're overlooking a key player here. Who the hell is the old guy with the gun?"

She finished the text and hit Send and put down the phone.

"After I was read in, the FBI, a DMPD detective named Sontag and I drove to Princeton, Missouri this afternoon, an hour and a half south of here, to the Willow Brook Family Living Center where Mr. Henry has been a resident for eight months."

"You spent three hours in a car with Donaldson? Ever hear of Stockholm Syndrome?"

"Focus, Will. Special Agent Donaldson, Detective Sontag and I interviewed the staff, looked at Henry's records, searched his room, and learned almost nothing about Mr. William Andrew Henry, age eighty-six. He has no family. He has no friends. He has had no visitors, as far as the staff can recall. He has no possessions of any significance, no photos, no mementos. He reads books and watches Fox news. To the best knowledge of his caregivers, he has no political leanings, never used a computer, and wouldn't have known Josiah James from Adam."

"Okay...where's his motive?"

"No idea. We're trying to track down his primary care physician to see if he's ill."

"You mean terminal? Huh. Maybe he decided to do some good before departing."

"If he did, he isn't saying."

"If you're going to go out with a grand gesture, wouldn't you want recognition?"

"He's not saying a word."

I considered the logistics. "How did he get from Princeton to Des Moines?"

Andy shook her head. "We haven't been able to piece that together. He has no car. He's living on Social Security. Donaldson's office is running a full background."

"Do you think someone put him up to this?"

Andy shrugged. "I thought he might be tied to Pemmick—that there might be a military link, but the initial FBI search shows no history of service."

Andy paused for a moment. Her eyes shifted to a point a thousand yards over my left shoulder.

"What?"

She lingered in the distance. I waited. After a moment, she blinked back into the room with me. "Something…something I thought I saw." She lowered her coffee mug to the table. "Hang on. Um. Just…I'll be back in a little while. I'm going to go write up that report. You'll be okay here."

She slipped away before I could ask why.

22

"Rise and shine, Sunshine."

"I wasn't sleeping." That's what my mouth tried to say. But since I had been sound asleep, the words tripped over my thick tongue and came out as muttered gibberish. Andy landed a kiss on my forehead, which triggered a panicked thought-memory of being late for school. It flashed and dissipated in a split second. I heaved myself upright on the small break room couch and collected memories of why I was here.

She stood over me, guarding against the possibility I might tumble back down for another snooze. I dug up three words for her. "I'm up. Coffee."

"No time. We have to go. We have a plane to catch."

I COMMITTED theft and walked out of the Des Moines police station with a coffee mug in my hand. It was either that, or curl into a fetal ball and refuse to go with Andy.

American Airlines had a six twenty-eight a.m. flight to Orlando via Charlotte with a 45-minute layover. I gathered that much from Andy as she hustled me to the rental car. My watch tried to tell me it was just after four a.m.

"Orlando?" I asked as we rolled toward the airport in the depressing darkness that comes before the dawn. The heat that cooked up yesterday's thunderstorms lingered, filling the air with humidity. Clouds of gnats and other flying insects fluttered around the street lights.

"I'll explain on the airplane," Andy said. She, better than anyone, knows the limits of my brain before it's been infused with coffee.

We dropped the rental car at the FBO, then walked our bags to the terminal. Andy identified herself as law enforcement and checked her bag in order to transport her service weapon. She is a stickler for arriving at the gate a full hour before check-in time, which in this case ended up making no sense because the TSA security check didn't open until six. We stood around with a few other fools who made the same mistake. I asked Andy again why we were going to Orlando, but she brushed me off, given the silence in the terminal and proximity to other ears.

"Do we have time for breakfast?" I asked after we cleared security.

"Nothing's open. We'll get something in Charlotte." She hurried through the terminal. I had time to be amazed that she functioned on no sleep, and that she looked as good as she did. She wore jeans and a light summer blouse. Her hair was tied back in a functional ponytail. She's not a heavy makeup user, which only means her light caramel skin looks as good on no sleep and no prep as it does any other time.

We breezed through boarding, stashed my carry-on and flight bag, and found our seats in the regional jet, which appeared to be less than half full when we eventually pulled away from the gate.

"Now?" I asked.

Andy looked around the cabin. I don't think it was paranoia as much as her long-standing policy of not talking about law enforcement or an investigation with strangers within earshot. Two young men dressed in business casual sat across the aisle. A woman occupied the window seat in the row ahead of us.

"Let's wait until we get in the air."

"I want you to recognize the absolute faith I am showing in you at this moment. Unless this is all a big surprise and you're taking me to Disney World for my birthday."

"It's not your birthday." She patted me on the arm and slid down in the seat to rest her head on my shoulder.

She winked out like a light before the captain pushed the throttles for takeoff.

ANDY SLEPT the whole flight with her head on my shoulder. Our connecting gate was mercifully close to our arrival gate. A genuine genius strategically stationed a nice coffee shop between the two. I was tempted to write an appreciative letter. Andy and I each bought a cup and a pastry and found a small round table for two. The coffee shop did a brisk business, but the steady stream of patrons hustled to catch morning rush hour flights. Few of them settled at a table. Andy glanced around and deemed the privacy adequate.

"We're going to USP Coleman," she announced.

"And that is…?"

"United States Penitentiary Coleman. Coleman I to be specific."

"There's more than one?"

"There are two."

"This is part of the James investigation, isn't it? Dee, I thought you were pulling out of that. You know, to focus on the bad people breaking into our home?"

"Yes…and no."

"Dee!"

"I *am* concerned about what happened. Deeply concerned. And to protect you I have moved you to a completely secure environment." She waved her arms at the terminal around us. "What better way to get off the grid than to launch on a crazy, unexpected cross-country trip with security provided by the TSA?"

"And is it your plan to hide out in a federal penitentiary? If so, I object."

"Well…" she tipped her head back and forth. "I might be using the opportunity to look into something related to the James investigation. Wait! Hear me out! I spent a lot of time on the computer last night. Do you know how many murders are committed annually by persons seventy-five and older?"

"A thousand?"

"Ninety-two in the latest stats. Do you know how many times this year a person over eighty years old stepped up and shot another person, then surrendered and made a full confession?"

Trick question. It had to be. "One?"

"Two, counting what we saw yesterday."

Thus prompted, I asked, "What was the other one?"

"Last March, in St. Augustine, Florida, an eighty-seven-year-old man walked up to someone and shot him six times with a revolver, dropped the weapon and turned himself in to police on the spot." I sipped my coffee and waited. She let the point hang for a moment, then said, "The victim was not just an ordinary citizen. He was Anatoly Malkin, a diplomat assigned to the Russian embassy in D.C."

"You found all this last night, while I was napping?"

"I already knew about Malkin. Vaguely. It was a bit of an international incident when it happened—but since the shooter was caught red-handed and confessed, there was no trial and therefore no media circus. Last night I looked up the details. The shooter was John Steven Allen, resident of a retirement home in Naples. No prior connection to the victim was ever found. No previous record. The weapon was traced to a gun show in Clearwater, but no connection to Allen was ever made. And no motive was ever determined. Allen confessed, refused representation, was convicted and now spends his remaining days at Coleman."

"Okay…" The depth of Andy's research didn't surprise me.

"Allen never explained his motive. He never revealed how he got the gun. How he traveled from Naples to Clearwater. Nothing."

"Coincidence?"

Andy ignored the absurd notion. "I want to talk to him." This was more than passing time while keeping me off the grid. Which made me wonder about something.

"How did you pay for these airfares?"

She dropped her eyelashes and fiddled with her coffee cup.

"Dee?"

"Credit card."

"What credit card?" She doesn't carry a copy of the Foundation's credit card—the one I carry for Sandy's business travel.

"Ours."

I regarded her for a moment. She raised her lashes and returned the gaze. "What?"

"Well," I said, "I know you're smart, and I know that you know using a credit card means there are certain individuals and organizations that can track that information, Donaldson included. So, while you say you're getting me off the grid, it sure looks like you're stringing out bread crumbs for someone to find us."

"Maybe." Her coy expression confirmed my assumption.

"Maybe, nothing!" I stopped to piece together what she had done. "Our credit card would tell someone where we are. But someone accessing that information more than likely doesn't know about the Foundation credit card. Which is why the guys at the house didn't know I was out of town. Because that's all on the Foundation card."

"That's the way I see it." Always a step ahead.

"So, you're putting bread crumbs on the credit card to see if someone—and by someone, I mean a certain FBI agent—follows the trail or sends his unknown associates after us."

"See, you got the looks *and* the brains, dear."

"Which conveniently lets you poke around a case with a striking similarity to the James shooting."

"Call that a side benefit." She leaned close and spoke urgently. "Will, we have to find out who came for you! Proactively."

If I had an argument, I didn't know what it was. "Tell me about Coleman. Did you arrange an interview with this guy, Allen?"

She reached across the table and cupped my hand under hers. The lashes fell to her cheeks again, then came back up like curtains on warm, inviting eyes.

"I called. He refuses all visitors. We need another way."

23

Our flight landed fifteen minutes early in Orlando. We blew the time gained waiting in line for an Avis rental car. It was close to one o'clock before we pulled out of the Avis airport lot. The directions on my iPad took us west on 528 to where it granted access to the Florida Turnpike. From there, another forty-five minutes put us at the Okahumpka Service Plaza. Andy parked under a line of trees on the northeast perimeter, as far from the busy plaza building as possible. I proposed grabbing a bite at the KFC, but Andy tapped her watch.

"We don't have time."

On the drive up, she described a long conversation she had in the middle of the night with a federal corrections supervisor. I wasn't privy to the call, but Andy can put a lot of 'friendly' in her tone of voice when she wants to. Among other tidbits she gleaned from the CO, she knew that Allen's afternoon recreation ended at three. The clock had just ticked past two p.m.

We wasted another five minutes loitering by the parked car, waiting for a moment when no one was near enough to be startled by two people vanishing. A programmable sign on the highway plaza gave the price of fuel, listed specials on fresh oranges at the convenience store, and told us the temperature was ninety-two. I felt every degree of it under the old fishing vest I wore for the purpose of carrying the power units.

Andy took a final look around and squeezed against me with both arms around my waist and her hands pressed against the center of my spine. "Ready?" I asked.

"Almost never."

Fwooomp! We vanished. The cool sensation wrapping itself around us was more than welcome.

I used the car mirror to push us to the rear of the car where I hooked my hand under the apex of the wheel well. This position placed us clear of the trees.

I flexed my ankles and we rose. Andy's grip tightened. Cars, the lot, the treetops all fell away. Above the tree line, we gained a sprawling view of flat central Florida, brown and scrubby. The lanes of the turnpike divided at the plaza, then rejoined and stretched into the hazy distance.

I pulled a power unit from my pocket, snapped a propeller blade on the motor shaft, tested it, and then slid the control forward. The unit hummed and produced thrust. Well clear of the treetops, we passed over the plaza, over the southeast-bound lanes of the turnpike, then over another thin band of trees bordering a barren stretch of land.

The grin on my face belonged to the moment of flight. The knot in my stomach belonged to our destination.

The federal correctional complex at Coleman had been built less than a mile from the plaza, as us crows fly. The land in between lies empty. To my right, a section of land showed a polka dot pattern of soil sampling. West of that, the earth had been scraped bare and raw new roads were laid out. Construction of a new subdivision appeared stalled, perhaps a hangover from the real estate crash. Only a fraction of the development sported shoulder-to-shoulder homes.

As we approached, I noticed stands of trees surrounding the prison complex, perhaps to shield it from outside view. The site had been well chosen. Most of the landscape for miles around Coleman lay barren. What small towns did exist were little more than wide spots in the state highways. Our choice of the plaza as a launching point had been forced. It was one of the few public parking spots where two strangers leaving their car wouldn't draw attention.

"Do you intend to speak to him?" I asked over the sound of the wind generated by our forward flight.

"Not sure. I want to get the lay of it first. The supervisor said he never alters his routine."

"Let's hope that's true."

The prison revealed itself to us like an opening aerial shot from a movie. Six guard towers lined the rectangular perimeter of Coleman I. A seventh, my target, stood at the geometric center of the complex. Coleman II, newer, sat in the distance. There was no mistaking the forbidding intent of this facility. High fences topped with razor wire outlined a shooting lane, with another fence line on the interior. The odd but orderly angled construction of the dormitories formed the next barrier. Within those buildings, a vast recreation yard contained a soccer field, basketball court, and open spaces that would appeal to no one—unless the alternative was a daily dose of painted concrete walls.

I aimed for the central guard tower. It reminded me of an air traffic control tower. I flew a tight course around it. We passed close enough to count two attentive corrections officers, each with a rifle strapped to his body in the current style favored by American combat troops. I felt Andy twist slightly, studying them as we passed within touching distance of the tinted windows.

"You did that on purpose," she said, speaking barely above a whisper.

"Damn right."

This place chilled me. I wanted it to have the same effect on her. If something went wrong here, we would have no options.

Inmates moved randomly below us in the yard. A few challenged the heat, playing a languid game of half-court basketball below us. The other half of the court lay empty.

A six-tier aluminum bleacher sat beside the basketball court. Today's game drew only one spectator—who showed no interest in sports.

"That's him," Andy said. "Same routine every day."

I flicked the power unit into reverse thrust and stopped us in a position midway over the basketball court. We hovered roughly forty feet in the air. I felt us rising on thermals created by the playing surface.

Andy had filled me in on the withered old man I now saw sitting below me. His thin white hair betrayed a scalp leathered by constant exposure to the Florida sun.

The CO supervisor told Andy that John Steven Allen never speaks to the other inmates, not even when spoken to. He has no visitors. He reads, mostly classic mysteries, sometimes westerns by Zane Grey. He shuns television in the common areas. He takes no interest in news or current events. Each day, during his designated recreation period, he climbs to the top tier of the small aluminum bleacher with a travel-size chess set, one of his only possessions. He plays against himself and has been known to turn down interested other chess players, one of whom once competed in a U.S. Chess Federation tournament.

No move seemed forthcoming now. Allen sat and stared. If not for the shallow rise and fall of his chest against a sweat-stained orange jumpsuit, the man might have been a statue. His face was long and thin. He fixed sunken eyes on the hand-sized chessboard unfolded beside him.

"Move closer," Andy whispered. She didn't specify. I had no idea what she was thinking or if she planned to make contact at all. I don't think she knew.

I flicked the power unit, arresting the thermal lift and initiating a downward vector. At the same time, I started a spiral arc with Allen at the center. I timed it perfectly and brought us to a hover less than five feet from the man.

Andy remained perfectly still beside me. I assumed she studied Allen. I examined the yard from as close as I ever want to be inside it.

The guard towers gained a more ominous presence now that they truly towered over us. Equally ominous were the sullen orange-clad figures moving through the sunlight on the asphalt and grassless turf. Men with hostile faces, branded by tattoos and scars. Men whose skin had been deeply etched by anger and aggression, desperation and resignation. Bursts of laughter and loud chatter came from inmate clusters. The voices sounded forced, guarded.

Andy moved beside me. I felt her lips against my ear.

"Camera." Barely a whisper. She all but communicated her wish to me with the movement of her lips against my ear.

I watched Allen to be sure he hadn't heard a woman speak, which certainly would have been mystifying. He remained statuesque in the sunlight. I still wasn't sure what Andy had in mind, but I shifted position to link arms with her, freeing both of my hands. She clamped her left arm against my right elbow and closed her right hand around my bicep.

I pulled my phone from my pocket. I double-tapped the main button and listened for the tiny, bird-like chirp indicating that the device had awakened in camera mode. For a moment, I feared Allen might hear, but then I noticed that he wore no hearing aids. At eighty-seven, chances were good his hearing wouldn't be top-notch. He didn't move.

This man came here to die.

Andy's lips found my ear again. "Three-sixty."

I wanted to protest. What she was asking was not easy. I still had the power unit in my left hand and now held the phone/camera in my right, aimed at Allen. The trick would be getting my right thumb onto the shutter button and catching a subject in an unseen frame while flying a maneuver known in pilot training as Turns About A Point.

At least there wasn't any wind. Not a breath of air moved in the prison yard.

I thumbed the power unit and moved sideways. Holding a radius of roughly six feet, we scribed a slow clockwise arc around the still life on the aluminum bleacher. Allen didn't move. He sat with his knees angled toward the game on the bench beside him, his hands folded in his lap, and his face locked on the chessboard.

I wasn't sure what Andy wanted from this, so rather than risk missing a shot, each time I pressed the shutter I held the button down to produce the burst effect that captures multiple images. As the shutter snapped, I flexed my hand. I hoped by spiraling the view of the lens it would cover Allen thoroughly.

We began from a position high and behind the bleachers, flying the clockwise arc. I shot a burst every thirty degrees along the arc. It worked well. The circle radius held steady. The camera chittered like a small animal. Allen paid no mind. I was well into memorizing a short speech for Andy on what a fantastic job I had done for her when I screwed the pooch.

Halfway around the circle, gliding over the bleachers, I lost my grip on the phone. Leaving a cold electric sensation in the palm of my hand, it snapped out of *the other thing*, became fully visible, and tumbled earthward under the influence of gravity. It hit the middle bench in the bleacher tier, clattered, fell to the foot plank below, danced for a moment, then fell to the ground.

Shit!

Allen startled. He craned his neck. From the way he looked between the aluminum bench slats, I knew he not only saw what had fallen, but where. He adjusted his posture, then stood and stepped over the seat in front of him. He paused there to gain a better look at the prize.

"Will!" Andy whispered harshly, as if I hadn't noticed what was going on.

I goosed the power switch and rose over the last seat, then started a tight turn inward and down. My hope was to maneuver in under the seats. It would be tricky. A metal framework barred the way to where the phone lay among sparse, struggling weeds.

Maybe if I grabbed the framework—

Snap!

Andy broke free of my arm and dropped three feet to the ground in full sight of anyone who cared to look in this direction. She landed on her feet, knees bent.

Allen spun his head and gaped at her.

"*Rada, ya tebya vizhu!*"

She pulled herself erect and looked at him, mustering a kind face. "Hello, Mister Allen. I'm sorry to disturb you. I—uh—dropped something." She gestured at the ground beneath the bleachers. "May I?"

He stared at her, his eyes wide. She didn't wait for an answer. She ducked under the slats and wove her way between the aluminum supports. Halfway in, crouching, she found my phone and slid it into her jeans pocket.

"YOU UNDER THE BLEACHER. STEP INTO THE OPEN." The commanding voice cut the air and pounded my eardrums, amplified by speakers installed with no concern for acoustic quality. "DO IT NOW!"

I glanced up to see both guards emerge from the central tower, weapons raised. The same movement took place at the perimeter tower nearest us.

"ALL INMATES ON THE DECK NOW!"

They didn't need to be told twice. The scattered yard population dropped to the dirt and asphalt and laced their fingers behind their heads.

Except Allen. He remained frozen, staring down at Andy between the slats.

"LAST WARNING! STEP OUT IN THE OPEN AND GET ON THE GROUND!"

Andy picked her way back through the support beams. She stepped into the sunlight and lifted her hands. Four automatic rifles fixed on her.

"Rada!" Allen cried out.

I didn't give him or the men with weapons another second. I slammed the power unit to full power and fixed a collision course on my wife.

We hit. I threw my arms around her and pushed. Hard.

FWOOOMP! Just before she vanished, Andy turned her head toward Allen. He looked at her desperately, stricken.

I kicked the ground, expecting gunfire. We shot up.

We were well above the height of the guard towers before I realized the pounding in my ears came from my pulse, not automatic weapons tearing up the air. No shots were fired.

I pushed the slide to full throttle to escape the airspace above the penitentiary. It was a mistake. As I passed over the central guard tower on the northeast side, one of the guards brought to full alert on the catwalk outside the tower shouted out, "We got a drone!"

He scanned the sky in vain for us.

I didn't let up until the turnpike plaza swept into view.

24

Neither Andy or I spoke.

Exhaustion and anger replaced panic. After landing at the Okahumpka Turnpike Plaza, we silently packed up and drove northwest on the turnpike, collecting our breath and checking the mirrors for no logical reason. A few miles up the road, Andy pulled the iPad from my flight bag and worked Google Maps.

"Exit on Highway 301," she instructed me. "For Wildwood."

"What's in Wildwood?"

"I need binoculars."

She offered no explanation.

"Are we going to talk about it?"

She didn't look up from the iPad. "Nothing to talk about."

"Jesus, Dee! They might have shot you! For a lousy phone!"

"A phone that identified you."

"You should have waited!"

"What? For him to pick it up?"

"Yes! If you don't think I'm capable of snatching a phone from some old coot's—"

"He's not an old coot!" Andy snapped at me. "He's...he's somebody. He was...somebody."

Before I could ask what the hell that meant, she ended the discussion harshly.

"I'm not the one who dropped the phone, Will."

ANDY NEEDED BINOCULARS. I needed a hamburger. We both needed to cool off. I figured when she located an inevitable strip mall selling outdoor equipment, fast food would follow.

We drove north on 301, which soon listed itself as Main Street, into Wildwood. Signs called out to my grumbling stomach. Woody's Bar-B-Q. Pizza Hut. Hardee's. I prepared to brake for Hardee's when Andy pointed.

"There! Just ahead. That red building."

It looked like a saloon in a tourist trap western town. I rolled past Hardee's, tossing it a longing look.

The sign over a western-style porch read *Nordic Gun and Pawn* and below that *Linda's Jewelry*. One stop shopping for a shotgun wedding. Images of a handgun, a Winchester rifle and a wedding ring lent credibility to the claims of the sign. I pulled in and rolled to stop at the overhang, feeling an impulse to tie a horse to one of the posts.

"I got this," Andy said crisply. She hopped out and left me in the sterile, slightly scented air conditioning of the rented Chevy. She returned before I had time to get bored and turn on the radio.

"Success?"

"I got a pair of cheap binoculars. Carmon. A Chinese knock-off of Canon." She pulled them out of the bag. "And this little tripod."

I backed out and wheeled onto Main Street with a purpose.

"Are we going bird watching?"

"In a way." She said nothing more until I applied the left directional. "Why are you turning here? We need to get back on the turnpike."

"No, we need fuel."

I rolled across the cracked asphalt to the Hardee's drive-thru order board.

ANDY REFUSED to consider eating in the car. Instead of doing the drive-thru, we took a short dinner break inside. Refueling provided new energy and let us ease the heat of the prison yard moment behind us. We supplemented dinner with coffee in an attempt to forestall drowsiness. I asked Andy if she wanted to look at the photos we shot of Allen. She said she preferred to wait. She did, however, return my phone, which notified me of a missed call from Earl Jackson.

Andy had one more trick up her sleeve before we settled in for the night. She had me rejoin the turnpike and drive northwest to the next exit, at I-75. As we rolled off the turnpike, she pointed at the Days Inn and said that's where we would spend the night. I looked for the best way to navigate multilane highways and medians to reach the hotel.

"Turn here!" she pointed.

"Motel Six? Really? Days Inn might not be the Ritz, but—"

"Turn! Turn! Turn! Here!"

I never argue with my wife when she barks commands at me while I'm driving. I pulled into the Motel Six lot and found the office.

Andy ran inside. She returned ten minutes later with a key.

"No," she answered my question before I asked it. "We're not staying here. Pull around and park in front of room fourteen."

I did. We climbed out of the car. She gathered her satchel and shopping bag. "Get the bags." She pointed away from the motel, across a vast parking lot.

A sea of asphalt sprawled behind a Pilot Travel Center bordering the motel lot. A couple dozen eighteen-wheelers of all varieties sat in rows, a few of them huffing diesel exhaust into the clear blue Florida sky. Beyond the truck stop lot, the Days Inn sat on the next property, adjacent to I-75.

"The car stays here, on our credit card. We stay at the Days Inn on the Foundation credit card." She gave me a self-satisfied smile.

25

A ndy hit the shower first, declaring an emergency need to get out of the clothes she'd been wearing for thirty-six hours—but not before rearranging some of the furniture in the second-floor hotel room. She moved the small desk away from its place by the wall and window, pulling it deeper into the room, toward the door. For a moment, I thought she intended to barricade the door, but then she set up the small tripod and binoculars.

"Why not closer to the window?"

I got a perturbed look. "Really? You think six extra feet will give a better view?"

It made sense to me.

"If you're doing surveillance, you want to set up farther away from the window. Less likely someone will see a pair of binocular lenses looking out at them."

"Smart."

She dropped into the desk chair and checked the line of sight. It seemed to satisfy her.

"I'll be in the shower."

"Need any help?"

She blew me a kiss and disappeared into the bathroom. The air kiss melted the lingering tension generated by my prison yard screwup.

I kicked off my boots, propped the pillows up on the bed, and pulled out my phone. The mattress sucked the remaining energy from my body as I stretched out. I touched the contact button for a call to Earl Jackson.

"What are you doing stealing my best pilot?" Earl demanded without preamble.

"Pidge? She'll be delighted you said so."

"Kelly said she took Sandy and the Foundation Navajo last night. Are you home sick?"

"No. I'm in Wildwood, Florida." I figured saying so over a cell phone line wouldn't make any difference, since Andy had decided to string bread crumbs with the credit card.

"Got arrested there once," Earl said. He didn't offer details. "I found the salvage company. Grab a pen."

I hopped over to the desk with the phone at my ear. "Go."

"Pelican Aviation Salvage. They're outta Alabama, near Tuscaloosa."

"That seems out of the way," I said. I wrote it down.

"Oh, hell no. They go all over. Use'ta have a big operation over in Africa, pulling old Soviet bloc shit outta jungles and swamps after some dipshit overloaded 'em and ran 'em off a runway, or flew some busted ass Tupolev into the side of a mountain."

"Why bother? I thought old Soviet stuff was a glut on the market after the wall came down."

"Sure. You could buy a nice MiG for twenty grand, but it'd cost you two hundred K in bribes and transportation fees to get it outta the country. These guys were hauling parts out of the jungle at cost. I think they might have put the gleep on a few planes, too. Whole. From the occasional warlord who bought one but didn't get an owner's manual or a pilot to go with it."

I wondered how much of this was first-hand knowledge.

"I talked to Walsh," Earl said.

"Connie Walsh? The woman from the NTSB?"

"Nice lady. She was under the impression that the airframe was still impounded."

"Did they finally issue a report?" It had been a while since the subject crossed my mind. Hard to believe we were approaching a year since my accident.

"She doesn't know diddly. All she can say is that the case file is out of her hands. Passed up to a higher authority."

"What's that supposed to mean?"

"She had no idea. Apparently someone has an interest in the case and they're not saying what."

"Boss, you ever get the feeling they reissued my certificate just to keep me from making waves?"

"Paranoid?"

"A little." *Ever since crazy women started stopping me on the street to tell me to run for my life.*

"Paranoia is the delusion that your enemies are organized. You're dealing with the government. Organized ain't their strong suit. Whaddya want with the salvage people, anyway?"

"Andy wanted to know. Something she's working on." It worked before. It worked again.

"Okay."

"You're not really pissed about Pidge, are you? It was her day off and I needed some help. She should be back tonight."

"Hell, no. Her gone just means I live one day longer."

Earl doesn't tend to say goodbye. I had to look at my screen to confirm he'd hung up. I put down the phone and tore my notes off the desktop pad. I folded the slip and slid it into my wallet behind the few bills I had left after the turnpike.

I might have dozed, waiting for Andy. Next thing I knew she bounced onto the foot of the bed and unfolded her laptop.

"Shower's all yours if you want it. Gimme your phone." She held out a hand and I complied. I lingered a minute to watch. She sat with her long bare legs folded beneath her, wearing a Green Bay Packers t-shirt. My t-shirt. Which made it long enough that I had to guess whether she wore anything beneath it. The tips of her hair hung damp, but she didn't wet it fully in the shower and it flowed onto her shoulders. She looked impossibly energetic and refreshed. She looked like a college girl about to tackle the paper she'd been putting off.

"You can't be serious about working now. You've got to be exhausted."

She didn't look up from thumbing through my photo gallery. "This won't take long."

I slid off the bed and headed for the shower. On my way, I stopped for a peek through the binoculars she had set up. The round image centered on the back of our rental car and the door to room fourteen at Motel Six several hundred yards away. Andy had been specific when checking in at the Days Inn. Second floor. Center. Facing south.

"You're not planning on staying up all night to watch this, are you?"

"Good lord, no. I just want to be careful."

THE SHOWER MELTED AWAY TENSION. Even though the clock read a little after eight and the sky remained bright blue, I felt capable of sliding between the sheets with Andy and sleeping a solid twelve hours.

"C'mere. Check this out." She gestured at the laptop with the energy of teacher's pet taking her turn at show-and-tell.

In a t-shirt and boxers, I padded across the carpet and hopped on the bed beside her.

"What am I looking at?" The laptop's screen presented a heavily pixelated image, an extreme zoom into a digital photo. "Is that a bar code?"

"Of sorts." Andy tapped the mouse pad and opened another tab. Rows of colored bars appeared. "Military ribbons. I've narrowed it down. I think it's either this one...or this one."

She pointed at two military ribbons on the screen. A website listed them for $1.65 each. I recognized them as the ribbons used to adorn U.S. military dress uniforms, representing medals and awards earned. The first, listed as the Korean Defense Commemorative Ribbon, alternated blue and white bars with a thin red bar down the center. The second, listed as the Distinguished Flying Cross Ribbon, exhibited the same pattern of blue and white but featured a thick red bar at the center.

"Go back to the other image, the fuzzy one." She flipped tabs. "What is that from?"

She danced her fingers across the mouse pad. The image zoomed away until it showed John Steven Allen hunched over his chess game in one of the photos I shot. The bar shrank to near insignificance on Allen's arm. I marveled that Andy caught it.

"You think he has a DFC ribbon tattooed on his forearm? Are you sure that's not some kind of bar code?"

Energized, Andy turned to me. "Will, I think I saw something like that, a pin, on the lapel of Henry's coat when he shot James!"

"That should be easy to confirm."

"No," she said. "It's not. I checked last night. I had the property officer show me everything they took from Henry. There was no pin, neither loose nor on his lapel. But I just have this—*this impression of it*! As he stood there. Just before James's private security grabbed him."

"Why? I mean—why the impression?"

Andy struggled for a moment to make it relate. "When he fired. My first thought—not even a thought—more like a *charge* running through my mind was *Shooter. Identify*. In other words, don't *mis-identify*."

"Don't shoot back at the wrong person."

"Exactly! I took a snapshot. In my head. I needed to have it mean something. When I see people like that, for the first time, I try to connect them to someone else I know. Everybody looks like somebody."

"Like a movie star? A celebrity?"

"Or a relative. Or the dentist. It happens in an instant—and in that instant, it was my Great Uncle Terrance. Daddy's mother's brother."

"Henry looks like your great uncle. I get it."

"No. He doesn't. Not at all. But that's the match that came to me. I didn't understand why until last night, when I told you that the first pass showed no history of military service. It hit me. I didn't frame Henry because he looked like my uncle. But because he had a pin like my uncle wore. My uncle was awarded the Bronze Star during World War II. He used to wear a miniature pin of it on his lapel."

"…like Henry…"

She gave a slow nod.

"You're saying Henry had a pin, and it's missing? Someone took it?"

"I don't know. Honestly, I was prepared to dismiss it entirely—until I saw this photo. It practically jumped out at me. Here! Compare the two!" Andy made the screen into separate windows showing the Allen photo beside the website with military ribbons for sale. "What do you think?"

"Jeez, Dee, this is pretty vague. But I guess of the two here, I'd say it looks like the DFC. That's a high award. Second only to the Medal of

Honor. You think both these guys were awarded the Distinguished Flying Cross?"

"What else can it mean?"

"Okay. But you also told me neither man has a military record. And frankly, you've got a website right in front of you that will sell one of these ribbons to anybody."

"Imposters? No," she shook her head vigorously. "Will, these are old men. From what I saw of Henry and read about Allen, they're men with backbone. Discipline. People like that don't falsely adopt military honors. Both men went out on a mission to kill someone. Performed the mission. Surrendered with zero resistance. Allen never said another word and Henry isn't talking. They had to know they'd be spending their remaining days incarcerated. Did Allen seem to be anything but at peace with himself?"

"Maybe he just loves chess," I said. "It should be easy to check. I bet there's a list of DFC winners somewhere on…" The look Andy gave me said she'd already been there.

"Neither man is on the list. And there's something else. Check this out." Andy clicked on a third tab. It opened to a translator application. I looked at the boxes.

The left box had words in the Cyrillic alphabet. Below that, in the English alphabet, the words *ya tebya vizhu.*

The right box contained, in English, *I see you.*

"He said that." Andy pointed. "He said that, do you remember?"

"Are you sure? I thought he said *Rada*-something."

"Rada is a name. A girl's name. He said, 'Rada, I see you.'"

I stared at Andy, at the energy in her gold-flecked green eyes and the electricity running under her light caramel skin. She dropped her hand on my forearm and clenched. "He looked at me—*like he knew me*—and said, 'Rada, I see you.'"

"What language is that?"

"Russian."

26

"Wake up, Will! Now!" My eyelids shot up, but to no avail—the room remained dark. Almost. A narrow band of light seeped in between the slightly parted curtains.

I twisted under the sheets and automatically reached for the lamp beside the bed. I found the switch. It flashed on and caught Andy fully dressed and standing over me.

"No! Turn that off!" I complied instantly. She disappeared into blackness until my eyes adjusted.

"Dee, what the hell?"

"She's here! Your looney with the Prius!" Her voice came from somewhere near the desk.

I threw my feet to the floor and stood up, squeezing muscles to wake my body and blinking to wake my brain.

"Look!" Andy's dim figure pushed back from the desk. She rose from the chair and pointed at the binoculars.

I hurried to her and leaned into the lenses. Sleep crud fogged my eyes. I blinked it away, then rubbed it away. The image came into focus. Andy left the binoculars fixed on a car—a Prius—sitting in the Motel Six lot, apparently running, with its lights on.

"Impossible. Who drives a Prius from Des Moines to Wildwood, Florida in…what? Ten hours? Twelve?"

"Nineteen."

"What time is it?"

"It's three fifteen."

"How long have you been up?"

She nudged me out of the seat. "Get dressed!" She slid onto the chair, leaned down and watched. "I've been up off and on, keeping an eye out. About an hour ago I saw her do a drive-by."

"You saw a Prius drive-by. That's got to be a first."

She looked at me, standing, staring at her. "Will, get dressed! It's her! She drove by once an hour ago. Repeated the maneuver half an hour ago. Now she stopped. Who else would it be?"

I grabbed my pants and pulled myself into them. "Someone stalking a cheating husband?"

"She slows down outside room fourteen every time! Now she's stopped."

"Dee, the travel time makes it imposs—"

"Will! She's getting out of the car!" Andy waved at me frantically. "Look!"

I hurried over and confirmed with a look through the binoculars.

It was her. Instead of a scarf, she wore a baseball cap. She wore the same silly sunglasses. She marched to the door marked 14 and began pounding.

"Let's go!"

Andy grabbed her satchel. I dove for my boots and pulled both on over bare feet. I grabbed a power unit from my flight bag, snapped on a propeller and shoved it in my back pocket.

We hurried out the door onto the second-floor walkway. Thick Florida air hit me. Andy dashed for the stairs. I raced to catch up and caught her halfway there. I hooked her arm.

"Wait! Two people running across that truck stop lot draws a lot of attention. Plus, we'll lose sight of her. My way."

I pulled Andy close.

Fwooomp!

We vanished. Instead of trying to fly up and over the railing, I clamped my free hand on the rail and used the core muscle running down my center to pivot us into a horizontal position, legs almost touching the wall of the hotel.

"I feel that! Will, I feel that!" Andy said breathlessly. "Like you said, like a muscle down my whole body!"

"Cool." I didn't know what to tell her. Now wasn't the time to experiment. I heaved us over the railing.

We launched silently over car roofs made satin by condensing humidity. I pulled the power unit from my pants pocket and pushed the slide forward. The prop whined. We accelerated across the Days Inn lot and then over the truck park behind the Pilot Travel Center. Big rigs of all kinds swept under us. Trucks with logos and advertising. Trucks with plain aluminum trailer boxes. Tankers. Low boys. Most had sleeper cabs and I assumed had men and/or women inside. No one wandered the lot, and if they did, I wasn't worried. The perpetual highway noise from the turnpike and I-75 covered the whine of the power unit.

I aimed for the last truck on the lot, a loner sitting at the perimeter directly adjacent Motel Six. Perhaps the driver wanted a real bed for the night. I hard reversed the power unit and bled off our speed in time to halt beside the dual rear axles of the trailer. We touched down—

Fwooomp!

—and staggered into sight.

"What are you doing?" Andy whispered at me urgently.

"We can't zoom right up to her and pop into sight, can we?"

Andy slipped her hand into her satchel. "You wait here."

"What? No—"

"I need you to watch my back," she said, putting her hand on my chest. "In case she's not alone. Plus, it might be best if she doesn't know you're here."

She pulled her service weapon from her shoulder bag, then slipped around the back of the truck.

I ducked down to watch from behind the trailer's rear wheels. The smell of rubber and grease oozed into the soupy atmosphere. Andy held her semi-automatic in a two-handed grip, muzzle down. She trotted lightly across the pavement toward the Prius that had been parked perpendicular to and behind our rental. She crouched, using the hybrid subcompact as cover.

When we had first seen the woman from our hotel room, she had boldly approached the room fourteen door and knocked on it. Pounded it. I had been afraid that when we failed to answer that she would drive off before we got to her. During our shuttle across the truck lot, she went back to her car, retrieved something and returned to the motel door. Now, instead of pounding, she hunched over the door handle, working a tool on the lock. A stark single parking lot light painted her twin in shadow beside her.

Andy crouched behind the Prius, checked on me, then scanned the terrain in all directions. I followed her lead and looked around. Except for the truck beside me, the only other vehicles nearby were nosed up to their respective Motel Six room doors. I looked for *Abcress Plumbing* vans, which I instantly decided would be either ridiculous or proof we were up against a band of idiots. No such clichés lay in sight. If someone watched us, they did so with the same skill Andy had employed. From where I crouched, the distant Days Inn formed a low, insignificant rectangle against the night sky. Our spy nest with the narrowly parted curtains was impossible to pick out.

Andy moved. Like a dancer, she swept around the back of the Prius and took up a direct line toward the door. She held her weapon low, aimed safely at the pavement. On long silent strides, she covered the ground in seconds using only the balls of her feet.

"Police!"

The woman uttered a clipped, "*Shit!*" She jittered and the tool in her hand fell to the threshold of the door. She reached for it.

"Leave it! Stand up—hands where I can see them! Now!" Andy maintained her distance, frozen, weapon at the ready. "*NOW!*"

"Alright, alright! Don't get your panties in a twist, Detective Stewart," she said, bringing her body erect, her hands level with her shoulders, and turning slowly to face Andy.

She wore black slacks and a dark t-shirt. As she had in my encounter in the street, she wore large-lens dark glasses. They looked ridiculous.

"Hands behind your head and turn around!"

"This isn't necessary."

"It is if you want to stay out of the hospital. Do it. Feet spread."

The woman huffed out a long sigh of resignation and complied. Andy holstered her weapon and produced a dual-loop zip tie from her satchel. In a matter of seconds, she secured the woman's hands behind her back and executed a rapid search for concealed weapons.

"You can show yourself, Will!" the woman called out. "I know you're here! God, you people are dumb!"

"I'm not the one standing here in cuffs under arrest."

"You don't have jurisdiction here and I've committed no crime. Come on, Will! Show yourself!"

Andy picked up the small tool the woman had dropped.

"Burglary. Illegal entry. Disorderly conduct."

The woman took up the chant. "Treason. Transporting fruits and vegetables across state lines. Removing mattress tags. Will! Do your thing! Appear! I'm dying to see it!"

I stood up and walked around the tailgate of the semi-trailer.

"See what?"

She leaned to one side to peer around Andy. "Well, that's disappointing."

"Do you have anything sharp in your pockets?" Andy asked. "Anything that will poke me or cut me?"

"Do I look like a heroin addict?"

Andy didn't answer. She produced a pair of blue latex gloves from her satchel. What my wife carries never ceases to amaze me. She began a methodical search of her prisoner's pockets.

"Did you seriously drive all the way here from Des Moines, Iowa in that Prius?" I asked.

She scoffed. "Hell no. It's a rental."

"Got a thing for hybrids?"

"I've got a thing for not contributing to one of the zillion ways we're all committing suicide on this planet."

"You do know that no one has yet developed a viable solution for the disposal of the millions of lithium-ion batteries that are about to flood landfills and poison the earth," I countered.

"That's what we're going to do? Stand out here in plain sight and argue eco-politics? Because following you two idiots was super easy, which means that people who want to do you genuine harm are equally capable of rolling up here at any moment. If they aren't already here." She turned on Andy. "You want to arrest me? Fine! Arrest me! Take me to the police. Anything's better than letting him stand out here in the open!" She flicked her head at me.

Andy ended her pocket search, having collected a set of rental car keys and a tube of lipstick. The lipstick prompted me to notice for the first time that she was an attractive woman, not quite as tall as Andy, with a wiry, runner's physique. I guessed her age between fifty and seventy. It gets harder and harder to tell and the one-source lighting didn't help. Her hair color flipped between blonde and light gray. On closer inspection, I could see fine lines at her eyes and lips, lines easily erased in a doctor's office if vanity compelled her, but which infused character when left untouched.

"Who's the other friend?" Andy confronted her.

"What?"

"The other friend. On the street in Des Moines, you told Will you were one of the only two real friends he had. Who's the other one?"

This brought a new look of incredulity to her face. "I don't know how you two are still breathing free air. You have to be two of the dumbest people I've ever met. Who do you think?! Doug!"

Andy spun and looked at me like it was my fault.

"Stephenson? Oh my God, Will! She's the UFO nut!"

27

"Huh. Maybe you're not complete idiots." Andy ushered the woman into our Days Inn room. She had removed the zip ties but maintained an arresting-officer posture behind her. The woman studied our surveillance setup. She bent at the waist for a look through the binoculars. "Cheap knock-off."

"Sit." Andy pushed the chair in place behind her and put a hand on her shoulder to emphasize the offer.

"Hey. Lighten up, Detective. I'm an ally, although the unlawful arrest card is mine to play." She took the seat. "Can we close that curtain, please? And can I get one of those bottled waters?"

"No." Andy gave no quarter.

"They're like eight bucks a bottle," I said, drawing the curtain halves together. "I'll get you a glass."

"Why are you two in Florida?"

"Police business." Andy sat on the end of the bed. "And I'll ask the questions."

"Nice guy—bad cop. I guess that works." She settled into the mesh-backed office chair. I filled a glass from the bathroom and gave it to her. She took a sip and made a face at the taste. A sentiment I agreed with.

"What's your name?" Andy asked.

"Lillian."

"Lillian what?"

"Lillian is all you get. Unlike you two, I'm not flinging my identity everywhere. Following you here was child's play."

Andy shook her head. "No. That's not true. Following us here was anything but child's play. Because it required you to obtain real-time access to secure credit card records. Unless you have our personal account information, which I doubt, you had access to the CitiBank data servers."

"Who doesn't?"

"Go ahead and be glib about it, but that's real-time penetration of sophisticated security and firewalling, which requires high-level technical skills. It's also illegal, unless you have a court order. If you're breaching private databases, it's a felony and I'm required to report it."

Lillian assessed Andy with sharp pale blue eyes. Her hair, in the light of the room, settled on blonde. She had a nicely proportional face that had been kindly touched by the lines I noted earlier. Mid-sixties would have been my revised guess, although the runner's body backed that down twenty years. It made sense that she was close in age to Doug Stephenson, my apparently unreliable confidant in the matter of *the other thing.* Stephenson had once proposed introducing someone to our circle of trust, someone with a science background leaning toward unexplained phenomenon.

A UFO nut.

That's how Andy put it. I attributed half of Andy's present hostility toward the woman to her original assessment and the other half to Stephenson's betrayal of trust.

The two of them locked eyes. A flammable gulf lay between Andy's earthbound legal and moral codes and this woman's paranoia and potentially challenging otherworldly beliefs. It would only take one spark.

"May I make a suggestion?" I asked, slipping onto the bed beside Andy and risking her ire for interrupting an interrogation. "How about if we agree that you're here with good intentions? And you, in turn, tell us everything? You came to me with a cryptic warning. I don't need cryptic. I need to know what and why and who."

Lillian pursed her lips.

"Without the Roswell conspiracy bullshit," Andy said. I held up a hand to gently request my wife not throw hand grenades.

"Fine," Lillian said. "It should be obvious. Somebody knows about you, Will. And they want to make you their lab rat."

Andy tensed. "Stephenson had no right to expose Will to you or anyone else."

"He didn't." Lillian sipped her water, made another face and stood up. "Screw this tepid swamp shit! I'll give you the eight bucks." She grabbed a bottled water from the courtesy tray on the dresser and snapped the cap open.

"Explain," Andy said.

Lillian sat down, drew the chair to the desk and settled her elbows on the wood surface. She rotated the plastic water bottle slowly in her hands.

"UFO nut? That's what you think I am?" She glared at Andy. "Detective, I have three doctorates: two in math and one in astrophysics. I have worked for NASA and JPL and half a dozen other abbreviations I'm not permitted to say out loud. And yes, the level of sophistication necessary to breach a major credit card database is just what you said. It's not some silly movie where a pimply kid speed types with one hand while holding a can of Red Bull in the other and says, 'I'm in!' like it's his World of Warcraft account. I know people, brilliant people, who have skills and access to servers and pipelines and backdoor portals, and it cost me a lot of fresh banana bread to get them to track you. Furthermore, I am part of a community of people whose beliefs—founded in hard, fucking science—stretch just a little beyond the flat-earth mentality of your average pickup truck driver! So, don't paint me as some tinfoil hat conspiracy nut, okay?"

Andy spread her hands in a gesture of reluctant neutrality.

"If you ever want to discuss the primitive notion that this insignificant speck of shit orbiting a half-assed star in a backwater galaxy is not only the center of the universe, but is exclusively blessed with intelligent life created by some benevolent genie-out-of-the-bottle deity, then I'll give you a five-hour lecture on the size and scope of the universe and the statistical probability that we're fucking morons compared to what's out there!"

"Okay," I jumped in. "Glad we got that out of the way."

"You said Stephenson didn't tell you. If he didn't tell you anything about Will, then—" Andy dropped her hand to my thigh and squeezed, her way of telling me to keep quiet "—what exactly is it you think you know?"

Lillian smiled. "I didn't say he didn't tell me. I said he didn't bring me in. Let's not dance around it. I know perfectly well what Will can do. Doug eventually told me—but he didn't come to me. I went to him —and he didn't give you up easily, if that's your concern."

Lillian paused, but we held our questions.

"Okay, look. I don't have a high tolerance for stupid. It cost me a few government jobs, but it also helped me cultivate a circle of friends and colleagues who can be counted on for higher level intellect—and high-level information. In a circle like that, you hear things. Word gets around. For a few months now the hot topic is a tech start-up seeking blind venture funding."

"Blind?" I asked.

"Blind. As in, 'you give me the money, I don't even tell you what I'm doing.'"

"How is that even a thing?"

"Because a new technology can be so revolutionary that refusing to disclose it is the only way to guard its value. The seller uses reputation to gain backing in the market. Absent that, they use back channels and rumors. In this case, the back channels are chattering about a break-through in stealth tech. People around the world who monitor these crumbs of information sat up and listened. The Chinese have been flooding dark markets with money for every bit of stealth tech they can grab. Pakistan, too."

"What's the source?" Andy asked.

"There is no source. That's the whole point."

"This is a waste of time!"

"Detective, this is not a world where you can scratch some DNA from under a victim's fingernails and catch the killer."

"No, but it is a world where programmers invest their ego in their code. And from what I know, that's its own form of DNA. There has to be a source. Furthermore, you're not talking about Twitter. You're talking about the dark web. Am I right?"

Lillian offered a smug smile. "Fine. Ajax370."

Like it was supposed to mean something to us.

"Is that a person, place or vegetable?" I asked.

"This is what I mean about dunces," she huffed. "It might be a person. Or an entity. Or a hive mind. It might be a government, working clandestinely, although they're usually clumsy and easy to spot. It might be any or all of the above. That hardly matters. What matters is that Ajax370 is the entity sprinkling clues about new tech, about stealth, and about an implied connection to a high-profile air disaster."

"Malaysia Air Lines flight 370," I said. "He put it right in his name."

"Yes!" Lillian flashed me a bright look, points for the correct answers. Then the light went cold. "And no, because that's obvious misdirection. Co-opting of a known aviation mystery—which isn't a mystery at all, once everyone gets their head out of their asses and accepts the obvious hypoxia hypothesis."

"That's what I thought," I said, grabbing the rebound. She ignored me.

"Seeding the rumor mill with a misdirection like that serves a purpose. The equivalent of a disrupting field in the flow of ideas. Or a filter." She stood up suddenly and paced the small space between the desk and the window. "Sucks away trivial thinking because of its size and overwhelming dominance. It sends the tragedy and conspiracy junkies off on their own tangent. Culling the herd."

She stopped suddenly and stared pointedly at me.

"What?"

"Air disaster, Will. Think smaller. A flash in the media pan."

"Me."

She pointed at me and my points were redeemed. "Yes! A bonified miracle. The man who fell to earth. Except physics and physiology scientifically deny the possibility of survival. Chart the odds of someone dropping from the sky at one-hundred and forty miles per hour from an altitude of 500 feet and you will not so much as hiccup from the x-axis. Yet here you are, Will Stewart."

"In the flesh."

"Mind you, all this chatter is only disguised as rumor. These are serious people trolling for even more serious funding in deep, deep channels. Stealth tech. An air disaster serving as a brick and mortar fact spicing a theoretical discussion—the pot begins to simmer. Now toss in something else, something wildly unaffiliated with any of this."

"Which is?" Andy prompted.

"Ajax370 linked in Pearce Parks."

"Our Pearce Parks?" Andy asked.

Lillian bobbed her head in the affirmative. "Your convicted murderer. A private prison CEO and black bag political operative taken down by a small-town detective." She nodded at Andy. "A man who suddenly loses his shit, pleads out, and suffers a mental collapse. Suddenly, he's crying in the night about his body disappearing, claiming he escaped from prison by floating in the sky. Talking about angels and demons. Absolutely crackers, until you Venn diagram him into a circle that shares space with a detective who happens to be married to…a miracle."

"Bullshit," Andy pronounced. "I don't care how many infinite monkeys on infinite typewriters you have, you can't possibly concoct a connection of those dots!"

"Yet Ajax370 crafted a blind funding venture opportunity inter-twining these exact elements."

"Obviously a scam!" I said.

"Really?" She squared herself at me. "Are you a scam? Is what you can do a scam?"

"Who is this asshole?" I demanded a little less politely than Andy would have.

"Ajax370. I told you."

"Right," Andy said sarcastically. "This is precisely what Will said. BS. Nobody gets funding, significant funding, like that by mashing up internet conspiracy crap. Maybe back in the dot com bubble days, but people have wised up. Tech start-up scandals are old news. Theranos, for heaven's sake."

"True, but do you think tech start-ups trundle over to the local bank and put on a nice dog and pony show?" Lillian laughed. "Imagine pounding away in your basement and one day realizing you have the code for the next Facebook. Or you have an atomic battery on your work bench. Tech startup funding at its highest levels makes the CIA's idea of secrecy look like passing notes in grade school. I know of tech ventures—astounding ideas—that sit locked away because their creators would rather forego development than reveal their work in order to beg for financing!"

"And for every one of those there are a hundred who have inflated value, falsified scientific studies and scammed people out of millions. You're taking random pieces and fitting them to some rumor you heard. Fitting the evidence to the crime," Andy told her, citing a cardinal sin of her profession. "It's nonsense."

"It's not nonsense to the high-level venture capital people who play this game. You mentioned Theranos. Yes, a con job. But it still took hundreds of millions from very smart people. Imagine what kind of money will come flying out of the woodwork when someone discovers what your husband can do."

I didn't need to remind Andy about the power of money.

Lillian shifted her posture, easing back slightly, perhaps wisely detecting Andy's stiffening resistance. "Look, Detective, absent my own access to facts, I might have come to the same conclusion. A scam. I may hold certain beliefs, but they are grounded in science, and I am a scientist, and therefore a skeptic. But—"

"But what?"

Lillian stopped pacing.

"But then I spent a long evening with my dear friend Doug Stephenson. Midway through the more intimate festivities I did what I normally do. I blathered on and on about anything and everything. I had been going on about blind funding venture when he—I swear—turned white."

"You have got to be kidding!" Andy exclaimed. "He got laid and spilled his guts!"

"You sell him short, Detective. I'll admit, at that moment he had nothing to hide, but he did not reveal your secret. He did, however, describe something quite impossible. And all the pieces fell in place." Lillian abruptly held her hand up in Andy's face. "Cool your jets, Detective. Even at that point, Doug adamantly refused to reveal your identity."

"Except he did," Andy said sourly.

"Eventually, but only a few days ago, after I showed him that the threat was real and convinced him that someone was coming after Will."

"What threat?" I asked.

"Money. Money is always the threat. And this is huge money. Either government money or very dirty money. A week ago, Ajax370, whoever it is, let it be known that he had secured more than enough cash to develop the tech—and then went dark—which in my world constitutes damned near ironclad proof. When I told Doug, he panicked."

"Why didn't he reach out to me?" I asked.

"It's not like he hasn't been trying," Andy said.

This startled Lillian. "What?"

Uh-oh.

"His office has been calling to make an appointment," I said quickly, catching a penetrating glance from Andy. "I don't think it's him calling about this."

"He better not!" Lillian snapped. "I warned him. I forbade him! Anyone who knows about Will, knows about Doug."

"How?" I asked.

"He filed your FAA medical reports, numbnuts! And since then, he's had calls asking questions about you. Did you know that, Will?"

"I didn't."

"One caller claimed to be from the Federal Aviation Administration Aeromedical Branch. Another one said he was from the NTSB. Doug ended both calls after asking qualifying questions they failed to answer. And of course, the most damning piece of evidence popped up just before I caught up to you on the street back in Des Moines."

"Which is?" Andy asked.

"Your new colleague, Detective. Special Agent Donaldson of the FBI. Did you know he's a minion of Bargo Litton, the energy billionaire?"

"Was."

"Really? You think those tentacles simply let go? Pick your poison, Detective Stewart. Donaldson is either an agent for some of the most sinister money in politics today—or he's an agent of the federal government, who will swoop in and snatch up every fiber of your lives if they think there's a stealth technology in your husband's head! Either way, that man's presence constitutes all the proof you need. And if you want to talk about someone who can follow the trail of your credit card without having to bake banana bread for some dark web programmers —I give you the—eff—bee—eye!"

Lillian's homage to Alan Rickman stirred a grudging respect in me. Andy missed the reference entirely.

"Litton pulled his money out of politics," Andy said.

Lillian scoffed. "Kabuki theater. A joke."

"He's also gone Howard Hughes. Total recluse," I added.

"Don't believe it for a second."

Andy brushed off Lillian's claim. "Special Agent Donaldson asked for my help on the James case."

Lillian let her eyes dance for a second, then shook her head. "It's worse than I thought. He's manipulating you. Stroking your ego. Letting the small-town cop play with the big boys. Detective Stewart, nothing good is going to come from contact you have with that man."

Andy buried her right hand in her thick hair.

"You're saying that someone knows what Will can do—"

"Ajax370."

"—and is raising venture capital—"

"*Has raised.* He also implied that he *has* the tech. And since *you're* the tech, Will—" she pointed at me "—it literally makes you overdue for abduction. Which gets a lot easier once someone has a few hundred million dollars to spend on private thugs and mercenaries—and with money like that in play, the law is a minor inconvenience, not an impediment."

"…someone's new 'shiny object'…" I muttered to myself, feeling a chill accompany the memory of the last time someone used those words on me.

Andy looked at me with renewed worry, as if I were something delicate.

Lillian planted her feet and put her hands on her hips. "They will come for you. You will be put in a place where you may never see the sun again. Or have a life. Or in your case, Detective, be alive at all—unless they decide to keep you alive as leverage to make him cooperate. It's only a matter of when and where they make their move. They—are—coming."

I traded glances with Andy. She sighed and nodded her head in response to my unspoken question.

"Lillian, I think we're already past that point," I said.

28

"Shit," I said.

Andy and I stood side by side, leaning on the railing half a dozen paces from the Days Inn room door. Lillian waited in our room. Andy fingered the VISA card Lillian had urgently handed her after I explained that we had one attempted abduction already on the books. *I came to give you this! Take it and run. Anywhere.* At least her plea put the woman's money—or Doug Stephenson's money—where her mouth was.

"Now what—we're supposed to run off to some island?" Andy asked. "Drop out of sight? Live out our lives looking over our shoulders?" Anger honed an edge to her words. She may not have intended it, but her anger translated into blame and it cut in only one direction. Lillian was not her problem. She was *my* problem.

"We're not." I said it quietly. I shook my head.

"We are if we take her seriously." She glared into the darkness. "I'm not ready for that. I mean it. For starters, I don't trust her."

I wanted to reach for her but knew better. When she's angry, it can be like reaching for a downed power line.

"When this all started, I never—I *never* complained. Or told you to bury it. I never asked you to weigh what it meant to *us.* But—" She shook her head slowly. "Will, we are *not* throwing our lives away! I just got my family back."

"Agreed. We're not doing what she says."

"Really? And what, exactly, do you propose?"

I turned to face her.

"Dee, what's the absolute craziest thing you've ever done?"

"I married you."

"Well, we need to up your crazy game."

29

"You're insane! Have you heard nothing I said?" Lillian folded her arms. I thought for a moment she would try to physically block us from leaving the room. Andy handed back her credit card and ducked into the bathroom and retrieved her toiletries. She zipped them in plastic bags and added them to her overnight bag.

"We appreciate your effort," Andy said.

"*Effort?!* This isn't a grade school essay contest, Detective! This is me trying to save your life. And if you don't care about that, give some thought to what happens when what's in your husband's head lands in the hands of people who are not pillars of morality. You can't let that happen!"

I jammed dirty laundry into my bag. Given that I was out of anything clean, it hardly mattered what mingled with what. I zipped the case shut and took up a position by the door. Andy held out her hand, palm up.

"Key."

I fished the plastic card from my pocket and turned it over. She added it to hers and left it on the dresser. "Got everything?"

"Flight bag. Overnight bag. Check."

She gave the room and the bathroom a final inspection.

"Good to go."

Lillian, helpless to stop this departure ballet, shook her head. "You're walking right into their hands."

"Hope so," I said.

Andy gave me the high sign. I reached for my two bags.

"Wait!" Lillian stepped forward and put her hand on my chest. "One thing before you go."

"What is it?" Andy asked with nothing resembling patience in her tone. I don't think she appreciated another woman putting her hand on me. Lillian ignored my wife.

"This is probably the last time I will ever see you two dumb shits. Not through any fault of mine, God knows! So..." She took a step back and faced me. "Let me see it."

Andy and I traded glances, checking each other for objections. She didn't look happy.

"Come on, dumbass," Lillian said. "One last time before you become a DARPA project."

I faced her.

Fwooomp! I vanished.

"Holy mother of God!" Lillian uttered breathlessly.

Fwooomp! She staggered back a step when I reappeared in front of her. A huge grin shattered the hardboiled expression on her face.

Andy pushed past Lillian for the door. "Time's wasting, Will. Let's go."

I didn't move.

"Did Stephenson show you everything? I asked. "The scans? His notes?"

Still grinning, Lillian nodded.

"Okay, Dr. Lillian of NASA and JPL...what is this?"

The grin widened.

"It's obvious! That's alien technology!"

"Told you." Andy lifted her bag and walked out.

30

Delta had an 8:25 a.m. flight to Tuscaloosa, but the airplane ride took us through Atlanta and Birmingham and consumed four hours of flight time, counting gate stops. I added to that the time it would take to drop off the rental car, process through TSA security and deal with checking at least one bag to handle Andy's service weapon, plus time to rent another car—and the decision to drive instead came easily. Google projected the drive to be eight and a half hours. We hit the road in the rented Chevy a few minutes ahead of four-thirty a.m. Allowing for comfortable breaks, a nice lunch somewhere, and no traffic issues, we anticipated arriving in Tuscaloosa, Alabama in the early afternoon.

I suggested to Andy that she sleep on the drive, but she jumped behind the wheel before I called it. She carried pent-up tension into our departure and released it on the car and the road. I revised my estimate to seven and a half hours, assuming we managed to evade law enforcement.

While Andy wheeled onto the turnpike, I stroked out a text message to Pidge, another to Earl, and a third to Sandy. I didn't expect replies, given the hour. I tucked away my phone, sipped the coffee we picked up at the Pilot Service Center next to the hotel and watched the amateur speeders glide past my passenger-side window in reverse as Andy powered the rental up the left lane.

31

"This is it?" Andy slowed the Chevy. The two-lane blacktop had been devoid of traffic for the last few miles of nearly empty countryside. I checked the traveling blue dot against the pin drop on my iPad.

"The great god Google says so. Turn in."

I checked my watch. Almost two. Arriving in Tuscaloosa, we decided to delay finding a hotel. We wanted to get to our destination before the close of the business day.

The property might have been a farm once. The house fronting the lot said farmhouse, but the outbuildings said industrial. A ten-foot fence constructed of corrugated metal ran between the buildings and away on each side, shielding the back of the property from the highway. Trucks of varying sizes and purposes sat randomly angled against or along the low metal buildings.

A small sign hung on the center of the three low outbuildings.

Pelican Aviation Salvage. Call for an appointment.

The sign offered no telephone number.

"Did you remember to call for an appointment, dear?" I teased Andy.

"Why no, honeybun. I guess we'll just have to rely on their Southern hospitality." She did a creditable imitation of the heavy

Southern accent we encountered when we stopped for breakfast in Dothan, Alabama. The waitress had been sweet and the food excellent.

"Do tell." I tried. Not nearly the equal of Andy's effort.

She stopped the car in the sun, nosed up to the building below the sign. Damp heat met us the moment we stepped out of the air-conditioned cabin.

Andy slipped her shoulder bag in place and walked to the door. She tested the knob. Locked. Beside the door, a rusty squawk box hung with the word "PRESS" above a greasy white button. Andy pulled a pen from her bag. She used the pen to push the button, which caused the box to emit a half-hearted growl.

I looked around. Nothing moved in the yard or the house. The stifling heat and past-their-prime structures reminded me of classic short stories by Southern writers. An old hound lying in the shade or someone's grandmother rocking on the porch would have completed the scene.

"Wazzit?" came from the speaker along with a burst of static.

"Police." She surprised me. I thought we might have tried some other story. FAA inspectors. NTSB field agents. Then again, my wife might have a better handle than I do on the consequences of impersonating a federal officer.

"Good cover story," I told her.

Behind the door, a latch snapped. The door opened.

"Kin ah hep you?" The face filling the space between the door and the jamb looked about twelve years old. The boy wore a sports team jersey over giant-sized baggy black shorts. Skinny legs spilled from the shorts into blown-out sneakers. He had a wide face with alert brown eyes under a shock of greasy brown hair.

"Detective Andrea Stewart," she said, stepping between me and the boy and extending her hand and a warm smile. He took it and shook like a boy who had been told a firm handshake is the manly thing to do. "And what's your name?"

"Jake."

"Jake, I need to speak to the owner or manager about an aircraft. Can you let us in?"

"Ahm th' only one here t'day." Jake's eyes must have adjusted to the bright sunlight because he now looked at the attractive woman standing in his doorway with something bouncing between awe and disbelief.

"You're running the show today? Then maybe you can help us. This concerns a Piper Navajo you obtained for salvage last winter. From Wisconsin."

"Okay."

"May we step in? Out of this heat?" Andy took a step closer to the door, which made the kid back away. She exploited the move smoothly. "Why, thank you!"

The building offered familiar cues to my senses. I recognized the oil-impregnated dirt underfoot and the scent of grease in the thick air. Greenish light fell from translucent roof panels onto airplane parts filling the space. Rows of wingless fuselages, ordered from small to large, lined the wall to my left. Beechcraft. Piper. Cessna. Wing panels stacked in wooden scaffolding lined the wall to my right. Faded old paint peeked through layers of dust.

Seeing these dismembered, flightless birds saddened me.

"Ah know th' airplane ya'll are talking about. D'you wanna see it?" the boy asked.

"That would be lovely."

The boy peeled his eyes off Andy and led us halfway down the narrow aisle between parked parts. He hooked left and opened a side door. We stepped outside, crossed a weed-choked space between buildings, and entered the side door to the next storage structure. The same filtered greenish light glowed on a sprawl of parts, engines, tarps, crates and unidentifiable pieces. We wove our way toward the back of the building where an inner space had been segregated from the rest by hanging sheets of scuffed white plastic.

"It's in here. They din't finish it," the boy told us. "On account 'a what AJ did."

The boy reached for the seam to grant us entry. I said, "Hold up, Jake." I caught Andy by the arm and stopped her. "Let me."

After the accident, Andy told me she never wanted to see the wreck. I had been inside the shredded and twisted remains of a once sleek aircraft. If that image took root in her mind, she would see it every time I climbed in a cockpit.

She stepped aside.

I gestured for Jake to proceed. He parted the curtain to let the two of us slip through.

Six Nine Tango had completed her journey to Hell.

After the crash, the airplane had been logically reassembled by the NTSB investigators and laid out in what is now the Foundation hangar. It may have been a wreck, but the arrangement of remains paid homage to what it had once been, nose forward, tail aft. It remained recognizable.

What I confronted in this depressing chop shop transcended butchery. Even the parts that retained their identity after the crash had been rendered to junk. Every panel had been sliced open. Control surfaces that survived the crash were shredded. The post-mortem damage had been inflicted in this aviation graveyard. This was not the aircraft the NTSB had pieced together.

I spotted an orange power cord on the floor and followed it to a Sawzall.

Christ, he eviscerated it!

"AJ was supposed to finish, but he din't 'cuz he did this to it. Trevor, that's the boss, liked to've killed him."

"What was AJ supposed to do?"

"You know. Take it apart. Sort the scrap from the resale. AJ 'specially worked on the avionics and 'lectrical. He's super smart with 'lectronics an' computers."

"Is he around? AJ?"

"He quit coming to work. Ah don' blame him. 'Cuzza all this..." The boy kicked at a piece of aluminum lying near his feet. The kid had something to say. I let silence hang between us until his need to fill it overwhelmed him. "Trevor thinks he was stealin' parts. Izzat why you're here? He call the cops?"

"Do you know AJ's full name and where he lives?"

The boy blinked. "Ah don't. But it's in the office."

32

"This is not what I expected."

Andy said nothing. She glanced at the house but didn't turn onto the driveway. Instead she rolled the rental to the end of the gently winding suburban street.

"You were thinking sharecropper shack? Dog in the yard? A couple banjo players on the porch?"

I didn't want to admit it. Instead, I said, "The middle class is alive and well in Tuscaloosa."

Tidy new salt box and Cape Cod homes lined the street on yards groomed to a degree of perfection more than likely demanded by home-owner association standards. Where vehicles occupied driveways, they varied only slightly between minivans and the current crop of small SUVs, all late model. None of the yards sported old pickup trucks on blocks or abandoned washing machines.

Andy found a circle court and used it to reverse direction.

"I need you to disappear."

"I'm not going in with you?"

"No. For one thing, you don't have law enforcement ID. For another, it works better if it's just me, especially if there's a wife or mother at home."

"What if what's-his-name is in there?"

"Alex John Rodham. If he's in there, I'll talk to him." Andy looked at me and lifted her eyebrows.

"As you wish," I said. I cinched down the seatbelt and worked the levers in my head to vanish. "Roll your window down."

Andy turned into the driveway and stopped on a slight upslope where recently sealed asphalt met a white two-car garage door. She checked her hair and face in the vanity mirror, blew me a kiss and hopped out. A few seconds after she pushed the doorbell, the front door opened.

A golden retriever leaped from the open door onto the concrete stoop. The animal whirled around Andy's knees, sniffing and smiling, swinging its tail merrily.

"Zephyr! Get in here!" the woman at the door commanded. The dog paid no attention. Andy reached down and let Zephyr sniff her hand, then rewarded her new best friend with a head rub and two-handed massage behind the ears. The dog found new reserves of joy. Its tail helicoptered wildly. "I'm so sorry! Zephyr! Come! Come!"

The woman, mid-forties and looking professional in neatly creased black pants and a white blouse, stepped through the door and hooked her hand in the dog's collar.

"He's so cute!" Andy gushed. "You're just one happy fellow, aren't you? I love dogs!" Andy does not love dogs.

"He's a pain in the you-know-what, but he is loveable." The woman pulled the dog back into the house. "I guess you better come in or he's just going to go bananas wanting to come out and play."

Andy followed the woman through the front door, which closed behind her.

I pulled my phone from my pocket and laid it on the center console. It snapped out of *the other thing* and became visible. I checked the time. Twenty minutes later, looking like a soccer mom leaving her best friend's home after an afternoon of finger sandwiches and book club, Andy emerged smiling and thanking her host. The dog leaped after her, prompting Andy to give him one more enthusiastic rub before his owner pulled him back by the collar.

"Well?"

Andy didn't speak as she backed out the driveway. She waved one more time at the woman smiling and waving from the front stoop. Andy put the car in gear and rolled away.

"AJ is her son," she said after making the first turn out of the pretty neighborhood.

"Is he here?"

"No."

"Does he sound like our guy?"

"He's a college dropout."

"Too bad. I had hoped AJ and Ajax were, you know, related. I suppose that would have been too on the nose."

"College dropout doesn't mean dumb." Andy smiled at the empty space I occupied. "In this case, perhaps the opposite. He's a computer nerd. Has been since he was in grade school. He studied coding at the university. His mother said he just didn't have the patience for classes where the professors delegated lectures to adjuncts who knew less about the subject than her son did in middle school."

Fwooomp! I reappeared. I leaned back in the seat and clapped my hands together. "And we have a winner! Where is this boy wonder now?"

"Mother wasn't sure. She's a bit put out by him right now. She said he went to visit a friend in Kansas. That was a few months ago. Mom and Dad let their disappointment be known and he hasn't been in touch since."

"Kansas?"

"I have notes. I need to do some research." Andy glanced at me. "Let's find a hotel. I'm beat and I'm starving. And I need to find a restroom. She made iced tea."

"Look at you. Making friends, both man and beast."

"I wanted to pepper spray that dog."

33

"Earl and Sandy both texted back and said yes," I told Andy while lifting the cover off a Hilton room service hamburger. Andy emerged from a quick shower wearing a fuzzy hotel robe. She slipped into a chair at the suite's small dining table.

"Yes to...?"

"Earl's letting us borrow Pidge. Sandy's letting Pidge bring the Foundation Navajo down to pick us up, but she won't get here until tomorrow night."

"I thought they were in Montana."

"Yesterday. Day trip. Sounds like it went well. Pidge flew Sandy and Arun back home last night."

"God, I hope she doesn't eat that young man alive," Andy said between bites.

"Amen."

Andy picked up her phone. "Six missed calls from Donaldson."

We traded unspoken agreement that she would not be calling him back.

I asked Andy about the interview with AJ's mother, but she told me we would talk after we finished dinner and I took my turn in the shower. She said she wanted to make a few calls.

After doing my best to use the Hilton's entire supply of hot water, I found Andy curled up against the headboard of the bed still wearing the hotel-furnished robe. Fresh energy glittered in her eyes. Her fingers danced on the keyboard of her laptop. I recognized signs of police work puzzle pieces falling into place.

"Can we tell Pidge to meet us in Memphis?" she asked without looking up.

I slid onto the bed beside her. Carefully. The room only provided one robe, so I opted to wear a towel. "What's in Memphis?"

"It's on the way to Wichita."

"What's in Wichita?"

"Wichita is where we will find Ajax370." She looked at me with thinly veiled pride.

"You mean the dark web phantom whose identity is an unsolvable mystery? The rogue hacker who is impossible to find? That Ajax370?"

"Yeah. Him. He's in an industrial park in Wichita, Kansas—near the airport."

"Oh, Lillian would be so pissed at you. How did you crack the code?"

"I called Greg."

"Wow. I knew the guy was a nerd, but Lillian made finding the Holy Grail sound easier than finding Ajax370. Kudos to LeMore for making *her* look like the dumbass."

Andy shook her head. "Greg didn't hack anything. He—we—came at it from another angle. Good old-fashioned police work, dear. With a digital twist."

"Lay it on me."

"I told AJ's mother I was a recruiter for a software company hoping to speak with her son about a job. That I'd been given AJ's name by one of his former professors. That perked her up. She all but pulled out his old school projects to show me how gifted he is. She blames his job at Pelican for his decision to drop out. She said things weren't going well at school and then some new project at Pelican had him all fired up and he started working long days and weekends and ignoring his studies. Then he quit school entirely to work full time at Pelican."

"Tearing apart Six Nine Tango. Where is the boy now?"

"Mom said he left to visit a friend, a high-school chum who, the mother said, was 'into computers' like her son, but not nearly as smart."

"Of course not."

"That was in March. I got a name. Mason Jeffords. I asked Greg to run a social media search on AJ and his pal. He confirmed they're both in Wichita. Or at least they were until a week ago. Greg said they were posting regularly in all the usual ways but then went dark."

"Around the time Ajax370 got the money. Maybe the investors told him to get off social media."

"Maybe. AJ's chum claims to operate a software development company. It probably only exists on the web, but Greg found an address. The phone goes to voicemail." Andy paused and looked closely at me "At the salvage place…what you saw…is it what you thought?"

I pictured the remains of Six Nine Tango and winced. "The kid shredded that airplane. I can understand his boss being pissed beyond belief. He destroyed valuable, salvageable parts. There's only one explanation that fits."

"You think he found something."

"Yeah," I said. "I do. I think he found a piece of whatever I hit. And when he found one piece, he tore the airplane apart looking for more."

"But that doesn't make sense. Didn't the NTSB go over everything?"

"They examine. Reassemble. They'll tear down components if the component factors in the crash—but they don't tear an airplane apart like that. What AJ did wasn't salvage. It was utter destruction."

Andy touched her laptop screen, initiating a shutdown. She closed the screen.

"Will, if he found something—do you think it's something, you know…something that has to do with what you can do?"

"His pitch is about stealth. That can't be a coincidence."

The answer offered neither of us reassurance. Andy said, "Whatever he's doing, there's a good chance it's put him in bed with some bad people. More than likely, the same people who came after you."

"Donaldson," I said. Her expression told me she wasn't convinced. "Look, I know you think he's a hotshot FBI agent working a case, but you have to consider the possibility that he used James—and brought up Mike—for another reason."

"To get to you?"

"To get to me through you," I said. Andy set her jaw. Her lower lip betrayed her slight underbite and warned me to tread lightly. "What Lillian said about the money—that's damning. Think about it, Dee. Who do we know that has a lot of money? And who do we know that *knows* we were in the desert when Litton was visited by the Ghost of Christmas Fuck You?"

She sat in silence. I didn't want to pound the point. I slipped my hand into hers. We flexed our fingers together.

"So, what's in Memphis?" I asked again.

Andy played with my fingers. She stalled. "I'm still a cop on a case…"

"What?"

"You're going to think it's crazy."

"Crazy is the codename for this mission, remember?"

"Will, *you know* I'm all in with you! Priority One is to track down these people and keep you safe. But since Pidge can't get here until tomorrow night, there's a little time to kill…"

"It's James, isn't it?"

She turned to me. "I'm sorry. I'll say it. I'm glad the bastard is dead. But there's something all wrong about Henry and Allen—I don't know. They're square pegs in a round hole. There's no explanation for why either one committed murder. Nearly identical murders. They don't belong. I want to know why."

"And Memphis?"

"It's on the way! Just a quick interview. There's someone there who might know Henry." She shifted her affect, worked her lashes on me, and leaned against me on the bed. Her hand came up and traced the contours of my bare chest. "It's just a two-hour drive."

"Maybe the way you drive."

"Pidge can meet us in Memphis. Then we'll go to Wichita."

"I dunno, Dee…I might need convincing."

She nudged up against me, leaned close and put her lips to my ear. "I might be willing to bribe you," she whispered.

Turns out she was.

34

We didn't make the drive from Tuscaloosa to Memphis in two hours because I insisted on driving. At times I saw Andy's right foot reflexively pushing the carpet to coax more speed out of me. I cruised at my customary twelve over the limit and let more than a few hotheads pass me.

I let fifty miles roll under us before asking, "This isn't something you could have called about?"

"She doesn't have a phone."

"Then how did she call the Des Moines police?"

"She used the office phone. At the nursing home. I called the number."

"Okay. Then why not just talk to her?"

Andy huffed a sigh in my direction. "Doesn't work as well as a personal interview. Look, I know this might be crazy, but there's just something…" She looked out the window at the passing scenery, a riot of green under a blue summer sky studded with cotton-candy morning cumulus. Thunderstorms at conception; benign now but by mid-afternoon the convection would toss water and ice high into the atmosphere. The mix would rise, then fall, then rise again, over and over until the accumulated weight of it brought tons of water, liquid and solid, to earth. I wondered if Andy's thoughts bloomed at the same infant stage.

Rising, falling, solidifying. I read her mood. Touchy about Donaldson. Tender where the question of someone pursuing us—pursuing me—intersected our lives. Distracted by elements of the James shooting.

"You don't think she's just another fruitcake?"

"I listened to the tip line recordings. At the DMPD station. After we talked about Henry not having a military record. Ninety-nine percent nutballs, but the lady who called and said he was her husband—who was shot down in the war sixty years ago—she sounded different." "How do you know DMPD hasn't talked to her?"

"Maybe they have. But I doubt it. They have the shooter. He confessed. It would be easy to lump her in with the rest of the loonies."

I thought it over. "There was no war sixty years ago. I did the math. Korea was over. Vietnam still had a French colonial hangover."

Andy didn't comment. She pulled out her phone, glanced at it, then put it away again.

35

The sign read Hamilton Green Family Living Center—an extravagant name for what looked like a pair of aging apartment buildings set on the fringe of a sixties-era residential neighborhood near Collierville, southeast of Memphis. The sign offered the reassuring slogan *We love your loved ones.*

So you don't have to, I added mentally.

A small parking lot joined a circle drive with an overhang sheltering the front door. I pulled into the all-but-empty lot. No rush of visitors today.

Andy and I eased out of the cool car into thick, humid heat. My empty stomach reminded me we had driven through the breakfast hour and my mind wandered to Memphis barbecue. I stretched the road stiffness from my legs, back and arms. Andy slipped her satchel strap over her shoulder and headed for the door.

I expected to find a reception desk guarding the facility, but aside from an office tucked to the right of the double front doors, nothing and no one challenged us.

"Hello?" Andy called through the office to an inner office. No reply. She looked down a long hallway. A dining room occupied the right side of the hall. A few residents sat in silence over a late breakfast. The arrangement suggested a kitchen nearby, which promised the best chance of finding staff. Andy set off in that direction while I looked over a large common area directly ahead of the front entrance. A staircase that reversed itself in mid-flight anchored the room, rising to an exposed second floor. On the wall farthest from the door, a flatscreen TV offered an endless parade of muted talking heads over a CNN logo. The room featured a piano, a ring of padded chairs and a fireplace. No one occupied the common area at this hour.

I picked up a conversation from the hallway. "...not supposed to use the office telephone." Andy returned in stride with a young woman in pastel scrubs. "We've talked with her about that."

Andy ignored the young woman's irritation. "Second floor you said? Room six?"

"Go right at the top of the stairs."

Andy thanked the attendant in a way that made it clear we didn't need or want company, but then stopped and called after her.

"What's she like?"

"Mrs. Hampton? Oh, she's nice. One of the nice ones."

"What about mentally?"

"Oh!" The girl laughed. "She's all there. She knows what day of the week it is."

DELICATE embroidered handwork adorned a bulletin board beside the door marked with the numeral 6. A five by seven color print dominated the center of the board—a gray-haired woman accepting a plaque from a group of men in suits. The photo's backdrop appeared to be a classroom. I recognized the look of school administrators. Unlike similar boards beside neighboring doors, this one lacked family photos.

Andy knocked. We waited a moment. Andy raised her hand to knock again when the door opened.

Adeana Hampton met us with friendly eyes under a halo of curled white hair. She had pale powdery skin. Her frame was smaller than it may have been in her prime, yet she stood erect without a walker or cane. She wore a white cardigan despite the way the air conditioning in the building labored ineffectively. Delicate fingers with thin bones hinted that this woman struggled to stay warm. An afghan draped over the arm of her recliner backed up my assumption.

"Ms. Hampton?" Andy asked.

"Yes?"

"I'm Detective Andrea Stewart." Andy held up her badge. "This is my husband, Will. He's working with me today. May we come in to talk to you about a call you made—?"

"To the police! Yes! Please, come in! This is about Armand!"

"Armand?"

"My husband! The man you arrested!" She backed a step into the room and waved us to enter. "Please, come in and sit down. Can I offer you a glass of water? I'm afraid I don't have anything else."

"No, thank you. That's quite alright." Andy took a seat on a small sofa facing the recliner. I dropped beside her.

The tidy studio apartment had a television, the sofa and two recliners. A stack of books leaned against the arm of the sofa. More books lined a small set of shelves against the wall. The kitchenette featured a half-size refrigerator, but no stove or microwave.

"Lord! I couldn't believe it when I saw him. I couldn't believe it!" Mrs. Hampton sat lightly on the edge of her recliner. She clapped her hands on her knees. "After all this time! After all these years! Is he alright? He didn't do what they said on the TV. He couldn't have!"

"Ma'am, the man who was arrested goes by the name of William Andrew Henry."

"Well, that's just foolishness. His name is Armand Lewellyn Hampton and he is my husband. We were married on November 16, 1958 in Chandler, Arizona, right before he shipped out." Her warm eyes softened, catching what might have been the millionth rerun of a memory.

"Did your husband live here? With you?"

"Oh, no. Dear me, no. We were only married for nine days. Just nine days…" Andy waited. "And then he received his orders. He had to go, but he wrote me. Every week. And then…well, then he was gone."

"Gone?"

"Yes. He's been gone now sixty years."

I looked at Andy to see how she planned to terminate an interview with a delusional woman.

"Hampton," Andy said. "You still have his name? You never remarried?"

"Oh…no…I suppose I always knew he would come back. I knew in my heart." She leaned forward slightly and looked Andy squarely in the eye. "Young lady, I know what you're thinking. That I've got fuzz between my ears. This place is full of old ladies with fuzz between their ears—lots of them younger than me. But I'm not like that. I taught high school English for fifty-three years and I remember the name of every student I ever graded. I remember the title of every book I assigned, every short story we read. I pray each night and thank the Lord for the mind and the memory he has given me. It is as sharp today as it was on our wedding day sixty years ago. It would have been our sixtieth anniversary last November. November the sixteenth."

"Well, ma'am, you answered my first question. But I'm confused about something. You said your husband was shot down in the war. Did you mean World War II?"

Adeana Hampton pursed her lips and regarded Andy in a way that left no doubt in my mind that this woman had been a teacher. "Dear, I did not teach history or social studies, but I can still give you an F if you think my husband, who would have been a boy in short pants during the Second World War, was shot down by the Nazis or the Japanese. No. He was shot down during the Cold War, which was quite heated at the time."

"You're saying your husband served…"

"He was a pilot in the United States Air Force. He flew bombers. He flew the B-29, but they had another number for it at that time because it wasn't a bomber any more. It was all very secret." She stood up abruptly. "Let me show you."

Andy glanced at me. "They flew the -29 well into the sixties," I told her. If she was impressed by my knowledge, she hid it well.

Mrs. Hampton stepped to her bookshelf. She touched her lower lip, searching the titles, then found what she was looking for. She tipped a slim volume out into her hands. A simple black cover bore the title *The Strategic Air Command: Evolution and Consolidation of Nuclear Forces 1945-1955*. She split the book open and lifted out a set of black and white photos with cracked edges. After a second of reverie, she came to the sofa and nudged us apart. She settled between us like a chaperone. I caught a whiff of perfume. Fresh bakery and lilies. I wondered if her new husband had welcomed that scent to his senses sixty years ago. If it existed sixty years ago.

"Here. This is our wedding photo." She held the precious snapshot carefully by the white-bordered edges. "It's the only one I have. The man at the chapel had a little Brownie camera and he took the picture right after the ceremony. Armand gave him a dollar and asked him to send the print to me. I had nearly forgotten about it...then one day it came in the mail."

I checked to see if Andy was seeing what I was seeing.

Two smiling kids held each other, one proud in his uniform, the other proud of the marital bond that had been sealed between her and her man. They were young and beautiful and full of life, yet old, from another age, frozen forever in black and white.

Andy's expression told me I wasn't wrong.

The young man in uniform with his arm around a pretty girl clutching a sprig of flowers was William Andrew Henry. Josiah James's murderer.

"This one," she shuffled the photos. "This was Armand's ten-man crew." She held up a classic bomber crew shot. Two ranks of smiling youth stood and squatted in front of a huge, polished aluminum fuselage. Six men in the front row wore sergeant stripes and enlisted man caps. Four men in the back wore peaked officers' caps, all with the ring removed to lend the caps a fifty-mission crush. "Armand gave me this picture. He wasn't supposed to. Everything was secret. But we were all such good friends. Such good friends. Even the enlisted boys." She pointed at the tall, handsome captain on the far left. "That's Armand."

"Who's that?" Andy asked. She pointed at the next man in line.

"That's Paul Lockwood. He was Armand's copilot. He was Armand's best man, too."

I thought sixty years might disguise a man. I was wrong. The handsome pilot standing beside Armand Hampton may have been Paul Lockwood in 1959, but twenty-four hours ago he was John Steven Allen who wore an orange jump suit and played chess against himself day after day at USP Coleman I.

36

"Let me," I lifted the phone out of Andy's fingers and gently took the photos from Mrs. Hampton. She had agreed to let Andy photograph the snapshots. One by one, I laid the precious images on my thigh and snapped pictures while Andy continued questioning the woman.

"Mrs. Hampton, did you know anything about your husband's duties? His missions? Was he flying over Vietnam?"

"Oh, no! It was top secret. He and Paul were not allowed to say anything about their flying. They joked about being sent to prison for mentioning what they had for breakfast. But it wasn't really a joke. The commanders were rigid about secrecy. But I can tell you for certain, he was not flying over Vietnam."

"How do you know?"

"He wasn't supposed to tell me, but he said they carried cold weather survival equipment. He told me about the extra winter suits they had to carry."

I spoke quietly. "We didn't lose our first American aircraft in Vietnam until 1961." I'm an encyclopedia of aviation trivia.

"That would have been more than a year after Armand and his crew were shot down," Mrs. Hampton said.

"They were shot down? What happened?"

She sighed. "I was never told. I received a telegram that said Armand and his crew had gone missing during a routine weather mission. Phony baloney. I called Colonel Wilmett—he was Armand's commanding officer—but he would only tell me the same thing and refuse to say anything more. I asked him where they were lost. He wouldn't say. I asked him if there had been a rescue mission. He wouldn't say. He wouldn't say anything. He told me I shouldn't ask questions."

She paused to skirmish with the emotion carried by the memory.

I waited, then handed the delicate prints back to Mrs. Hampton. She took one more look at the lost newlyweds, then tucked them in the book.

"Can I see him?" she asked Andy. "I'm willing to travel. I have savings. We never had the life we planned. I know we can't get it back. But it would be so good to see him again…"

"Ma'am, I don't know. That's an honest answer. I'm not sure what all this means, or why he did what he did—"

"Oh! He couldn't have!"

Andy reached out and took Mrs. Hampton's hands. "I'm sorry. I was there. I was only a few feet away. There's no question."

The woman read Andy's eyes and the truth therein. A glitter of tear formed in her own eyes.

"May I ask …what made you think it wasn't just a weather mission? How do you know he was shot down?" I asked.

"The other pilots and their wives—we all knew each other. They came to care for me. It was a Sunday. They came right from church. They were so kind. They didn't break any rules about secrecy, but there was talk. The other pilots were angry about the weather mission story. They were angry because of the missions they were asked to fly. They felt helpless."

"Against what?"

"Why, the Russians, of course. The Russian jets."

WE STAYED ANOTHER HOUR. Adeana Hampton plumbed the depths of a crystal-clear memory. She told us the names of all the men in the crew. She remembered their wives, their girlfriends. She told us how she and her future husband met on a blind date set up by a girl Paul Lockwood had been dating—a girl with a cute friend teaching English at the local high school. She remembered the restaurant where they met and the Hollywood musical the two couples watched at the local theater. She remembered quips and the color of eyes filled with love the instant she found them. In moments of reverie, she laughed. At a tale that included a flat tire and discovery of a possum in the rumble seat of an antique Ford coupe. At the funny, stumbling proposal her young husband-to-be made on the steps of a boarding house while the house matron fumed on the other side of the front door. Even in laughter, her eyes glossed with tears from a reservoir that had not run dry after six decades.

Andy shared what little she knew about what had happened in Des Moines. Adeana Hampton called Josiah James "a noisy little shit." Then she covered her mouth with her delicate fingers to hide the transgression and the startled smile that followed. She asked Andy again for a chance to see her lost husband, at which point Andy did what she always does. She made a promise she shouldn't have.

Drives me nuts.

When we parted, Andy traded hugs with the woman and assured her she would call soon. Mrs. Hampton needlessly reminded Andy that she would have to call the office and tell them to fetch her. As we stepped into the hall and the door closed behind us, I touched my wife's arm.

"Did you see this?" I handed over her phone. In addition to the wedding and crew photos, I had snapped an image of the back side of the bomber crew print. Faded blue ink captioned the picture.

Best of the 6091st.

"I think I know how you can find out more about this guy."

Andy stowed her phone, then stopped abruptly. She turned her head to listen to voices coming from the first floor below us. I started to ask, but Andy darted to the point where the hallway opened as a second-floor overlook to the common room below. She leaned over and spied on the source of the voices, then whirled back to face me, waving both hands urgently.

"Will! Disappear! Now!"

Fwooomp! The question forming on my lips vanished with me.

Andy turned away and marched to the top of the staircase. She hooked one hand on the finial topping the handrail and made a rapid descent out of my sight, headed in the direction of a familiar voice.

My abrupt disappearance left me floating in the center of the empty hallway. I hadn't expected to need my vest or the power units they contained. My only means of propulsion remained tucked in my overnight bag. I hung in the awkward position of having nothing to grip.

Screw this. I pulled the levers in my head.

Fwooomp!

I reappeared and dropped to the carpet. I hurried forward, then edged up against the wall where the second-floor railing met the hallway. I glanced over the railing. Andy stood on the stairway's mid-flight landing, her arms folded.

Facing Special Agent Lee Donaldson.

They spoke in low, harsh tones from guarded postures. Donaldson used his height to emphasize his authority—or tried to. Andy was having none of it. She abruptly pushed past him, descending the steps toward the front door. Donaldson rolled his eyes and followed.

Fwooomp! I disappeared and heaved myself over the railing. I curled my legs and pushed off with both hands. The short shot took me to the mid-flight landing. I grabbed the varnished wooden railing just as Andy stalked out of the building with Donaldson close behind. The electric motion-activated door swung wide for their passage and remained open in their wake. I saw my chance and shoved hard. I caught the doorframe, hooked left and grabbed a post supporting the building's overhang.

Andy and Donaldson faced each other a few steps into the parking lot.

"I thought we were working together, Detective." Donaldson opened with an accusatory tone.

"You can think whatever you like."

"You just up and left."

"A, I don't answer to you. And B, I had a personal matter to attend to."

"Personal?" He looked around. "Then what are you doing here?"

Andy stood frozen, studying Donaldson, eyes narrowed to slits. I knew the look. Thinking—and not about his question. She turned her head to one side for a moment and gazed into the distance, or into a memory. Donaldson waited. When she turned back to him, she took a step closer and held out her hand.

"Empty your pockets."

"What?"

"You heard me. Pockets. Now."

I thought he might laugh. Or invoke bravado and refuse. Instead, he gave it a beat, then offered a gesture I didn't expect. A nod of respect. He fished into a cargo pocket at the front of his thigh and pulled out what appeared to be a cell phone, but it had no screen. He handed the device to Andy.

Andy examined the slender rectangle. "This is a cell signal jammer. You jammed my phone. When we went to Missouri. That's why nothing came through until you left me at my hotel. What the hell, Special Agent!"

Donaldson looked around to reassure himself that they were alone.

"It wasn't about you. I was still running ahead of my SAC on the James case," he said.

"You told me you were golden!"

"Eye of the beholder. From where I sit, I am."

She held up the jammer. I pictured her throwing it at him.

"Look, on a professional level, I owe you an apology—"

"Big time!"

"And I will explain. Why don't you let me buy you a cup of coffee?"

"Not a chance! Explain right here, right now!"

"Fine." He spread his hands. "It was wrong. But like I said, it wasn't about you. On Monday I needed to stay out of touch with my SAC long enough to run down Henry's background. I didn't want certain outside influences stopping me. At face value, the James shooting is a slam dunk, which means nobody was going to endorse me spending time on it. I didn't want to get pulled off. I didn't want calls coming through you or that DMPD Detective, Sontag. We can't all say we had dead batteries."

"You lied! You weren't assigned to this case."

Donaldson equivocated. "There are aspects of what I'm doing, what I'm looking into—I have to be careful where I tread."

"Are you still off book?"

"Not entirely." Donaldson shrugged.

Andy rolled her eyes. "Jesus, how do you even have a job? Aside from a serious breach of professional ethics, we're talking about felony conduct here!" Andy waved the device between them.

"Can we please talk about this over a coffee?" Andy's posture gave him one guess. "Alright! Alright! Look, when you showed up in Des Moines, I was pretty sure you were on board about James. I just wasn't sure how far you would run with it. I needed to know, and you weren't sharing. You have a reputation, Detective."

"I don't know about reputation, Special Agent, but at this point there's very little chance I would share anything!"

"And I deserve that. What can I say? I apologize."

"Screw you. Did you follow me here?"

"Please. You're not the only cop capable of running down a lead."

"Really? Do you even know why I'm here?"

Donaldson's posture traded a touch of deference for a hint of restored superiority. "I'll show you mine if you show me yours."

Andy gave him a cold smile. "Thanks, but no. And I think I'll keep this." She tucked the jammer in her satchel. "Have a nice day."

She stepped off the sidewalk and started across the parking lot.

"You're here to see Adeana Hampton," he called after her.

She ignored him and kept walking.

"Because she thinks she was married to Henry!"

She fished the rental keys from her satchel and unlocked the car, never breaking stride.

"You also went to see John Allen at Coleman!"

That stopped her. She paused, then slowly turned around. He strolled toward her. I pushed off the post I'd been holding and glided to another, trying to stay close enough to hear the conversation.

"Keep talking," she said.

"You went to Coleman. You made the same connection to Allen that I did. You saw the similarities. I talked to the supervisor you spoke to. He called you a 'sweet thang,' by the way."

"Ear of the beholder."

"You flew down. I checked with TSA. The thing is…Coleman told me you never showed up."

"Allen refuses to see anyone."

"He doesn't have the final say on that, you know."

"Interviewing someone who won't speak is tiresome."

Donaldson flipped his thumb in the direction of the building. "The woman upstairs. She called the tip line. What did she tell you?"

"Find out for yourself."

"Let's save time. Share with me and I'll tell you what I know about Allen and the shooting of a Russian diplomat."

Donaldson watched Andy closely. She took half a step closer. "No."

"No?"

"No. You'll tell me what shooting a Russian diplomat has to do with James."

Donaldson's hands went up in surrender.

"Fair enough. I owe you. I'll share it all with you."

"First things first," she said. "What's your real interest in me and my husband?"

Donaldson looked around. "Yeah, where is he? I thought he was with you."

"He went home to Essex. Answer the question. Carefully. The remote chance of me having anything to do with you going forward depends on it."

"Okay. You really want to do this here?" He squinted up at the sun.

"I'm not moving until you explain." She folded her arms and planted her feet.

"Fine. You already figured it out. Your husband knew who I was when I came to your place in Essex. After Litton fired me for the break-in, once I got back with the Bureau, I checked. Flights. Hotels. Looking for anyone that might pop around the time our security was breached. And there you were. Flights in and out, and some cheap motel way out on the fringe. You and your husband. Right on the heels of the whole thing with Parks."

He paused to lure her into an explanation. Andy remained stone-faced.

"I'll admit, I liked you for breaking in on Litton. But I had no idea how. And then I found out about the Education Foundation. A cool hundred mil. Not bad. You were there to negotiate it, weren't you? For your friend, Sandra Stone. Am I right?"

Andy said nothing.

"Maybe negotiation isn't the right word. You connected the dots between Parks and Litton. So, you made him pay. I don't know how. The Bargo Litton I knew didn't pay off anyone. Plus, you never got in to see Litton. I know. I held the key to the kingdom."

"Are you accusing me of extortion?"

Donaldson waved his hands emphatically. "Whoa! Whoa! No! Crafty negotiating. That's what I'd call it."

"Then why bring it up?"

"I only brought it up to let you know that I knew you were there. And to show you that I do my homework."

Silence.

"Plus, I didn't want it hanging between us. That's not why I came looking for you. I meant what I said about Brogan, about James. I wanted your help. I still do. Pure and simple."

"And you were willing to use Mike Mackiejewski to get it."

"Don't play the indignation card on me, Detective. Please. You know what a piece of shit James was. And the role he played in your friend's death. You wanted him taken down, too. That's why you were in Des Moines. That's why you were at that show."

"James is dead. Your case is closed. Why are you still working this?"

"Why are you?" He repeated his gesture toward the building behind him. "Why are you interviewing an old woman who thinks she's married to the shooter?"

Andy didn't answer. Her phone rang.

"Wait! Before you answer that...I apologize. Again." Donaldson gestured at the phone.

Andy looked at her caller ID screen. She gave Donaldson a withering look and picked up the call.

"Yes, Chief." Andy held the phone close to her ear. I strained to hear. Chief Ceeves' voice tested the limits of the tiny phone speaker, but Andy stood too far from my position give his words clarity.

The Chief had a lot to say. Loudly. Andy listened, fuming.

"TDA to the FBI now?"

"Was his name Donaldson?" The chief answered and Andy glared at Donaldson.

"At the moment, Memphis."

"No."

"No."

Andy went silent. The Chief's gravel voice ground against her ear. Like a drivetrain bearing going bad, warning of trouble. She grimaced.

"I know."

"Yes, sir."

"St. Louis, sir. I need military service record information from the National Personnel Records Center."

"I meant 'I'…I haven't informed Special Agent Donaldson yet."

She winced as Chief Ceeves' voice rose. Andy nodded in silent acknowledgment, then shook her head.

"Not even for law enforcement?"

"Federal. Yes, sir."

"Yes, I will, sir."

"Right. The City of Essex, sir."

"No sir, just that family of raccoons. I'll talk to her again when I get back."

The grinding fell silent. Andy lowered her phone and stared at it.

Donaldson spoke softly. "I'm sorry about that. If I had known I would find you here, Andrea, I wouldn't have gone over your head. God's truth."

A lock of her hair fell across one eye.

"It's Detective Stewart," she said icily. "And I'm not sure you would know truth if it ran you over. Let's get something straight, Special Agent. I don't work for you. I'm not *with* you. And if you ever go behind my back to my boss again, we're done. Is that clear?"

She gave him a moment, but only just.

"I have a lead on a family of raccoons I'd much rather be following right now than lifting a finger to convict a ninety-year-old man of ridding society of that piece of crap James."

"Listen, I—"

"No, you listen to me. While you've been going behind my back with my boss, I've been ten miles ahead of you on *your* damn case."

He waited a moment, hands folded, head down. If his contrition wasn't genuine, it was a good act.

Andy's eyes darted to the posts holding up the overhang. She guessed correctly where I hovered and set off in my direction. She spoke without looking back.

"Get your car. I'm going to the restroom and then we're going to St. Louis."

She left him standing on the hot asphalt.

37

"Dee, what the hell?" I whispered harshly. She locked the door to the single-occupant Women's room.

Fwooomp! I reappeared and released my grip on the stainless-steel assist bar beside the toilet. Gravity pulled me to the floor.

"You're going with this son of a bitch?"

"Will, I am not happy about it, but at the moment this is the best course. I can't refuse to do my job."

"Really? Because if Crazy Lillian is half right, nothing in our past or present lives matters. Not your job. Not mine. Nothing."

"And you're just giving up on all that?"

"Exactly the opposite! I'm trying to save it!"

Andy took a breath and a step closer to me.

"What's the point of saving it if we blow it all up in the process? If I defy Donaldson and the Chief to go with you to Wichita, I might as well resign today."

"Well, I would think saving our lives beats saving your job," I snapped, instantly regretting it.

She had an opening to swing back. She didn't. Her hand came up to my cheek. "Love, nothing is more important than us. But I want to hold on to *all of it*, all of us, all of who we are." I drew a breath to argue, but she put her fingers to my lips and saved me from myself. "Shhh! Listen!

You still think Donaldson is a threat? Fine. Then what's better than dragging him off to St. Louis to keep him occupied digging through government records?"

"To hell with him. If Tom wants you on this case, why don't we go to St. Louis without him?"

"The NPRC only releases records to service members or next of kin —or a federal agency. I'm not federal."

"Dee, I don't trust him."

"Nor do I, but Tom and the whole FBI will be watching. I'll keep him busy and you go find this Ajax370 character." She pulled the keys to the rental from her satchel. "I'll get my bag and leave these under the driver's seat."

"Well, that sucks."

"Will, we're lucky he caught up to us here! Otherwise he would have followed us to Wichita! And if he really is involved in any of that, he would have tipped them that we were coming!"

She had a point, which I acknowledged by sulking.

She softened both her gaze and her voice. "This is the best way to keep tabs on Donaldson," she said. "If I bolt now, he won't be the only one wanting answers. How would I explain running off to Kansas?"

"It doesn't hurt that you have your teeth sunk into this business with Hampton, or Henry, or whoever he is."

It was the wrong thing to say. I felt heat rising in her affect. I watched her channel it into a dangerous calm.

She said nothing.

"Sorry," I said quietly. "Seriously, Dee. I'm sorry. That's not what I meant. You know how I get when things I don't want to hear make the most sense."

She eased me off the hook. "Go find him. Reconnaissance only. Promise me."

"There's a gigantic chance there's nothing there. If Ajax370 got his money, he's probably long gone along with whatever he found in that wreck."

"Reconnaissance. Promise me."

"Promise."

Her gold-flecked green eyes—Andy's lie-detectors—worked me

over. Satisfied, she reached behind my head and pulled us together in a kiss.

"I will join you as fast as I can."

A few minutes later, still tasting her lips on mine, from the window of the first-floor Women's restroom of Hamilton Green Family Living Center, I watched her take the wheel of Donaldson's car and pull away.

She may have been driving, but I couldn't help but feel she'd been abducted.

38

"That's what I'm fucking talking about!" Pidge exclaimed. "A heist!"

"It's not a heist," I told her through the intercom. She grinned at me across the cockpit. We took a jolt. Steady turbulence generated by late afternoon convection reached the puke bag point, making me grateful there were no passengers turning green in the back. Pidge ignored the bumps and jolts and guided us between boiling cumulus from her perch on the extra cushion she uses in the pilot's seat. I looked up through the windshield. The cloud tops rose well above our service ceiling. There would be no smooth air if we asked Center for higher. "I'm only going in to look—unless an opportunity presents itself."

"You really think this kid found something? Like something that explains what you hit?"

"Jesus, Pidge, you should have seen what he did to Six Nine Tango. It was a crime. There's only one reason for doing that, as far as I can tell."

"It's bad enough what you did to it." She said it smartly, but then shook her head in sympathy. No pilot can look at or imagine the ruins of an aircraft without feeling pain.

Center called and gave us a frequency change. I handled it while

Pidge flew. She prefers hand flying in rough air, rather than letting the autopilot chase itself.

She waited until I established contact with the next sector controller, then asked, "So, what's the plan?"

"Andy's cop friend in Milwaukee thinks they're set up in an industrial park by the airport."

"Inside or outside the fence?"

"Outside. No TSA. But close enough to the fence that I can just hop it and we can go. If we need to make a getaway, anyone following would have to get through the fence somehow."

"Who's gonna follow *you*?" She laughed.

I didn't share her confidence. Not after a paramilitary crew went through my house with a scanner.

The thought made me uneasy—or *more* uneasy. I looked out the copilot's window to the north, toward St. Louis. An hour before Pidge arrived at Memphis International, Andy sent me a text that she and Donaldson were boarding a flight for St. Louis.

Call you when I can. Reconnaissance only! she reminded me.

Fat chance.

39

The flight from Memphis to Dwight D. Eisenhower International Airport in Wichita took close to three hours, accounting for a headwind and deviations around isolated thunderstorm cells. Pidge denied feeling fatigue, but after flying all the way to Memphis from Essex County, then on to Wichita, she didn't argue when I took over the last third of the flight and managed the landing.

We shut down at Signature Flight Support just before ten. A side effect of the life I lead as a charter pilot is losing track of where I woke up on any given day. I had to concentrate to recall that the day began in Tuscaloosa. The memory mingled with a pre-dawn departure from the Days Inn in Wildwood and a sleepless night spent on a sofa at the Des Moines police station. Both Pidge and I were stiff and slow climbing out of the Navajo. I didn't like what that meant for the plan I had formulated.

Pilots live (and try not to die) by acronym checklists. GUMPS (Gas, Undercarriage, Mixture, Prop, Seatbelts) serves before landing. CIGARS (Controls, Instruments, Gas, Attitude/trim, Runup, Seatbelts) serves before takeoff. Pilots check their health and well-being prior to a flight with I'M SAFE, which forces the pilot to examine himself for Illness, Medication, Stress, Alcohol, Fatigue and Emotion. Being honest with myself, three of the seven items red-flagged my plan to find

Ajax370 tonight. Andy being in Donaldson's company had me stressed. Fatigue gnawed at my bones. And Emotionally, I was pissed. I would not admit it to Andy, but I had much more in mind than reconnaissance.

"Hold up," I told Pidge.

She stopped and read my face. "You're thinking tonight isn't the best time to hit those guys and make a run for it."

I shrugged. "What did you tell Earl? About being back?"

She laughed. "I told him you needed me for three days!"

"Three days! What the hell?"

"Fuck, Will! He had me scheduled to fly those stupid-ass photo-mapping flights in the 182. You know—for the university? I hate that shit. Plodding around the sky with a hole in the floor for that camera. It's cold. It's drafty. It's noisy. And that asshole from the university keeps rubbing his butt up against my leg while he's playing with his camera—or himself! I almost threw his ass out over Lake Winnebago."

It was my turn to laugh. I pictured her doing it.

"Yeah. I don't think tonight's the night to do this. Let's grab some sleep and come up with a plan over breakfast."

She heaved her overnight bag, a backpack, onto one shoulder. "Whose credit card are we riding?"

"Foundation."

She grinned. "Sweet! Do they have a Ritz in this town?"

"WHERE ARE YOU?" Andy asked.

"Holiday Inn," I said. "It's not the Ritz, but then what is? Where are you?"

"Same. I don't know how you do it, love. Living out of a suitcase? Although I did find one of those retractable clotheslines in the bathroom. All my underwear is hanging up." I wiggled the phone against my ear to bring her voice closer.

"Keep talking to me about underwear."

She laughed. It felt good. The cool breeze release of pent-up tension. I closed my eyes to imagine her in a room identical to mine, on a bed like mine.

"Did you get anywhere with the government?"

"The government doesn't open until eight tomorrow morning."

"Did Donaldson talk about the case? Did he tell you why he's gnawing on that bone? I mean, James is dead. His legacy is a fart joke."

I pictured her in my Packer t-shirt, long legs tucked, hair a little wild. I imagined an electric energy in her, the way she gets when a case gives her a charge. It didn't matter whether the investigation involved a murdered internet conspiracy fanatic or a family of raccoons under stolen cars. She can't help herself.

"Donaldson practically lit up when I showed him the crew photo. I think it corroborated other evidence he's been collecting. But he's holding back on his end."

"What do you mean?"

"Allen is Lockwood. Henry is Hampton. He's all over that. Doesn't question it one bit. So, I asked him to explain what it all has to do with James, but he held out on me."

"That's not the deal, Dee! He owes you!"

"He does," she said evenly. "And he promised to lay it all out for me as soon as we pull up the Hampton and Lockwood service records. He says he has a theory and those service records will tell us if he's right."

"Oh, that's such bullshit!" My wife has more patience than I do. "I told you not to trust him."

"Darling," she spoke softly, "I know what it's like. I know how it feels to build a picture out of fragments, but to hold it close until one more piece of evidence falls in place. I'm willing to give him the professional courtesy."

"You give him too much! Did you tell him about the DFC?"

"Uh-uh. I'm keeping that in my pocket. I think I know where he's headed, and if he is right, those medals might put a bow on it."

We fell silent for a moment. It happens sometimes, when we're apart. There's nothing awkward about it. Exactly the opposite.

"Thank you," she said at length.

"For what?"

"For trusting me to handle this. And for resting tonight. For waiting. For not charging in."

"Are you going to tell me it's 'reconnaissance only' again?"

"Would it do any good? You're going to do what you're going to do. I trust you."

"Damn, woman. Have I asked you to marry me lately?"

That ended talk of her mission, my mission, and of worrisome things. We joked about whether she would say yes to marriage or not, about having a big wedding, about taking a lavish honeymoon trip to a three-star motel in Wisconsin Dells. Maybe a river tour on the Ducks. Maybe visit the Circus World Museum in Baraboo. She pretended to swoon at the very idea. When we ran out of excuses to stay on the line, we traded I Love You declarations and reluctantly closed the cellular connection between us, each taking those words to bed in hopes they would bring restful sleep.

I gave up at two-thirty.

40

The Holiday Inn Express and Suites nestles behind a La Quinta by Wyndham and a Chinese restaurant—all lining a modern American airport perimeter with a host of similar businesses. A Texas Roadhouse, a Red Roof Inn and an Enterprise car rental office joined the lineup. To an inexperienced eye, the congestion and clutter is daunting, but to business travelers the signs and lighted parking lots feel comforting and predictable. Wichita. Indianapolis. Or a hundred other cities. After a long day of flying or driving, it hardly matters.

A short service road ran south outside the hotel entrance. Within a few hundred yards, the road formed a junction with another road that followed the airport perimeter. Beyond the asphalt, open field marked the start of airport property. The airport fence rose at that point to stop the merely wandering. I personally doubt such fences deter anyone intent on committing harm, but that's for Homeland Security to decide.

Before leaving the hotel room, I flew a simulated mission over the area using Google Maps. Not for the first time, I wondered what warriors in past centuries would have given to have this kind of aerial eye prior to plunging across unknown terrain into battle.

My target was a long warehouse containing multiple businesses. The overhead view gave no hint as to the kind of security I might face.

At two-thirty in the morning, the narrow blacktop road beside the

Holiday Inn lay empty and still. I walked south from the hotel through the last pool of street light, then passed into darkness, making a note of a string of power lines running parallel to the airport border. Despite the heat, I wore my old fishing vest. Beyond the last disk of street light illumination, I pulled out a power unit and snapped on a propeller. It tested perfectly. I patted the vest to assure myself I had two more charged and ready.

Fwooomp! The sound in my head announced my release from gravity. I flexed my feet against the pavement and launched, checking one last time to guarantee that I was clear of the last power lines. The nice thing about operating near an airport is that power lines are unwelcome within its borders. I reminded myself to be vigilant when approaching the target building.

I thumbed the slide controller on my power unit and aimed it toward the broad, empty black space that is Dwight D. Eisenhower International Airport in the night. Rows of blue taxi lights and lines of white runway lights offer confusion to the uninitiated but made perfect sense to my pilot's eye.

I flew a line toward the flashing Runway End Identifier Lights serving Runway 19 Left, not all that far from where Pidge and I parked the Navajo on the general aviation ramp. The distant windsock told me 19 Left and 19 Right were both active, but the airport slumbered at this hour. The package express flights launched hours ago and wouldn't begin their return cycles until just before dawn. Airline red-eye flights cruised high in the night air somewhere. Corporate or general aviation flights generally had the sense to avoid arriving and departing in the small dark hours. Beyond the fatigue factor of flying into the night, the fact is that services diminish after midnight. It's not uncommon to find yourself outside a locked FBO in the middle of the night. I felt confident crossing the active runway approach path without fear of a regional jet bearing down on me.

At the end of the runway, I turned east, followed the taxiway across its Hold Short line, then aimed myself across dry grass until I overflew the TSA fence. I estimated my height at one hundred feet. I slowed myself to get my bearings as the buildings of the industrial park flowed toward me. My target building ran parallel to the road LeMore named in the address he found.

Not impressive.

If Ajax370 scored the kind of money Lillian predicted, the structures below me seemed hardly worthy of a secret stealth technology project. I pictured something monolithic—concrete and glass surrounded by security fences, patrolled by guards with dogs. I had come prepared to breach such a building and seek out a secure vault, possibly slipping past stone-faced guards with automatic weapons.

This looked like a tire warehouse. Or appliance distribution center. The long cinderblock building featured half a dozen loading docks at even intervals. Beside each loading dock, a set of concrete steps rose to windowless metal doors. Some had keypads. Some featured traditional locks set in steel knobs or deadbolt cylinders. Each had a light above the door. A few cameras watched over the docks.

The asphalt lot beside the building lay empty.

I circled to check one last time for wires—it's a real paranoia with me, having once hit a set outside of Cedar Rapids. Assured of a clear path, I eased into an approach. The question was: Which door? The address Greg dug up appeared to be for the entire structure. I started at the end and worked my way from door to door.

Anvil Metalworks.

Rohan, Inc.

Zephyr Technology.

ABC Parts Expediters.

ABC Parts Expediters—Receiving.

Nesneros Outfitters.

I picked the obvious winner.

I eased closer until I floated in front of the door. The entrance had no camera, unlike several of the others. Security consisted of a simple knob lock. Not even a deadbolt. Nothing about this door suggested a secure facility.

Perhaps that was the point.

I pulsed the power unit and drew up to the door. This would be easy.

I closed my hand around the knob, then pushed *the other thing*, applying pressure to the levers in my head. A vague fuzziness, like a lack of focus, spread from my hand. The knob, and the door panel around it began to vanish as if a pool were spreading on the surface. The fringe of the now clear surface appeared *frayed.* I pushed until the pool reached the edge of the door and the location of the bolt, then stopped.

I tugged. The door released after soft resistance snapped the bolt like a strand of yarn.

I pulled the door open. The broken bolt tumbled to the concrete. I waited for the wail of an alarm.

Nothing.

Featureless black space filled the doorframe. Anything or anyone might be waiting in that black pool.

Decision time. If these guys have the ability to hunt me with a scanner, then why give them a win? Why not just walk in? After all, Will Stewart had a perfectly good reason for breaking in on them. *Quid pro quo.*

Fwooomp! I reappeared and stowed my power unit.

I groped the inside wall for a light switch. I found a box and a row of switches. I picked the first, figuring that by now, they knew the door had been breached. Might as well light it up.

I flicked the switch.

A single bulb burst to life above my head. I tensed, fully prepared to push myself back out the door, disappear and launch into the night sky.

The bulb illuminated a concrete floor. Directly ahead, a desk, a table and scattered chairs took up a space loosely divided by cheap office cubicle walls. Additional unused cubicle walls leaned against the cinderblock to my left. To my right, a foosball table nudged the wall. Pizza boxes had been stacked on top of the game table. A wastebasket beside the foosball table overflowed with beer cans and fast food bags.

Not exactly the sinister laboratory I imagined.

Probing deeper into the gloom, I spotted the glint of chrome and glass near the far wall. Headlights. A van. A blue van. It might have once worn a magnetic sign that said Abcress Plumbing, but its sides were blank now. I recognized the bumper from my unexpectedly close examination in the rain. Seeing it now, parked in this space, quickened my pulse.

I stood for a moment, expecting the light to trigger a response. If someone waited in ambush, they were well and truly alerted by now. Nothing moved. No one spoke.

I flicked the remaining light switches. A warehouse the size of a tennis court lit up.

That's when I saw the body.

The mound might have passed for a discarded tarp or pile of quilted moving van blankets. It lay at the foot of another set of walls near the center of the room. These walls were made of glass mounted in what looked like a freshly-constructed lumber framework. Forming a cube roughly eight feet on all sides, the cube anchored the center of the lighted space. The body lay at the foot of one glass wall.

Christ, a murder scene.

My first thought ran to Andy and the litany of proper procedure she would enforce. My second alerted me that my fingerprints stamped the doorknob and light switch. My third went to the decision I now faced.

Dammit.

The path I preferred allowed me to poke around and then leave. Let someone else deal with this. The path dictated by the Andy-voice in my head would have me call it in, wait for the police, then come up with a reason for being here. I gave myself the luxury of a brief debate, knowing there was no real choice.

I checked for cameras and didn't find any, which wasn't necessarily definitive. I used my t-shirt to wipe away my prints and made a note not to touch anything else.

The rest of the space, excluding the glass cube, consisted of a clutter of desks, lawn chairs, a small refrigerator and power cables. Empty beer cans littered the desktops, mingled with random keyboards and a few wireless mouse devices. No sign of computers. No hint of a lab. No equipment. No monitors running cryptic graphics or rows of code. The room contained nothing suggesting this might be the birthplace of a revolutionary stealth technology.

First things first.

I crossed the floor and approached the body. The victim had been rolled up in blankets. A tuft of hair protruded from one end. Articles of clothing littered the floor around him. I looked for blood but saw none.

Drawing close, feeling my throat tighten, I automatically held my breath against the inevitable smell of death. I bent over and reached out when the dead body spoke.

"Fuck, Mason! Turn off the goddamned lights!"

I snapped upright and took a step back.

The body rolled over. A face squinted up at me. "Who the fuck are you?"

"Who the fuck are *you?*"

I took another step back as the body scrambled and fought the twist of blankets, throwing them aside. He struggled, comically after a moment, until he found his feet.

Young. College age. He had a rat's nest of brown hair over brown eyes and a square-jawed face. He might have been one of the intruders at the house. He looked reasonably fit—a gift of youth, yet something easily squandered after a decade or two at a keyboard. He wore baggy nylon shorts and a horribly wrinkled black t-shirt with unreadable printing across the chest. The light made him blink and rub his eyes. I caught a whiff of stale body odor.

"No, who the fuck are you?" he insisted. "Did Mason let you in here?"

"Nope."

This put him on his guard. He looked past me at the door, which hung open.

"What you want? Did Lewko send you? 'Cuz he already got it all, man! There's nothing left to take!"

"Are you AJ?" I asked. "Ajax370?"

He blinked at me but didn't answer.

"Your mother is worried about you, kid." I took a breath and forced a wave of calm down the tight nerves in my neck, shoulders and arms. I flexed my fingers. The kid tightened his lips and said nothing. I stepped past him and strolled around the glass cube. One side of it lay in glittering shards on the floor. A small table occupied the center of the cube. A fish tank sat on the table. It had been covered by another piece of glass, but this had been smashed from above. Shards and slivers lay in the bottom of the tank. I was about to ask the obvious question when I decided to take another tack. "Where's the other van?"

The kid didn't answer. I turned to him. "Abcress Plumbing. Where is it?"

His eyes grew wider.

"Yeah. That was my house you broke into. And since you now know who I am, let's talk about who I'm married to. She's a cop. Which means that outside the knee-deep shit you're standing in, you've got some angry law enforcement coming down on your ass very soon. So, if I may, I'd like to suggest that we have a frank discussion, okay AJ? I'm sure you have questions for me, too."

He threw his hand up and furiously scratched the mop of hair on his head. "Aw, fuck!" He kicked aside the remnant of blankets tangling his bare feet and walked across the floor to a mini-fridge. He pulled open the door and rummaged through a few cans on the shelf. Without looking back at me, he asked, "Wanna beer?"

"Sure."

He pulled two cans and crossed the floor to me. He handed me a marginally cool can of Budweiser.

"You're Stewart," he said, popping the top.

"All day," I replied, doing the same.

"Well, fucking cheers to you." He held up his can. I tapped it. We both drew a slug of not-quite-cold beer. He smacked his lips and looked around. "You're a little late. They cleaned me out. Took everything."

His gaze drifted for a moment, like someone seeking an explanation in the debris path of a tornado.

"Did you really talk to my mother?"

"You should call her."

He shrugged, then sat down in his blanket nest on the floor. I found a rolling office chair at one of the desks and pulled it around the glass cube. I took a seat and another sip of beer.

"I was going to call her. Once I had the money. Once everything was set up."

"You got double-crossed."

He nodded.

"Tell me about it."

He looked up at me. "You tell *me* about it. I saw that wreck. How the fuck did you walk away from that? And don't bullshit me, because I think I already know."

"It is sad when we fail to realize the scope of what we don't know."

"Huh?"

I brushed off his confusion. "I don't know why I'm still upright, if that's what you're asking. I have no idea. Not a clue. I have no memory of the accident, the day of or the day after. Can't help you with any of that. But you can help me. Tell me what you found."

"Why should I tell you anything?"

"Because you're not sure why you shouldn't. And if it helps, I'll kick your ass if you don't. Let's not forget that you broke into my house."

"I guess." He chuckled. "That's the thing. I'm like you. I don't know. You're right—I found something. At Pelican." He glanced up at me. "That's the salvage company where I worked."

"Uh-huh."

"It was stuck up inside the fuselage. In back. I was trying to get at the autopilot servos, but I couldn't get my wrench around a bolt head. You know? How you can't see what you're doing, but you can feel around? Only I kept bumping up against something. I finally got pissed off and opened the fuselage with a Sawzall. And then…there it was."

I waited. Andy's trick. Let the other guy fill the silence. It worked.

"Or wasn't. When I got the panel open there was nothing there. I reached in and almost broke my middle finger. Because—you know—I couldn't see it. Broke the nail halfway down. That hurt like a mother-fucker. Then I started feeling around it. Craziest thing. I felt it but it wasn't there!"

"You think you found a piece of whatever I hit?"

"Gotta be."

"And you're saying you couldn't see it?"

He shook his head somberly.

"But you felt it. What did it feel like?"

"Like a chunk of a casting, but smooth. Thin on one end. Thicker on the other, but with these, I dunno, vanes…" He raised his hands and made a shape, roughly the size of a meatloaf. "It was wedged between the autopilot servo and the bulkhead. I got it loose and I had it in my hands—in my fucking hands! It had no weight! If I let go of it, it just kinda hung there. I don't know if it was composite—or metal—or God knows what!"

He pulled from the beer, long and hard. A little angry. He looked around.

"You know they came in here this morning and told me I have to the end of the week to get all this shit out of here. Told me if they catch me sleeping in here again, they'll call the cops. I owe like three months' rent."

"What happened next?"

He chuckled again. "Next? Next, I lost it! I had it in my hand and I fucking fumbled it and it was gone! I was like a maniac waving my arms around trying to find it again. I panicked and threw up those plastic sheets. I wasn't sure it didn't fly away somewhere in that damned Pelican warehouse—and then I'd never find it! But I figured if there was one piece, there might be more."

I nodded. "That's when you cut up the airplane."

"Yeah. I sliced open every piece. God, I must have cut my hands a dozen times on that fucking aluminum. I cut it apart, searched every chunk, every slice, every edge and corner and then I searched again. I don't know if you know what that's like. Like you found treasure on the bottom of the ocean and then dropped your GPS overboard."

I studied his face. Nothing suggested he knew about me and *the other thing*. He gave no hint of eagerness or expectation. No sign of having questions for me.

"That's why you broke in my house? Looking for treasure?"

"Hey, man, I'm sorry about that. It was mostly Mason's idea."

"Who's Mason?"

"A buddy. One of the guys. Mason, Leo and another Alex, only we call him Bones." AJ tapped himself on the chest. "On account of me being Alex, only everyone calls me AJ."

"Mason suggested breaking into my house? For what?"

"He thought you might have more. But that was after we figured out about the sound waves and we knew how to look for it." The look on my face prompted him to explain. "This was after we did some experiments with sound. And we found how—wait, do you know anything about wave form? Sound amplitude? Impedance?"

I shook my head. "High school diploma. Keep it simple."

"We found out that 'it' bends sound waves. Like, if we send a wave out, it bends the wave and alters the audio signal. Um—like a rock guitar player sends his signal through a pedal and changes it. You know?"

"Okay." I didn't know but wasn't going to tell him that. "Do you mean like sonar?"

AJ's face brightened. "That's what we first thought! I mean, we were pretty sure it wasn't going to show up on radar. But I thought sonar might work. The thing was solid, you know? I thought sound would bounce back, but it didn't. We think sound bent around it."

"So how does that help?"

"Because instead of getting a 'ping' like those old submarine movies, we got the absence of a ping. Kinda. We got a void. There's math involved you wouldn't understand."

I didn't care for the condescending tone, but let it go. "How did you learn all that if you lost the piece from the wreck?"

"Oh! Oh, no, man. I found that. This will make you laugh. After all I went through, after I tore that airplane to shreds and dug into the shreds over and over—after all that, it fucking hit me."

He looked up at me expectantly. Andy does that sometimes. She sets me up to prompt her.

"Hit you?"

"Yeah! In the face! I was in there for like the millionth time and it fucking hit me right in the face. Here!" He pointed at the bony corner of one eye socket. "It was just floating there. I walked right into it. It hit me and I grabbed for it and got it. After all my work! I wasted like a month looking for it! It was floating in the air, man! Gravity doesn't affect it one bit!"

I gestured at the glass cube and the fish tank inside. "That's what all this is for? Keeping it?"

AJ shook his head. "No, man. This was for show. Another one of Mason's ideas. Like the vans. The break-in. All that office cubicle shit over there. He's cinematic, Mason. He had us all dressed up like some fucking SEAL team when we broke into your place—and I'm really sorry about that. I really am. All this, though, this was for show, for the investor."

"If you had the piece you found, why did you break into my house?"

"Your accident—that's the origin. I mean, clearly you hit some-thing. Something that beat the shit out of your airplane and should have killed you. That piece—whatever it is—that's part of what you hit. *Has to be.* We got to thinking, what if that's why you didn't die? Like…what if you got your hands on a piece of this, too? And, I don't know, that's how you got down on the ground? What if you had a piece and knew how to use it? Dude! You don't remember *anything*?"

I ignored his question. "How did you expect to find something you can't see? At my house?"

"By that time, we had done all kinds of experiments. It was Leo who played with sound waves. He noticed just the tiniest shift, you know? Nothing you'd hear with your ears, but he found it. Anyway, we got to thinking you might have another piece. Or a bunch of pieces. Or a whole big, I don't know, like platform or shell or something you got into that landed you on the ground. Or maybe you had the whole thing."

"Whole thing? Like, what? An aircraft?"

"Dude! Aircraft! Ship! Have you not thought about this?"

I didn't answer.

"We thought there might be more. Okay, I *really* thought there might be more when we dug up that shit about that guy, Parks."

"Parks?"

"C'mon, man. You know what I'm talking about!"

I shook my head.

"Really? Parks! That guy your wife arrested! The one who got all wonky and went nuts?" He paused for me to confirm, but I gave him a blank stare. "He broke out of jail, he says, by disappearing…"

I said nothing.

"Disappearing! And flying through the air! We figured—I dunno— maybe that was you using this shit. That wasn't you?"

It sure as hell was. I shrugged innocently, although it disturbed me that this kid in Kansas put it together. "Sometimes a conspiracy just isn't a conspiracy. Sometimes a crazy person is just crazy."

"Well, that would figure, since we didn't find anything at your place." AJ stopped and tipped his head slightly. "Say, how did you find me, anyway?"

"I didn't."

He frowned. "Bullshit. Here you are."

"No. I didn't find you. Neither I nor my wife the police detective— and may I emphasize that again for you, just in case you think sharing a beer with me makes us pals—neither of us tracked you down for breaking into our home. No, I was approached by your new worst enemy. The man who double-crossed you."

"Fucking Lewko! That asshole! What did he tell you? Because he's a fucking liar! He fucking stole it! He said we'd be partners. I signed a contract with him, for shit's sake! Of course, they took my copy of that, too!" AJ finished his beer and threw the empty across the room. "You know what he said? He told me to go find a lawyer and try to prove any of it. He told me I would spend a fortune in court and never see a dime in return. He laughed his ass off at me and told me to try and prove something that can't be seen. And now I can't get past his company's phone menu! I shouldn't be surprised. That guy stole everything he ever did! He made a fortune on that Evermore App which he stole— everyone knows he didn't write the original code. I was such a fucking idiot!"

I didn't know the name, but I had heard of Evermore. Andy sometimes shopped through Evermore instead of Amazon. This was not good.

"He sent you here?" AJ asked. "Why would he do that?"

I saw an opening. "Because you told him all about me."

AJ's jaw dropped. "What? No way! I didn't tell him shit about you! God's honest truth."

"Why should I believe you?"

"Dude, if he found you, it's for the same reason we did. Don't trust him, man! He's a fucking liar! I never said word one about you!"

I checked that fear off the list.

"He wants me to work with him," I said. "Consult. I accused him of breaking into my house. He wanted to earn my trust, so he gave you up. That's how I found you here. That and the fact you put the name of your dog on the door." AJ shrugged. I pounded on. "He told me it was you at my house, and if I didn't believe him, come and talk to you first. I guess he wasn't lying."

"You can't trust him, man! Don't trust him!"

I shrugged. "I think that's his point. He's being honest about being dishonest. It kinda works. But you're saying you didn't tell him anything about me?"

AJ's hands went up. "No way! No way!"

"Well, if you didn't, he made the same assumption you did—about the accident—about me having pieces of whatever that is. But it's like you said—he's a liar, so he thinks everyone else lies, too. He thinks I'm holding out on him—and I'm gonna let him continue thinking that. Long story short, he told me all about you and threw you under the bus for the break-in."

"I can't believe he sent you here!" AJ's affect crumbled slightly. I realized the kid had been holding out hope of reconnecting with his double-crossing billionaire investor.

"Yup. He told me all about your dark web Ajax370 thing. How he connected with you." I decided to put another nail in the coffin. "He called it a silly amateur effort."

"Yeah, well...fuck him. He wouldn't know good code if it got rammed up his ass. The dark web is full of crooks, but at least you know they're crooks. Silicon Valley is full of crooks who pretend they're not. My work was anything but amateur! I hooked him, didn't I?"

"I'm curious. What was the deal? Was he really going to invest sight unseen?"

AJ snorted. "Oh, hell no. He talked a great game, but we did a lot of dancing. He insisted on seeing it—so to speak. I didn't want to, but it was put up or shut up. That's what this was all about. Building this cage. Trying to show him we were serious, that we had control. He came here and we let him put his hands on it in the cage. Big mistake. Right then and there he whipped out a contract for twenty million and I fell for it."

I whistled.

"Yeah, well...twenty-four hours later I was looking down the barrel of a gun while a couple guys smashed that and took it. They didn't even try to hide who they were working for. Cuz, who am I going to call? Cops? Lawyers?"

"You said he took everything. That include your research? The sound wave thing?"

"What do you think?" he replied sourly.

"No backups? In the Cloud?"

"We air-gapped this place, dude."

I stood up and placed the beer can, still nearly full, on a nearby desktop.

"So, that's it? You tripped over some treasure and then you and a couple gamer buddies played real-life dress-up black-ops and broke into my house? Then tried to scam a billionaire by pretending to be a bunch of Bond villains with this glass cage?"

AJ stiffened. His voice took on a sharp edge. "Fuck you. We were dead serious, man. Whatever that thing is—it's not a gamechanger. It's *the* gamechanger."

I leaned forward slightly and lowered my voice to a cold tone just above a whisper. "You know you scared me and my wife, kid. People break into your home and you feel violated. You feel like your life has been turned upside down."

AJ flinched and the bravado evaporated. He dropped his gaze to his toes. "Yeah, well...I'm sorry about that. I'm sorry about a lot of things."

I took one last look around, feeling a twinge of what AJ must have felt when the artifact slipped from his fingers.

"I should think," I said. I turned my back and started for the door. "Call your mother, kid."

41

I took the long way around the airport perimeter and walked back to the hotel. Partly to eliminate the possibility that AJ might follow me and watch me vanish, although he appeared to lack the heart for further involvement. He seemed gutted. Lost. I didn't have to try hard to feel a little of the same.

Partly to organize my thoughts and map the next moves.

By the time I approached the Holiday Inn, the eastern sky hinted at dawn and birds fired up territorial claims for the new day. My watch said four-forty. I wondered if it was too early for a phone call. I decided that even if it was, urgency outweighed decorum.

The phone rang long enough that I nearly gave up.

"Hello?" A man's voice, thick, having been dragged out of sleep.

"Hi, Greg!" I took some satisfaction in cheerfully greeting him, remembering a time when he called while Andy and I were amorously engaged.

"Will? Can I assume you know what time it is?"

"To the minute. This is important. What do you know about a Silicon Valley guy by the name of Lewko?"

"Uh, I guess only that he has more money than God, which may be the reason a lot of nerds think he is God. Why?"

The night's work flashed through my mind. The effort had produced good news outweighed by very bad news. Had AJ and his nerd friends been in possession of the artifact, I would have simply slipped in and stolen the item.

But I'd been beaten to the punch. And with that stroke the situation ratcheted to a new and more dangerous level.

I now had no choice but to do the same.

"Greg, you're going to get a call from a mildly crazy, highly paranoid woman who thinks everyone except her is a dumbass, and she may be right. Her name is Lillian."

PART III

42

I closed my eyes. I saw her, standing the way she does, head bowed just slightly. One hand holding the phone to her left ear. Her right hand at her temple with long delicate fingers buried in the thick waves of her auburn hair. She would have her eyes closed. Thinking. Silent.

She pulled in a long breath. I pictured her chest rising. She let the air escape through lips pursed as if for a kiss.

I waited.

"Spiro Lewko," she said again. "You're sure?"

"I'm sure about the Lewko part. Didn't know his first name was Spiro. LeMore thinks it's the guy you're thinking it is. The tech billionaire. Evermore?"

"Oh, Will. This is not good."

I had already received that memo.

"On the upside, the kid swears he didn't mention me. And he definitely didn't have any ideas about me. That's good news, right?"

"Spiro Lewko has unlimited resources."

"Okay. But he's not the government. Maybe it's not such a bad thing. Maybe he can figure out what knocked me out of the sky."

"And what happens when he makes that connection? Suddenly he and his research team will take an unwanted interest in you just like that kid and his pals. The man has his own space program. God, I sound like that UFO nut!"

I squeezed my eyes tighter, wincing at her pronouncement about Lillian. "Uh, yeah. About her. You might not like this but given that we're in agreement that things just got worse, I decided we need reinforcements." I explained to Andy that I called Lillian and gave her LeMore's contact information.

"Will, Greg doesn't know about you! What were you thinking?!"

"That Lillian can be trusted not to tell him, Dee. I told her to reach out and see if between the two of them, they can find out where Spiro Lewko would take a piece of secret stealth technology for analysis. They have insights into the guy's world that we don't."

"'Secret stealth technology'? What's Greg going to think?"

"I told him it might be tied to the reason James got whacked."

"Oh, so we're lying to Greg now?"

This was not going the way I had hoped. "If it gets the job done, then yeah." Andy gave me silence, which condemned my comment more than anything she might have said. I looked for an out. "How's it going there?"

"I don't know."

I waited for more. "What does that mean?"

"It means I don't know," she replied testily. "We put in our request. We've been waiting all morning for someone to process it, or more likely just come back to us and tell us that the records are classified, which is precisely what I expect to happen."

"Is that it, then? End of the line?"

"How would I know?" she snapped. More silence followed. Then I heard her let go of another long breath. "Oh, dammit, Will. I'm sorry. I don't like this. Any of it. I don't like being sent here. I don't like what's happened there. I don't like Lillian and her hare-brained ideas! And this place, it's like swimming in molasses here. Federal or not, FBI or not, we didn't exactly inspire a firestorm of activity by coming here. This place does not have a drive-through! And on top of that, my phone is dead when I'm in the building. They block wireless and Wi-Fi signals. I'm standing in front by the flagpole right now."

"Look," I said. "We're done here. I'll fly up to St. Louis and meet you. Whether you learn anything more or not, maybe Tom will let you off the FBI hook and we can just go home."

"And what? Don't you think we should still try to get that *thing* away from Spiro Lewko?"

"Why bother? Let him have it."

"We can't. Sooner or later he will find a reason to come for you. Or the government will. No. You and Pidge go home. Wait for Greg—and I suppose Lillian—to figure out what we do next."

"Let me pick you up on the way."

"Uh-uh. Whatever we find here, we have one more stop to make. Donaldson wants to go to Lincoln. He set up a meet with somebody who may have information we're not likely to get here. I have to go with him."

Have to?

I wondered if she really did but had the good sense not to suggest that she might be swept up in the chance to work with the FBI, even if it was with an agent she didn't trust. Maybe she simply found more comfort in exercising her law enforcement skills than in the prospect of acting outside the law in pursuit of Lillian's paranoid pronouncements. Bouncing back to square one in the matter of the missing artifact did nothing for our spirits.

"Go home, Will," Andy urged me. "I'll call you when I can."

"LET'S GO," I told Pidge. I stood on the threshold of her Holiday Inn room with the door open.

"Where?"

"Lincoln."

She stopped, turned and looked at me. "Nebraska?"

I didn't like the look on her face. "Why? What's wrong with Lincoln?"

"Dude, have you seen this?" Instead of reaching for her backpack, she grabbed the television remote from the dresser. She stepped back, aimed the remote and turned on the TV, waving me into the room.

The screen opened on the hotel's promotional guide. Pidge clicked in a number and the channel shifted to MSNBC. A talking head filled the left side of the screen. On the right side, various on-the-scene shots showed lines of people, lines of cars and what looked like a protest march in front of a towering government building. The headline across the bottom of the screen read, "Hate Groups Mass for James Funeral."

I looked closer at the shot of what appeared to be demonstrators. Most were young—in their twenties. Many sported tattoos. A few carried flags. Almost all were stoic and silent. All were Caucasian. None were women. The camera swung to another crowd. This group, made up of men and women of all ages with a noticeable racial blend, carried hand-made signs and were anything but silent. A line of police separated the two groups.

"Crap," I said.

"Yeah. Nazis. I hate those fuckers."

43

W e made the 194-mile flight from Wichita to Lincoln in just over fifty minutes with a blazing tailwind that kicked us to a 230-knot groundspeed. A strong low-pressure center marching across central Montana generated a spiral arm of storms stretching south all the way to Texas. Severe thunderstorm warnings, tornado watch boxes and predictions of a frontal line approaching Nebraska added urgency.

The images on Pidge's hotel room TV were disturbing on their own, but knowing Andy navigated a path directly into that shitstorm tied a knot in my gut. I tried to reach her, but her warning about the NMRC blocking wireless signals proved true. Multiple calls went to voicemail. Just before boarding the Navajo on the Wichita ramp, I sent her a text request to call me as soon as she arrived in Lincoln. I didn't tell her I planned to meet her there. That was news best delivered in person.

Andy would argue against a rendezvous, and she would be right. We both work hard to maintain faith. She believes in my decision-making when I'm airborne somewhere in the Midwest and word of powerful storms electrifies the local newscasters. I bite my tongue and trust her judgment when she works into the night as a police officer.

Faith or not, the sight of grim-faced men wearing armbands and standing in a line in front of the Nebraska capitol building turbocharged that need in me now.

44

Radar painted the storm front moving inexorably toward the western border of Nebraska when Pidge landed the Navajo on Runway 17L at Lincoln at just after two p.m. The model on my iPad suggested that the storms would hit sometime after dark. Before Pidge maneuvered off the runway onto the parallel taxiway, I pulled my phone and called the FBO to ask about hangar space for the night. By the time we stopped under the Phillips 66 sign outside Silverhawk Aviation, safe haven for the aircraft had been arranged, along with use of a crew car.

Twenty minutes later we were good to go.

"C'mon!" Pidge grabbed the car keys as I reached for them at the front counter of the FBO. "Let's shake it!"

I grabbed my two bags and hurried after her. I caught up to her making a bee line across the parking lot toward the blue Nissan Sentra the desk clerk had described.

"I'm driving!" she announced. Pidge is too young to rent a car, but that's no barrier for most of the crew cars FBOs keep on hand for visiting pilots.

"Fine. Just take me around to the main terminal. I'll wait there for Andy."

She used the fob to unlock the car and pop the trunk. She dropped her backpack inside, then turned expectantly to me.

"What?"

"So, let me see if I have this right," she said. "You're going to hang around the terminal for the next six to nine hours, then meet your police detective wife who is on a case and in the company of the FBI, and you're going to…what? Say, 'Hi, honey! What's for dinner?' when she walks into the terminal?"

"Uh, yeah. Maybe not like that, but…"

Pidge grabbed my bags, pulled them out of my hands and threw them in the trunk. "Have you met the woman? Jesus, Stewart, get in the fucking car!"

She slammed the trunk and danced around the fender for the driver's door. I gave it a moment, then slid into the passenger's seat and looked at her suspiciously. Something buzzed in her bonnet.

"Where are we going?"

She glanced at me long enough to expose the mischief sparkling in her blue eyes, then stabbed the push-button start.

"This is as close as we're gonna get," she declared. She pulled an abrupt U-turn in front of a car following close behind us. The driver didn't appreciate the maneuver and laid on his horn. Steering one-handed, Pidge flipped him off and wheeled into an open angle parking space on South 14th Street, two blocks from the Marriott Cornhusker Hotel. I chose the Cornhusker during the drive from the airport when she commanded me to do a Google search for a hotel near the city center. By the time we parked, I had two rooms reserved.

"C'mon!" She hopped out of the car. "We walk from here."

"To the hotel?"

"No, man! Let's go see this Nazi circle jerk!" She pointed south, toward the towering state capitol building two blocks away. Between us and the capitol square, the street had been barricaded. A line of white and orange sawhorses and a squad car with lights flashing occupied the intersection. From a glance at the Google map of Lincoln's perfect street grid, I deduced that the police had placed a one-block buffer around the capitol building.

"What? No. I don't want to go anywhere near those idiots."

"Oh, bullshit. C'mon."

"Pidge, it's not safe."

She stopped and planted her hands on her hips, full of judgment. "Don't make me call you the name of a lady part, Stewart. Besides, we might have a chance to get a little…creative."

"Oh, no. We're not doing anything to antagonize them. I mean it."

"Me? An innocent little girl like me? Antagonize those big strong manly men?"

"Said Pandora." I shook my head. She didn't move. I had just enough time to wonder what the choice of women in my life was doing to my backbone before I said, "Fine. Open the trunk. I want something."

She popped the trunk with the remote. I dug into my bag and found a power unit and propeller combination. I slipped both into the hip pocket of my jeans, then caught Pidge looking at the cylindrical bulge with a grin.

"Shut up," I told her.

We set off down the sidewalk and found ourselves joining other pedestrians headed toward the police barricades. The perimeter had been established to halt vehicles, but foot traffic flowed through easily. I glanced at the officer standing beside his parked cruiser. His eyes jumped from pedestrian to pedestrian, studying, searching, reading faces and posture for trouble. The radio attached to his tunic above his vest crackled, broadcasting codes and urgent jargon.

Beyond the checkpoint, the streets became sidewalks. People using both lanes converged on the capital square from all directions. The crowd thickened. Noise boiled and echoed off the buildings around. We followed the flow. I heard chanting, the bass beat of indistinguishable music, and random shouts. If I had not known the cause of the commotion, I would have taken this for a street festival or outdoor concert.

The Nebraska State Capitol can't be missed. The limestone tower, centered on a three-story square building the size of a city block, rises four hundred feet above the city around it. A park-like grounds takes up four city blocks around the statehouse building, with a sidewalk bordering the entire space. From forty miles away on the landing approach I had seen the proud structure. The design suggested an early twentieth century New York skyscraper. Approaching it now, its dominance over the city grew more impressive.

We pressed into a crowd lining the sidewalk across the street from the capitol grounds. I caught my first glimpse of the scene.

Stationed at thirty- to forty-foot intervals on the sidewalk bordering the capitol grounds, young men stood at attention holding large flags in honor guard fashion. More young men spaced themselves evenly between the flagbearers. Most wore sunglasses, denying eye contact. Many wore ball caps. Some wore t-shirts proudly displaying their deep patriotism and deeper racist beliefs. A few held canes at their sides, though I gave no credence to the thought that they were medically necessary.

The flags presented a mongrel mix of symbolism. I recognized the Confederate standard from the American Civil War. One or two mimicked the banner of Nazi Germany, but the swastika appeared to have been dropped in favor of some new secret glyph. An attempt at rebranding. Others were mysterious to me. The dominant color combinations were red and white with black accents.

The line of avowed racists stretched the length of the north perimeter of the capitol square, then continued at right angles down both side streets. They lacked the numbers to surround the capitol. The lines ended midway down each side of the capitol square. I estimated sixty to seventy sons of Adolf.

In contrast, the crowd opposing this bald expression of hate swelled to enormous numbers in both directions, down the side streets and well into the park-like fountain plaza across the street from the capitol building. Lincoln had turned out to let the world know that the men with flags didn't represent their city.

On the capitol side of the street, a cluster of men formed directly in front of the broad steps that ascended to the capitol building. One of the men held a megaphone and spoke fervently to the crowd filling the capitol fountain plaza on the north side of the street. Behind the speaker, two men propped up a giant image, easily four by eight feet, of Josiah James in one of his self-aggrandizing poses. The speaker frequently gestured passionately at the image. His eulogy had no chance. His oration was both distorted by the megaphone and easily drowned out by his unfriendly audience.

The crowd facing down this celebration of racism ran riot with color, skin and otherwise. Rainbow flags and streamers waved over people's heads. American flags waved. People sported colorful hats and wild costumes. In a few spots, people stepped off the curb and shouted at the stone-faced racists. In the plaza directly across from the men with the Josiah James portrait, dozens danced to music from a source near the central fountain. The crowd easily outnumbered the James gang by ten to one.

Another group also outnumbered the demonstrators. Police in riot gear formed a line down the center of the street between the two camps. The officers alternately faced both groups. The city of Lincoln had clearly decided that this would not become another Charlottesville. The police carried rifles, shotguns, rubber pellet guns, batons and plastic shields. Their protective border stretched out of sight, interspersed with police vehicles. A large, military-style vehicle with police markings anchored the corner of the capitol square. Within the square itself, a line of police officers guarded the entrance to the government building.

The demonstrators on the capitol property posed rigidly. The crowd opposing them flexed and shifted. Those who ventured too far into the neutral street were quickly ordered back by the police.

"Will!" Pidge shouted at me. "Check it out!" She pointed to the curb between the fountain and the capitol steps, hopping up and down to see over the heads around us. "That's fucking awesome!"

I looked in the direction she indicated and found the source of the music. A polka band had set up. They played loudly, contributing joyfully to the noise that drowned out the memorial oration. Bodies bobbed all around the band, dancing energetically. In this one spot, the police were less emphatic about enforcing the sidewalk limit. Dancers hopped and twirled in the street.

Bobbing to the music in the center of the street dance, someone wore a huge cardboard box costume in white, green and blue, like a college mascot if a college mascot were an over-the-counter medicine.

Gas-X. The product name ran across the top of the box in 2-foot letters.

I laughed, thinking, *Atta boy, Benny!*

News crews hovered and focused cameras on the box from all angles. The coverage seemed to delight the milling crowd who cheered on the *Gas-X* box as it hopped in polka time.

Pidge pushed her way through the crowd. I struggled to keep up. We moved closer to the epicenter. I wasn't sure what she intended but felt a need to stay close and wove through the crowd after her. She worried me. For the most part, the hate message intended by the James Nation was met with humor and music. A few in the crowd shouted and swore at the men on the other side. The James Nation standing vigil maintained rigid discipline. But it would only take one spark to break the peace.

Pidge stopped at the edge of the fountain plaza. We watched the dancers hop and spin. A few women wore skirts that flared as they whirled. Children imitated the dancers.

As the band's latest number wound down, the air broke with the sound of police whistles. I glanced at the cops, who turned their attention to the demonstrators on the capitol grounds. From the cluster at the center near Josiah James's giant head, several men wearing arm bands stepped forward. They blew whistles and waved their arms. From both directions, the ranks of the demonstrators closed in military fashion. What had been a sparse line stretching halfway around the capitol square now tightened until the rank of young men stood shoulder to shoulder on the north perimeter.

A hush descended on the crowd.

The whistles blew again, this time four shorts. A signal.

The flags rose and dipped. This had been rehearsed. As one, the demonstrators shouted.

"WE WON'T BE REPLACED!"

Compression made the ranks smaller, yet more ominous.

"WE WON'T BE REPLACED!"

A nervous tension rippled through the opposition crowd. People stepped back as if pushed.

"WE WON'T BE REPLACED!"

The menacing chorus dominated the street. Police officers lining the center of the street turned and faced the chanting men. Camera crews pushed forward seeking new angles. The lenses fixed almost exclusively on the demonstrators.

Pidge jabbed me in the ribs.

"I got an idea!" she shouted.

"WE WON'T BE REPLACED!"

She held up her hand, signaling me to stand fast, then darted away. I watched her short blonde hair bob in the crowd for a moment, then slip out of my sight.

Dammit, Pidge! I thought about bolting after her but decided leaving my spot was likely to have us chasing our tails in the crowd.

"WE WON'T BE REPLACED!"

A palpable mood change swept the crowd. People who had been spirited moments ago, facing down hate with color and energy, now shied away from the curb. A sense of trouble brewing flowed through the crowd like blood pulsing in a vein.

The police sensed it, too. As one, they adopted an alert stance, pulling batons from their belts and holding them at the ready.

"WE WON'T BE REPLACED!" A harsh drum joined the chanting, distorted as it strained whatever portable speaker system transmitted the sound.

I touched recent memories that stung like open wounds. Andy's pain and loss over the death of Mike Mackiejewski. Lane Franklin's agony when white supremacist hatred triggered the death of first adolescent love right before her eyes. Corey Braddock, bleeding in the light of a star.

My tension heightened, fueled by a brew of worry and anger.

The men across the street hurled their chant from mouths baring teeth. Veins stood out on their necks, at their temples. Fists rose into the air. Spittle flew with the words. The citizens of Lincoln shrank from the sound. The chanters grew more strident, louder.

"WE WON'T BE REPLACED!"

Someone grabbed my arm.

Pidge pulled me backward, away from the fountain plaza crowd. She led me out of the watching crowd to a building that bordered the fountain plaza. She pulled me into a narrow doorway.

"Here!" She pushed something into my hands. I looked at it.

"What do you want me to do with this?"

She flared her eyes at me. "What the fuck do you think?! Go and do your thing!"

"Pidge, no! That's—" I looked at what she had given me. "—no! I can't use this *and* hide it. They'll see it coming."

"I'll create a distraction." She glanced both ways. "Now! Nobody's looking! Go light 'em up!"

She made a spinning gesture with her hands that said, 'Get on with it!' and then darted back into the crowd.

I looked at the plastic Bic lighter in my hand. For a moment I contemplated tossing it.

"WE WON'T BE REPLACED!"

Like a bad accident, the scene across the street tugged at my attention. The chanting faces, the straining necks and bulging veins leaped straight out of Corey Braddock's skillful illustrations, portrayed perfectly on the pages of the graphic novel he produced as an offering of love for Lane Franklin. His illustrations came to life on the Lincoln capitol square.

"WE WON'T BE REPLACED!"

I looked around. The crowd stood tensely transfixed by the rage billowing from the capitol square.

"WE WON'T BE REPLACED!"

I thought about Lane Franklin who saw only love and life in skin, not color. I thought about the perfectly rendered Lane Franklin in Corey Braddock's graphic novel. A fighter.

She would fight these fools.

"WE WON'T BE REPLACED!"

Really, assholes? Nothing would make me happier.

I glanced at the area around the narrow doorway to see if anyone had their eyes on me. All eyes locked on the chanters.

I examined Pidge's impromptu weapon.

"Oh, what the hell!" I closed my fist around the lighter.

Fwooomp! I vanished.

The lighter vanished with me, but I didn't think it wise to ignite it from within *the other thing*. Using the lighter required making it reappear.

"Distraction..." I muttered. Pidge better come through, or else someone was about to see a cheap plastic lighter floating in the street.

I pulled the power unit and prop from my hip pocket. The prop snapped easily into place. I aimed the unit up and pushed the control slide. A growl quickly turned to a low whine.

I launched from the recessed doorway.

The building behind me fell away, I quickly ascended into sunlight. The crowd on the fountain plaza spread below me. Rabid chanting dominated the air all around me. Disorganized efforts to counter-chant sporadically erupted from the opposing crowd.

"WE WON'T BE REPLACED!"

"Yes, you will!"

Anger contorted faces on both sides of the street. In the center, police officers tightened their line. Four out of five officers faced the chanters, but heads turned to monitor both sides. Senior officers moved quickly up and down the ranks of the police in the street, issuing commands and urging calm. Despite their efforts, the air became explosive.

I crossed over the police line and dove into the space between the riot cops and the chanting men. A short cruise took me to the end of the James demonstrators. I turned and lined up on the row of flags hanging at forty-five-degree angles over the street.

I reversed power to slow myself to a crawl and vectored myself toward the first of the flags. Once stabilized, I jammed my power unit into my back pocket and fingered the unseen lighter into position. Dropping it from one hand to the other would break it free, make it visible and ready to use. I looked for Pidge. If something didn't change soon, this wasn't going to work. I waited.

"WE WON'T BE—!"

In mid-chant, the polka band struck a series of notes. Familiar notes. Percussive driving notes, immediately recognizable. I had no idea what the title was, if there was a title. But I recognized the pounding beat instantly. The unmistakable drum rift and brassy bellow of a burlesque strip tease.

I glanced in the direction of the fountain plaza. Pidge broke through the crowd at the curb. She took three strutting steps forward as if she had hatched a mad plan to crash the police line as a runway model. She stopped suddenly, cocked her hips suggestively and grabbed the bottom of her t-shirt. In one swift stroke she pulled it over her head. For a moment I thought she had decided to flash the crowd, but she wore a bright pink bra which glowed fluorescent in the sunlight. She spun her t-shirt in a circle over her head.

She began to bump and grind to the strip tease beat. The crowd behind her, which had lost much of its energy at the start of the intimidating chant, whooped and hollered in support of the brazen girl in the street.

Pidge strutted to the thumping strip tease percussion, twirling her shirt, wiggling and grinding. She moved up and down the line provocatively as the band continued pounding out the brassy song. Whoops and cheers rippled outward from the center and soon became a tidal wave of noise competing with the chanting from across the street.

I looked at the young men. They were helpless; their eyes locked on the girl. A few hesitated, losing the meter and momentum of their chant. Pidge's gyrations tugged at their attention and their hormones and weakened their wall of sound.

Jesus Christ, Pidge! Dumbfounded young racists stared at her. And she knew it. She thrust her hips at them, turned and swung her cute butt at them, wiggled herself and strutted for them. She blew them kisses. She wiggled her fingers at them, teasing and inviting them to come over. The polka band bellowed the bawdy tune and filled the street with its grinding beat.

I caught myself staring at Pidge, then jarred my attention loose. I needed to move.

I floated closer to the line, close enough to hear individual voices trying to sustain the chant, which had been largely drowned out.

Time to do this.

I cupped one hand under the lighter and released. It snapped into view. I caught it and quickly thumbed the striker. A tiny jet of flame appeared. The lighter floating alone in the air—as small as it was—looked gigantic and obvious to me. I gave the tiny gap between lighter and flame a moment's thought, then impulsively closed my hands around the lighter. An electric snap bit my palms. The lighter vanished, but the flame remained, fed by the gas jet and floating in the air above the vanished plastic vessel.

Much better!

I pulled the power unit from my pocket and maneuvered to the nearest flag. The floating flame was lost to the sight of the young men, unable to pull their eyes off Pidge.

I pushed the flame directly under the bottom seam of a black, white and red flag. In an instant, combustion bit into the fabric. The power unit pulled me forward to the next flag. Then the next. At each, the flame bit hungrily into the flag. The flag bearers' eyes, drawn to Pidge, failed to catch the yellow flicker in the sunlight.

Three. Four. Five. I held the lighter in my left hand and worked my power unit with my right. God bless these idiots for standing in a rigid line.

I misjudged my speed and skipped a flag. Lit up number six, then seven. A shout broke the air behind me.

Fire!

Eight. Skipped another. Nine. Only a few more.

Shouting in the flag line killed the already weakened chant. I glanced back and saw flames rise and swirl when the first of the flags became engulfed. The second and third quickly ignited. Flagbearers mistakenly tried to extinguish the burning flags by waving them. The flames whipped through the air and devoured the banners. Flaming pieces broke away and fluttered like aimless bats.

Confusion broke the line. Flagbearers awoke from the lock Pidge had clamped on their attention to stare incredulously at their burning flags. One man grabbed the pole from his transfixed neighbor and threw it down in the street. He stomped on the Confederate banner. He hopped and jumped, but the flammable nylon defeated him—not before his futile dance drew cheers from the crowd. News crews rushed to get the shot.

Chaos broke the ranks. Burning flags fluttered then fell into the street, onto the grass. More men tried stomping, eliciting more cheers. Others stood by clueless. The police remained at the center of the street, poised for trouble. The man with the megaphone who had been leading the chant now screamed at the police to bring fire extinguishers. None of the cops moved.

A flagbearer holding the flag I skipped threw his banner into the street as if it too had caught fire. Another flag, fully engulfed, was thrown on top of the untouched flag, drawing it into the merry bonfire.

Two for one, I thought happily.

The men holding the few untouched flags now retreated onto the grass, away from the flames. They furled their flags and studied them, searching for spontaneous combustion. I found the part of valor that is discretion and elected not to pursue them.

But there was one more move to be made.

Behind me, the opposition crowd found new momentum. I caught a glimpse of Pidge, urged on by a cheering, clapping crowd. She joined their outcry, howling and spinning her shirt above her head. Elsewhere in the lineup, another girl jumped forward and pulled off her shirt, mimicking Pidge's moves. Then another, this one either uninhibited or simply forgetting that she didn't wear a bra.

In the chaos among the demonstrators, the men holding the Josiah James portrait stood their ground, sending confused glances in all directions, as if they expected attack. I aimed lower, almost scraping my knees on the sidewalk as I approached the cardboard-backed poster. I had to lay the lighter flat on the concrete at the bottom edge of the cardboard to get the flame to lick the image. The men began to move backward. For a second, I thought they had seen the flame and might run. Instead, they hesitated, confused and transfixed by the fires around them, uncertain whether to stand fast or bolt. I held the flame steady. The poster suddenly heaved out of my reach when they abruptly stepped back, retreating from the chaos.

I decided to clear out. Too much longer in this position, and someone was going to trip over me.

I didn't bother with the power unit. Instead I kicked the ground and shot upward. I rose to a safe thirty or forty feet and released the trigger on the lighter. The flame winked out.

I considered hurling the lighter into the crowd, but instead slipped it into my pocket. No sense leaving evidence. I aimed the power unit for the sky and pushed the slide. The unit hummed then whined. I rose alongside sparks and fluttering ash.

Below me, the men had stopped chanting their racist mantra and fractured into directionless clusters. Some of them hurled curses at the crowd across the street. Some taunted, inviting a fight. Others sprinted away across the grass. A few darted forward on the attack. Before reaching the first lane line, police closed in and drove them to the ground. Bold compatriots hinted at joining the fray, but a dozen officers surrounded the men on the ground and false secondary bravery evaporated.

Police advanced and began detaining the flagbearers. Arms were clasped, hands joined, and handcuffs applied. It was impossible to hear what the officers were saying but I imagined it had something to do with an unlawful bonfire on public grounds. Or perhaps burning without a permit. Cheers from the opposition crowd rewarded the officers for their effort.

On the street below, a group had formed and lifted Pidge to their shoulders, still lurching and heaving to the strip tease music. She laughed and twirled her shirt over her head.

On the grass of the capitol grounds, the men holding up the James photo staggered away. I watched for a moment, and my faith in karma was restored as flames gnawed the bottom of the giant poster, quickly rising and licking at Josiah James' silly statuesque pose. The poster blackened and curled, but the men holding it were loath to let it go until the flames reached for their hands. They dropped it and backed away. One man half-heartedly kicked and stomped at the fire, but wisely decided it was too much for his rubber-soled athletic shoes. The man that had been speaking into the megaphone dropped his instrument and raced to where the portrait burned on the concrete. Uttering a feral cry, he fell to his knees and began slapping at the flames with his bare hands. The effort only seemed to spread the blaze. His companions pulled him away.

The portrait peeled and bubbled. The burning poster delivered a satisfying private image to me.

Josiah James burning in Hell.

45

I lost Pidge.

Last I saw her, she floated on the shoulders of an adoring mob. She rode in glory in her short denim shorts and gaudy pink bra, gyrating to a beat from the polka band.

I felt oddly energized, hovering above the crowded street. I'd never done this before, not in daylight, not directly above so many. My flying has been largely private, secretive. Often conducted at night. I felt buoyed by the music and celebration, and by the release of tension. Energy from the crowd rose palpably around me.

I lingered and enjoyed the drone's-eye view. Even if I wanted to land, my options had narrowed considerably. People milling the streets below me eliminated any notion of reappearing in the recessed doorway —or anywhere else near the capitol square.

Remnants of the James Nation remained. A core group surrounded the ashes of the memorial portrait. They huddled and argued, eying the street crowd nervously. One of the men pointed at retreating comrades and called after them. A few stopped, confused. Others ignored him and called it a day.

I drifted closer, although I had no hope of picking up their conversation over the music and advancing crowd.

One man stepped away for a moment, pulled a phone from his

pocket and took a call. He held his free hand up against his other ear. He nodded quickly in response to the caller.

He looked familiar. Large. Muscle-bound. No neck. Hair cut close around three sides with a scruffy patch on top. He wore a white t-shirt with a broad Confederate flag across his chest, but I readily pictured him in black tactical attire.

Josiah James Security.

I'd seen him first at the rally, then again at the shooting. He had a square, chiseled face with dark, deep-set eyes.

He was the goon that grabbed Andy's gun.

If his street racist resumé wasn't enough, the memory of him putting his hands on my wife cemented my dislike. I wondered how he'd feel if his pants caught fire. I tapped my hip pocket to reaffirm that I still had the lighter.

His phone call ended. He pocketed the phone, turned to the still-arguing cluster and poked two fingers into his mouth. He blew a power-ful, shrill whistle. All heads turned in his direction. He performed a twirling motion with one hand and pointed away from the front line.

Retreat.

Now we know who's calling the shots here, I thought.

The group did not question. They broke up, shouting out to their followers. Like NCOs corralling foot soldiers, they waved for the young men under their command to move out.

Linebacker watched the action for a moment. Then he did some-thing that raised the hair at the back of my neck.

He pulled out his phone and took a few steps forward, aiming the phone at the crowd moving across the street toward the capitol. At the crowd still bouncing and cheering, carrying a bold blonde girl on their shoulders. At Pidge.

He took the shot, examined the result, adjusted the zoom and took another. Then he stowed his phone and spun to follow his retreating troops.

I watched Linebacker march away across the broad lawn. I thought about following him to his vehicle, wherever that might be. Perhaps to shoot photos. Get his license plate number. Information for Andy to —*what? Investigate? Arrest him?*

I didn't need my wife's voice in my head to point out the futility in that plan, but she chimed in nonetheless.

What do you want me to do with these? So, he's a shot-caller, so what? These hate groups are full of Gruppenfuhrers and Oberleutnants and whatever they call themselves. Let it go.

Let it go.

I tried to do just that as he and his comrades hiked away across summer-green grass.

Having no option to reappear on the street below, I aimed my propulsion unit in the general direction of the angle-parked crew car. If there were any chance of a rendezvous with Pidge, it would be there.

In less than a minute, I glided over the spot, trying to remember the color and make of the vehicle we had driven. After settling on a likely suspect, I waited, pulsing the power unit occasionally to maintain position, hoping Pidge might appear. She had the keys.

After what felt like ten minutes, I developed an itch to access my phone. To call her.

She's with a thousand new friends. Let her have her fun.

I gave her another five minutes. When she didn't show, I headed for the hotel. The position of the sun suggested late afternoon. A cold drink and something to eat seemed like proper reward for a good day's work.

On reaching the hotel I flew a circuit looking for a discreet place to reappear. I selected the upper deck of the adjoining parking garage and came to a smooth landing between two parked minivans.

My watch said four-forty.

My phone said I had one missed call from Andy and one text message.

Boarding Delta to Lincoln. Call you from Atlanta. LuvU!

"Atlanta? Who's the damned pilot? Wrong-Way Corrigan?" I muttered. I get the whole airline hub system, but in my air charter world, A simply goes to B.

Sans luggage, I checked in and obtained a room key. Instead of going to the room, I found an empty booth by a street-side window in the hotel's Miller Time Pub & Grill. The cheery server took my order and hurried away to fetch a Corona and a cheeseburger while I fingered my phone. I double-checked the time stamp on Andy's message, then scrolled through Delta's website and found the likely suspect. Flight 1782 departing Atlanta—arriving at Lincoln Airport at 7:22 p.m.

I tapped the screen and launched a call to Pidge that rang its way to voicemail, which she never checks. I switched to text and thumbed out a message. *At the hotel. Where R U?*

Not that I expected a response. Pidge is a two-hundred pound exhibitionist packed in a ninety-pound girl. I might not hear from her for the remainder of the day.

Suddenly the thought made me worry.

Let it go. She can take care of herself.

The server arrived with refreshment and promised the burger would follow in short order. The first slug of Corona went down smoothly and reminded me I hadn't eaten all day.

My phone vibrated. Pidge. The degree of relief I felt surprised me.

Nice bonfire. Big party. What's beer cutoff?

Pidge might party like the twenty-three-year-old she is, but she abides by the FAA's mandatory eight-hour interval between bottle and throttle, even if she might clock it down to the minute.

Andy had earlier mentioned meeting with someone tonight. I might not see her until late in the evening. She'd be tired and looking for rest, and therefore delighted that I was here to greet her with a room all squared away (I told myself).

FBI can find his own damned hotel.

Whatever business she still had with Donaldson might wrap up tonight. Maybe that would be the end of it. I'm an optimist. Once done with Donaldson, James and the FBI, Andy and I would be free to go home, regroup and deal with our other pending crisis. Perhaps by then, Greg and Lillian might have meaningful information to share.

So, what to tell Pidge? At the earliest, we might fly out in the morning. More likely, the afternoon. And even then, I saw no reason for her to act as pilot with me on board. It would be easy to turn her loose to party all night.

The disturbing image of Linebacker shooting photos of her came to mind.

I tapped the screen.

Come to the hotel. Need my bag. Car keys.

A full ten minutes passed without answer. I finished half the Corona before the phone vibrated again.

Pub crawl! Sucks to be U! ;)

Not helpful. I thumbed the screen.

Andy arriving tonight. Need the car.

My dinner arrived. Three bites in, the phone vibrated yet again.

Screw you. Uber.

Still not helpful.

I thumbed the screen again, something I'm not good at.

B careful. Those shitheads were watching you.

Send.

The phone sat and stared at me, taking Pidge's side, defiant. I worked on the burger and the Corona and tried hard to trust that she would be fine. Just as the server came to ask how everything was tasting, the phone vibrated again.

Pidge.

Boy were they ever!

46

"Did you see this girl?"

The young server caught me staring out the window. I glanced up and read her name on a plastic badge above her left breast. Raejean. She pointed at the flatscreen above the bar. On the left half of a split screen, Pidge danced in the street. On the right half, the James Nation memorial line fractured into chaos as flags went up in flames.

The subhead beneath the news footage said, *Hot Girl Ignites Demonstration.*

"How on earth did she do that?" Raejean asked with genuine wonder—she seemed barely out of her teens and utterly guileless.

"Do what?"

"Get those flags to catch fire."

I looked up at her. She stared at the screen like a child looking at a department store Santa Claus. Believing.

"Um, I doubt she had anything to do with it."

"No!" Raejean pointed again. "Look at that. They got it on video!"

I blinked. On one hand, this young woman clearly lacked a grasp of simple physics. On the other hand, well, my part in the equation brokered no explanation.

I decided to throw in with the local news channel which had no qualms about reporting fantasy. "Maybe she used her mind."

"She sure used *something!*" she said with a wiggle of her hips and a smile. "Another beer?"

An automatic Yes nearly slipped from my lips before I stopped myself.

Believing.

The young woman standing beside me believed—or at the very least, didn't question—that Pidge lit up those flags.

Shit.

"Uh, no thanks. Just the check."

Maybe Raejean wasn't the brightest bulb. Maybe it wasn't her fault. Maybe her education had been so focused on passing standardized tests that it forgot to teach her how to think, but surely any reasoning human would know that nothing a street dancer did, no matter how provocative, generated combustion. Television news might play up the *Hot Girl* angle because it powers their never-ending quest for ratings numbers, but if challenged, even they would surely admit the headline had been tongue in cheek.

Yet this girl *believed* Pidge had something to do with the fires. At the very least, she did not ask the next question.

I wondered who else watched this without asking the next question.

Pidge put on her show for a chorus line of True Believers. Believers in the supremacy of light pigmentation. Believers in a ridiculous rash of conspiracy theories doled out in streaming bursts by an internet con artist. Believers in racist, xenophobic tweets. Believers who don't ask *the next question.*

Shit. My pulse picked up speed.

Even if James's idiot followers didn't actually believe that Pidge lit their flags on fire with her hips, they wouldn't be stopped from believing she was responsible.

I pulled three singles from my wallet and dropped them on the table, slid out of the booth and pulled my room key from my pocket. Halfway out of the pub, I caught Raejean's eye and waved the key at her.

"Room three eighteen," I called out. "Gotta go! Charge it for me, okay?"

If she wanted to protest or get my signature, she wasn't fast enough.

I ducked out of the restaurant, through the lobby and hit the street, pulling my phone as I walked. Traffic remained heavy, perhaps as a result of the closed-off streets around the capitol. Foot traffic was heavy, too. People streamed toward the capitol area. In the distance, I heard live music.

I dialed Pidge. Her voice joined the line after eight rings. *"Seriously? Voicemail? Don't bother. Text me."*

Dammit.

The low-angle afternoon sun overpowered my screen. I ducked around the corner to hold the phone in shade.

Pidge would be at the epicenter of a crowd. That didn't necessarily make me feel better. In a crowd, just about anyone might get close to her.

I tapped out four numerals, the transponder code for Emergency.

"She's not gonna like this," I told myself. I glanced at my watch. I had less than two hours before I needed to get to the airport to meet Andy.

I hit send, pocketed the phone and set off down the street.

47

The street festival had grown. Except for smudges on the sidewalk between the capitol and the fountain plaza, all signs of the James Nation were gone. The police anti-riot line had dissolved. Alone and in pairs, officers still wearing heavy tactical gear strolled among the crowd. Half a dozen officers remained on sentry duty at the entrance to the capitol building.

I followed a route that first took me back to the crew car, hoping I would find it gone (and subsequently valet parked at the hotel). It remained angle parked against a meter that had no time. I dumped the few coins I had in the meter and moved on.

Retracing our original steps, I emerged from a cross street facing the capitol square. To my left, the polka band continued their impromptu dance festival on the fountain plaza. In both directions, citizens strolled the street. People wandered the lawn of the capitol. Families and couples spread blankets to catch the sun.

I checked the buildings facing the capitol square. None of them suggested a pub or bar. No sign of telltale neon.

I veered left for the fountain plaza and wove through the mixed crowd, marveling at the demographics represented. The legion chanting in favor of a homogenous white society were definitely barking up the wrong tree. Even more amazing, men and women pushed strollers adorned with American flags as if attending a Fourth of July Parade. Bringing a child to the scene of potential violence seemed like a very bad idea.

I found the *Gas-X* box dancing in the plaza, hand in hand with a circle of children. Sight of it answered my question. Perhaps this win belonged to people with children, people with vision and hope.

I spotted and angled toward the nearest police officer, catching his attention with direct eye contact. Young, athletic and a lot like Mike, he gave me a quick once-over as I approached.

"Have you seen that girl. The one who did the street dance." I held my hand out, palm down, to mark Pidge's height. The officer instantly understood.

"What's your interest in the young lady?" I liked his automatic instinct to protect Pidge.

I slowly, a little exaggeratedly, pulled out my wallet and slipped my pilot's license out of the sleeve. "My name is Will Stewart. Chief Pilot for Essex Air Service. Pidge—Miss Page—works for me. She's a pilot." I got the look. "Yeah, I know. But she's the best there is. We're here on an air charter. We just happened to catch this show today and she got a little…enthusiastic."

He lifted his eyebrows, registering the understatement.

"Anyway, we got separated. Rather, she got carried away—literally. I hoped you might know which direction they went."

He handed back my license and I stowed it.

"She really a pilot?" he asked, letting a hint of smile lift the corners of his mouth.

"Airline Transport Rating. She can fly the pants off anybody I ever met. And all the ones I haven't. I need to catch up with her. We might have to fly out tonight. I might, that is. She may not be legal at this point. She texted me that her new friends were taking her on a pub crawl."

"No pubs around here. We've got churches." He pointed at the Catholic Church and school flanking the plaza. The school had provided me with the recessed doorway. "You'd want to head up that way. Take K. Go right on 11th. You've got The Old Pub, The Hot Mess, Thirsty Bar Lincoln. And over at the Cornhusker Hotel, there's the Miller Time."

Back the way I'd come. Figures.

"Thanks," I said. "I appreciate it."

"Hey." He stopped me. "Your friend know anything about how those fires started?"

I flipped up a shrug, probably a little too enthusiastically. "I don't know how she would. From where I stood, she was dancing in the street."

"Where were you standing?"

"Sidewalk," I said. "Over there." I pointed in the direction of the sidewalk where Pidge first announced her idea, hoping the element of truth would sell the lie. If it had been Andy doing the interrogating, I would have been toast.

This young officer looked me over, then nodded. "You stay safe."

"I will."

"And tell your friend…thanks. Unofficially, of course."

"I'm sure she was happy to help. Thank you."

I walked away, painfully and ludicrously aware of my pace, trying not to hurry, trying to look casual without looking like someone trying to look casual. I simply ended up feeling awkward for about twenty paces.

If there was ever a time I wanted to vanish and traverse the route the way the crow flies, this was it. Instead, the busy streets and sidewalks presented a constant stream of faces, all of them looking at me. It was infectious. People smiled at strangers. The absence of the James demonstrators felt good, the way the absence of pain feels like relief. More than a few people threw me a "Hello" as I wove through bodies on the sidewalk beside K street.

The police cordon around the capitol remained in place. A ring of two streets around the square prohibited vehicle traffic. Beyond that, traffic grew heavy. Vehicles looked for parking so their occupants could join the spectacle unfolding at the capitol. The memorial for a xenophobe turned into a block party for diversity. Remembering the hint of despair I felt when I watched the sad James faithful line up to hear their hero at the Coliseum in Des Moines, this reversal cheered me.

Turning right on 11th Street as instructed, I headed north. Ahead, in front of several street-side establishments, patrons spilled out of limited bar space onto the sidewalk and into the parking lanes. Each corner held a small throng waiting for traffic light permission to cross.

Finding Pidge wouldn't be easy, but the revelers on the sidewalks handed me a hint.

The Old Pub came up first on the right. Patrons holding drinks filled the sidewalk and spilled into the alley alongside the rectangular building. The bar had the look of a place ordinarily that belonged to a handful of regulars. It probably hadn't seen a crowd like this…ever.

"Hey, is that girl here? The one that did the street dance?" I asked the first person who accepted my eye contact.

"Who?"

"Never mind." I moved on and tried again. This time I not only got a firm "No," but the young woman pointed up the street.

"She was. That whole bunch went up to Thirsty Bar, I think."

"You're sure she was with them?"

"Yeah! That girl who did the strip tease? Yeah, she went up that way with a whole big group. Did you see her? Amazing!"

I thanked her and angled into the street between parked cars. I jogged toward the human cluster in the next block. Almost in traffic, I made much better time than on the busy sidewalk.

The sign said Thirsty Sports Bar. The shotgun shack layout, long and narrow at mid-block, abutted an alley that doubled as a path for power lines. Here again, the crowd spilled out the front doors onto the sidewalk, into the alley and into the angle parking lanes. A banner across the sidewalk awning offered riches at Keno.

I looked for an opening and jogged across the street on an angle, then crossed against the light at L Street. I dropped out of the jog because people started looking at me. *What's the hurry, pal?*

For the second time in an hour, I tried to look casual as I walked, and realized it only made me look awkward and tense.

As I approached the bar, a white pickup on a jacked suspension wheeled into an open angle spot on the other side of the street. Horns blared when the pickup driver scooted into the spot, cutting off another driver coming from the opposite direction. I heard shouts, then an engine rev as the offended driver expressed himself with a squeaky peel-out. I glanced at the initial offender who stepped out of his pickup with a fist high and his third finger higher.

Linebacker.

His confederate flag t-shirt was either gone or covered up by a University of Nebraska hoodie. He shoved both sleeves up to the elbows, revealing Popeye forearms. He strolled across the busy street between passing cars and trucks.

Linebacker reached the sidewalk crowd first. He would have made it into the bar ahead of me, but he stopped and looked in both directions. Following his gaze, I saw two men on the sidewalk react to him. One simply nodded. The other thumbed at the bar. Linebacker considered the scene, then pointed at the two men and made a circular gesture that ended with him pointing at the alley beside the bar. They hurried out of my sight. Linebacker resumed his march toward the door, which I reached ahead of him.

Thirsty Bar packed its patrons wall to wall. Heads bobbed and bodies shifted and squeezed each other starting at the front door. A tiny sign near the entrance advised of a maximum capacity of one hundred fifty. At least that many stood between the front door and the bar, and more stretched into dimly lit dimensions.

I squeezed, angled and elbowed my way deeper into the room. The noise was overwhelming. Rock music played loudly through speakers mounted near the cheap acoustic tile ceiling. A row of flat screens projected color and motion above the bar. At present, the stations earned their keep by running commercials. A fourth seemed incongruously stuck on The Golf Channel, a quiet game played out before a loud crowd. Tables and booths lined the wall on my left, every seat taken, every booth overflowing. Finding Pidge in here, by far one of the smallest people present, might have proven impossible if the commercial breaks had not ended. Returning to programming, one of the stations ran the split screen video again, the one Raejean pointed out.

As video replayed Pidge's dance, a cluster midway down the bar erupted in cheers. In the center of that cluster, a head of short blonde hair bobbed up and down, one arm high.

Gotcha!

Something solid jarred my elbow from behind. I smelled stale sweat and cigarettes. Linebacker pushed past me without sparing a side glance. Between his rigid bulk and an utter absence of courtesy, he moved effortlessly through the crowd.

I had no hope of pushing past him to reach Pidge first, so I slipped into his wake and followed him through the crowd like a remora on a shark. He jarred a few drinkers, drew harsh looks and ignored them all. Those with an impulse to confront the stranger bumping them from behind quickly swallowed their anger after one look at his hard-angled face.

Linebacker pushed into the circle around Pidge. For a split second I feared he would harm her in full view of a dozen witnesses.

The music and the hoots and cheers for Pidge's replayed performance on the flatscreen challenged my hearing. Linebacker leaned toward Pidge and spoke directly into her ear. His body blocked mine. Pidge hadn't seen me yet. Whatever he said hooked her attention. She looked toward the back of the bar, and pointed, questioning. He nodded. She turned to move through the crowd. He put his hand on her shoulder and gestured for people to make way.

I reached—lunged, really—past him and grabbed her upper arm. She flipped a glance back at me.

"Hey!" I shouted at her. Linebacker reacted to the intrusion by shoving, as if to protect her. He caught me reaching, off-balance. I bumped into a woman to my left, knocking a splash of beer onto both of us.

Pidge stopped, puzzled by the scene.

I stumbled a little closer, apologizing quickly to the woman and squeezing closer to Pidge. Linebacker fired a cold glance at me.

"What are you doing here?" Pidge shouted at me. She looked glad to see me. I attributed that to her long-standing belief that I'm old and don't have a clue about partying.

"Where are you going?" I shouted back, bumping closer, still trying to get around Linebacker who, although Pidge didn't seem to notice, did his best to barricade her from me.

Pidge thumbed toward the back of the bar. "TV interview!"

I weighed the odds of a good outcome from confronting Linebacker here, in these tight quarters, and decided I'd have better luck at the electronic Keno games mounted like robot sentries on the wall.

"No shit?" I tried to sound enthusiastic. I gave Linebacker a quick grin while I edged still closer to Pidge. "What station are you with?"

"Fox," he said. "Wanna get outta the way, pal?"

"Sure, just a sec! We work together." I looked at Pidge. "Hey, before you do this, check your messages."

"My what?" Pidge shouted. She pointed at her ear and squinted at me. Subtlety and inflection were not going to work here. I opted for pantomime. I pulled out my phone and pointed.

"MESSAGES!" I shouted. Linebacker started to move again, almost pushing Pidge, reaching past her to move someone aside. I waved my hand in his face and shouted. "Hold up one sec!"

Pidge's eyes clouded over with annoyance. She jabbed her hand in the pocket of her shorts and pulled out her phone. My text to her appeared onscreen as soon as she brought it to life. Her eyes darted. Message to me and back to message, then to Linebacker.

Pidge leaned toward me. "Is this that fucking … I'm a … wheel again?"

I couldn't hear her. "What?"

"I SAID, IS THIS THAT FUCKING HYATT DEAL AGAIN?"

"Real close!" My eyes shot to Linebacker.

"Hey! They're waiting!" Linebacker tried to move. Pidge abruptly shoved his hand off her shoulder.

"Getting a little handsy, pal!" she said. "I think I've had enough fame for one day! Tell 'em thanks anyway."

People in the tight circle encouraged her. *Do it. It'll be great. You were awesome.* She locked her eyes on me for a moment and I gave her my best eye flare.

"Won't take long!" Linebacker claimed, although his attention shifted, along with his stance. He squared up on me. "Wanna let the little lady go?" Wrong thing to say.

"*Little lady?*" Pidge planted herself.

Linebacker shifted a cold gaze at me. I stared at him. A chilling silence fell between us, even though the noise level in the bar had not diminished in the least.

I've been in two full-fledged fights in my life. Neither ended well. Linebacker easily carried fifty pounds more than me and none of it was spare tire. As his television interview gambit evaporated, so did all pretense. The next few seconds would determine if this would become a bar fight—one I would lose badly—or not.

I didn't care if the whole bar bore witness; if it came down to grabbing Pidge and vanishing, I was ready.

Linebacker took an eternity to decide.

His stale body odor and the second-hand smoke smell on his clothes filled my senses as he leaned closer—close enough that only I heard the words slipping from a mouth that barely moved.

"This ain't over."

I gave it a beat. Better to let him have the last word, a meaningless win. He pushed me aside, into the same woman with the same spilled beer now losing another third of the glass. I steadied her quickly.

Oh, what the hell.

"Hey!" I called to him before he penetrated the first layer of the circle around us. He glanced over his shoulder. His eyes squeezed to frigid black slits.

"You dropped something." I fished the Bic lighter from my pocket, flicked the flame to life and held it up between us. We locked eyes for a second. His stare delivered an unmistakable message, then he heaved himself through the crowd, quickly disappearing from sight.

Pidge punched me on the shoulder.

"That was fucking stupid!"

I stared in the direction he had gone—toward the back of the bar. No doubt to meet his friends waiting in the alley outside.

"Yeah...well...he's an asshole!" I surveyed the immediate circle of people around Pidge. They were young, her age, looking like a group of pre-marital friends. Most of them held a drink in one hand. All of them now stared at the two of us with the look bystanders get when they're half scared and half awed by unexpected behavior.

I grabbed Pidge by both shoulders. "Listen to me! You get ten of your new friends here to walk you back to that crew car. Stay tight. Stay in a group. That was one of those fucking Nazis, and they're not happy with you. Get that car and beat it back out to the field and get through the security fence to the hangar. Hole up at the FBO or in the cockpit. That guy has your picture and he and his Nazi pals have it in for you. Copy?"

A protest formed on her lips.

"Pidge, goddammit, don't fuck with this! I mean it! I gotta go! Keep your phone handy. Copy?" I let her go and started to back away. "Ten of them! Now!" I shouted at her.

"Copy!" she cried flashing equal measures of anger and fear in eyes that told me what I needed to know.

I hustled through the crowd, drawing a bead on the front door, hoping to get through it in time.

48

I reached the bar entrance doing a weird sideways hop that squeezed me through the knots of drinkers. A three-hundred-plus pound man waddled into the doorframe and held me up. He moved through slowly. The sidewalk remained busy with drinkers and a few smokers and just outside the door, the man paused. I had no room to the left or right of the huge man. My frustration grew. Then I saw the plus side of the plus-size-man. He blocked me to the front; the door blocked me to the rear.

Fwooomp! I vanished, using as much cover as I was going to get. If anyone saw me, let them try to explain.

Just as I was about to stomp my feet and shoot up, I remembered that the bar had an awning. I would have smacked right into it. The big man blocking my way forward apparently decided to stop and take in the sights.

I tapped him on the right shoulder. He rotated his torso. I grabbed his left shoulder and pulled myself around him and into the street on an angle that took me above the heads of a dozen drinkers occupying the angle parking in front of the bar. My feet, trailing behind, knocked the big guy in the back as I passed.

"Sorry!" He spun his head, searching for the disembodied voice, utterly bewildered.

On the rise, I pulled the power unit from my pocket along with its propeller. I snapped the prop in place, trying not to let the fact that I was on a collision course with a light pole rush me into dropping the device. It was the only one I had.

I reached the centerline of the street. A quick blip on the power changed my vector to the bed of the white pickup truck parked below.

Linebacker's pickup truck.

Like many men who never got over playing with trucks, Linebacker had rigged his ride with a jacked suspension and a heavy roll bar festooned with lights. I aimed for the bar behind the crew cab and came to a halt with my free hand wrapped around it. My haste paid off. I landed with time to spare. Linebacker was nowhere in sight. I waited, using the time to handle some equipment business.

I pulled a Bluetooth earpiece from my hip pocket, slipped it into place on my right ear and switched it on. This also served to silence my phone ringer, always a good idea when lurking around people who can't see me.

I kept the power unit in my right hand, expecting to need it at any moment.

Linebacker appeared at the mouth of the alley beside the bar. He walked in animated conversation with the two other men I'd seen. His companions offered a suggestion or two, but he brushed them off. One of them advanced another suggestion. Linebacker snapped at him, ending all discussion. The two men parted from him, clearly under orders from someone they either obeyed or feared.

Linebacker ignored the traffic and marched angrily across the street to his truck. Two vehicles stopped abruptly, to my regret, letting him have the right of way. He hopped behind the wheel and slammed the door. I braced for the inevitable quick start and angry peel out. The start came, but he didn't move the truck. He cracked the windows, including the rear glass. I ducked down to watch and listen.

He touched a button on the steering wheel.

"Call Bossman," he commanded the voice-recognition system.

Beeps and chirps followed. A mechanical female voice said, "Calling Bossman." He waited. Through the speaker system in the truck, a phone rang. Once. Twice. Three rings. Then a faint click.

"It's Kellen," Linebacker said. "You lookin' for me?"

"I want you up at Leo's. It's on. Nine o'clock." I didn't know the voice but ventured a guess that it belonged to ex-Marine Corps General Winslow Pemmick.

"Like you wanted?"

"Yes. Be there and be ready, but *do nothing* until Connie confirms with me, got it? Nothing until he confirms and clears it with me."

"Got it. Are you coming?"

"No."

"Ulysses?"

"Tomorrow. Which is why I want you handling this."

"Yes, sir."

"Kellen. Nothing can fuck this up. Not now. I do not want any wrinkles. Do not fuck this up."

"No, sir."

Pemmick let his underling stew for a moment, then said, "I got word you were chasing after that little chippie from the street. Tell me you're not that stupid, son."

I looked at the rearview mirror, at the eyes staring ahead, at a man caught in the act, thinking hard about the next lie he planned to tell.

"Not stupid, sir." Kellen paused. "Sir? I think she was working with somebody. Some guy."

"Doesn't matter. You hear me, son? It doesn't matter. That street shit doesn't matter. That was show."

"Yes, sir."

"After Connie confirms, you clean up."

"Yes, sir."

"This is not a drill."

"No, sir."

A click, a beep and the mechanical female voice announced, "Call ended."

Linebacker—Kellen—did whatever he needed to do to disconnect the call. He hit the start button and the diesel engine powering his truck rattled to life.

You need to get off this train, I told myself. *This has nothing to do with you or your problems. It probably has nothing to do with Andy or Donaldson or anything else remotely related to you.*

A quick kick and I'd be off. Up and away while Linebacker simply drove off on whatever errand his boss intended for him. Float free, hit the power unit and glide back over to the hotel for another beer. Then catch an Uber out to the airport and regroup with Pidge. Maybe spring Andy loose from Donaldson and include her in a discussion on how to best safeguard Pidge until we can get out of Lincoln.

Linebacker was an asshole, but he wasn't my business.

On the other hand, maybe he was headed in the direction of the airport. If so, why not hitch a ride? Save the cost of an Uber.

I decided to give it a few minutes, to see which direction he drove. I held on to his gaudy light bar as he maneuvered the one-way streets of Lincoln.

LINEBACKER DROVE to a perfect jump off point for Lincoln Airport. From the street in front of the bar, he made a right, then another right onto 10th Street, which flowed directly into I-180, which morphed into Highway 34, The Purple Heart Highway, according to a sign that flashed by.

As the highway eased out of Lincoln, I caught glimpses of the airport to the west. I considered jumping, but Highway 34 promised to take me closer as it curved left, eventually heading west across the north end of the airport. From my perch behind Kellen's truck cab, I saw down the centerline of Runway 18, less than a quarter mile away.

Jump off point.

Or it should have been. Except I was thinking about Frozen Yogurt.

49

A year before I met Andy, Earl Jackson called me into his office on a bright winter morning. Early January. I remember the air being crisp and dry, leeched of all moisture by high pressure and overnight temperatures below zero. The kind of day when you can layer up and still never quite feel warm.

Earl's office was frigid, as it always is in winter. Yet he sat at his desk wearing a flannel shirt; no vest, no jacket. Except for complaining that his coffee is cold, Earl never notices that his office runs ten degrees cooler than the rest of the building.

"I need you to take John Bader up to Houghton. Take Six One Nine."

"On Lake Superior? Jesus, Boss. Why not a trip to Moose Jaw instead? Or Ice Station Zebra?" *How come it's never Miami?*

John Bader had been a student at Essex Air. A good pilot. He'd been renting for a year or so after passing his flight test. He progressed nicely, obtained his instrument rating and had moved up into the high-performance Piper Arrow that Earl keeps on the line. He'd talked to me about a multi-engine rating. Money didn't seem to be a barrier.

"What's he want in Houghton?"

"He bought an Aztec." Earl mixed mild surprise with his perpetual scowl.

"No shit," I said. So, he decided to go multi-engine. The Piper Aztec is a solid machine, sometimes called an Az-Truck because it hauls a lot. It's not as fast or sexy as a Baron, but I liked the models I'd flown.

"He wants to bring it here. Have you teach him how to fly it."

"Huh. What...am I supposed to fly him back in it?"

"Naw. The guy selling it to him is going to fly him down in it after they close the deal. John wants us to inspect it."

"Um, isn't that letting the horse out of the barn before the cart—oh, hell, you know what I mean. Why doesn't he just have the guy fly it down here, then we go over it and give him the report before John writes the check?"

Earl shrugged. "'Cuz his heart's all pitter patter over the goddamn thing, I guess. Can't wait to get his hands on the throttles. Not how I'd do it, but it's not my money."

Earl always has an opinion and he's not shy about giving it, but he doesn't break a sweat when people choose not to listen.

That winter morning, on Earl's instructions, I flew John Bader, a nice man in his mid-fifties who managed an engineering company—a man who seemed too young to show off the pictures of his grandchildren that he kept in his wallet—to the Houghton airport. Houghton sits on a forbidding peninsula jutting into a very dangerous-looking Lake Superior. It must have been early in the season, because I remember sea smoke rising from patches of water that remained open, despite the deep cold.

John met the seller of the Aztec, introduced me and invited me to see his new toy. It had been stored in a heated hangar overnight.

I remember almost nothing about the airplane. If asked, I would probably say it was mostly white, possibly with blue trim. But it's a blank to me except for one image I will never forget.

After a quick walk-around, Bader and the seller asked for the hangar door to be opened. I helped push the airplane into the heatless sunshine on the ramp. It was too damned cold, so I hurried back into the FBO for a warm-up coffee. I planned to hop in the Beechcraft Baron for the return trip to Essex before it sat long enough to require preheating the engines. Allowing for a coffee and a leisurely departure, I figured I would still beat them back to Essex. The Baron is decidedly faster than the Aztec.

Inside the FBO, I traded cliché comments about the cold with the young woman behind the counter. She laughed.

"That's funny, because guess what we have."

"I give up."

She gestured for me to follow her into a small break room. I expected to find the coffee there. I didn't expect what she showed me.

"Our own frozen yogurt machine. Check it out!" She pulled a plastic cup from a stack and pushed a button on the front of what looked like a small refrigerator perched on a countertop. She swirled a cup of soft-serve vanilla frozen yogurt and handed it to me. "C'mon! It's a perfect day for it! It won't melt."

Frozen yogurt.

I was eating that frozen yogurt in the FBO main office, standing by the windows, when I watched that Aztec taxi for takeoff.

That's the last time you'll ever see that airplane.

I might have turned around to see who was talking to me—the voice came so clearly out of the blue. But it spoke in my voice, in my head. As firm and intractable as anything I've ever said aloud.

The Aztec rolled away, bobbing her tail, showing me the symmetry of her engines, the squarish shape of her fuselage. The wings blazed white and blinding in the sunlight.

The image I've never forgotten.

I've since talked with Earl about "gut" feelings. A man with his breadth of aviation experience will be the first to tell you he's only upright and breathing because he listened to his gut when it counted—sometimes without a shred of logic to support what the voice in his head told him.

My gut did two things that day. It told me I would never see that airplane or John Bader again. And it made its voice known to me, for the first, but not the last time. It spoke so clearly, so unquestionably, that I would never harbor doubt if it spoke up again.

Standing with a frozen yogurt in my hands, watching its wings glint white, I was one of the last people, possibly *the* last person, to see John Bader and his new airplane. It never arrived in Essex. It never opened a flight plan. It never transmitted a distress call. The best guess is that it went down in the waters of Lake Superior. No one knows.

Frozen yogurt.

My gut.

Which told me not to jump off the back of that truck.

50

Time is problematic when I vanish. I can't see my watch. I wasn't sure how long I rode in the bed of Linebacker's truck when I decided I needed a time check, and while at it, a phone check.

I'd been holding the light bar, crouching with my feet on the pickup bed, exerting pressure between my hands and my feet to keep from flapping behind the light bar like a banner.

My plan to reappear meant ducking down on a line directly behind the driver's seat and staying in his blind spot, clear of the mirrors and the rear window. No real problem. Shortly after passing the airport, Linebacker veered right off of Highway 34 onto a two-lane blacktop marked as Highway 79. Signs indicated the distance to the towns of Raymond and Agnew ahead. The highway carried little or no traffic. If there had been, I wouldn't have worried about anyone following us close enough to see someone in the pickup bed. Linebacker drove fast.

I squeezed down, switched my grip from the light bar to the rim of the pickup bed, and checked to ensure that my head was well below the bottom perimeter of the cab rear window.

Fwooomp! My weight settled on the ribbed steel floor of the pickup bed. I quickly rotated, planted my butt and hunched down.

My watch said seven forty-eight.

I pulled my phone and swiped the screen.

Message from Pidge: *At LKN. WTF?*

Message from Andy: *In Lincoln. On our way to a meet. Call you from the hotel later. LuvU!*

I checked for a missed call from Andy but found none. That told me she didn't want a direct conversation with me, something I don't take personally. She often uses text—and the tone within a text—to say, *Can't talk now.* It signaled that she and Donaldson were on the trail of something. St. Louis must have rendered results. Had the NMRC been a complete bust, she would have expressed it.

The wind roaring around me prohibited me from making a call, but I decided it was time to let her know I hadn't gone home.

Cornhusker Hotel in Lincoln. Room 318. Surprise. See you later. Love you.

However this little side trip with Linebacker turned out, I felt sure I'd be back at the hotel with Andy tonight. I held the phone in my hand for a while, but Andy didn't reply. Another sign that she was preoccupied.

The tone of Linebacker's conversation with Pemmick suggested he would be returning after fulfilling his mission. James Media kept its offices in Lincoln. I assumed that's where Pemmick would be found, and that's where Linebacker would ultimately report in. I wondered if Andy and Donaldson planned to meet with Pemmick. She would tell me later, of course, under the terms of our Usual Disclaimer. I could wait. I anticipated having something of interest to share.

Linebacker had something up his sleeve. Since his Plan A had been to lay hands on Pidge, finding out his Plan B seemed like a good idea.

Unless, of course, Plan B was to drive to North Dakota.

LINEBACKER DIDN'T DRIVE to North Dakota. He went left on Highway 92, then right on Highway 81, then most of another hour up the highway. He drove through the small city of Columbus without stopping. He drove through miles of flatland farms on an arrow-straight four-lane highway toward the town of Norfolk before slowing down unexpectedly. He turned right on Airport Road, which gave me an idea. After a country mile he turned right again onto 556th Avenue, a name that struck me as odd since the two-lane country road bisected nothing but farmland.

Almost nothing.

Linebacker eased off the gas. Time check. Just past eight-thirty. I poked my head up for a look.

Linebacker slowed the truck and veered left, off the highway, into a broad gravel parking lot surrounding a long, low building with a road sign that read "Leo's Roadhouse – Fish Fry Friday – Live Music Saturday." Orange neon beneath the sign proclaimed the establishment open for business.

Shit! Poking my head up, I looked directly at three men loitering near the grille of another parked pickup. A dusty sedan sat beside it on the gravel lot.

Fwooomp! I pushed hard and vanished quickly, hoping they had been too absorbed in conversation to notice me. I threw my hand up and grabbed the rim of the pickup box before the swirling wind took me.

Linebacker rolled to a stop in front of the two vehicles. I clung to the truck bed and studied the men. I recognized three of his comrades from the capitol square. All were young, muscle-bound and dressed in the uniform of the day, a t-shirt (color and political statement of choice) over camo or cargo pants. Two of the three wore ball caps. The third man had what looked like white athletic tape on his hands. Closer examination revealed the tape to be bandages. I recognized the man who had tried to put out the flames consuming Josiah James's face. He got no sympathy from me.

Linebacker killed the engine and climbed out of the truck. As he did, one of the boys went to the back of the waiting pickup and lifted a military-style AR rifle from the bed. He held it up for Linebacker to see and, I presume, admire. He lifted a rectangular magazine from the pickup bed and slapped it into the rifle.

"What the fuck are you going to do with that?" Linebacker asked.

"Take care of business," Rifleman replied.

"Put it the fuck away!" Linebacker barked. He didn't wait to see if Rifleman had an argument. Instead he opened the rear door of his crew cab and pulled out a duffle bag. "I've got everything we need in here." The bag's contents rattled as he lifted it.

Rifleman complied, reluctantly.

"D'jou bring the plastic?" Linebacker wanted to know.

"Uh-huh." The man with the bandages gestured at the car.

Linebacker looked over his comrades.

"Jesus, Harv, an AR? You put a round through someone with that and it goes through the wall and half a mile down the road. The fuck are you thinking?"

Rifleman shrugged.

"How many you got back there?"

"Three," Rifleman admitted. Linebacker laughed.

"Holy Mother of God, Harv! You planning on starting World War Four? What—were you gonna spray those things around like the fucking St. Valentine's Day Massacre? Right through the fucking walls. How do you think Leo would like that? Probably would'a shot up my truck and then I'd have to cut your balls off!" He laughed again, but without humor. Rifleman shoved his hands in his pockets. Linebacker's laugh stopped abruptly. "We get the word on this and we take care of it with what I got here." He lifted up the bag. "No ballistics. No casings. No noise. Got it?"

I examined the bag. It reminded me of something.

"I want these two vehicles outta sight. Put 'em out back," Linebacker commanded. He checked his watch. "They should be here soon."

Not-Rifleman jangled a set of keys and jogged to the driver's door of the rifle-bearing pickup. Linebacker, without another word, turned and trudged away on a line toward the front door of the building, swinging the bag at his side. No other cars or trucks occupied the gravel lot. Rifleman and his bandaged companion climbed into the pickup and car respectively.

I made a snap decision and shoved myself across the gap between the two trucks. I grabbed the second pickup's bedrail just as it lurched forward, rolled across the uneven gravel lot and drove around the corner of the building.

Gravel dominated the back of the property. Tire impressions and a lack of weeds in the gravel suggested that Leo did a fair business on his Fridays and Saturdays.

A small shed stood near the end of the building. Near a central rear entrance, two cars nosed up against Leo's gray wood siding. Linebacker's comrades parked the pickup with the weapons and the dusty sedan beside the cars already present.

Vent fans and a litter of crates and dumpsters suggested a kitchen. An off-center loading dock featured a single roll-up door, currently closed. The gray building stretched off in both directions like an homage to an Army barracks. I pictured a central bar, a restaurant area going one way and possibly a rental hall in the other direction. Weekend weddings and retirement parties. Steady beer trade to pay the bills the rest of the time.

The wooden walls had no windows. This place was one headline away from fame as a fatal fire trap. Rifleman, Not-Rifleman and The Mummy (the guy with the bandages) climbed out of the vehicles and filed into the building through a rear screen door that slapped the frame when it closed behind them. I heard voices, a laugh, then silence. I listened for kitchen sounds but heard nothing. No pans banging. No water hissing. No dishes rattling. The sign said Open, but the empty parking lot called the sign a liar.

I pulled my power unit from a pocket, snapped on the propeller, and thumbed the slide.

It fired up, but the whine of the electric motor told me I'd pushed the batteries too far. This was the same unit I used in Wichita, and again at the rally in Lincoln. I should have switched units, or at least charged the batteries.

A drugstore or convenience store selling C-cells would have been handy, but this roadhouse occupied the middle of nowhere.

I pushed off and made a short flight up to the apex of the low-angled roof. Checking to make sure no one remained outside the building, I settled near what looked like the remnants of a dish antenna mount, grabbed it and—

Fwooomp! —reappeared, dropping to sit on the peak of the roof.

"Shit!" The roof was hotter than hell. I hopped to my feet, quickly getting my butt and hands away from searing asphalt shingles that had been baking in the sun.

Not for much longer. The sun kissed the high edge of towering cumulus clouds to the west. I'd nearly forgotten about the storm warnings. Judging by the anvil tops approaching, I anticipated a thunderstorm assault on central Nebraska within the hour.

"Perfect," I said to myself, thinking about the return trip to Lincoln. A vague plan to borrow Linebacker's truck formed in the back of my mind. Disappear and snatch up his keys. Maybe wrap it around a telephone pole when finished with it...

I pulled out my phone and crouched beside the aluminum frame on the roof. I called up the map function and reviewed my options. After some scanning and scrolling, I touched up the phone function and tapped Pidge's name.

"Who was that motherfucker?" she demanded the instant the call connected. My worry meter dropped back to zero at the sound of her voice.

"Hello to you, too."

"I mean it, Will. Who was that?"

"One of the *Gruppenfuhrers* from the demonstration. While you were celebrating after they broke up, he took pictures of you. You're not very popular right now with the sons of Adolf, and all that TV coverage painted a target on you."

Pidge didn't speak, which is rare.

"Listen," I said, feeding her need for a change of subject. "I need a pickup. Has to be kinda quick because that front is coming. How much did you have to drink?"

"Two Cokes."

"Come on. Be honest."

"Two fucking Cokes, Stewart. I was pacing myself. Where do you want me, and when?"

"Looks like Norfolk. The map says I'm not too far from there, and there's an airport. Seventy, maybe eighty miles. You can be here in half an hour and we'll have it back in the barn there before the shit hits the fan."

"What the hell are you doing up there?"

"I don't really know. I had a bad feeling about that guy, so I hitched a ride with him. He's up to no good. I'm thinking about just calling the cops on him and then bugging out to the airport." *Assuming I have the battery power.* I paused for a moment, mind spinning out ideas, thinking again about Linebacker's pickup truck keys.

Pidge waited for further explanation. I had none so I went with "It seemed like a good idea at the time."

She remained silent for a moment, then said, "I have it. Kilo Oscar Foxtrot Kilo. Be there in … half an hour."

I caught a glint on the highway. A car rolled north toward Leo's dance hall oasis.

"Good. Gotta go. See you there."

I broke the connection, stowed my phone and vanished well before the approaching vehicle closed enough distance to spot someone on the roof of the roadhouse.

I grabbed the old satellite dish frame and held on.

The small silver sedan slowed. At the entrance to the gravel parking lot, it pulled in, wheeled across the gravel, then parked facing away from the building in the shadow of Leo's roadside sign.

The driver's door opened. A man in khaki pants and a white golf shirt climbed out, stretched, then examined the building beneath me with mild disgust. He wore black-rimmed glasses beneath a hairline that had receded to the crown of his skull. His round face matched a round bulge at his belly. His pale skin suggested an office-bound existence. He seemed reluctant to enter the rough-looking roadhouse. After carefully locking his late-model car with the key fob, he hiked across the gravel, collecting dust on expensive-looking shoes. A moment later, I heard the front door open and close below me.

I read him as either sales or officious upper-middle-management. Probably annoying as hell. Possibly part of the James executive team. I wondered if the reception Linebacker had in mind was intended for this newcomer. If so, he didn't stand much of a chance.

I was about to call the cops when it struck me that I'd have a hard time explaining the call. My phone would be identified by the county's 9-1-1 system. What do I tell them? That I happened to be driving by and saw men with guns? Men with a bag of—what?

Sports equipment! That's what the bag looked like. It looked like a duffle full of equipment, something the assistant coach would carry out to the field.

So, what do I tell the cops? I saw some guys planning a softball game at a bar and oh, by the way, they have a trio of semi-automatic rifles in the back of their pickup…not necessarily news in this part of the country.

"And Mr. Stewart, can you tell us what you were doing at that bar, and how you got there...?"

Shit.

Another car winked into view; its chrome and plastic fascia tossed back reflected last rays of sunlight. A white Nissan approached in silence on the seemingly endless ribbon of highway. It decelerated abruptly and heaved right, off the road, onto the lot. It parked beside the silver sedan that had just arrived.

A meeting? This required a little eavesdropping.

Pidge wouldn't reach Norfolk airport for a while.

I calculated that I had enough time to poke my head into the building for a quick look. The back door offered the best entrance. I prepared to turn in that direction when the car doors opened.

Donaldson stepped out on the passenger side. My immediate thoughts rushed to *You're part of this troop, you son-of-a-bitch!* Mixed up with James. In with James all along!

I watch too much TV.

The driver's door opened.

I recognized Andy's long legs before she pulled herself from the driver's seat.

51

The backdoor screen opened, but the solid inner door refused to budge. I considered the trick of using *the other thing* to break whatever bolt held the door, but this door had no deadbolt. A black plastic pad beside the door betrayed an electronic, magnetic lock. My trick doesn't work with magnetic locks.

Shit!

I pushed off, floated backward away from the door, then rotated and pushed the slide on my power unit. The prop whined. Gauging the sound against the position of my thumb on the slide, the batteries didn't have long.

I opted for the shortest route, up and over to the main entrance to the building. To conserve power, I aimed for the gravel in front of the entrance and simply collided with the ground without using reverse power. Two steps, and—

Fwooomp! —I reappeared on the move, trotting a few steps before stowing the dying power unit and moving to the door.

"This is a bad idea. This is a bad idea," I muttered to myself. I stepped across a short concrete walk to a set of double doors. Like the rest of this building, the doors had no windows. On the plus side, nobody would see me coming. On the minus side, I had no idea if Linebacker or one of his pals waited on the other side of the door.

A door my wife had just walked through.

Fwooomp!

I made the decision to vanish as I pulled open the door. Screw it. If someone standing inside saw a door open mysteriously, let their rational mind fill in the blanks. Wind. Air pressure. Whatever.

I slipped through a minimum opening and immediately found myself in trouble. The double front doors accessed a vast barn-like interior. Dark wood walls spread in both directions beneath a flat ten-foot ceiling. Sparse incandescent lighting bordered the entire space. Recessed light pots in the ceiling cast yellow puddles of illumination on a scuffed wooden floor. The room lacked central posts or beams. I would have credited thick beer-and-sweat-scented air with supporting the roof.

To my right, a dance floor stretched away uninterrupted until it reached a small stage at the far end of the building. A few high-top tables dotted the perimeter, serving as drink rests. No chairs. A cloudy plastic tarp had been spread on the dance floor, suggesting maintenance work in progress.

The space to my left, occupying the other half of the building, contained an L-shaped bar, half the length of the building. The money-maker. The main line of the bar traced the longitudinal centerline of the building, then hooked at ninety degrees toward the back wall. It stopped short, leaving room for a hallway with signs for Guys and Gals, and a set of swinging doors that opened on what I presumed to be the kitchen. I made out only two other exits. The one I just traversed, and the roll-up door on the back wall, the loading dock I'd seen from the outside—a convenient way for the band of the night to load and unload.

Goddamn fire trap, I thought again. Or at the very least, trap.

Stools nudged the bar. Scattered high-tops without chairs filled most of the bar area. A few standard-height tables lined the front wall, and a row of red-leather upholstered booths connected to the wall itself. Above the booths a collection of electric signs hawked beer and spirits, interrupted only by posters for the Nebraska Cornhuskers in cheap frames under sheets of cloudy scratched plastic.

Andy sat at the first table along the front wall, facing the bar. She looked professional in a white blouse and blue blazer. Definitely out of place in this roadhouse, at least to my eye—probably because I never take her to places like this. The heat of too many men staring at her, planning approaches to her or plotting my murder, is too much.

Donaldson held down the Godfather seat at the table, facing me and the front door. He gave me a start because he stared directly at me, then I realized he had noted the front door opening and closing. He maintained a state of alert and monitored the door despite the fussing of the only other person in the room.

A man, rail thin with a moonscape complexion, hovered over the table with a tray in one hand. With the other hand he dropped three glasses onto cardboard coasters on the table—two carbonated colas and a clear carbonated drink for Andy. She takes ice water most often; Sprite when the water can't be trusted. The server pulled a narrow, laminated menu from his back pocket and dropped it on the table. He said something to Andy and Donaldson about the menu. The words were lost beneath music—Roy Orbison struggling to describe his Mystery Girl. Andy and Donaldson shook their heads, no. The bartender dropped a single nod and walked back to the bar where he passed through the flip-up panel. Back at his station, he busied himself with whatever bartenders do to keep the ship running. He stayed close, perhaps expecting the two patrons to change their mind about ordering nachos or chicken tenders.

That was it. Andy and Donaldson.

Good news and bad news. Where was Linebacker? Where were the Rifle twins? The Mummy?

Where was the guy in the white polo shirt?

I checked the kitchen doors. Maybe Linebacker and his comrades were engaged in something that had nothing to do with Andy and the FBI man. Maybe the corporate casual bureaucrat who arrived ahead of them was just a bar supply salesman pitching swizzle sticks in the back office.

Maybe the beer in this place wasn't watered down.

Andy maintains an intractable position on the subject of coincidence. She ranks the likelihood of coincidence on par with the likelihood of unicorns. As an aviator, I dispute that position. Every mid-air collision I ever heard of or read about is the coincidental occupation of the same airspace by two different aircraft. Yet at this moment, I saw nothing coincidental about the convergence of Linebacker (on a very specific mission), Andy, Donaldson, and the man in the white polo shirt.

Who suddenly appeared near the rear of the building.

I had gone back to watching Andy engage in cop talk with Donaldson—I recognize it when I see it. I missed seeing the man's point of origin. Was it the Guys/Gals hallway? Or the kitchen?

Neither kitchen door wiggled behind him. Was he relieving himself after a long drive? Or was he conspiring with Linebacker?

He put on a business grin and returned to the table. He took the chair facing Andy. His affect was that of a glad-hander. My worry meter needle swung into the red.

Roy's song volume suddenly dropped. Behind the bar, the bartender rolled the dial on a big old tuner.

"...feel like I need shots in this place," Bureaucrat said as he sat and pulled his chair up under him. "And I've been to Africa."

"Alright. We're here," Donaldson said, reeling his alert eyes back from the mysterious front door. "What does the Department of State want with us? And why are you here? In Nebraska? I didn't think we had an embassy here, although I'm not sure it isn't a good idea."

"Trip wires, Special Agent," he replied. He lifted his cola for a sip, holding Andy's and Donaldson's attention hostage. Sparing no drama, he lowered the glass back to its condensation ring on the table before continuing. "Your inquiry at NMRC touched trip wire records. Records which carry automatic notifications."

Donaldson squared his upper body by folding his arms across his chest. "I'm familiar. I also know that unless the subject is part of an active investigation, trip wires wind up generating messages that drop onto a low-level bureaucrat's desk and can take days, weeks to reach the right eyes, if ever. They're overused and often ignored. Your call came within an hour of us poking into those records. You got out here in the hinterlands in one good goddamn hurry."

Andy, playing second fiddle to no one, leaned on the table and chimed in. "You were here ahead of the trip wires, Mr. Conway."

Conway? I replayed her words in my head. *As in Connie?*

"Yes, I was already here," Conway admitted. "I've been interviewing General Pemmick."

"About what?" Donaldson demanded. "How are military records a State Department issue?"

Conway tented his fingers, striking a cliché pose he probably practiced in the mirror. "I'm afraid, Special Agent, that's not how this is going to work. I'm not here to answer your questions. You're here to answer mine."

"Bullshit!"

"Anything but," Conway said. "You're probing highly classified material. Material well above your pay grade. I called you this morning and arranged this meeting for two reasons. First, I need to know what damage has been done—"

"And by damage done, you mean you want to know what we've uncovered," Andy said.

Conway nodded condescendingly at the pretty lady. My dislike for the man grew. He said, "Second, I need to lay out the boundaries for you. For the FBI and for local law enforcement. While not compromising the classified material, I must clarify for you where that classified material begins, and where your unsanctioned investigation ends." He aimed the latter at Donaldson. "I also require a complete list of everyone you have included in your investigation, everyone you have reported to, everyone you have commented to and everyone you shared a bull session with regarding anything and everything related to your inquiry at NMRC. A *complete* list."

To make his point, he reached into his hip pocket for a small notebook, the kind with *Keep Calm and Carry On* imprinted in foil on the cover. He extracted a pen from his shirt pocket and clicked to extend the tip, working hard to make the click sound like judgment itself.

Donaldson launched into an "If you think…" speech, but I stopped listening.

Be there and be ready, but do nothing until Connie confirms with me, got it? Nothing until he confirms and clears it with me.

Conway. *Connie.*

This building was a trap, alright. Conway had come to probe Andy and Donaldson, to find out what they knew, and establish whether they had passed information on to others or not. His job was to assess whether my wife and the FBI agent were loose ends.

And Linebacker was here to tie up the loose ends.

I glanced at the pock-marked bartender. He stood behind the bar, sorting garnishes, slowly, idly.

Friday night, fish fry. Saturday night, live music. Even for a Thursday, it seemed impossible that the place would be empty at nine o'clock—unless the place was never open on Thursdays. Unless the "Open" neon had been ignited solely for the benefit of two unsuspecting patrons told to meet a man from the State Department in a public place.

Donaldson continued arguing that the exchange of information had to be a two-way street. A clock ticked in my head, counting down. Linebacker and his pals in back wouldn't wait forever.

Hung up at the front door with nowhere to go, my options sucked.

I made a rash decision.

I grabbed the door handle on the right to gain leverage. I pushed the left side door open—wide open. I heaved myself out into what had become a much darker world. The sun had been swallowed by high, anvil-topped cumulus clouds the color of cold lead. Distant, weak lightning flickered.

Fwooomp! I reappeared, dropped to the concrete and spun quickly. I hurried back through the door. Conversation ceased and all eyes, including the bartender's, met mine.

"Sorry! Sorry!" I said to everyone, hands raised. Andy blinked at me. I said to her, "I know you told me to stay in the car."

My boot heels knocked out a confident beat on the wood floor. I swept up behind Andy and bent to give her a peck on the cheek.

"Will..." She did a creditable job of remaining stoic. "What...what are you doing...?"

"I don't mean to interrupt. I came inside because my phone battery died," I said. I glanced at Donaldson. "And to use the restroom."

Donaldson stared at me, unreadable. I stared directly back at him, then flicked my eyes toward the bar as a warning. It probably looked ridiculous. He gave no indication of getting the message.

This might require a more direct approach.

"Can I borrow your phone?" I asked Andy. Without waiting for permission, I bent over and lifted the flap on her satchel. She hates it when I go in her purse or satchel, and this instance was no different. She stiffened, but it was too late. I jabbed my hand inside, felt the hardshell internal holster protecting her weapon, and kept rummaging. I felt her phone and fingered past it. *There!*

I pulled out the cell signal disrupter she had confiscated from Donaldson. I had feared she may have returned the device to the FBI. My thumb found a slide switch on the side of the device; I moved it and caught sight of a green LED light.

"I just need to make a quick call," I said, waiving the device at Andy and Donaldson, hoping they got a good look at the "phone" in my hand before I pantomimed punching the non-existent screen. "Only take a sec!"

"Who is this...person?" Conway asked, finding the limit of his patience.

"Oh! Sorry!" I said. "I'm her husband. Really didn't mean to interrupt. She told me to wait outside, but—you know, the phone thing. Can't live without it." I held the device up to my ear. I took a step away from the table, using the move to scan the back wall and kitchen doors. No sign of Linebacker. I checked on Bartender. He had moved slightly closer. He oozed exaggerated disinterest.

I paced a couple steps, then turned back to the table. Andy and Donaldson watched me, silent.

"Hey! It's me," I said to the lifeless device. "We're here...uh-huh... now? Right now? Okay, I'll tell them...thanks!"

I made a show of touching the "screen" again, then looked directly at Andy, locking on her gold-flecked green eyes. They met mine under long lashes held high and open.

"Dee," I said slowly, "we have to go." I stared at her. We held the optical connection open, transmitting urgency in one direction, understanding in the other. Her acknowledgment came without hesitation.

"Alright, then," she said. She pushed her chair back and stood.

"Our business here has not been concluded!" Conway objected. "Whatever *that* is can surely wait."

"I'm afraid not," Andy said. She dropped her right hand to her satchel. Donaldson watched her and noted the move.

"Special Agent, I cannot allow you to leave without a complete accounting of who you've shared classified information with. It is in your best interest to nip this in the bud before it becomes a prosecutable matter."

Donaldson swung his gaze to Conway, narrowed his eyes, and used the chiseled angles of his face to respond to the threat. His message carried clearly. Conway flinched.

Donaldson's chair shrieked in the weighty silence as he pushed it back. I saw his hand fall to his hip, where he carried his service weapon in a hard-shell belt holster instead of his customary shoulder rig. He began to rise.

Bartender moved fast. Too fast for any of us. He may have had practice. In one swift dip and rise he swept a black and brown arm's length of a shotgun up from behind the bar and onto us, onto Donaldson specifically.

"Leave it!" Bartender ordered. "Hands up where I can see 'em."

Andy's hand froze. She had already slipped it under the edge of her satchel flap. Her fingers no doubt touched the contours of her Glock.

Bartender abruptly shifted the shotgun onto me. The soulless black eye of the barrel came to rest on a line directly at my face. "Lady, pull anything outta that bag and your husband here gets a face full of 12-gauge. KELLEN! Hands up and out! Now! KELLEN!"

The kitchen doors swung open and Linebacker, followed by his three-man posse, emerged. The mystery of the duffle bag evaporated. Each man carried a baseball bat. Kellen casually swung a blue aluminum bat at his side as he walked. The Rifle twins and The Mummy seemed to prefer the traditional wooden Louisville slugger. Bartender moved, slipping through the flip-up gap in the bar and sliding to his right to remove Conway from his line of sight.

Donaldson drew himself fully erect now but eased his hand away from the weapon on his hip as Andy withdrew her hand. I edged sideways toward Andy.

"Don't fuckin' move, asshole!" Bartender snapped at me. I froze.

Conway slumped in his chair, muttering. "No, no, no, no."

Linebacker and Rifleman spread out between me and the dance floor with the now ominous plastic tarp. Not-Rifleman and The Mummy flanked Bartender on the other side of the table, closing the circle around us.

"You get what you needed?" Linebacker asked Conway. "You call him?"

"No, I did not fucking get what I needed!" Conway snapped, jerking his chair back and taking to his feet. "Dammit! Your man here was premature. Premature!"

"They were leaving," Bartender pled his case to Linebacker, who made a face.

"Georgie, please take that fucker's weapon before he gets any ideas. Hers, too."

The Mummy tucked his bat under his arm and approached Donaldson from behind. Bartender swung the shotgun again, making sure that Donaldson had a clear view down the black length of the barrel. Donaldson didn't blink or flinch as The Mummy fumbled first with his holster strap, then had to pull three times to extract the weapon. He backed away quickly, a thief stealing eggs from a rattlesnake's nest.

"Just take her whole fucking bag," Linebacker instructed The Mummy when he approached Andy and hesitated. "It's gotta be in the bag 'cuz she ain't hiding nothing on that body."

Andy slipped the strap off her shoulder, gathered it, and held the bag out. The Mummy snapped it out of her hands and moved quickly out of reach.

"Jack, take that shit out back. Put it in the back of the truck."

Bartender didn't move. He held the shotgun high, swinging slowly back and forth between Andy and Donaldson. "You sure you want me to go?"

"I'm sure Leo doesn't want fucking buckshot and blood all over his walls. Go. We got this." Linebacker slapped the aluminum bat against the palm of his hand. "Wait outside."

Bartender slowly lowered the shotgun into the crook of his left arm. He took Donaldson's weapon and Andy's bag from The Mummy, who quickly resumed a stance with his bat in both hands.

"You didn't call it in?" Linebacker asked Conway.

"I told you! Your man was premature! I don't have the information!"

Linebacker shrugged.

"You two," he gestured at Donaldson and me. "Phones on the table."

Donaldson shot me a look laden with message. I made a guess and leaned forward for the table, keeping the cell signal disruptor concealed by my hand. I moved slowly, allowing time for Donaldson to carefully pull his phone from his hip pocket. He leaned forward in synch. I laid my device down first and he lowered his directly on top. We moved back holding our collective breath.

"Call him now. Ask him what he wants us to do." Linebacker told Conway.

"Fuck." Conway reluctantly pulled a phone from his own pocket. While he worked the device, I edged slightly toward Andy.

"You move again, dipshit, and I'm going to limber up my swing on your skull. Got it?" Linebacker muttered to me. He took a second look. "...do I know you...?"

Blessings upon all bullies who don't bother to see their mark as anything but a victim. He had looked me in the eye at the Thirsty Bar, but to him I had been just another asshole looking for a beatdown.

I shook my head but avoided lending my voice to the identification process.

"I'm not getting a signal," Conway said. He stared at his screen. "I'm not getting a signal!"

"I heard you the first time."

"You have crossed a line here!" Conway snapped. "I'm compromised! You fucking idiot! I'm compromised here, no matter what! And now we don't know what we absolutely, positively needed to know! This is NOT good!" Panic slipped under his skin, pushing out sweat.

"Call me an idiot again and you won't have a worry in the world, Connie. This ain't over yet. We still have time to find out what we need to know." Linebacker slapped the bat on his palm. "You kids ever been in a bar fight?"

None of us spoke.

"You know why drink slingers keep a baseball bat behind the bar? It ain't for some gangbanger sticking a gun in their face and demanding everything in the register. For that shit, they give 'em the money and good riddance. Nope. It's for when the fists fly. 'Cuz a baseball bat in a bar fight trumps all the poking and slapping. Couple swings and it's over. It's hard to go all Chuck Norris on somebody when you got a broken arm dangling from your shoulder. Or you got a big dent in your skull."

"I'll take that action," Donaldson told Linebacker. He adjusted his stance. "You and me. You keep the bat. Let's go."

Linebacker smirked. "If you were hittin' on my girl, or spilled my drink, it would be my pleasure. Hell, I'd even leave the bat on the bar for a pussy like you. But there's still some questions my friend here needs answered, so we're going to take a different approach. Let's try one time, all friendly-like." He gestured at Conway.

"Special Agent, I need to know the names of everyone you've reported to in your investigation of Lockwood and Hampton."

"And I'd rather kick this dickhead's ass and arrest the lot of you."

Linebacker flexed the tree trunks connected to his wide shoulders. "On what charge?"

"Well, that's the point of jumping on this offer now. I arrest you before you do anything, and you've got nothing to worry about. You're out before the ink dries on the arrest report. You start swinging those bats around and you're down for assaulting an officer, attempted murder. A whole different game," Donaldson said smoothly. "You boys up for some hard time?" He aimed the question at the men who had been standing by silently.

Conway shook his head angrily. "I need to know who you've talked to!"

"Are you even with State?" Andy asked. "If you are, this is a sad end to whatever career you've had. At least if you end it here, before anyone gets hurt, losing your job is a better outcome than doing time in a federal prison."

"I got a better idea," Linebacker offered. "We'll take the lady cop over there for a dance on the plastic. Give her some of that love all the liberals have for Mexican piñatas. Arms first. Then knees. Then feet. Then legs. Hands. Keep her screaming until you answer the fucking questions. How's that sound?"

Rifleman, who showed no sign of weakness to my eye, took a menacing step toward Andy. She tensed and repositioned to face him. He wasn't Linebacker's size, but he had sixty pounds on my wife. That wouldn't save his face and eyes from her hands, now tightly curled at her side.

She would fight.

I gauged the distance to Andy. Too far. Rifleman held the ground between us. The instant I moved in her direction he would react. They would all react. I saw a different clear path.

"Whoa! Whoa! Whoa!" I cried out, holding up both hands. "You guys are making a huge mistake and I for one don't want to be here when the real shit hits the fan. It's bad. You lay a hand on her and things get really bad, really fast. She can't control it." I started to move away from Andy.

"Shut the fuck up," Linebacker dismissed me.

I waved my arms at him. "No, no! You gotta listen. I'm a grade A coward. You scare the shit outta me, but she—!" I turned to Andy. "I gotta tell 'em, honey! I'm sorry!"

"Will, shut up!" she snapped at me.

"No! If you lose control, we're all screwed. Guys! She's telekinetic! I mean it. Like that girl in the movie, Carrie."

No one spoke.

"Yeah! I know, it sounds crazy."

"Will! Enough!"

"Baby, if you had any control over it, you'd just pop all their eyeballs and we'd walk outta here," I said. Rifleman flinched. "Guys! I shit you not! She is one hundred percent telekinetic! And when she gets threatened, attacked, she can't control it. I'm talking shit flying through the air! Tongues jerked out of heads! She can pop a human heart like a balloon. But once she gets going, she can't stop it. I don't want to die like that! You gotta back off! Back off and let us walk out of here!"

"Are you fucking kidding me?" Linebacker scoffed.

"I've seen it happen. She's a cop, and they cover it up. But I've seen the bodies. Mutilations. Horrible. I told you. I'm a coward. You do what you want—or try, anyway. I'm taking cover!"

I ducked and broke into a run. A clear path—five steps to the bar. I prayed it would come off as so stupid that no one would make a move against me. I passed behind Conway and leaped over the polished, glossy bar surface. I looked clumsy and idiotic. I dove over and crashed down on an array of sinks and coolers behind the bar. Bottles tipped off low shelves and followed me to the floor, which was covered in a thick rubber mesh. The corner of something jabbed my ribs. One shin caught the edge of a sink and it hurt like a sonofabitch.

I dropped to the floor with a thud.

"Ow!"

Someone laughed.

A bottle fell to the floor beside me and rolled away, unbroken.

Silence.

"Did you see that shit?"

"Hey asshole!" One of the men, not Linebacker, called after me. "Are you shitting for real?"

"Dude, are you really going to let us beat the shit out of your wife while you hide back there?"

"There's nowhere to go, you dumb fuck!"

"Leave him!" Linebacker barked. "If he wants to hide while we tune up his chick, fuck him!"

FWOOOMP! I threw the levers in my head forward. The sound filled my mind like thunder. I heaved myself away from the floor, rotated my legs and grabbed the tray beneath a row of beer spigots to steady myself.

"You can't stop her!" I shouted.

They grinned at each other and the empty space I occupied, unseen.

I reached for the nearest bottle on the shelf and lifted it. I "floated" the bottle forward, then held it in space over the bar.

The grinning stopped.

Everyone in the room stared at it, except Andy, whose eyes darted to the dimensions around her, calculating.

I flipped the bottle and sent it sailing against the front wall. It hit with a dense thump, then dropped onto the booth below. Not being made of movie glass, it failed to break, but instead bumped and knocked its way to the floor, spinning.

I grabbed another and held it out, making it float. The men in the room stood transfixed.

"What the fuck?" Not-Rifleman mumbled.

I covered my mouth with one hand. "I warned you! It's happening!" I flipped the bottle against the wall. "She's doing it! She's doing it! Don't go near her! She'll rip the spine right outta your body! You gotta get the hell outta here!"

Andy took a step back, away from Rifleman, expanding the distance. She adopted an eerie, wide-eyed expression, a frozen stare. Like most women, she can't do sound effects, but I would add that she's also not good at making faces. I forced down a burst of nervous laughter at her attempt to appear possessed.

She stared in the direction of the bar and I prayed she wouldn't do anything goofy like lift her arms or start moaning.

Rifleman shot his attention between the next floating bottle and Andy. He fidgeted on his feet and lifted the bat, either to protect himself or to attack. He drew back to swing. I hurled the bottle at him. He shrieked and threw his arms up. The bottle hit his forearms and clattered to the floor.

I grabbed another and hurled it. Then another. I aimed for Rifleman, sensing his composure cracking. He danced out of the way, away from Andy.

"Get away from her! Get as far away from her as you can!" I shouted. Rifleman darted toward Linebacker.

The men behind Donaldson jumped back involuntarily. Conway moved out of the bar area seeking safe ground behind Linebacker. He backed toward the kitchen door. I grabbed a bottle and threw it in his direction. He turned and ran.

Donaldson edged toward Andy, his head jerking back and forth, assessing the moves made by the men closest to him, watching Andy and watching the levitating liquor.

Grabbing as fast as possible, I rained bottles on them. Bottles flew and banged into the wall, into the booths. One hit a Cornhusker poster and sent the frame crashing down. One hit the corner of a booth just right and shattered, spraying brown spirits all over the upholstery. The rest clinked and clattered to the floor, spinning away.

Linebacker ducked into a crouch. The bat came up.

"RUN!" I shouted. "Save yourselves!"

I grabbed a bottle of something that looked expensive and swung it down onto the bar. It thumped—unbroken—and sent a jolt into my wrist. I raised it again and smashed it against the corner of the beer tapper. This time it shattered. Golden liquid cascaded away from me, down the surface of the bar.

I shoved my hand in my pocket and pulled out the Bic lighter. One flick, and the trusty flame joined the fight. I held the flame to the liquid and was instantly rewarded with a blue-yellow flash that danced away on the flowing wet surface.

The burst of flame was too much for The Mummy. He broke and ran, chasing after Conway, disappearing around the corner.

"Motherfucker!" Linebacker shouted.

I resumed my rain of bottles but broke the cadence when I caught Donaldson looking in my direction. I grabbed a liter of Smirnov and bobbed it once, then heaved it gently toward Donaldson, upright.

The FBI agent reached and caught it one handed. Carrying through, he whirled, flipped the bottle to gain hold of its neck, and brought it crashing down on the crown of Not-Rifleman's skull. His victim managed to get one hand up to impede the blow, but the hand suffered, and the man screamed, pulling smashed bleeding fingers away from shattered glass. Donaldson drew back and jabbed the broken bottle neck into the man's shoulder. It stayed. Still screaming, now drenched in vodka, he bolted past Linebacker in full retreat.

Linebacker ignored him. He focused on Andy and charged. She saw him coming and heaved her chair in his path. I grabbed everything not tied down and threw it in his direction. Bottles. Trays. A box of swizzle sticks. What he saw coming, he flicked away with his arms. The rest ricocheted off his body.

He stomped toward her. The chair tumbled against his legs. He kicked it aside, then ducked as a bottle sailed past his head.

He pulled back to swing the bat. Andy dove away.

Donaldson lunged across the table. He threw his arms around Linebacker's waist. He gained temporary advantage by driving one shoulder into Linebacker's belly, knocking him backward, doubling him over. They dropped to the floor. Linebacker let go of the bat and grabbed Donaldson by the shoulders to heave him off. As fit as Donaldson was, it was an uneven contest. I hurled a bottle that hit the floor short but bounced into the side of Linebacker's head, drawing blood. Donaldson punched and kicked. Linebacker grappled. They rolled away toward the dance floor.

Rifleman backed away—all the way to the front door. He stared at the bottles lifting off the shelves, drawn back and hurled forward. His eyes were golf balls with constricted irises, unblinking. Just when I hoped to count him out, he charged the clawing, rolling fight on the floor. He drew back the bat to swing.

Andy found her feet and grabbed another chair. She heaved it around herself, spinning like an athlete throwing the shot put. She let it fly. I aimed a liter of brandy at Rifleman's head. On the floor, Linebacker grabbed Donaldson by the throat with one hand and shoved him upward.

Rifleman swung. Hard.

The chair connected with the center of his spine. The bottle simultaneously hit him in the shoulder. He folded, but not before the bat swept through an arc and caught Donaldson near the top of his head.

Donaldson dropped, limp, onto Linebacker.

Andy screamed.

I didn't wait. Our odds had gone bad.

Heat told me the bar behind me was in flames. I grabbed another bottle and twisted off the top. I found a stack of paper napkins and jammed one in.

Linebacker sucked in a breath and heaved Donaldson aside. He scrabbled backward on the floor, bunching up the plastic that had been intended to catch our blood and chips of our bones.

Fwooomp! I reappeared and dropped onto the rubber mat. Twisting, I touched the paper napkin to the flame. It caught. I moved fast, never having done this before and not at all sure the thing wouldn't blow up in my hand. I ducked through the open flap in the bar and charged forward.

Andy found her feet and made a move as I did. She darted forward to where Donaldson lay motionless. She clamped her hands on his ankles and pulled. I leaped over his limp body.

Linebacker saw the flaming bottle in my hand. He fought the plastic sheet to put distance between us. Rifleman struggled to his feet moaning and holding one hand to his back.

I drew back, coiled the muscles in my right arm, and slammed the bottle to the floor. For an instant I feared it might clunk and bounce harmlessly away, but the bottle shattered. The flaming napkin ignited liquid spray and a satisfying wall of flame erupted at my feet, forcing me backward.

My aim was off. I had hoped to catch Linebacker and tangle him in burning, melting plastic. When the bottle shattered, it sprayed to my right. The spray caught Rifleman full-bodied. The flames jumped to his legs, to his belly. He flapped his arms screaming. He staggered backward. His burning legs tangled in the plastic. He wobbled and fought the flames.

Linebacker gaped at his comrade for a moment, then danced away as the flames withered the plastic under his feet. He hopped backward toward the kitchen doors. I saw flames on his shirt.

"Will!" Andy cried out behind me.

Rifleman went berserk, screaming and slapping himself. The plastic tripped him. He fell to the floor. He tried rolling, which glued burning plastic to his body. In a moment he was fully engulfed, flailing helplessly, throwing off burning bits in all directions. His screaming continued until his head became a torch.

"Will! Help me!"

Andy's outcry broke the spell. I turned. She dragged Donaldson toward the front door. A trail of dark red blood marked the path of his head.

"Help me get him out!" she cried.

"Open the door and hold out your hand!" I pointed at the door behind her. "Go!"

She jumped to her feet, pushed open the door and propped one foot behind her, holding it open. She turned back to me and held out her hand.

I dropped to my knees and picked up Donaldson. The man was solid and heavy. Carrying him out was not an option.

FWOOOMP!

I pushed *hard.* The sound only I can hear reverberated in my head.

I vanished and took the FBI agent with me. Unfolding my knees lifted us both and gave me a slight vector toward the door that Andy held open against the darkness outside. I hooked Donaldson's weightless body with my right arm and reached for Andy with my left.

The flames in the bar area jumped to the ceiling. Panels ignited and dropped.

Andy reached. Our fingers met, then our hands. She clamped hard and I held on. She pulled too vigorously and heaved us out the door, nearly tumbling to the concrete.

"Easy!" I cried out.

She didn't answer. She found her footing and marched us toward the parked car.

"Wait! Your keys! Your bag!"

"Right here!" Andy pulled a set of car keys from her jeans pocket.

Smart girl. She aimed the fob at the car and summoned the unlock chirps. The lights blinked. She pulled open the rear door. "In here!"

I grabbed the door frame. "Back up," I said. She moved aside and I floated Donaldson's body into the back seat. I held on until I felt his legs, then released. An electric snap touched my hands when he reappeared and dropped on the seat. I shoved his legs in. Andy's face tightened with fear for the man, then fixed with cold resolve.

Fwooomp! My feet dropped to the gravel. I whirled around to watch the front door and braced myself for Linebacker to burst through.

"Get in!" She pulled open the driver's door.

I slammed the rear door and darted around the car. I was barely inside when Andy threw the vehicle in reverse. She floored it, spinning the front-wheel drive on loose gravel and using the broken traction to whip the front end around, parallel to the building. Without windows, the slab-sided roadhouse betrayed no sign of the fire inside.

"Which way?" she asked.

I pointed. "North. Norfolk will have cops! Maybe an EMT!"

Andy dropped the car in gear and shot forward, then slammed on the brake.

"What?'

She said nothing but dropped the car in reverse and stomped on the gas. We lurched backward. She whipped the wheel around and we cut an arc across the gravel that ended in a resounding crunch. The left rear corner of the car connected with the silver sedan Conway had driven.

"What the hell, Dee!"

Andy threw a glance over her shoulder at the sedan. White clouds of airbag filled the cabin. She dropped the gear shifter into drive and hit the gas again. We shot forward, but once again, abruptly stomped the brake. We ground to a halt.

This time I didn't question.

The second pickup, the one Rifleman had driven, burst from behind the building. It too slammed on the brakes and skidded to a broadside stop in Andy's headlights. On instinct, she flicked the lights to bright.

Linebacker leaped out of the driver's seat. He stood for a split second. One side of his face was black and red on a line divided by his nose. Most of his shirt was gone, exposing cords of muscle and more blackened skin. He stood only for a second, then ran toward the back of the truck.

"Go! Go!" I cried to Andy. "They have guns!"

She didn't bother to voice a reply. She threw the car in reverse and floored it. We shot backward, screaming to the far end of the parking lot where she again whipped the wheel around, breaking the front wheels loose and spinning the car. Without missing a beat, she dropped the car in Drive and floored it again. We flew out the gravel entrance, hit pavement on squealing tires, and heaved left, the wrong direction. Andy's foot went to the floor. The four-cylinder engine screamed.

Not good. The car, a four-banger Nissan meant for trips to Starbucks, accelerated unimpressively. The truck behind us sported a V-8.

Not good at all.

Andy settled in the seat, fixed both hands on the wheel at nine and three, and glanced in the mirror. I looked over my shoulder for headlights onto the road behind us. Nothing yet.

She pushed the little car up over a hundred miles per hour. I thanked Nebraska for building their highways straight and true. The downside of that meant we would remain visible for miles. As if reading my mind, Andy flicked off the lights. Or tried to.

"Shit!" I said.

"Driving lights," she calmly announced. "I can't turn them off." She flicked the lights back on and upped them to bright. The broad, empty highway stretched away in the darkness ahead, sweeping under us at an outrageous rate. "What do they have?"

I watched the highway behind us. Still no headlights.

"Will! What do they have? What guns? Besides the ones they took from us?"

"Three AR's."

She bit her lower lip. "Dammit. They don't have to catch up. If they get within half a mile of us, all they have to do is throw rounds at us. Sooner or later a lucky shot will come right through this piece of tin."

"Well, that sucks."

I checked the speedometer. One-oh-five. If bullets came our way and blew a tire or—*God forbid!*—hit Andy, this would end fast in a rolling ball of aluminum, plastic and glass.

I watched, hope rising. Still no headlights.

"What was that business of hitting Conway's car?"

Andy ceased checking the mirror. Her body, her whole being, fixed on the highway flying at us, under us.

"Late model Volkswagen. It has impact sensors. I hit it hard enough to set off the airbags, which automatically cuts the fuel to the engine. I thought if we were going to be followed, it would be in that. I didn't know about the truck."

"They have a truck," I said. "Parked in back."

"Oh. Good to know. Thank you. At least Conway won't be going anywhere. Anything?"

I watched through the rear window for Linebacker and the truck.

"Not yet. Maybe that guy passed out. He looked a little crispy."

I spoke too soon. Deep in the receding distance, a pair of pinprick lights joined the black.

"Shit! Here they come!"

52

Andy looked like violence in a bottle. Her eyes blazed. Her steering wheel movements were microscopic. She had the look of a goddess going to war. The vehicle windows were closed yet I swear I saw her hair flowing in a wind.

"Will."

I stared at the lights behind us.

"Will! I need you up here. Crossroads. I can't keep us on the road at this speed and watch for traffic. You have to call it out."

"Right." A Stop Ahead sign flashed by. I looked both ways into darkness. "Clear!"

We shot through a four-way stop intersection.

"Now isn't the time, dear, but what on earth were you doing there?"

"I hitched a ride. And you're right. Not the time."

"Do you have your phone?"

"Damn! Yes!" I jabbed my hand into my jeans and pulled out my phone. The tension wrapped into every muscle in my body made my fingers quiver. I swiped the screen and drew a long deliberate breath, exhaling slowly. I pushed a calm down the back of my neck, down my shoulders, down my arms. I flexed my fingers.

The screen came to life, blindingly so. I tipped it away from Andy's eyes.

"I'll call 9-1-1."

"No!" she said. "Map first. Where are we? We need to give our position, and we need to know which way to turn if they tell us to drive toward a patrol officer."

"Right!" I tapped the map app. It took forever—two, maybe three heartbeats—to open. It took even longer for the genie in the phone to talk to the gods in space and come back with a pinpoint location. Hours went by. Days. "C'mon! C'mon!" I muttered.

"Intersection!" she called out. I checked both ways. Darkness.

"Clear!"

The tiny blue dot appeared on my phone map with its quaint head-light effect showing direction of travel. It moved at a remarkable pace down the electronic line representing the road beneath us.

I glanced over my shoulder. The headlights had grown. They were two distinct lights now. I estimated a little over two miles behind us. I checked Andy's speed. One-ten. The engine howled.

"Can you go any faster?"

She shook her head tightly. "It's governed. The tires on these things are only rated to about one-fifteen. Intersection!"

"On it!" I cried out. I checked left and right. A set of headlights approached from the right. I gauged the speed. "Clear!"

"What about that truck? What's his top speed?"

"Higher," she said. She didn't elaborate. "Where are we? On the map."

"Uh…here. Southbound on 556th Avenue. This goes straight for a while, but there are no towns. Eventually we run out of road. We'll have to turn. About ten miles."

"Okay, get a fix on the next crossroads and call 9-1-1."

The phone rang in my hand. The bar at the top of the map announced a call from Pidge.

I answered it on speaker. "Not now, Pidge!"

"Are you at the airport?"

I glanced back. The spread between following headlights widened. Gaining on us.

"I gotta go! I need to—" I stopped.

"Will, stop fooling around with Pidge and call 9-1-1!" Andy snapped at me.

"Hi, Andy!"

"Pidge, where are you?" I held up my hand, begging Andy's patience. "Are you on Bluetooth?"

The headsets in the Navajo allow users to connect a phone via Bluetooth. It's not hard to take or make calls while flying, it's just hard not to drop a call since cell towers change fast at two hundred miles per hour.

"Yeah. I'm ten minutes out. I'm calling to tell you to be ready to rock and roll. We got a fuck load of weather coming! I can't sit on the ground for long if we're gonna outrun it!"

"Pidge listen to me! Pull up the iPad and switch to road maps. Do it! Andy and I are in deep shit. Do it!"

I feared for a second that the connection had been lost. She didn't respond.

"What are you doing?!" Andy demanded.

"9-1-1 will never get here before those bullets," I told her.

"Got it!" Pidge announced. "Bullets? What bullets?"

"Do you see Highway 81? Runs south from Norfolk. Right past the airport?"

"Yeah."

"Jog to the east. One road over. A two-lane road called 556th Avenue. Straight as an arrow running north and south parallel to 81. See it?"

"Intersection!" Andy cried.

I checked. "Clear!"

"Got it," Pidge said. "About fifteen miles ahead."

I did quick math, adding the Navajo's speed to ours, coming up with close to three hundred miles per hour. A mile every twelve seconds.

"Say altitude."

"Three thousand."

Andy shot a glance at me. "What are you doing?"

I checked our six. The lights widened, growing larger, closer. I checked the Nissan's speed. No better than before. I estimated the closure rate with our pursuers. Right around the time we would have to drop our speed to turn left or right, they would be on us.

"Pidge, drop down to about two hundred AGL. Get over that road. 556th Avenue. Can you do that?"

"What the fuck!"

"Can you do that?!"

Pidge gave me a moment of silence. She spoke calmly. "Do you need to ask?"

"Drop your gear and show me your lights!"

"Buy me dinner first. Oh, sorry, Andy!"

I leaned forward and searched the black sky through the windshield. Lightning flashed off to my right. Pinprick landing lights winked on in the night sky low ahead.

"I have you in sight! Kill the lights." The landing lights disappeared. "Get over this road and get down as low as you can."

"What the fuck are we doing?"

I swallowed. I needed to get this right the first time. "Remember that story about the World War II pilots? The guys training in the desert who used to find trains at night?"

Time ticked away in my head. Pavement streaked beneath our wheels.

"You mean that gimmick where they'd scare the shit outta train engineers?"

"Yes!" I pumped my fist. "There's a car full of assholes with guns about half a mile behind us. They're closing on us and they have AR's and they don't have to get all that close to hit us."

"Fuck, no they don't! What do you want me to do about it?"

"Same stunt. I want you to drop down on this road, pass over us and then light 'em up. Scare the shit outta them. Head-on!"

She said nothing. If Andy had been able to peel her eyes from the road, she would have set them on me with the look she reserves for when she thinks she has a twelve-year-old for a husband.

"Pidge?"

"Uh. You're shitting me, right?"

"Dee, flash your high beams."

Andy flicked the light stalk. The landscape roaring toward us expanded and contracted with each flick. I didn't know which view was scarier.

"Pidge, do you see us? We're flashing our brights. Only a couple miles. We get one shot at this. See us yet?"

"Yeah, I see you."

"Do you see the lights behind us? Southbound, about half a mile."

"Got 'em! Shit. Are there any wires?"

"West side of the highway. Power lines, about thirty feet off the edge of the pavement on that side."

"Wonderful. What about crossing?"

"I guess you'll know when you hit them. Best I can offer. If this is gonna work, you're going to have to be skimming the pavement. Use both sets of lights for perspective. The road is flat as a pancake."

"Put yours on low beam! Here I come! Gear down. Three green!"

I searched the black sky ahead. Nothing. I looked back. The pickup closed on us rapidly. I estimated five hundred yards. It wouldn't be easy at this speed, but if they had someone in the bed, or leaning out the window, they might be able to fire on us. Aiming wouldn't matter. One lucky shot would do the job.

I stopped breathing. Andy straddled the centerline and held the car rock steady.

Seconds ticked by.

Pidge roared out of the black and over us like thunder. The deep sonic tremor of her engines touched my spine. The belly of the airplane flashed white in our low-beam headlights. Spinning propeller discs cut the air on either side of us. I instinctively ducked. Andy screamed, but held steady, ignoring what looked like an inevitable collision. I braced for the nose wheel to smash through the windshield. It missed.

I whipped my head around and saw the highway behind us explode in light when Pidge snapped on the airplane's landing lights. The Navajo's silhouette instantly dipped lower. I swear she touched the wheels to the pavement. In time measured by heartbeats, the grille, hood and windshield of the pickup truck following us appeared, caught naked in the blazing landing lights of the Navajo. The pickup's headlights winked wildly, then flew off the road, tumbling and flashing at impossible angles. Then disappeared.

The white position light on the tail of the Navajo rose into the night. Green light winked on the right wing, red on the left wing. Pidge soared skyward. Lightning fractured the entire western sky and painted the white fuselage with a split-second glow.

The road behind us lay black.

Andy checked her mirror and immediately released the accelerator. She blew out a long-held breath.

"FUCK ME!" Pidge cried over the phone. *"Did you fucking see that?"*

I couldn't speak. My mouth had gone dry.

53

C loud to ground lightning stabbed the earth off to my right.
"Will, 9-1-1. We need help. We need to get him to a hospital," Andy said. She snapped a glance at the back seat.

Pidge chimed in. "I'm outta here. Screw Norfolk. The shit is here! I'm headed east."

"Nice flying, Pidge," Andy said.

"Fucking magnificent flying!"

The connection ended. I worked the map screen on my phone, struggling to keep my fingers steady. I noticed for the first time that I had blood on my hands and forearms.

"Take the next right," I said. "Go west to 81, then hit it hard. There's a hospital in Norfolk. You'll get us there before anyone can get to us. Go."

Andy found the first crossroad, blew through the stop sign and launched westbound. I checked the road behind just to be sure. Nothing followed. Lightning bolts raced across the bottoms of menacing clouds.

I searched the northern horizon. Joining the lighting, a hesitant yellow glow reached for the bellies of the ragged, racing clouds.

Fire.

54

Andy touched my knee. "Hey."

I must have dozed. I climbed out of a foggy well. My wife sat beside me wearing a red t-shirt with *Norfolk Area Strides for Stroke* imprinted across the front. It looked better on her than on me. After taking excessive steps to confirm that the blood all over her blouse and jacket, and my shirt, was not the result of injuries—at least not our own injuries—someone on the hospital staff bagged our bloody clothes and dug up a pair of left-over charity event t-shirts.

Andy gave me a look that was both loving and amused.

"What? Was I drooling?"

She smiled. "No. I just...I know you can do the disappearing thing and all, but I don't think I've ever been more impressed than I am by your ability to sleep in a plastic hospital chair." She handed me a cup of coffee. I tipped the blessed brew to my lips, expecting the worst. As if my wife's unearthly beauty—even at this hour in a borrowed t-shirt— had exerted magical influence, the coffee tasted superb.

"Any news?" I checked my wristwatch. Three-forty. Middle-of-the-night semi-silence draped the hospital atmosphere. Low voices mixed with white noise. Andy sipped from her own cup of coffee, a signal that sleep was not on the agenda.

"He's stable. They relieved the pressure from the swelling. An air ambulance is on its way to take him to Omaha. They had to wait for the storm front to pass," she paused. Her lips closed, giving the lower a lush prominence. I caught a damp glint in her eye. I reached for her thigh and stroked it. She put her hand on mine and said angrily, "People see these dumbshits on television knocking each other over the head. Getting 'knocked out.'" She flicked air quotes. "They have no idea the cranial damage that does. We had a guy, about a year before I met you…he and his best friend argued in a bar. He hit his friend in the head with a beer bottle. The bottle didn't break, but his friend's skull did."

She paused. Andy sees things in her job. She tells me some. But not all. This was one I never heard. I waited.

"His *best friend*. They grew up together. Went to Maple Avenue grade school together…he left his friend with the cognition of a toddler. For life. And for what?"

I didn't answer because she wasn't looking for an answer. She squeezed my hand and composed herself.

"The helicopter should be here soon. Finish your coffee. We need to go."

"What?" I'd been a little out of touch once the initial frenzy of arriving at the hospital with Donaldson.

The moment hospital staff took over, Andy launched rapid calls to the Norfolk Police Department and the Madison County Sheriff's office. Law enforcement duties immediately pulled her away. She abandoned me with instructions to keep my head down and not talk to anyone without her. Shortly after that, she met a sheriff's deputy at the emergency entrance door and escorted him toward the trauma unit. I found and made friends with a plastic chair in a sparse ER waiting area and waited. At some point, sleep ambushed me.

"We're leaving," Andy repeated.

"Where are we going at three-thirty in the morning?"

"Away from here. The FBI is coming, and I don't want either of us here when they arrive."

"Aren't they the good guys?"

"Yes, but not so much when you've illegally obtained highly classified information."

"Huh." I took a sip. "Can I get this to go?"

55

The storm system that crashed down on us when we delivered Donaldson to the emergency entrance at Faith Regional in Norfolk had stopped rumbling sometime during my nap. Long gone, it left behind glistening roads and steamy rising mist.

The catnap proved surprisingly refreshing. I felt alert and confident, aided by the coffee. I hustled to the driver's door when Andy *feeped* the lock. Her driving tonight had been a lifesaver, but I felt that giving her a break would do us both good.

I flipped the wipers occasionally to deal with road spray and lingering raindrops. I also cracked the rear windows on the damaged rental to evacuate the scent of blood. The back seat had a lot of blood. Between that and the crushed left rear corner, I uncharitably hoped the rental was on an FBI credit card.

"Where are we going?" I asked.

Andy glanced back at the hospital and seemed satisfied to see it fall behind us. "I don't know. We need to talk."

"As in...*we need to talk*?"

"No, as in we need to talk about staying out of federal prison."

"Oh. *Phew!*"

"Give me your phone," she held out her hand. I produced it. She swiped the screen. "Your battery is almost dead."

"There's a lot of that going around. Which reminds me. Holler if you see a 24-hour convenience store."

Andy worked the phone, then gave me directions. "There's a Hampton Inn."

"Bless you! I need a bed!"

"We aren't checking in. I'm just going to ask if we can hang out in their breakfast room. Turn left at the next light." She pointed, then switched her concentration to me.

After an uncomfortable moment, I asked, "What?"

"Telekinetic? Really?"

56

The young man working the graveyard shift behind the counter at the Hampton Inn traded a shamelessly long look at Andy for the use of their breakfast room. He exaggerated his largess by explaining that he wasn't supposed to let non-guests use the facilities, but she was welcome to go right ahead. She tipped him with a sweet smile. I knew without looking back that he stared at her ass as we walked from the front desk to the pint-sized cafeteria. A sign in the lobby raised my hopes by announcing a continental breakfast. Blank countertops, a cold coffee machine and the absence of anything edible dashed those hopes.

"Dee, what are we doing here?" I asked.

She stopped, turned, and stepped close to me, sliding her arms beneath mine. She pulled me against her.

"This." She laid her head on my shoulder. I drew her in. One of the things I love about my wife is that we fit, physically. She's taller than many women, but just right for me. My hands find the contours of her waist inviting. My chest welcomes the press of her breasts. We can kiss without her having to stretch. She can drop her cheek to my shoulder for solace as if it had been made for her.

I stroked her hair and breathed in her scent, which was tainted slightly by smoke.

We held each other. Heartbeat to heartbeat. When it ended—when she had refueled the engine we share—she backed away and found a chair. I dropped in the chair beside her. Our hands met and clasped on the Formica tabletop.

"Usual Disclaimer?"

"Uh, not if it means federal prison," I said, then added, "Yes. Usual Disclaimer."

She surprised me. "You first. Any news from Greg or Lillian?"

I shook my head. "I think that's going to take some time. I hate to say it, but this Lewko guy is in a different league. That kid in Wichita was an idiot."

Andy didn't comment.

"What's the deal with running from the FBI?" I asked, shifting gears.

"We're not—" She stopped abruptly and searched the adjacent lobby. She lowered her voice. "We're not running from the FBI. Lee's boss is coming down from Sioux Falls. I don't want to get tangled up with him. Not yet." She glanced at the front desk. No sign of her ardent admirer. "Again. You first. What in Heaven's name were you doing there? Why didn't you go home?"

"I told you. I hitched a ride." I explained in brief how I made the impulsive decision to fly to Lincoln and the events that followed on the Capitol Square and later at the Thirsty Bar.

"That big guy? He tried to get at Pidge?" she asked.

"Rather crudely. Any idea what happened to him? I'd like to make sure Pidge isn't still a target."

"I don't think that's an issue. I spoke to Norfolk PD," Andy said. "Madison County deputies found the truck. They estimate it left the road at a hundred and twenty miles per hour. There were three bodies. They're guessing the first one had been riding in the box, got ejected, and then crushed by the truck when it rolled. The other two are balled up in the cab. DOA. Word is it's going to take a lot of cutting to get all the pieces out."

"Linebacker," I said. Andy threw me a quizzical look. I corrected myself. "Kellen."

"They found my bag, my phone and weapon. They haven't found Lee's weapon, but they know to look for it. There's something else…"

they found shell casings on the road. Two-two-three." Andy and I traded raised eyebrows. "I guess they were firing at us."

We gave that knowledge a moment of silence. I resolved to examine the car for holes. "That can't be easy at a hundred twenty miles an hour."

"I wouldn't want to try it," she said. "Norfolk PD also picked up Conway. He's been lighting up their night watch commander, screaming about his State Department rank and threatening everyone in sight. They don't quite know what to do with him. I suggested they hold him until I can make a statement. Then they can determine charges."

"Probably wants diplomatic immunity."

"Nebraska's not a foreign country."

"I dunno. Donaldson might be right. Maybe we should have an embassy in Nebraska."

"Filing charges means coming back here," Andy said unhappily. "Oh, my God. I just realized—did you hear from Pidge?"

"She's fine," I said. "She made it to Des Moines ahead of the squall line."

"Des Moines. Huh…full circle."

"She said she's pulling the battery out of her phone until tomorrow afternoon, er, today."

"She can sleep all day as far as I'm concerned. Excuse me, what was that business about World War II"

I laughed. "Okay. Pidge likes to claim she's the greatest pilot ever. Notwithstanding the fact that she might be, I thought I'd knock her down a peg. I gave her some books. Chuck Yeager. Bob Hoover. Doolittle. Some others. I told her that's the competition. She loved it. Anyway, there's a great story in the one of them about training, I dunno, in Texas or the desert somewhere. When they were flying at night, they'd see a train going across this big empty landscape. So, they'd get out ahead of it, dive down right above the tracks and about half a mile out turn on their landing light. Make it look like another train coming!"

Andy looked horrified. "That's not funny!"

"It's hilarious!" She wasn't buying. "Okay, maybe a little hard on the engineers, but that trick saved our bacon a few hours ago."

"My Lord! That girl!"

"Your turn. What the hell did you and Donaldson stir up at the National Military Records Center?"

Andy heaved a long sigh. "A hornet's nest. This is why we need to talk." She checked the lobby again, then leaned forward in her seat, winding up the story with her hands. "We found the records, and of course they're heavily classified. There was no information on the missions they were flying, other than that lame cover story about the weather mission. The men are listed as Missing. Felt like a dead end, but Lee wasn't deterred. The man is a walking Rolodex. He spent most of yesterday on the phone, outside of the NMRC. Honestly, I can't say for certain who he called, or how many calls he made. Some of them were overseas."

"As in…intelligence community?"

Andy lifted her eyebrows and bobbed her head. "Heavyweights. People he knew from his time in L.A. who have moved up the ladder. A few he knew from his time with Litton."

"Anybody with information about Hampton and Lockwood? What really happened?"

"Yes, although I only heard half of the conversations." Andy paused. She winced. "This is where things get Classified."

And here's the wall, I thought.

"Okay. Here goes. I'm now committing a federal crime by telling you. This is what Lee pieced together." Andy shifted anxiously in her seat. She checked the line of sight to the front desk. "In November of 1960 an Air Force ELINT flight designated Racehorse Blue entered Soviet airspace. That flight, a reconnaissance RB-50, which most people would recognize as the B-29 bomber that dropped the first atomic bomb—"

I clutched Andy's thigh. She startled.

"What?"

"God you're sexy when you talk airplanes!"

She slapped my arm, but a thin smile escaped her intense expression. "That flight was flown by Captain Armand Hampton and Captain Paul Lockwood, with a crew of eight more officers and enlisted men. Their job as part of the 6091st Reconnaissance Squadron was to penetrate Soviet airspace and map electronic defenses. ELINT means Electronic Intelligence."

"I know what ELINT means."

"Well, I didn't. They were sent to find out where the Reds put their radar and their anti-aircraft missiles and their fighter bases. A lot of flights went into Soviet airspace on similar missions. A lot more than the public was ever told. Some never returned. Captain Hampton's ten-man crew was one of the lost. But because it was the Cold War, those losses were kept secret. That's why Mrs. Hampton got the runaround."

Nine days. I pondered the size of the hole it would tear in my life had I been given just nine days with Andy. Her hand squeeze suggested she shared the thought.

She continued. "Some of the lost men were killed. Some were captured and held by the KGB. It isn't like we didn't know. Air Force command and the highest levels of the intelligence services were aware of the fate of those men and others like them. We had active prisoner exchange programs with the Soviets."

"Francis Gary Powers," I chimed in.

Andy gave me a blank look.

"U-2?"

"The band?"

I shot back in my chair. "Dee! Tell me you know—"

A dimple appeared and I knew I'd been had. Punishment for interrupting.

"Yes," Andy said. "Captain Powers—who was flying for the CIA as a civilian, not a member of the military—was exchanged, but only after the Soviets inflicted public humiliation upon the United States. The Soviets chose between executing him in secret or making a show of the U.S.'s failure and letting him live. So, yes, he was exchanged. As were others. But some were not exchanged, or even acknowledged as prisoners, because the Soviets wanted them for one reason or another. On our books, those men simply disappeared. One of Lee's sources is a former Moscow station chief for the CIA. He thinks Hampton's crew went into a secret KGB installation in Staroturukhansk—they call it *Staro* for obvious reasons. He thinks the six enlisted men were killed—either in the crash or made to 'disappear' later—but the four officers were kept."

"Four?"

"We now know about Hampton and Lockwood. The other two…uh,

Captain Brent and Lieutenant Hillerman...unknown. Possibly dead. Possibly still being held."

"Jesus."

"This former station chief is also the one that told Lee about The Glass Wall."

"Time out!" I put up two hands in the accepted signal. "You've got a lot of anonymous people telling Donaldson a lot of stories. Do you trust all this?"

"Not anonymous. People Lee knows. People who owe him. Trust him."

"But why are they giving him this information? If it's Classified?"

"Because there's something bigger going on here, which I'll get to."

I shrugged away any further objection.

"The Glass Wall," Andy said. "This is the icky part."

"I would have said anything to do with the KGB is 'icky,' but go on."

"The Staro facility exemplifies the long view taken by the KGB and the Soviets. Yes—they practiced brutal methods of torture and prisoner mistreatment, but they engaged in other methods as well. Staro is rumored to have invented a technique called The Glass Wall."

"What the hell is that?" I asked.

"The prisoner is placed in solitary. For years. Years and years. No human contact of any kind. I don't mean some sort of hole. An ordinary cell. The idea wasn't physical torture, it was mental deprivation. Utter silence. No human contact. Food coming in, waste going out. Clothing and showers provided. I don't know how they handled medical or dental needs, but the point here is deprivation of identity, of existence. The twist is that the cell has a glass wall. For years the wall stays black. And then one day the other side of the wall lights up and reveals the interior of an American-style home. Some accounts said they even piped in American TV. Suddenly after years alone, the subject sees this tableau of normal life. Except for the glass, he becomes part of it, as if he's there. There's a woman posing as a wife like nothing is out of the ordinary. She knows the subject—they had full dossiers. She might even look like a wife left behind, a girl back home. Can you imagine? After years there's a normal woman on the other side of the glass—sometimes English-speaking, sometimes Russian—depending on the long-term objective for the subject. Chatting away, cooking, talking about her day, talking about family, friends, the hometown. Trading jokes. Complaining. Pretending it's all perfectly normal."

"Playing chess…?" I wondered.

Andy pointed a finger at me. "If the subject steers the conversation to anything about the prison, the wall goes dark. Punishment. Not just for a few days or weeks or even months. For years. Then they start over."

"Years?" I asked, trying to swallow the concept.

Andy nodded solemnly. "Years. Long enough to make it all seem like an illusion. A hallucination. Long enough to make the man desperate to get it back. Remember, Captains Hampton and Lockwood were captured nearly sixty years ago. If they were subjected to The Glass Wall, this cycle would have repeated countless times. For decades. They trained the men to accept this fantasy as reality. They rebuilt their identity."

"Wow. That's horrible."

"It gets worse. Sometimes, as one means of breaking the subject down, the fantasy ended gruesomely. Word is they murdered their own actors while the subject watched. The fake wife. The fake family. Children. Babies. Horrible. The wall would go black, leaving the subject in despair. Then they would repeat the cycle with look-alike women."

Andy's eyebrows lifted.

Rada, ya tebya vizhu.

Rada. A woman's name. Lockwood's un-reality Russian wife. Given. Taken away, horribly. Over and over. How many times? How many cycles?

"My god," I said. "Lockwood saw you and thought it was happening again. Why? Why would they go to all this trouble?"

"Why did they do anything? Weapons. They made these men into weapons. In point of fact, both men eventually came to the United States and committed murder."

"Dee, they're almost ninety! The government that started all this is long gone. What possible interest does the current regime have in the murder of one of their own diplomats and an internet looney-tune from Lincoln, Nebraska?"

"Patience, love," she pressed a hand to my arm. "This is a twisted road. I literally watched Lee put it together after picking up bits and pieces from his sources and from what we learned at the NMRC."

"Sheesh."

"It's not the government—not directly. They, the Soviet government initially and the Russian government that formed after the breakup, didn't send those two octogenarian assassins. The Staro facility and its program became an orphan when the Soviet Union broke up. But in the vacuum that followed, if it had value, it became a target for acquisition. How do you think Putin, a former KGB agent—essentially a cop—became one of the richest men in the world? Staro became a private facility, under private ownership. Privatization started under Yeltsin. The *apparatchiks* who preached collective sacrifice under the communists gave birth to the oligarchs. The *Semibankirschina*—the Seven Bankers. Ultimately it led to Putin and his ilk. Under CAATSA, the Countering America's Adversaries Through Sanctions Act, the U.S. Treasury published a list of 96 known oligarchs. The sanctions you hear about today are directed at many of those individuals and their companies."

I must have been gawking at her.

"What?" she asked. "Okay. Fine. I spent a ton of time on Google while Lee was on the phone."

"CAATSA?"

"Lee told me to look it up," Andy said. "That's where he showed me the name of Valentin Berezovsky. Berezovsky was mentioned several times by Lee's sources. Valentin Berezovsky is one of the richest of the rich. His father was an *apparatchik* under Yeltsin…" Andy paused for effect "…and his grandfather was commandant of a network of KGB prisons that included Staro."

"Sonofabitch. They kept it in the family. So, who is Berezovsky and what does he have to do with…all this?"

"I'm getting to that. Remember how Lee had one piece he didn't want to share? It was General Pemmick's record at the NMRC. He was convinced the Pemmick record was a lynchpin."

"And?"

"United States Marine Corps General Winslow Pemmick was assigned to the Moscow embassy—ostensibly as part of the Marine security detachment—right around the time of the breakup. His real assignment was to persuade the survivors of the breakup to curry favor with the U.S. by turning over secrets, and more importantly turning over U.S. military personnel they had been holding, sometimes for decades. A Schindler-type mission. Save those he could. The Soviets had a lot to hide and their favorite method of hiding things was a bullet in the head and a body dumped in an unmarked pit. Pemmick forced the hands of more than a few by persuading them that their crimes would be exposed, and they would face international tribunals once full-fledged democracy took over in Russia. Of course, democracy didn't have a prayer, but they didn't know that. Pemmick did a lot of good and received commendations for his efforts."

"Pemmick tried to recover Hampton and Lockwood and the crew?"

"No," Andy said. "At the time, the United States had no idea Hampton and Lockwood were still alive and didn't know about Staro —*at the time*. Lee said most of what we know about Staro comes from bits and pieces of intelligence picked up in recent years. But when Pemmick served in Moscow, he knew Berezovsky, Senior. He negotiated with him for the release of other men in other facilities. Fast forward to now, and Berezovsky's son, Valentin, is one of the oligarchs on the CAATSA list."

"Who now owns Staro," I said.

"And all of Staro's assets. Hampton and Lockwood, property of an oligarch. Weapons. Possibly Brent and Hillerman, too. Maybe others. Lee thinks Pemmick looked up his old contact Berezovsky—"

"Or vice versa," I offered, then ducked aside to let Andy continue.

"Lee made the connection between Pemmick's negotiations with Berezovsky in the eighties, his son today, and the appearances of Hampton and Lockwood here in the United States. Lee thinks Pemmick secretly gained the release—or perhaps use—of the two men. Not back then, but now. This is where the Distinguished Flying Crosses come in. We searched the records. They were never awarded to these men. Lee thinks Pemmick gave the medals to the two men. On his own. Part of the charade of secretly bringing them home."

"Why not? I mean, what's reality to them? This is some twisted shit," I said. "But why would Pemmick do all this now?"

"Lee thinks Pemmick funded his buy-in with James with laundered money from Berezovsky." Andy let the point settle for a moment before continuing. "Pemmick used it to turn James into an internet *phenomenon,* then for the Nedritch purchase—the foundation of a new media empire. Remember, it was the Nedritch abduction that sent Lee down this rabbit hole in the first place."

"You're saying Donaldson thinks Berezovsky is in bed with Pemmick? And that Berezovsky brought Hampton and Lockwood to the deal?"

Andy nodded. "Hampton and Lockwood helped remove two roadblocks."

"Hold the phone!" I interrupted. "I don't get that. Why kill James? The golden goose? Why kill some minor diplomat—what's his name—Malkin, in St. Augustine?"

"Lee said, 'To understand Malkin's murder, you have to know the players.' Everyone in any position of authority in today's Russia owes their allegiance not to the state, as it once was, but to the family. To the benefactor. The oligarch. Malkin was someone else's boy. To understand his murder, look at his replacement. One of Lee's calls went to the State Department—no, not to Conway. He confirmed that Malkin's replacement is loyal to Berezovsky. They slipped him into Malkin's position to facilitate moves by Berezovsky. Guess who on our team counterparts Malkin's replacement?"

I looked at Andy and smiled.

"Conway," she said. "That's why there were trip wire notifications on the Hampton and Lockwood records—and why they routed to Conway. That's why he came here. That's why he called Lee and set up the meeting in Norfolk. Conway's job was to guard against anyone finding the link between Pemmick and the Russians."

"You knew going in that last night was an ambush?"

"No. And if Lee suspected, he didn't tell me. Lee thought Conway was just a source—one which might cement his theory that Berezovsky is the money behind Pemmick. Conway blindsided us."

No kidding.

"Okay. That explains Malkin's murder. What about James?" I asked.

"James…James was a clown. We—you—made him a fart joke. He had no more value. James needed to be turned into something more."

"Martyr," I said. "But still…"

Andy's eyes sparkled. I saw in her the police academy student that shot to the top of each class and caught the attention of her instructor, now her boss, Chief Tom Ceeves. Knowing the answers electrified her. "James the Clown was an impediment. James the Martyr is galvanizing."

"Galvanizing for what?"

"The next phase."

"Which is?"

Andy jumped to her feet. She spoke with her hands flying. A lock of her hair fell across one eye.

"The part Lee saw through all this clutter. The real game. *James Media!* Buying up radio stations! And no doubt in the months ahead, television and print. Using money laundered and channeled in from Berezovsky with the help of a wheel-greaser in the State Department— someone in the position to lift sanctions, to make it easier for an American businessman like Pemmick to hide doing business with a name on the CAATSA list!"

"But why the short game?" I asked. "Why put on a neo-Nazi demonstration? That's not going to win him any friends."

"Yes, it is! Hate groups. He's didn't put on that demonstration to make a political point or to win new support from the general public. These days, most hate groups eschew those tactics. They've switched to the gospel according to social media. Disinformation. Tactics right out of the Russian playbook. Pemmick staged that display to build up the memory of James the Martyr, and as a gesture to unify the hate groups gathering here for the James funeral. That demonstration threw a bone to the skinheads and twenty-something supremacists while he reeled them in for something bigger."

I held up a hand for her to pause while I struggled to extract a memory. "James. Where did he live? Where will he be buried?"

"His offices and studio were in Lincoln," Andy said, "He lived in a little town north of Lincoln. He called it a 'Slice of Real America' in some of his speeches. A town called—"

"Ulysses!" I chimed in. "Right?"

"That's where he'll be buried," she said. "They're planning a processional from Lincoln to Ulysses."

"That's where Pemmick has a meeting. Today."

"What do you mean?"

I repeated what I overhead in the bed of Linebacker's pickup, then added, "But this can't just be Pemmick fashioning himself as a new David Duke—making a coalition out of a bunch of white supremacists," I added.

"Oh, trust me, it isn't," Andy said. "Jump to 2016 and the Russian role in the U.S. presidential election. The Russians pulled off one of the greatest attacks on democracy in American history. Will...!" Andy slipped back into her chair, clutching my arm. "This is going to sound crazy, but—look at what Pemmick is doing and who he's doing it with. Building a coalition of hate groups when Nationalism is trending all over the world. While you have nationalism coming out of the White House and simultaneously being pumped equally hard by Russian troll farms. Those tactics rendered an impossible, unexpected success in 2016. This time, instead of bankrolling some troll farm in Russia, Berezovsky is funding Pemmick so he can build a political movement right here in the U.S. Something along the lines of America First in the thirties!"

I whistled.

"Lee's intelligence sources told him Berezovsky is currying favor with Putin. If he can pull this off and keep Putin's choice in the White House..." Andy slipped back into her chair. "Will. We have to stop him."

"Pemmick? *We* have to stop him? *You and me?*"

Andy struggled to find the words for a moment. "Look. The Russians aren't stupid. They were outed by Mueller and half the intelligence community. But then a miracle happened. The administration denied it ever happened. Look at the Mueller Report! They tried everything to spin it or bury it."

"Dee, this president would take Satan's endorsement if it meant winning. That's not exactly a secret."

"But that's the point! Lee's intelligence sources told him the Russians were ready to call it a day; they thought they were blown. But, now they're even bolder. Mix in General Pemmick, a coalition of hate groups, fresh Russian money and a media machine that will saturate middle America and they have a whole new blueprint for swinging the election. Not like last time. Better!"

"Jesus," I said.

"I didn't want to believe it, Will. Nobody does. The man in the White House will deny, deny, deny, like last time. But at the same time, he's been pushing non-stop to lift sanctions against Russian individuals and companies. Lee believes it was White House intervention that fast-tracked FTC approval of the Nedritch purchase."

"So, why didn't Lee marshal the forces of the FBI and blow this up?"

"Because that's the most insidious part—the FBI and the men and women serving the FBI and the laws of this country have been denounced and marginalized. They can't afford to be accused of cooking up another 'Russia Hoax.'"

"But not Donaldson...?"

"He saw the big picture from the start. That's the real reason he worked off book. That's the real reason he came to me. He knew he had no option to take this to his superiors. The FBI cannot and will not risk pursuing another Russia investigation that can be framed as politically motivated. Today's Justice Department is certainly not going to sanction one. Will, don't think I don't know how this sounds. Lee Donaldson's effort notwithstanding, in this political climate—on *this specific issue*—the FBI is powerless."

"What about Hampton and Lockwood? They're in custody."

Andy gave a dismissive sigh. "Russian spies, perhaps. Russian tools, yes. The FBI will certainly look at them differently now. But, short of a miracle, you'll never connect them to Pemmick, or for that matter Berezovsky. For God's sake, Pemmick will claim he was a *victim* of Hampton. And even if you got the two men to testify—what defense attorney wouldn't attack their state of mind? On top of that, prosecution would take years. They'll be dead before the law clerks start labeling folders."

"What about Conway?"

Andy shrugged. "If it was up to me? I'd charge him in the attempted murder of a police officer and an agent of the FBI. But unless he's a fool, I doubt we'll find any kind of trail linking him to Pemmick or Berezovsky. The fact that he counterpoints certain Russian diplomats will be painted as nothing more than Conway doing his job."

"The Racehorse Blue mission? The true story of what happened?"

"Classified. Same with The Glass Wall. Lee's sources warned him. At best, it's a fanciful story from the Cold War that no one can prove. At worst, blow the whistle on Staro, and Berezovsky will bulldoze it overnight." Andy flexed a finger back and forth between us. "You and I can't reveal Staro, either. They'll wave federal prison time in our faces faster than we can make a call to *The New York Times*."

"Pemmick tried to kill us last night," I said coldly.

"He sure as hell did. Your point would be?"

"He tried to kill an FBI agent! And he may yet succeed! Doesn't that mean anything?"

Andy didn't have to answer, but she did. "You know it means some-thing to me. This is still about Mike. And Corey Braddock ...*You know my feelings*."

I stood up. I had to think. I paced the small room. "Jesus, Dee…"

"I know."

She waited while I dealt with the Tetris cascade of pieces in my head. Not for the first time, I considered how absolutely convincing a conspiracy sounded in the darkest hours of the night.

"You don't think Conway can be flipped?"

Andy shook her head sadly. "Lee might have had a shot, if he got to him before anyone else, and if he broke a few rules. But no, not at this point."

"What about us? We were there. We can testify."

"We can…but Conway can legitimately claim he was only there to assess the degree to which Classified secrets were being compromised by a rogue FBI agent with a political agenda, and a local cop with delu-sions of grandeur. Honey, I think you'd be treated to seeing your wife crucified, maybe arrested."

That stopped me in my tracks.

"Fuck that."

"Then you see what I'm saying. *If* all of Lee's conclusions—all of this—is even close to being on target, it's the perfect crime. It's protected. It's deniable. It has high-level political muscle either behind it—or determined to turn a blind eye to it. All the evidence can and will be denounced as 'fake news' with the two key witnesses discredited as mentally malfunctioning."

"Well, that fucking sucks!" I channeled a bit of Pidge. "Now I get why we're running from the FBI."

"Not running. Avoiding." Andy rose and stepped around the small table. She slid her arms around me again, pulled herself close again. "I can't let this go, Will. I can't. Whether he lives or dies, Lee deserves to have this finished."

I squeezed my wife tightly. She looked up at me.

"I can't ask you—"

"I'm in. All the way. Always."

She put both hands on the side of my head and kissed me.

"Uh, hi?" The hotel desk clerk spoke up tentatively behind us. He framed himself in the doorway to the lobby. "Do you two want some breakfast?"

57

The desk clerk hustled about, setting up the morning's continental breakfast of sweet rolls, fruit, dry cereal in miniature boxes and, praise be to the Lord, coffee. He then miraculously appeared carrying two plates heaped with scrambled eggs and bacon, grinning from ear to ear and staring at my wife nonstop. From that point on, he popped in and out often, fussing with the countertop buffet and attempting small talk, eyes wandering to Andy again and again. I came close to the limit of my patience. I wanted to call him on it, I really did. But the man brought bacon.

During one of his trips to the kitchen, I leaned over to Andy and said, "You know, if you unbutton the top two buttons of that blouse, he might offer you a room."

"With you or with him?"

Toward the end of the glorious meal, I realized our mistake. Our bodies betrayed us, and deep fatigue settled in.

"Let's try that button trick and get a room," I suggested.

"Let's not. From what you overheard in that pickup truck something is happening in Ulysses today. It's not the funeral. That's tomorrow. We need to get down there."

"Okay but take a step back. We're both shot. Neither of us will be operating at our best, and since my best is fifty percent of your normal, that puts my tired normal in the negative. I might screw things up more than usual."

"Stop it."

"Also, whatever is happening in Ulysses, it's not going to happen at six in the morning. Let's grab a few hours of rest and get there this afternoon. Who knows? It might happen tonight. Or it might be nothing. Point is, I think we have time."

"No, I—"

"And finally, we have no plan." She bit her lip, frustrated. I had her there. "Sleep would be a plan. A good plan. Otherwise, we have no plan."

"Stop saying plan." She planted her elbows on the table and pressed her eye sockets into the heel of her hands. "God! Fine. But I'm not unbuttoning anything."

We finished breakfast and presented ourselves at the front desk. Andy insisted on the precaution of leaving our credit cards dormant and paying with cash, which led to the comical—at least I thought so—discovery that I had forty-three dollars and she had nothing. We asked to rent half a room, with a guarantee we'd leave by noon.

"Here," the clerk slid a plastic key card across the desk. "No charge. Really. Two-fourteen. Elevator's around the corner. Use it as long as you want." He pointed. I peeled off a twenty and laid it on the counter.

Andy asked to borrow a phone charger. He produced one from a drawer full of them. Andy tipped his kindness with a radiant smile.

We hit the pillows hard and fast.

Andy woke me five hours later.

58

"Well, there's one upside to losing my bag. I didn't have anyone blowing up my phone," she said, tossing my recharged phone onto the bed and then fussing with her hair in front of the mirror on the wall. "They blew up yours instead."

I spent a moment getting my eyes to work before noting the time—seventeen minutes after eleven o'clock. Able to read the screen, I poked at the phone.

"Five missed calls from a number I don't recognize—"

"That's the FBI. They've figured out that my phone is at the Norfolk PD so they're calling you." Andy made a face. "Will, you have six missed calls from Stephenson from last week! Six! You've got to call him back!"

Dammit! Forgot to delete those!

Six missed calls had nothing to do with an appointment.

Stephenson was my silent research partner. It was Stephenson who discretely inquired with hospitals I visited about recent unexplained successes in cancer treatment. The information was hard to extract, but his reputation as a nationally known neurologist opened doors and prompted results.

Stephenson wasn't pestering me for an updated scan. We agreed to use missed calls to signal success. *Six!* I prayed that the number included Benny and Anastasia.

None of this helped me with Andy.

The curative characteristic of *the other thing* frightens her more than anything else. After the first visit to Children's Hospital in Milwaukee, she begged me to be careful. She knew she couldn't tell me not to save children's lives. But this scared her.

I promised Andy, vaguely, that I would be careful, that I would try to learn more before rushing ahead.

Andy continued talking. "I know you don't agree with me on this, but—"

I plucked the phone from her fingers. "Sweetheart, I promise. Can we just deal with a few more immediate things first? Here. There's a text from Arun. A text from Earl, uh...looks like Pidge is fired."

"What?"

"Yeah, don't worry about it. Earl fires her twice a month. Uh-oh. Three missed calls from the Chief."

"Looking for me," she said. "Probably because Lee's SAC is lighting him up."

"Ha. Joke's on Lee's SAC. The Chief doesn't get lit up. That's an exercise in futility. Do you want to call him?"

Andy dropped on the bed beside me. She picked up the phone and looked at it, as if it might render a sign. After a moment, she handed the phone back. "Better if I don't. For both me and the Chief. Get up. We need to go."

"Really?" I stretched and flopped back on the pillow. "Why don't we stay here?" I patted the mattress. Andy flipped a look over her shoulder that derailed the amorous offer forming in my head.

"Move it."

"Does that mean we have a plan?"

"We do."

59

"Well, I did not expect that," I said.

Andy studied the roadblock. A pair of late-model pickup trucks angle parked across both lanes of the narrow gravel road. Young men in black tactical clothing and matching ball caps loitered in front of the white and gray trucks. Each carried a military-style semi-automatic rifle slung across their chest. We stopped a quarter mile away. One of the men lifted binoculars to his eyes. I slid down in the seat, not for any logical reason.

"Can they do that? I mean, this is a public road," I pointed out.

"Would you like to go up there and tell them that?" Andy put the car in reverse and backed into a Y-turn. She motored placidly away from the scene.

"No plan survives first contact with the enemy," I said.

"Our plan is fine. We just need to park a little farther away."

"Von Moltke said that, you know."

"Thank you."

"Prussian guy. One of those antique pointy-helmet generals."

"I know." Andy drove south, away from the roadblock. It may have been a public road, but it consisted of little more than one and half lanes of pressed gravel, as were many of the roads between the arterial highways in this part of the state. Farm fields filled chest high in corn spread on both sides of us.

At the first intersection, she turned right onto another gravel road. This, like all its linear Nebraska brethren, ran true to the compass, due west. Nebraska's road grid sectioned off individual square miles of farmland. Most road sections lay uninterrupted. On others, a few mailboxes in varying states of tilt marked driveways.

This section ran through endless corn, but it had one interruption. A round aluminum corn bin with a conical roof sat on the right near the center of the country mile.

Andy slowed and pulled the rental off the gravel. We bumped over shallow ruts. She maneuvered the car around the circular structure and parked between the curved aluminum wall and the wall of green-leaved corn. The car wouldn't be hidden to anyone driving by, but it would be unseen from a distance. Good enough.

Prior to leaving the Hampton Inn, Andy used the room key and a code provided by the front desk to access their "Business Center"—a PC tucked in a nook off the breakfast room. She opened Google Maps and we spent a quarter hour studying the small town of Ulysses, Nebraska, the land around it, and the square mile section Josiah James had purchased to build his estate.

The aerial images offered a mixed bag, shot at varying times. Most showed construction of a large structure in the center of a cornfield, the majority of which remained intact. A long driveway bisected the southern half of the square mile, leading up to a single building. Street views exhibited a two-story, pillared, mansion-sized home with white walls and dark green shutters. Zooming in on the house pixelated the image to the point of making it useless. The corn growing around the estate was dry and tan, suggesting the images had been taken in the fall, but which fall? Neither Andy nor I knew Google's schedule for shooting or updating their ongoing reconnaissance of the Earth's surface. We assumed enough time had passed to allow completion of the ostentatious house.

We'd soon find out.

Andy and I stepped out of the car and gathered at the trunk. She took a moment and scraped a shallow groove out of the dirt behind the left rear tire. She dropped the keys into the depression and covered them with dirt.

"New batteries in?" she asked, brushing the dust from her hands.

"Check."

"Give me your phone." She held out her hand. I turned over the device and pointed.

"Two taps on the button—"

"I know, I know." She held the phone out and double-pressed the main button. The phone screen came alive in camera mode.

"Then press this button to—"

She fixed a perturbed look on me, took a step back, aimed the phone at me and touched her slender index finger to the shutter button. The phone emitted a familiar camera-shutter click.

"Oh, look," she said, "a picture of the common blue-eyed know-it-all. I can check this one off my list."

I ignored her cheeky grin. I pulled my sole power unit from my hip pocket and snapped the propeller in place. With fresh batteries from a pit stop at Love's Travel Stop on the way out of Norfolk, the power unit gave out a strong, satisfying test buzz.

"One second," she said. She worked the phone screen, swiping, touching and chasing menus. "I want to kill this camera click sound... okay...there. You ready?" She looked at me expectantly.

I held up the power unit. "Alright, I've put a lot of thought into this." I levied a solemn gaze on her. It seemed like the right time to tell her. "Basic Linear Aerial System for Transport, Electric Rechargeable." I held up the power unit.

The world around us held its breath. Distant calls from crows and hawks fell silent. As if she commanded nature itself, Andy stopped even the wind rustling corn leaves by affixing a motionless stare on me. Or maybe it just seemed that way in the instant it took for her to pass judgment on my brilliant new name.

"No." She turned her back to me and took a step backward into position directly in front of me. Her sweet scent kissed my senses. "Ready when you are."

"Okay. Here we go." I slid my left arm around her at the waist and hefted my BLASTER in my right.

No way I was giving up that name.

Fwooomp!

IT'S the change in perspective. The way the earth falls away, the immediate area at first, then everything stretching to the horizon—the way the landscape pretends to reveal itself, only to taunt with greater and greater dimension as you rise. That's just one reason flight takes my breath away. I tapped my toes and the corn stalks beside us dropped. The gravel road changed angles until it became a tan seam through a quilt of lush colors. The corn turned into a table of green all around us.

I didn't aim the power unit straight up. Height entices me, but not Andy. I snuggled against her. As our feet cleared the plateau of corn tops, I pushed the slide throttle forward and held the power unit out, past Andy. She closed a grip on my arm where it wrapped around her slender waist. She would have preferred facing me, with a death grip around my neck. But we agreed that this plan called for her to assume the duties of camera operator, which I had artfully flubbed at Coleman I. She would work the phone, snapping what we hoped would be damning photos of General Winslow Pemmick at his summit meeting of hate groups.

"Take us over the roadblock, Will," she commanded. "I want to scope it out."

I altered our flight path slightly, cutting a diagonal across the corn-field toward the roadblock on the field's eastern border. Sun glinting on chrome and high-gloss paint quickly revealed the two pickup trucks choking the road. I altered course slightly to the right and pushed the speed control forward, accelerating. Andy's ponytail danced between us, tickling my neck.

We skimmed the tops of the corn until it slid away beneath us, replaced by the ribbon of gravel road. We broke out over the spot where Andy had Y-turned. I flexed my hand to the left and the power unit pulled us toward the parked trucks. I pushed harder, building speed. When I reached a point where the whine of the prop might be heard I sharply cut the power.

We sailed silently. Voices and laughter reached our ears.

"...how he came up with the dumb idea to buy that piece of shit," Sentry One said. He sat on a tubular running board with his back to the driver's door of the white truck, making use of the shade that stretched onto the gravel as the sun began its dive for the horizon. "The head gasket's shot, the struts are bad, and I swear that tranny is eating itself alive."

"He never listens," Sentry Two shook his head, strolling slowly past his companion. His rifle, an ugly black semi-automatic made of grips and angles, hung across his chest. I noted a small radio in his breast pocket.

We passed directly over them. I checked the truck bed for additional arms. Two athletic bags lay on the ribbed surface. Range bags. Extra clips and accessories for the weapons at hand.

"That's the fucking truth," Sentry One agreed heartily. "Only I'm the one's always gotta bail him out. What my sister sees in that asshat is…"

The conversation faded as distance grew between us and the sentry post. I let us glide north at a comfortable altitude of a dozen feet above the road. Wind resistance eroded our speed. When we no longer heard them speaking, I thumbed the power unit slide control and turned the prop, first at a low growl, then slowly increasing to a healthy whine. I angled my hand to the left. We left the road and returned to a path that skimmed the corn. A few of the plants showed signs of tassels, which seemed early to me until I realized we were nearing mid-July.

"We have an anniversary coming up," I said softly. I know from experience that a voice can seem startlingly loud when there is no engine noise and little wind noise to overcome.

"This is something you want to discuss right now?"

"I don't want you to get me anything," I said.

"Is that your way of telling me you're not getting me anything?" I couldn't see the spark in her eye or the dimples that dance at the corners of her mouth, but I heard the smile in her voice.

"Oh, no. I already have the world's greatest anniversary gift for you," I said.

"No, you don't."

Shit. I can't even lie to her when she can't see me.

She stiffened. "Okay, button it up. There it is."

I saw what she saw, the James house—mansion—rising in the distance.

"Jesus, Dee! Do you know what that is?"

"Uh…it looks familiar."

"That's a freakin' replica of Tara! The house from *Gone With the Wind*! Seriously!"

White walls, green shutters, and stately square pillars dominated the sprawling green landscape ahead. The house rose from the flat center of the six-hundred-forty-acre square mile defined by gravel roads on all sides. Google's photography was clearly dated. A finished asphalt drive began at a gate near the road and ran between sapling trees directly on a line anchored by the mansion's double front doors. The drive formed a neat loop at the house. A rich green carpet of lawn spread around the home, ending at a low brick wall that separated the estate from the corn on all sides.

"Don't they all look like that? You know…Southern?"

"No, I'm not kidding. I saw a place in New Orleans that was built to reproduce the façade they built for the film. This is the same façade! The porch. The windows. Take some pictures. We'll look it up when we get back. You'll see!"

"Weird."

"Not really. What better statement for James to make than to construct an homage to the glory days of slave ownership?"

"Okay. *Shhhhhhh*…more guards. See 'em?"

I had been gawking at the house, thinking about how James proclaimed himself to be such an average Joe while he poured money into a mansion on a square mile of land. We passed through Ulysses on the drive from Norfolk, the small town that James liked to praise. Nobody in Ulysses lived on this scale. I wondered what they thought of this white whale rising in the sea of corn.

I pulled my attention off the house and spotted two more sentries at the gate. I changed course to the right, keeping us over the corn and wide of the asphalt drive and gate.

Andy broke the silence, speaking just above a whisper.

"Where is everybody? The news said that hundreds of these guys were closing in on Lincoln, camping out. Wouldn't you have thought they'd be here? Somewhere around here?"

"Yeah. Camping. Tents. RVs. It looks like Pemmick isn't letting anyone near the place."

"I've got vehicles in front of the house," Andy said. "A serious cliché, don't you think? Blacked out SUVs?"

"Like something in a Michael Bay movie," I said.

Andy didn't comment. She sleeps through action films.

Three vehicles crouched in line astern formation in front of the house. Tahoes or Suburbans. All black, all with heavily tinted windows.

"Pemmick's? Or do you think he has visitors?" I asked.

"I had hoped for dozens of visitors. I wanted to be able to get facial recognition on the leaders of his pet hate groups. Show him fraternizing."

Except it appeared no one had come to the conference. Maybe we missed the meeting. The few vehicles, more than likely belonging to Pemmick himself, didn't support the idea that this was the birth of a political force.

What if we missed the critical opportunity because I pressed for a nap?

If Andy was thinking the same thing, she didn't say so, although I anticipated hearing her thoughts on the subject later.

"Sentries by the vehicles," she reported in a whisper. "I see two. Take us in. Let's check the windows."

I goosed the power and turned the BLASTER at a sharp angle. We left the corn behind and crossed a few feet above the border wall. After cruising half the distance to the house, I killed the power for a silent glide across the lawn. The house loomed, and with a touch or two of reverse-thrust to slow us, we floated up to the brick corner of the building.

We stopped. I clamped a grip on the bricks and rotated us to watch the sentries stroll back and forth beside the parked vehicles. These men differed from the men at the roadblock and gate. These wore white shirts and ties under dark windbreakers. They wore dark glasses and looked older than the young supremacists that had formed the flag line on the edge of the Nebraska Capitol square or the team at the road-block. They looked like contemporaries of Donaldson and carried them-selves with his level of professionalism. Neither man walked with a long gun. Both sported bulges under their windbreakers. I expected one of them to touch a hand to his ear or speak into a wrist microphone. They didn't. They strolled and watched. Not just over the cars, but over the lawn, at the house, even at the sky. What did they expect? Aerial assault?

This didn't look like Pemmick's crude linebacker security detail. These men looked serious.

"Dee," I leaned forward and found the side of her head. I spoke into her ear at a level spanning the line between breath and whisper. "I think these guys belong to someone who is meeting with Pemmick. Whatever meeting they had planned is happening. Right now."

She turned her head until her lips found my ear.

"Windows."

I pushed against the bricks, gently. My thumb eased the BLASTER control slide forward—just a hair. The prop turned silently. We moved. Slowly.

We traversed the four-pillared two-story porch. A double-hung, munton-barred window passed on our right. Curtains obscured the interior. I decided not to risk increasing the power to scoot across the arched, double front door. Slow passage meant not having to use reverse thrust at the next set of windows. After an interminable glide we passed the second set of windows. More curtains.

Andy tugged on my arm. I read it as "Go up." We were close enough to the boards of the porch that I was able to extend one foot and tap to push us vertically. We rose. The second-floor window on the left side of the façade slid into view.

Curtains.

I slipped the BLASTER into my hip pocket, grabbed the sill, steadied us, then pushed on a line that would take us back across the porch at second-floor height. Once moving, I found the core muscle I feel in the vanished state and I rotated. Andy let out a clipped hum and gripped my arm. I had forgotten that she feels that same sensation when we're together within *the other thing*.

The center windows over the door lacked curtains and revealed an empty hallway. The right-side windows exposed a bedroom, also empty.

I found Andy's ear again.

"Let's go around to the back."

I felt her head nod.

The glide took us to the corner of the house, then slowly past it. I pulled the power unit, aimed and gave it minimal thrust. Propwash pulled us in an arc around the corner. It quickly became apparent that this "mansion" was little more than a two-story rectangle, much smaller than the first impression suggested.

A fake, much like James.

As I calculated a vector that would render a silent glide past two second-story windows, I heard the front door of the house open. Footsteps pounded across the wooden porch.

Andy gripped my arm.

I know, I know! I answered her by flexing the core muscle and rotating us to face the front lawn. We continued moving backward. I pushed the BLASTER power, setting up a low growl that risked being heard, but which also brought us to a stop and then reversed course. I sent us downward and cut the power as we drew even with the corner of the house.

Half a dozen men hurried down the steps toward the vehicle. Three men took the lead. Two on each side matched the sentries strolling in the yard. The man in the center was smaller, younger. He wore suit pants, a leather jacket and a ball cap pulled low on his forehead. I felt Andy aiming the phone, but the angle was bad. The flankers blocked her shot. The man in the center faced away from us and walked with his head down.

One of the sentries hurried around the rear of the center vehicle and pulled open the second-row door.

We're gonna miss him! Shit! I pulsed the power to accelerate. It was a mistake. Another of the sentries stopped in his tracks and lifted his face to the sky.

"Drone!" he called out.

The alarm had the instant effect of accelerating the man in the middle. He all but leaped into the back seat. His feet hardly cleared the scuff plate before the man holding the door slammed it shut and scrambled for the driver's seat.

"Dammit!" I whispered. Missing the shot wasn't our only problem. The grass came up to meet us. I straightened my legs and extended my toes to cushion us without kicking us off into space. It worked. We leveled off but continued forward.

Directly into the path of the vehicles.

The drone warning sparked action. Engines turned and started. Tires squeaked as the vehicles leaped forward.

The balance of the party—three more men—hurried to the third vehicle. The first two vehicles launched.

I had a poor choice—kick off and shoot upward or hit the BLASTER and force us to stop. If I did neither, our path ran into the rapidly accelerating lead Tahoe.

"Will!" Andy saw it, too, but not with the same intent. "Get us over the roof rack! On top!"

I tapped my toes, induced an upward vector, then aimed the BLASTER left and hit the power. We surged and rose on an intercept course, and at the same time I rotated us to a horizontal position to swing our legs clear. The first black Tahoe swept under us, just out of reach. I turned my wrist to alter course. The second Tahoe slid under us. It heaved to the right, following the curved driveway loop. I felt a jolt. We shot forward, locked in motion above the vehicle.

Andy! She had reached out and closed a grip on the roof rack of the second Tahoe. We accelerated rapidly. I scrambled to stuff the BLASTER into my hip pocket. The prop caught my shirt. I wiggled it free and jammed the power unit home. With my right hand free, I reached around Andy, who clutched the roof rack beneath me. I grabbed a roof rack crossbar. Relative wind increased rapidly and blew past us as the drivers, reacting to word of a drone, accelerated.

"Pull us close!" I instructed Andy.

We both pulled until the glossy black roof nearly touched us. Our legs extended over the rear lip of the roof. The wind tore at us. Reacting as trained security drivers, the men behind the wheels pushed their vehicles hard. We may have hit sixty on the half-mile driveway. They slowed for the gate, knowing that a hard turn onto gravel offered dire consequences. Clear of the gate and the turn, they kicked it again. I closed my eyes against a wind that made them water.

Andy didn't move or speak. There was nothing to do or say. We held on.

I thought about the situation.

Pemmick traveled with the group. I caught a glimpse of his white-haired head among the three men going for the last Tahoe. Slowest to react to the Drone Alert, they trailed at a distance.

Why fear a drone?

This bunch exhibited a serious obsession with security. Did they fear attack? An attack from the sky? But from whom? Neo-Nazis certainly have enemies, but almost never violent enemies. I knew of no white supremacist gatherings invaded by an active shooter.

Why fear a drone?

Common drones don't attack, not outside of a war zone. Common drones take pictures and shoot video.

Cameras.

The passenger in the vehicle beneath us did not want to be seen.

I thought about slipping over the side to shoot pictures while in motion. The roaring relative wind posed problem number one. It prohibited communicating my idea to Andy. Tinted glass introduced problem number two. Holding the camera added problem number three. Too much chance of dropping it. Better to wait.

The likely destination had to be Lincoln and the headquarters office of James Media. That put us roughly an hour away from stopping. I wondered if it was worth it. Maybe it would be better to release, push off and get back to the rental car. From there, drive to Lincoln, regroup and reconsider our approach.

I twisted slightly and pressed my lips to Andy's ear.

"What do you want to do?"

Her right hand, still closed on my left forearm, squeezed a grip and held it.

Stay!

"Roger that."

60

Twenty minutes into the trip, the caravan slowed for the town of Seward. The lower speed limit came as a relief. At a stoplight, I reconsidered shooting pictures of the man in the cabin below us. I realized there wasn't time to reposition and the risk of the vehicle pulling away without us was too great. Andy and I simply hung on.

Exiting town southbound, the three vehicles picked up the pace again. Just as I settled for another half hour of wind, the Tahoe abruptly decelerated. I lifted my head and opened my eyes. A set of metal buildings with a row of vertical agricultural storage tanks passed on my right. Ahead, more low metal buildings lined a service road. I instantly recognized them.

A portable lighted sign parked on the roadside grass offered *Airplane & Helicopter Rides*.

Airport.

The lead Tahoe turned onto the service road. We shot forward several hundred yards, then hooked left. We passed a set of hangars, slowed, and turned onto a short driveway that opened onto the Seward Airport ramp.

A white executive jet kicked flashes of sunlight to my eyes as the three vehicles rolled across the concrete. I expected the black SUVs to pull up to the open airstair on the twin-engine Cessna Citation, but they veered right abruptly and darted into an open, empty hangar. They stopped side by side, out of sight.

All three engines stopped. Silence pressed my ears, exaggerated by the sudden absence of wind noise.

"Let go. Get the camera ready. I'll get us in position." I pushed against the roof rack and floated vertically. The hangar had a high ceiling with room to maneuver. I rotated to a comfortable vertical position and pulled the BLASTER from my pocket.

Doors below us opened in concert. Men stepped out. The security team fanned out on the concrete floor. The two with Pemmick took up a position at each side of the full-span door. They held black rifles at port arms. The team with Pemmick's guest formed a four-man box, facing outward.

Without wind or engine noise, and with no activity on the airfield, the hangar lay in sullen silence, making it almost impossible to give the power unit more than a few revolutions. We eased forward slowly. I made a spiral turn to my right to bring us around and down, hoping for a shot of Pemmick and his visitor.

The visitor emerged from his vehicle just as Pemmick did the same. Neither man spoke. I rotated to give Andy a frontal view of the men.

The visitor abruptly stepped past Pemmick without acknowledging him. Hat pulled down over his face, he took a position in the center of the box formed by his security team. Without breaking stride, the second rank of security men closed in, gripped his arms and marched him forward.

No! No-no-no-no!

If Andy was shooting, she was getting nothing. Bodyguards and the ball cap shielded the man. Pemmick stood nowhere near him. Andy tapped my forearm urgently.

I saw no other choice. I pushed the power unit slide. It struck up a whining note and we surged forward.

"Drone!" One of the men called out again.

"Go!" Pemmick ordered.

The squad around the visitor closed ranks. The two holding his arms all but lifted him off his feet. The man threw a hand to the brim of his hat and pulled, obscuring his face. The security unit broke into a synchronized trot. Jet engine noise joined the sound of the BLASTER. The Cessna Citation engines spun to life.

Shit! This guy does NOT want to be seen!

Andy rapidly tapped my arm. We shot forward, chasing the upright rugby scrum that darted across the ramp.

"I'm trying!" I whispered. "Be ready!"

She stopped tapping and moved. I took it as preparing the camera, holding it in position.

I accelerated and swung left to put working space between us and the cluster of men. I simultaneously rotated, giving Andy the best angle to shoot.

For a moment, I thought we had them. I swept through an arc that brought us to a halt near the nose of the jet. The team still had four or five paces to cover before reaching the plane. I steadied us with a loud power reversal on the BLASTER.

The lead security man on the right leaped forward, took two long strides and hopped the airstair to enter the jet. Perfect. In a second, either the next security man would follow suit, or more likely, he would urge his charge forward. Either move would put the man in the clear.

The second security man made his move, but not the move I hoped for. He shrugged out of his windbreaker and threw it over the head of his charge. He then bear-hugged the man and lifted him onto the steps like cargo. The lead man reached out from the cabin and pulled the principle from view.

It happened in a pair of heartbeats.

Andy gave up an angry jolt and tugged at my arm.

"Let me go! I need to stop this!"

I tightened my grip. "They see you. They shoot you."

She stopped. We hung helpless in the air as the rest of the team boarded. A moment later, hands pulled the door closed and the engines wound up to taxi breakaway power.

I glanced into the open mouths of the twin jet's engines and saw the blades spinning, drawing in air. In the vanished state, without weight, we were less than a dandelion fluff in the air—air now being pulled into the jet engines in huge gulps.

I rotated the BLASTER and shoved the power slide. We rose.

"Take me to Pemmick!" Andy ordered. "No! Take me to that goon on the right. Put me down right in front of him!"

I didn't question. I halted our ascent, rotated us, and lined up a path to the man Pemmick had dispatched to stand guard at the corner of the hangar door. Our target, his counterpart, and Pemmick stood in a line across the front of the open hangar watching the jet roll across the ramp.

Jet engine sound covered the whine of the BLASTER. I gave it a shot that powered us directly at the sentry standing with his rifle across his chest. Andy turned her head to me.

"Right up to him. When I say the word, let me go."

We pulled up directly in front a pug-nosed linebacker type with what looked like one lazy eye. I had a split second to wonder how good this guy was at watching out for his master with that eye.

"Now!" Andy's voice, less than a meter from the man, startled him. He searched for the sound.

I let her go and felt the electric snap that follows. She winked into view with her hands gripping the sentry's rifle.

She smashed her knee into his balls. He doubled. She pulled the rifle toward her, then reversed it into his face. He took the blow across the bridge of his nose and blood spurted. His body didn't know whether to suck in air or cry out. The result was a strangled guttural heaving sound. He tumbled forward. She backed up, bumped into me and knocked me away. In full possession of the rifle, she swept it right, then left, connecting the butt with the man's jaw as he fell. She then danced away from him and brought the rifle up to bear on the other sentry who had scarcely noticed that his teammate just folded onto the concrete with his hands clutching his groin. Too late, he blinked at the woman pointing a rifle at his face.

"DROP IT!" she shouted. He hesitated. She didn't. She jerked her rifle to the left and lowered it. She fired. The report shocked my unprotected ears. The shot chipped concrete a yard from the other sentry's boots. Before the echo trapped in the hangar died, she had the rifle back on target.

He pushed the weapon away from his chest, then slowly lowered it to the concrete.

"Kick it away!" He kicked. The rifle skidded and clattered forward. "On your belly, hands behind your head!"

He knelt slowly, lowered himself to the concrete and interlocked his fingers behind his head.

"Call them back, General!"

Pemmick, unmoving at the center of the hangar door, looked calmly at Andy. Mild surprise rode a slight squint.

"Get on your phone and call them back!"

Pemmick shook his head slowly, thoughtfully. "I don't know what you're talking about, Detective Stewart. I don't see anyone here except a woman who has not identified herself as an officer of the law—who just committed assault and battery. Who is brandishing a firearm. Who just threatened me and my security staff by discharging a weapon. I'd go so far as to call that attempted murder."

The jet rolled onto the taxiway and began the long trip to the departure end of Runway 16. The tail bobbed as it crossed seams in the taxiway.

Andy shifted the rifle onto Pemmick. "General, I'm not going to ask you again. Call him. Berezovsky. Now."

Pemmick shrugged. "I don't know who you mean."

I eased up beside Andy and tried hard not to startle her. "Dee, are you sure about this?"

Neither her eyes nor the rifle sight moved from Pemmick.

"Valentin Berezovsky is on that plane, General. He's sanctioned against travel to the U.S. That's why you don't want him seen."

"Dee," I repeated softly, "are you absolutely certain he's on that plane?"

"I'll be going now," Pemmick said.

"Dee?"

She took a breath, then spoke softly, only to me. "No. I'm not certain. But I can't take a chance that he is and let him leave."

A strand of hair danced across her left eye. Her jaw reflected her stance, set and stubborn. Her lower lip gained prominence and her long upper and lower lashes moved to meet in a deadly squint. She held the rifle's sights on Pemmick's heart with her trigger finger ready to pass judgment.

"Okay. Keep him busy. Try not to shoot him." I shoved the throttle slide forward. The BLASTER jumped to a whine that caused Pemmick to look skyward for the spying drone. I didn't care. I aimed for the hangar and swept inside, searching.

"Not another step, General!" Andy snapped.

A tool bench lined the right side of the hangar, but someone kept a tidy shop. No tools littered the metal surface. A quick glance upward ended my search. I curled my knees to keep from barking my shins on the bench. I aimed high, pumped the slide control, then killed the power once the BLASTER sent me on a collision course with the hangar wall. I hit hard and scattered several rubber drive belts hanging from nails. Momentarily clumsy, I fumbled with the one I wanted and nearly dropped it. It was the shortest of the collection, still new and wrapped in red, white and black cardboard around the center. I grabbed it. A mistake. The weight immediately drove me down to the bench, which I hit with my still folded knees.

I jammed the belt down into my shirt and felt an electric snap when it vanished. Once more entirely free of gravity, I pushed furiously away from the bench and wall. As I shot toward the center of the hangar, I rolled, extended my legs, and put my arm out, aiming the BLASTER at the open hangar door.

I went to full power. Pemmick instinctively ducked as I shot past him. I didn't look back.

For a moment, I thought I had this handled. The jet continued to bob its tail on the taxiway. From my perspective, it had not reached the runway hold-short line, which gave me ample time to catch it.

I was wrong. What I thought represented more taxiway proved to be an illusion created by a stubby stretch of pavement created to allow the unpaved northeast/southwest runway to intersect Runway 16/34. The jet completed its taxi run, abruptly turned left and showed me its full length in profile.

I crossed mental fingers and prayed the crew needed a minute to copy a clearance or finish a checklist before rolling onto the runway.

They didn't.

The jet eased forward on the roll. Its white nose swung sharply to align with the runway centerline.

Shit!

Jet engines spooled up. Heat wrinkles blossomed in the air behind the engines. The crew held her in place for a moment to accumulate extra thrust against the short runway. The nose bobbed briefly when the brakes released. The Citation begin its takeoff roll on the four-thousand-foot runway.

I accelerated.

I haven't figured out a reliable method of gauging my speed, but on test runs I've out-paced traffic on Highway 34 in Essex County, which typically hits close to sixty-five miles per hour. Racing forward, I rapidly reached my maximum. To reduce wind resistance, I rotated my legs so that they trailed behind me. I held my right arm fully forward and had an instant to imagine that this was it—the classic superhero pose. Too bad no one could see me.

I ran out of ramp and raced across the grass, then across the taxiway. I crossed the median between the taxiway and runway. The Seward Airport ramp sits at midfield beside its primary runway. Guessing at the acceleration and required takeoff distance for the Cessna Citation jet, I knew they would still be on wheels when they reached me. The problem would be the closure rate. And my aim.

I reached out and switched the BLASTER to my left hand, immediately wobbling thanks to a lack of practice driving lefty. I plunged my right hand into my shirt front and pawed for the rubber belt. The move increased my wobble and I dipped perilously close to a runway light. The short belt—probably an alternator belt—had slipped down and threatened to slide around my left side. I shoved harder and felt a button snap. My fingertips brushed the crisp edge of the unused belt.

The jet lunged toward me.

I shoved harder, broke another button and grabbed the belt. I yanked it free.

On the run or static? I had a split instant to decide. I chose on the run and shifted across the runway centerline to favor the airplane's right side.

Only one question remained. With the engines running at takeoff power, they sucked in great gasps of air. Depending on its size, a jet engine can suck a man off his feet. A man with weight.

I weighed nothing. If I got anywhere near the flow of air racing into these two screaming engines, I'd go in before I knew it.

The jet approached midfield at close to one hundred miles per hour.

Add my sixty-plus, and our closure rate came down to a blink. There would be no second chances.

I skimmed the pavement. The jet's wings became razors to my eyes. *Now!*

Making two moves at once, I flipped the belt forward, aiming for the oval of the right engine. I snapped the BLASTER straight up. My fingers tingled as the belt broke from *the other thing* and reappeared. The jet's wing flashed under me. The black open mouth of the engine swallowed the tumbling rubber belt.

I soared. Induction air feeding the engine tugged at my legs. I instinctively curled them up. The BLASTER pulled me free, climbing. *BANG!*

Sharp sound stabbed at me from behind and below. I whipped around. Racing away on the runway centerline, the jet trailed black smoke and furious sparks from the right engine. I watched the shadow beneath the wings. If it separated from the wings, it signaled the jet lifting. The shadow clung to the airplane as if weighing it down. Fragments and turbine pieces blew through the pristine cowling of the right engine and arched into the sky like summer celebration rockets. A large chunk of the cowling broke free and flipped away, spinning and fluttering.

The engines abruptly cut. The crew pulled the throttles. They wouldn't know for certain what had happened, but by virtue of *something* happening before calling for the aircraft to "rotate" they had one choice: Abort. On a longer runway, it would have worked.

Smoke curled from burning brakes. Three quarters of the runway lay behind the wheels. Nothing would stop this aircraft from an overrun. I cringed, hating what was about to happen to an innocent airplane. The Citation shot over the numerals painted on the departure end of Runway 16. White wings jumped and jerked when the wheels hit the turf at the end of the pavement. At the last second, the crew tried to slew it around, intentionally ground looping to kill the forward speed. The maneuver succeeded—partially. The nose made a sixty-degree swing to the left before the right main landing gear snapped and tumbled out from behind the wing. Both remaining gear legs snapped in rapid succession. The jet dropped to its belly and left the turf at the end of the runway. It slid down a shallow embankment into corn. Leaves and stalks sailed skyward. A dirt cloud enveloped the jet.

Everything stopped.

Smoke billowed from the ruined engine. Dirt and sliced-off corn stalks rained down. Inside a brown cloud, the undamaged engine continued to run until the crew assembled their wits and shut it down.

My high-speed climb approached five hundred feet before I realized the BLASTER pulled me skyward at full power. Rather than try to stop, I flipped my wrist and followed the power unit into a dive. As the turf approached, I pulled out and skimmed the airport surface.

Andy stood where I left her. Two security men sprawled on the concrete. Pemmick remained frozen in her sights. He stared at the smoking wreck.

I pulled the power into reverse, gunned it, and killed my speed in a near-perfect approach that ended in a perfect landing beside Andy.

"...told you, I don't know who you're talking about!" Pemmick argued. Some of his cool demeanor had slipped away. "But I can *guarantee you*, Detective, that your actions here will be held to account!"

"Is he being a pain in the ass?" I asked softly. She blew out a sigh of relief.

"Are you okay?" she asked just above a whisper.

"Peachy."

"Are *they* okay?"

"Oh, yeah," I said confidently. "They might've spilled their drinks, but they're fine, if they don't catch fire. What do you want to do with him?"

"Hold him. We need to call for backup and hold him until they arrive," she said. "We need to get the FBI out here, too." Pemmick tilted his head, confused by Andy's nearly sub-audible conversation with empty air. His expression darkened when he caught mention of the FBI.

"You have no authority here. I'm leaving," the general announced, his composure slipping, his complexion reddening. I grew more confident in Andy's instinct that Berezovsky was the man in the leather jacket. Pemmick barked an order at his bodyguard. "Get up!"

The bodyguard twisted his thick neck to check Andy who rewarded his caution with a look down the barrel of the rifle. He wisely chose to ignore the general.

"Get up!" Pemmick repeated. "That's an order!"

No one moved. The bodyguard nearest Andy huffed for air and

gripped his testicles. I noted a puddle of vomit and my stomach rolled in sympathy.

Seeing that Andy trumped his chain of command, Pemmick turned sharply. "Shoot me, then, Detective, if that's your plan. Or add false arrest to the charges I will be levying. Otherwise, I'm leaving."

He stepped off to march across the polished concrete hangar floor. Andy made a move to go after him.

"Hold up," I said. "I got this."

I gave the BLASTER a power shot and angled toward the hangar interior on an intercept course. Pemmick grew bolder after the first few steps and picked up the pace toward his black Tahoe. I wondered if he'd really thought this through. Unless the keys hung in the ignition, he wasn't going anywhere.

It didn't matter. A better idea had already crossed my mind.

I applied power and accelerated until the angle of my short flight met the line of his indignant march. I hit him from behind and threw my arms around him. He coughed out a clipped, "Woomph!" that perfectly synchronized with the *Fwooomp!* I heard in my head when he vanished.

He tensed and struggled using solid, corded muscles. I held him tightly from behind with one arm. His feet lost contact with the concrete and he flailed. I poured on the power and twisted my wrist to the left. His resistance didn't last long after we shot out the hangar door and began to rise, and full realization dawned.

"What the—?!"

I was tempted to answer. A slick speech about the stain he put on the uniform of the United States Marine Corps ran through my head.

I was tempted to explain that one of the flags his new political base had waved at the capitol square represented a nation and ideology against whom the United States had legally declared war and paid in blood and national treasure to defeat.

I didn't.

We rose quickly. Pemmick stopped flailing and became rigid.

"What is this?! WHAT IS THIS?!"

I leveled off at roughly twenty feet in the air and aimed for the thin pillar of smoke rising off the end of Runway 16.

"WHAT IN GOD'S NAME—!"

I was tempted to call Pemmick a raging asshole.

I didn't.

We flew over the runway, over the gouged path left in the turf by the jet, over the crushed corn. We approached the crash site. The men in the Citation had evacuated. Some worked their way back over bent corn stalks toward the runway. Some loitered near the open cabin door. A white-shirted crew member attended to the man with the leather jacket who sat in the dirt holding a cloth to his face.

I didn't speak to Pemmick

But I was tempted.

I was also tempted to drop him.

That, I did.

61

I watched the show from a lawn chair with a cold beer in my hand. The summer evening staged a spectacular sunset, enhanced by the emergency lights clustered at the end of the runway. Three engines belonging to the City of Seward Volunteer Fire Department arrived, along with two ambulances and half a dozen patrol cars belonging to the Seward police department and the county sheriff's office. Individual vehicles driven by volunteer firefighters joined the scene. The airport saw more traffic in one evening than it had all year. That according to Ken Wilson, owner of the lawn chair and generous distributor of cold beer. Wilson had silver hair, a former fighter pilot's stature, and a pristine Beech Model 18, the kind with the twin tail and round engines that require drip pans when it's parked. (*How do you know when a radial engine runs out of oil? When it stops dripping.*) He happened to arrive at the airport just as Andy suggested I disappear. I spotted him after he opened his hangar two doors down. Wilson stood with one hand hooded over his eyes, watching the emergency vehicles tear down the runway. One look at his airplane and I decided I had to meet this man. I told Andy where to find me if she needed me.

After I dropped off General Pemmick, literally, I did several turns around the crash site. My heart sank to see the gleaming twin jet on her belly, her sides streaked with dirt, her right engine looking like a dog's chew toy. The fuselage appeared intact, but that was no guarantee that some insurance adjuster wouldn't declare that repairing the airplane would cost more than replacing it. I pictured Pelican Salvage arriving with a small crane, and after removing the wings and lifting the pieces onto a flatbed, trundling the poor bird off to their warehouse for a few decades of dust accumulation and slow dismemberment.

The first of the emergency vehicles pulled onto the ramp just as I finished a final circuit and aimed the BLASTER in Andy's direction. When I arrived at her side, I noted a significant change in the hangar. Two of the Tahoes, along with Pemmick's security detail, were gone.

"Where's the brute squad?"

"I told them each to take a vehicle and get as far away from here as possible, or be arrested as an accessory to murder," Andy replied.

"They just took off? You didn't want to arrest them?"

She shook her head slowly. Mischief danced in the gold flecks of her green eyes.

"You do know what you just did, dear," she said, tipping her head toward the crash scene. An ambulance whizzed by on the ramp, lights flashing. Tires squealed when it made the turn onto the runway.

"Uh...this sounds like a trick question, but yeah...? I added the general to the flight manifest. He can try to deny it, but I'm afraid he might have been injured in the crash, which makes it hard to claim he wasn't on the plane. And I'd like to hear him try to tell someone how he got there."

Pemmick reappeared the instant I released him twenty feet above the left wing of the jet. He shrieked, pinwheeled his arms and dropped like a stone. One leg hit the leading edge of the wing, the other didn't, which made for a very bad landing. He tumbled and twisted into the dirt, screaming. When I left, although clearly alive, he lay immobile. The flight crew, still attending to one injured passenger, now turned their attention to another, probably wondering how they missed him earlier.

"Will, from here it looked like you dropped him from thirty feet up!"

"You saw him fall?"

"Yes!"

"Well, it was more like twenty."

"Is he still alive?"

"Oh, hell yes. Not very mobile, though." I shrugged. "He's not going to get anyone to believe he wasn't on that plane. Even if everyone on board testifies that he wasn't."

"I get that. I got that the minute you—you know."

I slapped my forehead. "Ah! *That's* why you didn't want his security guys around."

"I'm going to catch a ride down there and see who was on that plane." She put her hands on my cheeks and pulled me into a kiss. I joined the effort, thinking, *Beautiful woman. Beautiful evening. Airport. How could this get any better?*

Of course, the answer to that was beer.

Andy wrapped up the kiss by telling me to get lost. Not really the first time that's happened to me with a girl, but I got her meaning. She kept my phone and brushed a hand gesture at me that said go away.

An hour later my new friend Ken and I sat trading stories and watching the excitement when Andy returned from the crash site in a Seward PD squad. I sipped a second cold pale ale while Ken nursed a Coke since he planned to fly a few night-currency takeoffs and landings later. I didn't think the runway would reopen any time soon.

"Ken," I said, "my wife, Detective Andrea Stewart."

Ken popped to his feet and wiped soda can condensation from his hand to his pants. "Delighted to meet you, Detective."

"Please. Andy. Nice to meet you, too, Ken. I see you've been keeping my husband company."

"Swapping lies. Be careful where you step. It gets deep around some of the stories we aviators tell."

"I'm aware." She dazzled him with a smile, but I detected an uneasy undercurrent. She turned to me and said, "I just got off the phone with Lee's boss."

I hesitated to ask, "Any news?"

She shook her head. "Nothing yet. But he wants to see me."

"When?"

"Yesterday. He's in Lincoln and he's not happy. He went there to track down General Pemmick."

"He called you?"

"I called to fill him in on what happened here."

"Is that who was on that plane?" Ken asked. "That Pemmick guy?"

"Yup," I said quickly. To Andy, I asked, "Is he coming here?"

"He was. But I told him they're transporting Pemmick and one other passenger to Lincoln for treatment—in custody. He's sending a team to meet them at the hospital."

I raised my eyebrows. I wasn't sure what she did or didn't want said in front of a bystander.

"In custody?"

"There seems to be some question of illegal entry into the United States by the flight crew and/or the passengers. The flight originated in Toronto, but things get a little fuzzy from there. I asked the deputies to collect all the passports and detain everyone until this gets straightened out." She lifted her phone for me to see the screen. "I did a search. This is a photo of the gentleman we discussed. The one from overseas." The screen showed a rugged looking man with crew-cut hair, gray eyes and too much mouth for the face. "He wasn't on the plane."

Berezovsky.

"Shit," I said.

Andy put her hand on my arm. "We need to get down to Lincoln right away. I'm going to see if I can get one of those deputies to set up transportation."

"Lincoln, you say?" Ken asked. "I don't mean to butt in, but..." He looked at me and waved at his airplane. "Ever fly a D-18?"

62

It was a rare instance of wishing I hadn't accepted a cold beer, because it meant turning down Ken's offer to let me take the pilot's seat. His Beechcraft was a beautifully restored executive version of a twin-engine utility ship built in the thousands to train pilots for action in World War II. The radial engines sang the way only round engines can. Ken took off on the grass runway, avoiding the crash scene. The night sky welcomed us and the ride to Lincoln Airport proved too short. I would have preferred cruising for a while.

Andy, not so much. I felt her tension. She sat with her face to the cabin window, intently studying nothing in particular.

We received priority handling on arrival. The tower gave us special taxi instructions that took us to a corner of the general aviation ramp where they advised that a vehicle waited for us. Andy had called Special Agent in Charge Neil Rayburn to let him know we were coming. A car with the authority to enter the security zone idled on the ramp.

I heartily thanked Ken and told him not to bother shutting down, but he insisted. He helped with the cabin door and cautiously wished us well when two agents from the Federal Bureau of Investigation met us. I told him I'd look him up some day and tell him the whole story.

The FBI ushered us into the back of a silver Honda Accord, which disappointed me. If the bad guys got Tahoes, why not the good guys?

63

"No." Andy folded her arms and planted herself on the bland hallway carpet. "This is not happening. This is not an interrogation!"

The room exceeded broom closet dimensions, but only barely. It had an aluminum table, bolted to the floor and wall. Several plastic chairs. A camera, high-mounted in a corner. The agent attempting to usher us into this drab cube within the Lincoln FBI offices froze. Andy refused to move. I followed her lead.

"Tell Special Agent in Charge Rayburn that I am a law enforcement colleague, not a suspect. Go find an office where we can meet like professionals. Go!" The young agent's complexion took on a rosy hue as Andy whirled around and stalked back the way we had come. I fell in step with her, not at all sure where she planned to go.

From behind a new voice called out, "Detective!"

We stopped. At the far end of the hall a middle-aged man in a short-sleeved white shirt and monotone tie waved at us. He amiably gestured for us to return. Andy hesitated, mostly to make a point, then reversed and walked past the flustered agent who ducked into the small interrogation room.

The man waving at us stood about Andy's height, looked fit with nothing hanging over his belt, and had a genial, academic appearance.

He wore rimless glasses and a government-issue haircut. His shirt pocket contained a pen and a cell phone, contributing to an early-sixties-NASA fashion statement.

"Apologies," he said, extending a hand. "We live and die by protocol, and sometimes we don't see it happening when it shouldn't be. I'm Neil Rayburn. We spoke on the phone."

"Andrea Stewart." She shook hands. "My husband, Will."

Rayburn looked me over. "If you'd like to wait in the—"

"He stays with me," Andy said. Rayburn lifted an eyebrow. "What I mean to say, sir, is that he's been a part of this from the start. He was present in Norfolk. He's the one that pulled Special Agent Donaldson out of the fire. He *belongs* in this debrief. Will knows everything I know."

Rayburn extended his examination of me, then shrugged mild-mannered acceptance. He waved us into a tidy, airy office overlooking the empty, lighted parking lot of the Robert V. Denny Federal Building.

"We'll borrow this office," Rayburn announced. "Please, have a seat. Can I offer you anything? I know it's late, but coffee? Water? Uh...that might be all we have."

"Nothing for me," Andy said. I shook my head.

Rayburn slipped into the chair behind a desk with a placard for someone named Schebylski. Andy and I took the only two facing office chairs.

She looked impossibly good, given the length of the day and the long, windblown trip from Ulysses to Seward on top of Pemmick's truck. She sat in the chair at attention, alert. She opened her mouth to speak, but Rayburn interrupted her.

"Agent Donaldson's condition is unchanged," he said. "They're maintaining an induced coma and monitoring the swelling. The surgery to mitigate that part of it seems to have been successful. It's all about time, now."

"Thank you, sir. I appreciate the update," Andy said.

"At Agent Donaldson's request, it seems."

Andy blinked. "I'm sorry...?"

Rayburn wasn't playing this the way I expected. I thought we'd be given the stick-up-his-ass squad commander straight out of central casting. All bluster and blast, but no logic. This man came off as a friendly uncle.

A thin smile cracked his face. "Agent Donaldson is my problem child. He doesn't play well with others and we have not always seen eye-to-eye. I'm aware that he initiated an unsanctioned investigation and has read in a police detective wildly out of her jurisdiction."

Okay. Here it comes.

"However, he left me a message two days ago that, among other things, called your role in his investigation 'invaluable' and strongly suggested that I consider anything you have to contribute highly credible."

"I don't understand," Andy said. "Two days ago? That would have been just before we went to Norfolk…"

"Yes," Rayburn said. "I know what you're thinking, but I doubt very much that Agent Donaldson anticipated his injury or anything worse. He is, as I said, a problem child, and he knows it. I think he simply wanted to establish you as a witness to actions that were sure to be called into question. You were his unwitting insurance policy. So, Detective Stewart, why don't you start at the beginning and read the FBI in on its own investigation?"

"Maybe I will take that glass of water, sir," Andy said.

64

Pidge picked us up at noon the next day. After Andy briefed Rayburn, starting as far back as the role Josiah James played in Ben Braddock's attempted bombing of the DNC search committee in Milwaukee, and the subsequent dual tragedy of his son's death and Mike's suicide. She walked him through the complex story of Racehorse Blue and an Air Force flight crew lost sixty years ago. She told him everything Donaldson had uncovered, leading up to her failed attempt to catch up to General Pemmick to question the man. She told Rayburn she narrowly missed Pemmick when he boarded a private jet at Seward Airport. Andy is a human lie detector, but I noted how effortlessly she wove this part of the tale. Something I hadn't seen in my wife before. She finished her briefing by asking Rayburn if the men on the plane with Pemmick had been identified. It was at this point Rayburn slipped into the role we had anticipated. He ignored her question. He told Andy to provide his office with a detailed written account of everything she just told him, then politely but abruptly rose and ushered us out of the small office, and out of the Lincoln offices of the FBI. After a perfunctory warning not to disclose anything to anyone, he bid us a good evening, thanked me once more for my role in saving his agent from the fire, then closed the door behind us. We had to call a taxi to get to the hotel.

I was pissed, of course. For most of the ride to the Cornhusker Hotel, I embellished a description of Rayburn that began with ungrateful. I declared loudly that Lee Donaldson had been right—the FBI was running scared from anything with the appearance of political motivation, which only gave a green light to genuinely evil people. Eventually, Andy put her hand on my arm and said, "Stop. I think you may have misjudged the man." She punctuated the comment with a cryptic smile and said nothing more.

We crashed hard at the Cornhusker Hotel. I showered away whatever held me up. Andy curled up against me on the bed and we talked for a while, reviewing what we had done, what we might have done, and what we hoped the FBI would do. At some point we stopped talking. In the next instant, morning barged in through the seams in the hotel room curtains.

Checking out, we were surprised to find several large, sealed FBI Evidence bags waiting at the front desk. One contained Andy's travel bag and my motley collection of recently purchased clothing, both having been rescued from the rental we parked behind a corn bin on a gravel road in Ulysses. Another, smaller bag contained Andy's shoulder satchel with her badge, phone, and service weapon. I was surprised that the FBI would leave something like that with a hotel desk clerk, until I saw two men in suits get up and leave the lobby once we collected everything.

Andy wanted Pidge to fly us to Omaha, but she called the hospital first for an update on Donaldson's condition. She was informed that the patient was in the protective custody of the FBI and no visitors would be allowed under any circumstances. Standing in the FBO lounge at Lincoln Airport, Andy ended the call and turned to me with a sad smile.

"Let's go home."

EPILOGUE I

I stole a moment to stare at my wife as she walked beside me in the sun. She wore her hair in an intricate French braid, prompting me to wonder how she accomplished such a wonder working in a mirror. She wore a light summer sun dress, the hem of which kissed her tan legs in a way that made me jealous. The top of the dress dipped nicely on her chest, sharing curves I surreptitiously studied from behind my Ray Ban Aviators. The breeze rippled her dress. I took her hand, for which she paid me a radiant smile.

Pidge strolled behind us. She wore a startlingly feminine summer dress and shoes that lifted her and clicked on the apron surface. Earl gawked, unsure of what he was seeing.

Arun walked beside her and stared helplessly, quickly dropping his eyes whenever he thought someone noticed, then letting his gaze be pulled magnetically back.

This was nice to see after the two of them nearly collided with an entirely different outcome.

The day we returned to Essex, Pidge casually asked if I thought Arun would be at the hangar when we arrived. I teased her with a frustrating "Beats the crap outta me" reply, knowing that the smitten young man had texted twice asking for our ETA. What I didn't expect upon arrival was the way Arun had closed himself in his office. Pidge helped me move the Navajo into the hangar, then fussed over unloading the bags. After half a dozen overtly casual glances at the closed office door, Pidge said, "I'm just going to … just say Hi to … you know…"

Andy and I traded suppressed smiles.

We were on a path to the door when Pidge blew out of Arun's office and bolted into the hangar. She wore a dark, rigid expression I would have taken for rage if not for the wet glitter spilling onto her cheeks. She stormed past us in silence.

Andy raised one eyebrow and said, "You better go find out what he just did."

Reasons why this was none of my business rapidly assembled on the tip of my tongue. My wife shot down every unspoken argument simply by staring at me.

"Hey," I stuck my head in Arun's office. He sat like a soldier on a battlefield wondering where his legs had gone. "What the hell did you just do?"

Muscles quivered in his jaw. "This is no concern of yours!"

"The hell it isn't. I've only known you a couple months. I've known that girl for years. She saved my ass. Twice. I've seen her do things no man I've met can pull off, but one thing I've never seen her do is cry. You need to explain that to me or we're going to have a problem."

He looked like a boy on the verge of tears.

"She—I saw—*I saw her on the television!*" he blurted out. "*I saw what she did!*"

It took me a second.

"You're kidding me. You mean what she did in Lincoln?"

"It was all over the news! For everyone to see! Out there on that street, like—"

"Like what?!" I snapped. I began to think I might be able to punch the poor kid after all.

"Will! Oh, damn everything! *My mother saw her!*" He sank in his chair and pressed his face into his hands. "Oh, damn everything!"

"Aw, Christ," I muttered, realizing I wasn't going to knock the kid around. I felt Andy's touch on my shoulder, which turned into a gentle push.

"Go on," she said, then backed out of sight.

What do you want me to do? I demanded of my wife, silently, in my head so she wouldn't hear me.

"Hey!" I barked at him. "Hey! Look at me!"

He raised a face made glossy by a damp sheen on his cheeks.

Jesus Christ.

I stepped up to his desk and planted my hands on the spotless surface.

"You're the wrong color, did you know that? For some people in this country, you're just a little too tan. You talk funny. You're here to steal their jobs and make their daughters pregnant with inferior little brown babies. Yeah. Even around here, you're gonna get some of that. Don't tell me you haven't already. And that thing in Lincoln? Those guys were hard core. Those were the real deal. Guys who will beat someone like you to death for looking at a white woman. Those guys lined up on a street chanting scary shit *specifically about you* and holding up flags to make the point that you don't deserve to eat, sleep or breathe their idea of free American air. That life and liberty only belong to people who burn easily on a beach. And that little girl, that ninety-pound ball of fire-breathing female, completely unarmed, stepped into a street lined with those motherfuckers and knocked them on their collective racist asses with the only weapon she had. I don't know what you think you saw, or what your mother thinks she saw, but I was there, and I saw an act of courage and defiance performed not just for you—but for humanity. So, get your head out of your ass, Arun!"

He stared at me, wide-eyed.

"Get up! Go! Fix this! Or I'll kick your ass, I swear!"

He moved in a way I'd only seen once before, when he sent Sandy into a meeting with the wrong summary folder. I followed him out of his office. He nearly clipped his head ducking under the wing of the Navajo.

"You're such a romantic," Andy said, slipping her arm in mine.

"Ain't I?"

Her words came back to me as we walked hand-in-hand toward the flight line that paralleled Runway 13/31. I stole another look at her and if *romantic* covered *lust* I was fine with it.

We stopped in a small group where the grass met the asphalt of the main ramp. Andy checked her watch. Pidge chatted with Arun, smiling in a shy way that just looked wrong on her face, but which held him captive. Earl gawked yet again, occasionally scratching the leathery surface of his skull. Once or twice he looked at me and begged confirmation that someone else was seeing the same thing he was. Rosemary II hovered beside Earl, clutching a small packet of tissues against what was coming and holding the arm of Adeana Hampton, who looked fine as sunshine in a dated blue dress, her white hair shaming the few puffs of cloud in the blue sky. Doc, our chief mechanic, and half a dozen others spread out between us and the empty office, checking wristwatches and scanning the sky.

I spotted the government plane before I heard it.

"They're here," Andy said, pointing at the approach to Runway 31.

A sparkling white King Air turboprop lowered itself to the asphalt runway. The combined jet whine and prop noise reached our ears as they made the turn onto the taxiway. Turboprops sound like they idle at full power.

I looked at my watch and then over my shoulder. Chief Ceeves wheeled his SUV into the airport parking lot. The Chief knows the way. He rolled through the gate, around the hangar and across the ramp. He pulled up and parked beside our small gathering. By the time the turboprop rolled to a stop on the ramp, the Chief took up station standing behind us.

"I still don't know how you pulled this off," he said quietly to Andy.

"I'm not sure I have," Andy confessed.

We waited. The pilots ignored the small milling crowd and did what pilots do, closing out checklists and shutting down engines. When the turbines slipped into silence, Andy started across the ramp. The Chief and I followed a step behind. This was her show.

The King Air's cabin door dropped. The door operator wore pilot's epaulets. After performing his duty, he ducked back into the cabin. In his place, a woman wearing a dark business suit stepped lightly down the airstair. She spotted Andy and marched directly to meet her.

"Detective Stewart?"

"Yes." Andy accepted her outstretched hand.

"I'm Special Agent Torrance."

"Where's SAC Rayburn?" Andy asked.

"He wasn't able to make the trip," the woman said.

Bullshit. He wanted nothing to do with this. I held my tongue but caught a side glance from the Chief. Andy nodded as if this came as no surprise.

"I'm senior assistant to SAC Rayburn. I represent his interests."

"His interests?"

The woman gave Andy a *don't be coy* look. She drew a breath for dramatic effect.

"Detective, my job today is to deliver a message and to confirm a certain understanding."

"What message?"

"You've been...persistent. SAC Rayburn wants assurances that by doing...*this*...today, that your *persistence* is at an end."

"It is."

"He also instructed me to remind you of your role going forward."

Andy's shoulders flexed, betraying a suppressed laugh. Dimples appeared at the corners of her mouth.

"No need. You may report to your boss that I have no interest in the case he is putting together against General Pemmick or in wherever that case may eventually lead."

"Not good enough." The woman held Andy in icy stare.

"Or in making my involvement known to the media—or to anyone," Andy added. She shook her head. "Your boss really sees Pemmick as his ticket to the top, doesn't he?"

"There's a lot at stake for the Bureau."

"One question. What about Brent and Hillerman? SAC Rayburn said he would try."

"Consider it ongoing. However, he did tell me to tell you that Staro is gone."

"Gone?"

"Demolished. It's been confirmed. He said you would know what it meant."

"Berezovsky is cleaning up after himself," Andy said soberly. I knew what she was thinking—that two of the faces in the crew photo would never return.

"I can't comment on that," Torrance said.

"Hey." I pointed at my watch. "You're cutting this a little close."

Special Agent Torrance turned her attention to me for the first time. "This understanding goes for your husband, too, Detective."

I opened my mouth to make a rude comment when Andy closed her hand on my arm.

"My husband will honor the commitment I made."

The FBI agent looked me over. Then she spared a glance up at Chief Ceeves. For an instant her confident demeanor cracked. The Chief can have that effect.

She quickly restored a stony expression. Without looking back, she waved one hand at the King Air's cabin. She took a step closer to Andy. "Off the record, Detective, I think you're pissing in the wind here. These two have had nothing to say. They're one hundred percent brainwashed. One hundred percent in the pocket of a foreign power."

"We'll see." Andy said.

Torrance shook her head. "They committed murder, Detective. They betrayed their country."

"I'm not sure it isn't the other way around."

"It doesn't matter. They're never going to see the light of day. They haven't said a word, not even in their own defense."

Andy leaned closer to the FBI agent. She lowered her voice.

"You spend sixty years in the hands of the KGB. Then sit in judgment."

Torrance didn't respond. Instead, she said, "One more thing. No contact with Agent Donaldson. Is that clear?"

"I want to know his condition."

"Unchanged…" Torrance suddenly betrayed a hint of humanity. "Look…we all know what you did for him. And we're grateful. But this situation—the Bureau's position—it's highly sensitive. Highly sensitive. You have to appreciate that. Agent Donaldson is in good hands."

It was Andy's turn not to respond.

Torrance glanced at the cabin door and hardened her tone again. "You'll see, Detective. This is a waste of time."

"You're right. I will see."

A second FBI agent appeared and hurried down the airstair. He wore a nylon windbreaker with bold yellow lettering across the back. He stopped at the bottom of the steps and reached back to help his charge.

Slowly, carefully, a frail old man lowered himself, step by step. His unsteady movement was hindered by steel handcuffs binding his wrists.

"Lose the restraints," Andy ordered.

Torrance hesitated long enough to register her objection, then nodded at the second agent. In a flash, he produced a key and removed the handcuffs.

Captain Paul Lockwood stood in the sunlight wearing a simple blue suit over a white shirt and gray tie. He planted his feet and stabilized himself. He blinked briefly at Andy. I expected him to recognize her, but he gave no hint. I expected him to speak but he remained silent. He turned to watch his friend and flight commander.

Captain Armand Hampton slowly descended from the aircraft. A third agent steadied him from behind. At the bottom of the airstair, the second agent removed his handcuffs.

Captain Hampton drew himself erect.

He looked directly at the only other person in his sight, the only other person in the world.

Adeana Hampton put her hand to her lips. She took a hesitant step. Then another. And another. Then she took all the remaining steps she needed to cross time, distance and war to reach her husband.

They came together and filled each other's arms without a word.

Andy sniffled beside me. A small crowd had gathered behind Chief Ceeves. Rosemary II hitched a loud sob. Some damned thing, jet exhaust probably, made my eyes water. Earl Jackson angrily examined his shoes.

Captain and Mrs. Hampton held each other as if not a moment had passed since someone snapped their nuptial photo.

I glanced at Andy. The fulfillment of a promise to an old woman painted a serene look on her face. Her eyes met mine. Her hand found my hand and squeezed.

"Here they come!" Pidge announced. She pointed.

All heads turned to search a line extending northwest from the centerline of Runway 31. Pidge has better vision than most, so it took a moment, but soon everyone saw the two sets of black dots representing radial engines. Then the glint of silver wings and the sparkle of all-glass noses. Deep in the distance, the thunder of eight powerful Pratt & Whitney engines paved the way toward us.

Two Boeing B-29 bombers, flying museum pieces from a war that ended three quarters of a century ago, hung in the blue sky. Their size belied their speed. For a moment they simply hovered. Then, as if drawing a giant breath, the silver wings expanded. Four massive propeller discs on each aircraft bounced back sunlight. The roar of the engines grew louder and louder.

Captain Hampton parted from his wife and stepped beside her. Captain Lockwood fell in beside his crewmate. Both men stared skyward, eyes squinting away the years.

The two airplanes swept through the sky, indominable. Chance had placed the only two operational B-29s in the world at the annual Experimental Aircraft Association convention in Oshkosh, not far from Essex by air. Andy, the FBI and forces unimaginable put them on a path over our heads. Their thunder shook the air and reached down into my bones.

Drawing closer, the speed of the bombers became evident. In loose formation, they looked as if their wings spanned the entire Essex County Airport.

Unprompted, as one, Captain Lockwood and Captain Hampton drew their near-ninety frames to full attention. As one, their hands snapped to their brows in salute.

The airplane they had mastered, flown and given their lives to roared overhead, saluting back.

EPILOGUE II

General Pemmick hadn't lost a step, despite the wheelchair. If anything, the granite Marine bearing appeared stronger, more defiant. The marble halls of the federal courthouse framed him as a potent wounded warrior prepared to do battle against his accusers. Reaction to his arrest polarized along political party lines. Half denounced another "Russia Hoax." The other half demanded reviving the investigation into foreign meddling in the American political process. Endless speculation by 24-hour news cycle talking heads suggested Pemmick might make a deal with prosecutors—and that his cooperation would lead to a wider investigation. The White House tweeted its support for the general, calling him a great American and urging him to stand fast.

On camera, the white-haired general fired volleys of ice back at the videographers who dogged him in the courthouse hallway. His jaw jutted. His upper lip curled. He adamantly maintained that he had never been aboard the airplane that crashed in Seward. His claim that he had been kidnapped and planted at the crash site drew ridicule from mainstream journalists, but found a following in the remnants of Josiah James' media empire, which continued to broadcast, alternating between "encore" presentations of Josiah James's previous work and new broadcasts using on-camera actors posing as journalists. Hard-line James supporters ignored reports that the other passenger on the plane was Gleb Sokolov, a known associate of a Russian oligarch named Berezovsky. They called it another FBI lie and demanded the President fire the Bureau's director. Mainstream media described Sokolov as Berezovsky's personal banker, bag man and the force behind world-wide Russian money laundering. *The New York Times* posted an article connecting Sokolov to recent low-key administration efforts to ease sanctions against Russian oligarchs.

I looked for Andy to express satisfaction that she had been right. That the risk we'd taken at the Seward Airport had been justified. The most she would give me was a coy smile.

I asked, "Why? Why would they take the chance and meet like that?"

"In person? That's easy. No evidence trail. No transmission that can be intercepted. They needed to arrange the laundering and transfer of hundreds of millions of dollars. Do you know how hard that is?"

I didn't, but Andy balances the checking account, so I trusted her on that one.

Pemmick's alleged connection to Berezovsky was painted by James supporters as an elaborate conspiracy meant to smear the great General Pemmick and the immortal memory of Josiah James. The argument gained little traction. Sokolov sat in federal custody, first arrested by Seward County deputies, then quickly handed over to the FBI. He faced a long list of charges starting with illegal entry into the United States.

Special Agent in Charge Rayburn sank his career teeth into Pemmick and Sokolov, stockpiling FBI fuel for a juggernaut investigation. One that could not be marginalized or dismissed by an uneasy Justice Department. Andy commented more than once that she expected to see Rayburn rise to high echelons in the Bureau.

The White House and its dedicated voices vainly suggested political bias, an argument aimed largely at those who followed their antics on Twitter. Faced with detailed questions from the press, they presented stony silence.

Pemmick and his attorneys joined the conspiracy chorus with perfect pitch—at least for the cameras. Their blatant denial angered me, but Andy brushed off the outrage as all show. She told me more than once that Neil Rayburn had been in a very good mood the last time she spoke to him, despite the way she bent him to her will regarding

Hampton and Lockwood—who had both been transferred to a minimum security federal facility. It told her that Pemmick struck a deal with the Feds and that the outward defiance was a cover.

Pemmick's rapid release from hospital care surprised me. His equally rapid arraignment gave me hope that justice would make haste and the truth, for once, would emerge. Live coverage of the court appearance dominated the morning news broadcasts.

I ordinarily avoid television news. Most outlets commit the sin of shaving a complex story down to a few sound bites. I can't listen to a news story without thinking it would take days of study to truly understand what happened. Or without wondering which direction the news channel is spinning their report. Yet our proximity to this story made me tune in even as minor events unfolded. Andy showed less interest. She preferred to read the police summary or the court record.

While Andy puttered in the kitchen over breakfast, I lingered in the living room with the remote in hand. The screen screamed out "Breaking News" and "Pemmick Press Conference" and captioned the location as Lincoln, NB—*idiots.*

I opened my mouth to call Andy in case she wanted to see Pemmick talk to the cameras, but figured if it came to anything, relentless cable news would play it to death. On that, I was correct.

Flanked by a squad of lawyers, Pemmick rolled his wheelchair up to a stand of microphones that had been lowered to his height. He looked left and right, posing, reminiscent of a Josiah James performance. The man had been paying attention.

He cleared his throat.

The cameras on Pemmick didn't catch it. Later, video from another angle would show the world what happened, over and over.

In relentless replay, an elderly man stepped forward, slightly stooped, almost completely bald and wearing a poorly fitting suit over a thin frame. The moment he appeared, my mind erased the brush strokes of age and saw him as a young officer proudly posing with Captains Hampton and Lockwood in an old black and white photo. Brent or Hillerman—I wasn't sure which. A Staro survivor. A graduate of a Russian oligarch's twisted training. A tool. In one swift motion, the old man raised his arm and fired six shots into Pemmick's chest from a revolver. The shooter dropped the weapon the instant the sixth shot left the muzzle.

The live broadcast—the one I watched in my living room—showed the General acknowledging the shots with a simple nod. He dropped his chin to his chest and showed the white cap of his head to the cameras.

Case closed. Rayburn's star witness—gone.

My mind flashed on Andy's words.

Berezovsky cleaning up after himself.

I stared at the screen. Even after panic broke out and the image devolved into shaken camera confusion, I remained transfixed. The cameras whipped around to fix on the old man. Someone grabbed him.

Brent. Second row. Third from the left in the ten-man crew photo.

His face was serene.

"Son of a bitch," I said aloud.

"Oh—my—God!" Andy's voice jarred me as she stepped into the room.

"I know!"

She wasn't looking at the television. She had no idea what had just happened. Instead, she held up my phone.

"You just got a text from Lillian. They know where Lewko has the piece of debris!"

DIVISIBLE MAN
TEN MAN CREW

Sunday, October 21, 2018 – Friday, May 17, 2019

ABOUT THE AUTHOR

HOWARD SEABORNE is the author of the DIVISIBLE MAN™ series of novels as well as a collection of short stories featuring the same cast of characters. He began writing novels in spiral notebooks at age ten. He began flying airplanes at age sixteen. He is a former flight instructor and commercial charter pilot licensed in single- and multi-engine airplanes as we as helicopters. Today he flies a twin-engine Beechcraft Baron, a single-engine Beechcraft Bonanza, and a Rotorway A-600 Talon experimental helicopter he built from a kit in his garage. He lives with his wife and writes and flies during all four seasons in Wisconsin, never far from Essex County Airport.

Visit www.HowardSeaborne.com to join the Email List
and get a FREE DOWNLOAD.

PLEASE ENJOY THE START OF WILL AND ANDY'S NEXT ADVENTURE

Caught up in a series of hideous crimes that generate national headlines, Will faces the critical question of whether to reveal himself or allow innocent lives to be lost. The stakes go higher than ever when Andy uncovers the real reason behind a celebrity athlete's assault on an underaged girl. And Will discovers that the limits of his ability can lead to disaster.

A Kirkus Starred Review.
A Kirkus Star is awarded to "books of exceptional merit."

Available in print, digital and audio.
Visit us at **HowardSeaborne.com**

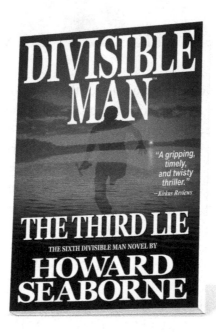

DIVISIBLE MAN: THE THIRD LIE

— 1 —

"Lie to me once, you're on my shit list.
"Lie to me twice, we're done.
"Lie to me a third time, I'm coming for you."

—Earl Jackson

"Stop." My wife pressed her hand against my bare chest where a moment ago she had been idly tracing three capital letters with the tip of her index finger.

"What?"

"You can't start a story like that." She rolled to face me. "That's the original cliché."

"Whoa, whoa! You asked me how it went. I'm telling you how it went." I picked up her hand. "Go back to doing what you were doing."

"What...this?" She traced the three letters slowly, starting at my navel and ending just above my diaphragm.

"Yes," I said. "That. Now let me tell my story."

Gold-flecked green eyes warned me of undisclosed mischief. She dropped her cheek to my shoulder. Her hair spread on my skin and I drew in the intoxicating scent she uses to enslave me.

"Fine," she said. "You may begin again."

"Okay. It was a—" her hand slipped down to my ribs, then up into my armpit, where I am ridiculously ticklish "—about an hour and fifteen minutes after civil twilight and radar showed widespread convective activity across most of lower Michigan and Ohio. In other words… it was dark. It was stormy. It was night. I don't know how else to put it."

Her hand slid back to my chest. Reprieve.

— 2 —

I scanned the engine instruments. Oil pressure looked good, but the right engine oil temperature wiggled on the high side. I tabbed through several screens on the Insight engine monitor and stopped at the display for individual cylinder head temperatures.

Gotcha.

I checked our position on the moving map. Nine thousand-plus feet below, the northwest shoreline of Lake Erie slid behind me. I touched the audio panel to join my headset to the in-cabin intercom.

I glanced back.

Sandy Stone and Arun Dewar faced each other across a small foldout table. They traded Education Foundation papers back and forth under a cone of warm light from the cabin overhead. Sandy pushed aside a tired lock of blonde hair and glanced toward the cockpit. Catching her eye, I tapped my headset. She untangled hers from the seat's armrest and slipped it on. Arun followed suit.

I said, "We've got a problem."

Arun's dark eyes grew wide. "What kind of problem?"

His reaction tempted me to reply with *It looks like the right wing is loose* but it's bad form to screw with sensitive passengers.

"I've got a cylinder running hot." Arun opened his mouth to panic, but Sandy raised a calming hand. "I'd like to put down in Detroit and have it looked at."

Sandy trusts my judgment.

"Will there be anyone to work on it at this hour?"

"No. I know a shop on the field at Willow Run that will give us priority in the morning. If it's minor, we could be on our way by noon. If not, Arun can get us a flight out of Detroit Metro. Either way, it's an overnight stop."

It had been a long day, our third on the road. The Pennsylvania trip followed closely on the heels of two trips last week and one the week before. With the start of the school year nearing, Sandy seemed determined to cram in as many Education Foundation trips as she could before returning to teaching kindergarten.

"Whatever you think is best, Will," Sandy said.

"Arun, do your logistics magic. I recall a nice Holiday Inn close to the Willow Run airport."

"On it." He reached for his phone.

I returned to the flight controls and flicked off the autopilot. My fingertip hovered over the push-to-talk switch on the control yoke, waiting for an opening on the busy ATC frequency. The sector controller had his hands full helping flights work their way around the weather. He wasn't going to appreciate my request.

The cylinder head in question suffered a stuck valve. A sharp Willow Run mechanic named Nolan knew it before he had the engine cowling off the next morning. He said he could take care of it but needed a few days. I called Doc, the resident Airframe & Powerplant mechanic at Essex County Air Service, for a second opinion. I hoped he would put together a parts-and-tools kit and get Earl Jackson, our boss, to run him across the big lake for a ramp repair. Instead, Doc asked to speak directly with Nolan. The two gearheads agreed that Nolan was better equipped for the job. I broke the news to Sandy. Arun pulled out his phone and booked three seats on an 8:20 p.m. Delta flight that had us arriving in Milwaukee at 8:27, accounting for the time change.

I don't like flying commercial. Flying a Piper Navajo cabin-class twin for Sandy Stone's Education Foundation means I can deliver Sandy from the stairs of the airplane to the door of a waiting car at any of ten thousand general aviation airports. Commercial flying, laden with the cattle-drive process of check-in, security and reporting to the gate for boarding, takes far longer. In the hours required to make a commercial flight from Detroit to Milwaukee (only forty minutes of which consist of actual flying) I could have flown us over and back again and still met Andy for dinner.

After threading our way through the eye of the TSA needle at Detroit's Wayne County Airport, the airport tram and people-mover combination carried us to our gate with relative efficiency. I began to think the process wouldn't be as painful as I anticipated.

I was wrong.

"Is that...?" Arun pointed at the wall of windows as we strolled to the gate.

"Some serious weather," I finished his thought.

Bruised and boiling clouds loomed over the western perimeter of the Detroit Metro airport. Lightning crawled between giant cumulus buildups and stabbed the earth. An angry line of aerial violence blotted out the setting sun.

We found seats in the waiting area. The terminal grew darker. Anxious passengers swiped device screens. Arun pulled out his iPad and studied ugly blotches of radar imaging.

"There's a tornado watch in effect," he reported, his voice high and tight. Born and raised in Britain, Arun didn't have much experience with Midwestern tornados. I was less concerned with a twister than the fact that the jetway for our gate had no airplane attached.

"*Watch*," I said, "means conditions *might* produce a funnel cloud, but it does not mean an actual tornado has been spotted."

Arun buried his nose in his screen, looking for better news.

The gate agent picked up her microphone.

"Ladies and gentlemen as you can see, we have a bit of weather approaching. We've just been informed that air traffic control is holding arrivals until these conditions pass. It means that the aircraft taking Flight 1931 to Milwaukee has not landed yet and will be late reaching our gate. When it arrives, we will unload and service the aircraft quickly and try to get you on your way. We appreciate your patience."

"Aw, fuck that shit!" A loud voice behind me turned heads. "*What the fuck!* Let's get this show on the road!"

Someone laughed. The loudmouth had an audience.

I twisted in my seat.

They were a party of three. Two men and a woman. Loudmouth stood at the center of their small cluster. I guessed his age to be in the mid- to late-twenties. He easily topped six-feet-six and showed off a heavily muscled physique with a tight silver t-shirt that advertised a fitness club. He wore crewcut hair bleached bright white with three horizontal black stripes on each temple. Thick gold chains hung around his neck. Gold bands adorned one wrist and a heavy, multi-dialed watch —the kind of watch people think pilots use, which we don't—weighed down the other.

The young woman on his arm wore bright pink tights that left nothing anatomical to the imagination. On top, she bundled a pair of abundant breasts into what looked like a yellow elastic bandage. She covered a minimum of it with a tiny leather jacket decorated with dozens of silver studs. Her scarlet hair and heavy makeup spoke as loudly as her boyfriend.

The third star in this constellation wore long hair in a man bun and squeezed himself into a "tiny suit"—a jacket three sizes too small over trousers tapered to a snug fit at the calf. Under the glossy suit jacket he wore a black t-shirt weighed down by gold chains, although not quite the mining haul the trio leader draped across his chest.

Loudmouth carried on.

"C'mon! Get us some pilots with balls and let's bounce! I'll fly the motherfucker!" The girl tugged on his bulging arm.

"Derek, buy me another drink!"

Derek gave it a beat. Then he turned to a heavyset man who had been trying hard not to pay attention from a nearby seat.

"Dude watch my stuff," Derek commanded. He pointed at the man and then at three bags laying in the aisle. "I'm holding you responsible! Anybody fucks with my stuff it's on you."

The hapless man stared at Derek's thigh-sized arms.

Derek and his troop set off for the bar on the other side of the next gate.

I thought about reporting the unattended bags. Airport police destroy first and ask questions second. The policy struck me as perfect justice for an ass of this magnitude. I decided instead to watch the other storm—the one dumping sheets of rain on the runways. Lightning speared the earth while thunder cracked. The absence of delay between flash and boom betrayed the proximity of the strike.

I checked on Arun. He was staring at the trio strutting toward the bar. He wore an alert expression, the sort one might adopt when encountering a snake. Arun is a small, bookish young man. I wondered if hard experience had outfitted him with a visceral wariness of bullies.

It took another two hours for the weather to clear, for our plane to reach the gate, and for the aircraft to be unloaded, serviced and made ready for boarding. No imagination was required to see that most, if not all, of the Milwaukee-bound passengers were on the last leg of a long day of travel. Listlessness and too much carry-on luggage weighed people down. Only a few passengers, universally under the age of six, exhibited anything resembling energy by the time we lined up to board.

Before stepping into the jetway, I glanced back at the cluster of carry-on bags orphaned between two now-empty rows of gate seats. I crossed my fingers that Derek and his pals were too busy chumming with Jack Daniels to notice that the flight had been called.

Thanks to last-minute booking, our boarding passes took us to uncomfortable seats in the rear of the plane. Arun and Sandy squeezed into the window and middle seats on the right side of the aisle. I slid into a left-side aisle seat one row back. A woman in her sixties or seventies nestled politely beside Sandy, who tossed me a relieved glance.

Sandy Stone is a remarkably attractive young woman who has confided in me that her greatest fear when flying is sitting beside a man attempting to generate enough conversation to justify a marriage proposal by the end of the flight. She, like everyone else on this flight, simply wanted to go home.

My watch said we would land in Milwaukee after eleven. It would take several hours after that to reach Essex.

A loud voice erupted from the forward section of the plane.

"Move it or lose it!"

I looked up. Derek and his dominoes lined up in the aisle. Derek towered over everybody. He bobbed and danced impatiently to a beat in his own head. A family ahead of him hurried to settle themselves. His shuffling steps were unsteady. His eyes, bleary.

"Let's go people," he said. "Let's light the fuse on this rocket!"

His girlfriend giggled and jiggled. Her heavily lidded eyes scanned the faces of the men she passed, daring them to gaze at her chest. The third wheel in the group shuffled along wearing mirrored sunglasses and a stone face, wobbling slightly, as if the still earthbound plane navigated light turbulence.

Derek compared his boarding pass to the seat numbers. "Ariel, baby, *what did you do?* You got us sitting in fucking Siberia!"

"It was all they had, honey!"

The trio worked their way past me trailing a cloud of cologne and whiskey. They found their assigned seats two rows aft of mine. The new issue became the packed overhead bin.

"What is all this shit!" Derek jerked open one plastic door after another. He tried shoving bags sideways to make room. "Fuck!"

"Sir, your bag will fit under the seat." A flight attendant ventured into the fray. "If you would please take your seats now."

"If you would please take your seats now," Derek mimicked. "Bitch, where'm I gonna put my feet?"

The flight attendant, whose day had probably started four cities ago, chose not to engage.

After aggressive jostling and maneuvering, the carry-on bags were stowed under the seats. Third Wheel took the window. Ariel took the center seat and immediately flipped the armrest up to snuggle against her man. Derek dropped in the aisle seat with one leg in the aisle.

The show might have been over if we had pushed back from the gate. Instead a voice from the flight deck told us that although the heavy weather had passed, ground control remained backed up.

"Folks," the captain said with a marked lack of enthusiasm, "we are now holding for clearance to push back."

It gets like that. The storm may have moved on, but the effects of diverted and delayed traffic, compounded by the late hour, stacked up against us.

We waited.

"Fucking plane is overloaded," Derek announced. Someone shushed him. It might have been Ariel. He paid no attention. "I saw this shit online. They overload the plane and it messes up the gravity. Puts all the controls out of balance."

Idiot, I thought.

"This one plane, they put too much baggage in the back. It took off and the front end went up and then it did a big old nosedive right into the runway. Splat!" Heads turned to issue reproachful looks. I gave the effort small odds. Subtlety is lost on those who wear loafers without socks. "Every freakin' person on board died," Derek continued. "They couldn't tell which body parts belonged to which passenger. Fucking goo."

"Sir," a woman said quietly, "please. There are children here."

"That's what happens, lady. They overload these planes and they just fall outta the sky!" Inexplicably, Ariel giggled, which made Derek laugh.

"Hey!" A man's voice this time. "Can you keep it down, pal?"

"Pal? Are we pals? Cuz' I don't remember having any pals with such an ugly-ass face."

"Just keep it down."

"Or what?"

The man did not reply.

"Fucking pilots don't know shit and that's why people get turned to jelly in these things, *pal*."

I unsnapped my seatbelt. Sandy shot me a warning glance, but it was too late. I took to my feet and stepped into the aisle. At the back of the plane, a flight attendant caught sight of my move and started forward. I didn't wait for her. I turned and hurried up the aisle to the forward cabin. The lead flight attendant, preparing for the safety briefing, saw me coming.

"Sir, you need to—"

I pulled my wallet from my jeans pocket and flipped it open. I held it up and gestured for the woman to step up into the space behind the cockpit door, which had already been closed. The wallet move—hinting at law enforcement—threw her. She stepped back.

"I'm a pilot." I held up the plastic flap that showed my FAA license.

It wasn't what she expected. She rebounded quickly. "Sir, you really—"

"Listen," I said softly. "You've got a problem passenger in row forty-three. He's drunk and he's running his mouth and frankly, he's upsetting the other passengers. He's also looking for a fight."

Her gaze shot to the back of the plane and landed on Derek. I hadn't told her anything she didn't already know.

"Here's the thing," I said. "Federal Aviation Regulation ninety-one point seventeen states that 'Except in an emergency, no pilot of a civil aircraft may allow a person who appears to be intoxicated to be carried on that aircraft.' Now, I don't want to cause you trouble, but it's going to get ugly back there. I for one don't want to be cooped up in this pressurized tube with him when it does. That man and his companions are clearly drunk. He is menacing and scaring the passengers around him."

She sent a resigned look in Derek's direction.

"Listen, I don't want to be an ass about it. But you've now been made aware. If things go bad—and I sincerely believe they will—this crew will be operating in violation of FAR ninety-one seventeen."

She looked at me like I was the bigger asshole. I didn't blame her.

"No one wants that. May I make a suggestion?"

The flight attendant handled it beautifully. A few moments after I returned to my seat, she strolled back, leaned down, and spoke softly into Derek's ear.

"Yeah, baby! That's what I'm talking about! Grab your shit, sweet-cakes. We're movin' on up!"

The flight attendant backed away. Derek stood up a little too quickly and lost his equilibrium. He leaned into the row across the aisle. His hand went wandering. A woman shrieked. "Whoa, lady!" he muttered. "Don't get your panties wet. You ain't got anything special up there anyway."

Ariel threw the woman a superior look and pushed her boyfriend forward. The forward attendant met them in the aisle. "We just need a few minutes to clear the seats and restock with fresh pillows and blan-kets. Please follow me." She dished out a big smile. "Can I offer you a complimentary beverage?"

Derek ordered a whiskey sour and weaved his way forward, pinballing off the seatbacks as he went. At the front of the plane, the smiling lead flight attendant said, "We'll just have you wait on the jetway while we prepare your seats in First Class." She ushered all three through the still-open door onto the jetway.

I leaned over and tried to see out the nearest side window. The view wasn't great, but through slit windows on the jetway I caught sight of law enforcement uniforms. Almost immediately, the attendants closed the forward door, a chime sounded, and a tired-sounding voice welcomed us aboard for what the crew hoped would be a short, smooth flight to Milwaukee.

A cheer rippled through the cabin.

"What did you tell them?" Arun asked.

He hurried to keep pace beside me, anxious to learn a new secret. Except for the stream of passengers exiting our flight, the Milwaukee terminal lay empty. The shops wore metal grates for the night. A maintenance worker pushed a vacuum across a sea of carpet.

"I told them to offer the asshole a first-class accommodation. They did. First Class courtesy of the Wayne County Sheriff."

We followed the subdued flow of passengers to the escalator that descended to the baggage claim. Arun grinned.

"I've never seen that before! Brilliant!" Something about the episode charmed him.

"It's against federal law for a pilot to operate an aircraft carrying someone who appears to be intoxicated."

Sandy laughed. "That's got to be one of the least enforced laws on the books!"

I hopped the escalator and shrugged. "Maybe. Flight crews don't like confrontation. They *really* don't like to remove a passenger. It's bad for business, especially with everyone carrying video cameras. Most often, if they can just get a plane in the air, it quiets people down. That guy was not going to settle down. The crew got lucky, getting him off the plane."

Approaching the bottom of the escalator I spotted a familiar face.

"Hey, Lyle! What are you doing here?"

Lyle Traegar works with my wife as a part-time patrol officer on the City of Essex Police Department. He served under her supervision when she still wore sergeant's stripes. I hadn't seen much of him since she moved up to detective, although I remembered him in uniform at Mike Mackiejewski's funeral.

Lyle stood with his overweight frame stuffed in a black suit, white shirt and black tie. The neatly printed sign in his meaty hands told me that if he was still working for the Essex PD it remained part-time.

"Hi, Will!" he grinned. "My other job." He wiggled the sign.

"You're a driver? Chauffeur, I should say."

"'Til I can get Chief Ceeves to hire me full time. Tell your wife to put in a word for me. How 'bout her making detective! That's something!"

"She never ceases to amaze me." I sidestepped his request that I nudge my wife on his behalf.

Arun tapped me on the shoulder. "I'll get a car." He bounded off toward a row of rental car desks with more energy than seemed possible at this late hour. I didn't like his odds. The desks looked deserted.

"You just come in from Detroit?" Lyle asked. "Flight 1931?"

"Yeah."

"That's the flight I'm waiting for. Jesus, you're like three hours late. I've been cooling my heels here forever. What happened?"

"Weather." I read the sign in his hands. "D. Santi? That wouldn't be a Derek Santi, would it?"

Lyle looked at me like I'd just done a magic trick. For a big man, he had a boyish veneer—the perpetual look of someone who didn't quite get the grown-up joke. I wondered if that might be the reason Chief Ceeves hadn't offered him a full-time position with the department. "You know him?"

"Nope. Wild guess. I'm afraid you may have a really long wait." I explained what happened. Lyle dropped the sign to his side and shook his head.

"Yeah, that sounds like the guy. He was an entitled ass on the phone. Demanded top shelf liquor in the car." Lyle cast a glance up the stairs. The last of the passengers from our flight had already descended and milled around the baggage carousel. "Crap. Yours is the last flight from Detroit tonight."

"Oh, he won't be flying tonight. Not commercial, at least."

"I guess I'm dead-heading back up to Essex."

"Want company?"

"Sure!"

I waved at Sandy. "We have a ride! In style, I might add. I'll go fetch Arun."

Three hours later, in bed, I finished explaining to my wife why a stretched limousine dropped me at our back door. She said nothing. Her hand lay motionless on my chest. Her breath came and went in a slow, steady cadence. I estimated she had fallen asleep around the time I got to the part about the cylinder head temperature.

— 3 —

The war council gathered around my counter-height kitchen table. A light evening breeze whispered through the open kitchen windows. Andy sat to my right. A slim blonde woman with a low tolerance for fools took the seat opposite Andy, which represented more than just a seating arrangement. Most of what Lillian—whose last name she refused to divulge—had to say landed in direct opposition to my wife. Lillian may have been a rocket scientist and mathematician with multiple doctorates, but Andy continued to refer to her as "The UFO Nut."

The fourth member of the council floated on Andy's laptop screen. Dr. Doug Stephenson joined us from his home office via Facetime. Andy propped the laptop on an empty Evermore shipping box.

Stephenson inadvertently introduced Lillian to our lives and my secret after she got wind of someone who had tripped over a piece of debris from my accident. The debris shared the characteristics of *the other thing*—a mystery unresolved.

Lillian, in what had become a pattern, dominated the floor.

"Evermore, North Carolina. Lewko built the town from scratch and named it after his company. Christ, I think he'll name his firstborn after the company. The state had a collective orgasm when the press reported the location as the new site for Evermore's corporate headquarters. Imagine their surprise when Lewko announced it was only a research facility and shipping hub. Things got testy between the bureaucrats and the billionaire because the state gave him a huge package of tax incentives. When the legislators suggested rolling back the tax package, Lewko threatened to drop the whole thing and the state caved. The corporate welfare check came to well over a billion. The state picked up the tab for the infrastructure while Lewko retained the deed to all the land. It's the same playbook Foxconn used here in Wisconsin. And may I say, you guys really got hosed on that one."

Andy ignored Lillian's political leaning. "How sure are you that he took the *thing* to North Carolina?"

"It's there."

"A little proof would be nice."

Lillian huffed. "Lewko dropped out of sight. Going to that kind of trouble means he's doing something important. Nothing, believe me, is more important to him than the piece of debris from Will's crash. I've got sources that put him in Evermore, so that's where the artifact is."

"What sources?" Andy demanded.

"Dark web sources."

"That doesn't prove anything."

"Dark web?" I asked. It always sounds like something from a comic book to my ear. "What? Do they follow the guy?"

Lillian looked at me like I was stupid. "They follow all those guys. Bezos. Zuckerberg. Brin and Page. Gates. Jobs, back in the day. They'd get stool samples if they could. It's all about trend, and no piece of intelligence is insignificant. Knowing where the major players nibble their *foie gras* is golden. It gets checked against other players—financiers, bankers, Senate committee chairmen. It signals conversations, coalitions, chemistry. Every discarded Dixie cup is a clue. Can you imagine the stock run if you had intel that Larry Ellison booked the same B&B as the CEO of Southern California Electric?"

Lillian says everything like she thinks you should know what it means. After tolerating a moment of blank stares, she blurted out, "Nuclear power! Oracle in bed with nuclear power!"

Stephenson patiently reeled her in. "Is there any intel on his team?"

Lillian shook her head, but she eyed the screen suspiciously. "Spill it Big Bear. What are you groping for?"

"Big Bear?" I looked at Stephenson. The neurologist may be in his seventies, but the man looks twenty years younger. Andy and I knew he and Lillian were casual sexual partners.

Stephenson hesitated. The video connection made it hard to tell who he was looking at. "Do we tell her, Will?"

I guessed it was me.

"Tell me what?" Lillian stiffened. She shot glances between Stephenson and me. "What?! Are you two holding out on me? That's not our deal!"

I wasn't aware we had a *deal.* Stephenson raised a hand to calm her.

Andy shifted uncomfortably on her chair. This was touchy for her. It had not gone over well when I confessed to her that Stephenson and I were testing one of the unexpected characteristics of *the other thing*. Andy wasn't against it. She also wasn't for it.

"Either we're all in or I'm out!" Lillian declared.

"Relax, Honeybee," Stephenson said.

I clamped my jaw against a grin.

"Will?" Stephenson asked.

Lillian fixed her laser-focused glare on me.

"Okay," I said slowly. "You know about the disappearing act. You know that when I vanish, gravity lets go, which is good and bad. You know that I lose my mass—"

"Inertia. That's different," Lillian corrected me.

"Inertia. Fine. I'm not subject to the laws of inertia and mass and gravity."

"We went over all this, Will. What are you holding out on me?"

"He wasn't holding out on you," Andy said tersely. "We've just been cautious about revealing too much. I'm sure you can appreciate that."

Lillian gave no sign of reading Andy's tone. "I don't solve equations in the dark. What haven't you told me?"

I swallowed. "It turns out I can take people along for the ride."

"Like the little girl in the fire. What's-her-name."

"Lane," Andy said sharply.

"At first, I thought I had to wrap them up. You know, like wrap my arms around them. But it seems like all I need is a good grip on someone. If I push hard—in my head—they vanish with me."

"And?"

"And…it has a side effect," I added. "Last Christmas, well it's kind of a long story, but I had an Angel Flight—a charity flight where we take—"

"I know what Angel Flight is, Will."

"Right. So, we had this little girl with leukemia, and we were trying to get her into Marshfield for treatment, and the weather was shit, and we couldn't make the landing. She was going downhill, so I did my thing—and I bailed out of the plane with her and dropped her off at the hospital."

"You bailed out?"

"No, not like that. I didn't abandon the airplane. Jesus! Pidge was flying the plane."

"Pidge. Who the hell is Pidge?"

I explained. Then added, "Pidge and the flight nurse stayed in the plane."

"Christ!" Lillian slapped her hand on the table. "Two people saw you?! Why don't you just take out an ad in the *New York Times*? What about Greg LeMore? Does he know? Because you told me not to tell him why we were looking for Lewko! He's going to think I'm a bumbling—"

"No. Greg doesn't know."

Lillian rolled her eyes.

"That's not the point here, Lillian," Andy said.

"No," I jumped in before something caught fire. "It's not. The point of this story is what came after. That kid, that little girl—"

"What about her?"

I shrugged. I didn't know how to put it.

"Lillian," Stephenson came to my rescue, "the child emerged from the effect in remission."

Three of us gave Lillian a moment to calculate. She turned to Stephenson.

"Partial?"

"Full."

"N.E.D.?"

"Appears to be."

"Cellular regeneration?"

"Regeneration. Cleansing. I don't know. I wasn't privy. She exhibited Polycythemia Vera, which metastasized into Leukemia, which—simply went away. Will climbed out of the aircraft with a dying child in his arms. He handed a child in full remission over to the staff at the hospital."

Lillian stared at the screen. I knew better than to think of her as speechless.

"I've done what I could to follow up," Stephenson continued. "I know her primary. He can't stop talking about her. It's been over six months. The child is healthy. Better than healthy."

Her gaze slowly shifted between me and Stephenson.

"Subsequent testing?"

He nodded.

"Blind?"

"Ish."

"Quantifiable results?"

"We don't have access. We think eighty-eight percent."

"How many subjects?"

"To date…twenty-nine."

I thought about a girl named Anastasia, who drew pictures of her own death. I thought about a little boy named Benny, who giggled when I took him flying. I thought about others I'd held in my arms in the dead of night. Frail. Light. Pale skin that seemed to glow in near darkness. I didn't think of them as *subjects*.

Numbers crunched behind Lillian's eyes.

"This is bad," she said slowly. "This is very bad. I need some air."

Lillian slid off her chair and stepped out of our kitchen without another word. We heard the screen door slam. Andy and I traded glances.

"Give her time," Stephenson suggested. "Call me later."

The screen winked out.

ALSO BY HOWARD SEABORNE

DIVISIBLE MAN

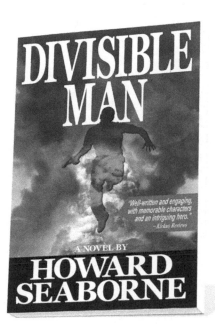

The media calls it a "miracle" when air charter pilot Will Stewart survives an aircraft in-flight breakup, but Will's miracle pales beside the stunning after-effect of the crash. Barely on his feet again, Will and his police sergeant wife Andy race to rescue an innocent child from a heinous abduction—*if Will's new ability doesn't kill him first.*

Available in print, digital and audio.

Learn more at **HowardSeaborne.com**

ALSO BY HOWARD SEABORNE

DIVISIBLE MAN: THE SIXTH PAWN

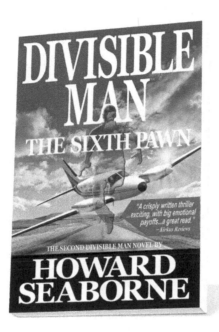

When the Essex County "Wedding of the Century" erupts in gunfire, Will and Andy Stewart confront a criminal element no one could have foreseen. Will tests the extraordinary after-effect of surviving a devastating airplane crash while Andy works a case obstructed by powerful people wielding the sinister influence of unlimited money in politics.

Available in print, digital and audio.

Learn more at **HowardSeaborne.com**

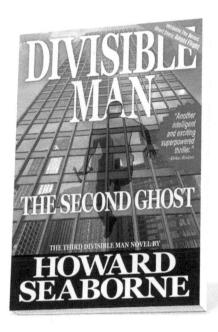

ALSO BY HOWARD SEABORNE

DIVISIBLE MAN: THE SEVENTH STAR

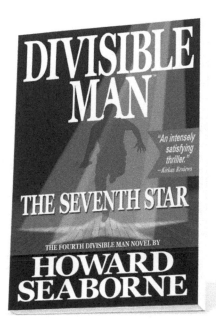

A horrifying message turns a holiday gathering tragic. An unsolved murder hangs a death threat over Detective Andy Stewart's head. And internet-fueled hatred targets Will and Andy's friend Lane. Will and Andy struggle to keep the ones they love safe, while hunting a dead murderer before he can kill again. As the tension tightens, Will confronts a troubling revelation about the extraordinary after-effect of his midair collision.

Available in print, digital and audio.

Learn more at **HowardSeaborne.com**

ALSO BY HOWARD SEABORNE

DIVISIBLE MAN: TEN MAN CREW

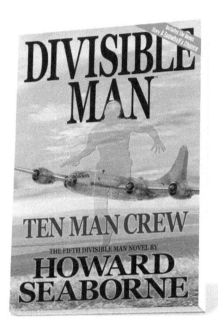

An unexpected visit from the FBI threatens Will Stewart's secret and sends Detective Andy Stewart on a collision course with her darkest impulses. A twisted road reveals how a long-buried Cold War secret has been weaponized. And Pidge shows a daring side of herself that could cost her dearly.

Available in print, digital and audio.

Learn more at **HowardSeaborne.com**

ALSO BY HOWARD SEABORNE

DIVISIBLE MAN: THE THIRD LIE

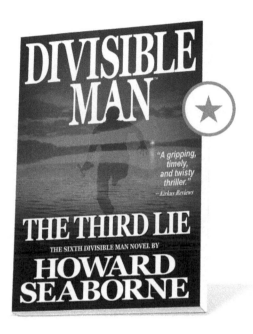

Caught up in a series of hideous crimes that generate national headlines, Will faces the critical question of whether to reveal himself or allow innocent lives to be lost. The stakes go higher than ever when Andy uncovers the real reason behind a celebrity athlete's assault on an underaged girl. And Will discovers that the limits of his ability can lead to disaster.

A Kirkus Starred Review.

A Kirkus Star is awarded to "books of exceptional merit."

Available in print, digital and audio.

Learn more at **HowardSeaborne.com**

ALSO BY HOWARD SEABORNE

DIVISIBLE MAN: THREE NINES FINE

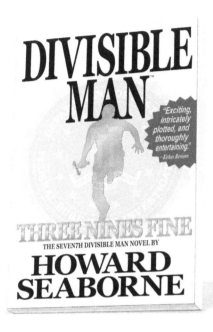

A mysterious mission request from Earl Jackson sends Will into the sphere of a troubled celebrity. A meeting with the Deputy Director of the FBI that goes terribly wrong. Will and Andy find themselves on the run from Federal authorities, infiltrating a notorious cartel, and racing to prevent what might prove to be the crime of the century.

Available in print, digital and audio.

Learn more at **HowardSeaborne.com**

ALSO BY HOWARD SEABORNE

DIVISIBLE MAN: EIGHT BALL

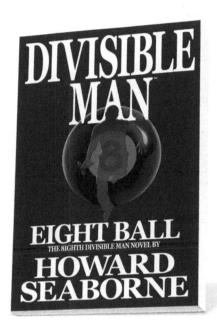

Will's encounter with a deadly sniper on a serial killing rampage sends him deeper into the FBI's hands with costly consequences for Andy. And when billionaire Spiro Lewko returns to the picture, Will and Andy's future takes a dark turn. The stakes could not be higher when the sniper's true target is revealed.

Available in print, digital and audio.

Learn more at **HowardSeaborne.com**

ALSO BY HOWARD SEABORNE

DIVISIBLE MAN:

ENGINE OUT AND OTHER SHORT FLIGHTS

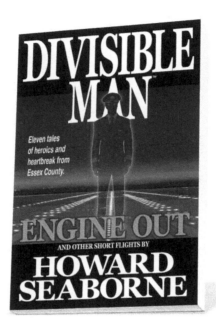

AVAILABLE: JUNE 2022

Things just have a way of happening around Will and Andy Stewart. In this collection of eleven tales from Essex County, boy meets girl, a mercy flight goes badly wrong, and Will crashes and burns when he tries dating again. Engines fail. Shots are fired. A rash of the unexpected breaks loose—from bank jobs to zombies.

Available in print, digital and audio.

Learn more at **HowardSeaborne.com**

ALSO BY HOWARD SEABORNE

DIVISIBLE MAN: NINE LIVES LOST

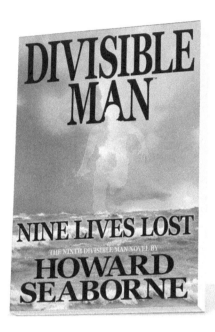

AVAILABLE: JUNE 2022

A simple request from Earl Jackson sends Will on a desperate cross-country chase ultimately looking for answers to a mystery that literally landed at Will and Andy's mailbox. At the same time, a threat to Andy's career takes a deadly turn. Before it all ends, Will confronts answers in a deep, dark place he never imagined.

Available in print, digital and audio.

Learn more at **HowardSeaborne.com**

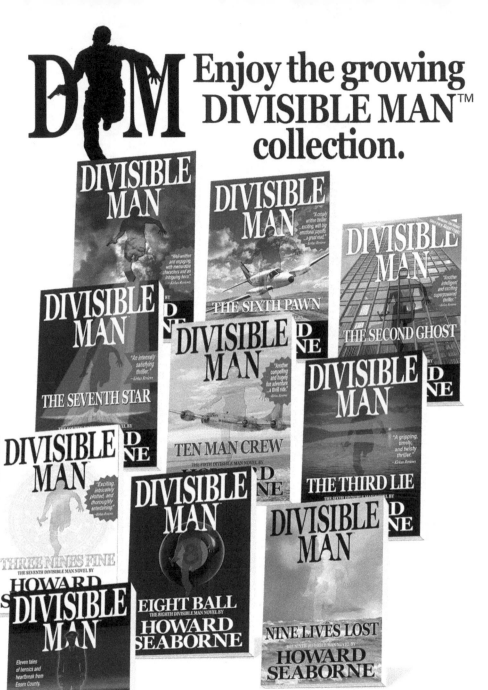

CPSIA information can be obtained
at www.ICGtesting.com
Printed in the USA
LVHW081235180922
728646LV00025B/1006/J